Belonging

Alexandra Raife

coronet

CORONET BOOKS

Hodder & Stoughton

First published in Great Britain in 1999
by Hodder and Stoughton
First published in paperback in 1999
by Hodder and Stoughton
A division of Hodder Headline PLC
A Coronet Paperback

10 9 8 7 6 5 4

A CIP catalogue record for this title is available
from the British Library

ISBN 0 340 73830 8

Typeset by Palimpsest Book Production Limited,
Polmont, Stirlingshire
Printed and bound in Great Britain by
Mackays of Chatham PLC, Chatham, Kent

Hodder and Stoughton
A division of Hodder Headline PLC
338 Euston Road
London NW1 3BH

Alexandra Raife has lived abroad in many countries and worked at a variety of jobs, including a six-year commission in the RAF, and spent many years co-running a Highland hotel. She lives in Perthshire. Although she has written stories for years, *Drumveyn* was her first published novel, followed by *The Larach* and *Grianan*. Vividly depicting the West Coast of Scotland, Alexandra Raife's new novel, *Belonging*, returns to the sea-lochs and hills of *The Larach*.

Praise for Alexandra Raife:

'A real find . . . the genuine storyteller's flair' Mary Stewart

'A welcome new storyteller' Rosamunde Pilcher

'Warm, friendly, involving . . . lovely' Reay Tannahill

'*Drumveyn* had me hooked from the first page' Barbara Erskine

'A love story with an unconventional twist [. . .] a very readable novel' *The Times*

'A compelling read' *Woman's Weekly*

'The power of a natural born storyteller' *The Lady*

'An absorbing story with a perfectly painted background' Hilary Hale, *Financial Times*

Also by Alexandra Raife

Drumveyn
The Larach
Grianan

For James,
who quite likes this one

Chapter One

Thin morning sunlight flooded into the high kitchen of the Edinburgh flat through the long window open to its tiny balcony. The kitchen was bright, orderly, immaculate, the smell of freshly ground coffee and *petits pains* warm from the microwave mingling agreeably with the scent of the freesias Esme liked so much. The sunlight glowed back from the orange juice in its fluted jug, struck rich colour from the dark marmalade, laid a line of light along the fold of a professionally starched napkin.

Rebecca sat at the table not attempting to do anything, routine already broken, allowing herself to be looked after as people setting out on an important journey do, with a hollow feeling inside her at the thought of the stripped flat above, the packed bags, the lost territory of the office where someone else already had a one-to-one relationship with her computer.

It had worked well, she thought, bleakly for her, the balance she and her mother had achieved between closeness and independence over the past few years. It had probably been so successful because Esme was a highly occupied person herself, and had been sensitive enough and wise enough to ask no questions when Rebecca had so carefully restructured her life those seven years ago. There had been a lot of affection, a lot of laughter, and Rebecca watched her mother now with love as she stood beside the coffee percolator waiting to snatch it off the ring the moment its strenuous bubbling hit the right note and her nose told her that the full flavour of the grounds had been released at the precisely desirable moment.

Esme was wearing well-cut fawn slacks, cream cashmere sweater, bright silk scarf; the dark springing curly hair which Rebecca had inherited, greying now, was crisply shaped, her make-up perfect. She looked very much the well-heeled Edinburgh lady about to make up a four at Bruntsfield, have lunch in the clubhouse, perhaps play bridge in the afternoon.

Esme brought the steaming, still-bubbling percolator to the table and sat down with a small rueful smile at Rebecca which did not pretend that this was a morning like any other. 'That emptiness above,' she said. 'Strange how it makes itself felt.'

Rebecca nodded, her eyes stinging for a moment. She would drive away from it; her mother would come home to it, though she knew Esme had not been making any bid for sympathy. 'I shall miss this too, you know,' she said, her voice not quite ordinary.

'You wouldn't prefer to keep your options open for a while?' Esme asked. 'Let the flat stand empty till you're sure what you want to do? It would be next to impossible to find anything so convenient for us both again and you could afford not to sell immediately.'

'I know.' Rebecca hesitated. She had not put the flat on the market before she left to save herself the hassle of showing people round. And to keep life as normal as possible for as long as possible, knowing that this workable and acceptable existence could never be re-established in its present form. She had not told her mother about the events that were driving her from the city, the reason for her desperate haste to be gone. But she had not fabricated any explanation either and Esme knew there had to be some compelling motive behind the move. Once more she had asked no questions.

'It has to be a clean sweep,' Rebecca said, the muscles of her face tight. There was not one detail she could give which would not open floodgates to a huge torrent of facts, unstoppable, destroying the whole meticulous fabric of her present self. Their eyes met; appeal and compassion.

This had all been said; Esme had wished only to make clear that her love and sympathy were there. It could be no small thing that would drive Rebecca to dismantle her enviable, successful and apparently contented life so ruthlessly.

'And you won't find it hard to be at Ardlonach again?'

'I actually don't know the answer to that,' Rebecca admitted. Ardlonach, the much-loved family home on the West Coast. Rebecca's father Francis had been the second of the three Urquhart brothers. He and the youngest, William, had been swept away by an avalanche while skiing in the French Alps seventeen years ago and neither had survived. The eldest, Kenneth, who had never married, had lived at Ardlonach till his sudden death after a heart attack seven years ago at sixty-three. He had left the house and what remained of the small estate to the only nephew, William's son Tony, the youngest of all the cousins, and Rebecca, for whom Ardlonach was one of the great passions of her life, had found this very hard to accept. Also it had come at a time when she was intensely vulnerable to emotion, her usual realistic good sense not quite in place, and her mother knew how much she had minded Kenneth's choice.

'You're sure you'll be able to cope with finding Tony there?' Esme asked now. 'Tony owning it?'

'Owning it because he's got a cock and I haven't,' Rebecca said disgustedly, jerking marmalade crossly onto her plate.

'If that's the only way you can find to describe male succession, then yes,' said Esme, unmoved.

Rebecca laughed. 'Oh, I've had time to get over all that. Now I just think it would be sad if I let it cut me off from Ardlonach for ever. I've stayed away for far too long as it is. I can't think of anywhere I'd rather spend a few weeks regrouping and though Tony can be a pain I do enjoy Una.'

'Yes, Una's delightful,' Esme agreed, smiling with quick

affection. 'Though I absolutely cannot see her running a hotel. Nor Tony, come to that, other than the bar-propping side of it. And finding the house swarming with strangers might come as rather a shock.' She spoke lightly, but was concerned that Rebecca, usually the most clear-sighted of people, might in her evident need for refuge be shutting her mind to the changes that had overtaken the old house. That sudden need deeply worried and puzzled Esme. There had been no signs in Rebecca's full, organised and apparently emotionally unflurried life that some sort of crisis was imminent.

'They don't open for three weeks,' Rebecca reminded her. 'If I find I can't stand the customers I can always clear out.' And go where, the panicky question immediately presented itself, with a map-like vision of Scotland, and beyond it the whole of Britain, stretching blank and flat, empty of any focus point, with one dark area which must be avoided at all costs. She stood up abruptly. 'I should be on my way.' Untrue; she had all the time she chose to take.

'And heavens, so should I,' Esme exclaimed, looking at her watch.

Their goodbyes were brief. Esme was not a contact person. Her love expressed itself in trust and reticence and loyalty.

When the outer door had closed behind her mother, Rebecca went through to the drawing-room overlooking the crescent and opened one of the French windows to stand on the balcony of black-painted, fleur-de-lis ironwork and watch her mother walk swiftly across the cobbles to her car. Her back in the soft green leather jacket was straight; she walked like a young woman. She was nearly sixty and she was a plumber. That is to say not only did she run the business she had inherited from her father but was a time-served plumber herself, as well as being a qualified teacher and having a degree in history.

Before getting into her car she raised a hand towards the severe curve of the high stone terraced houses as Rebecca had known she would, and Rebecca felt the lump in her throat harden painfully and for a shaken moment longed to call to her to stop, to come back, to talk, not to leave these wastes of unsaid words between them.

But I can't tell even her about those shattering encounters, she thought in anguish, waving. I can't tell anyone. And I can't live in the expectation of another one, anywhere, at any time, here in the familiar streets of home. He promised. It was the single absolute condition and he promised. Now he had broken that promise, and seemed to think because he had done so that the reason for making it could no longer have any validity. To Rebecca it seemed that all sense of safety has been destroyed and there was nothing she could do about it except remove herself.

Perhaps in any case it was time to go, she thought more practically, as she had many times in the past few weeks. Her life had become too predictable, too satisfactory and successful. It needed a shake-up. Oh, don't be so sensible and bracing, she mocked herself. Anyway, it's decided, it's happening, just get moving.

Esme drove round the corner and pulled up, blind with tears. The packed demanding day stretched before her, arid, exhausting and pointless. And after it she would come home to silence, to the sensation of absolute aloneness. Oh, don't be a fool, she protested angrily. There were many days when she and Rebecca never saw each other at all. And she had been alone when Rebecca was taking her qualifying degree in accountancy at Glasgow and for the three years spent afterwards as a trainee with a firm in Aberdeen. Rebecca had not been the sort of student to commute home every weekend with a pile of washing, nor Esme the sort of mother to wash it if she had. But this was different, for now she knew Rebecca had suffered some serious blow and she had been unable to help her. She was so much in the mould of non-interference, careful never to invade Rebecca's space, that she was afraid she had lost the capacity to help her. What use was mute loving support when something was torturing her outgoing and robustly pragmatic daughter? Torturing her enough to make her resign from the hard-won partnership in Athole Finance Services, sell the functional convenient flat so exactly suited to her needs. And had hardly bothered to furnish, Esme reminded herself, managing a trembly smile. Clean lines, simplicity and everything in working order was what Rebecca aimed at. She left domestic perfection to her mother.

Oh, my darling girl, Esme cried to her, folding a tissue over her little finger-tip and carefully running it under the lashes along each lower lid in turn, I want to see you laughing again. I don't know how to live without your trenchant comments, your irresistible humour, your warmth and generosity. Esme took a couple of deep breaths, squared her shoulders, pulled the Mondeo out from the kerb and headed for Leith.

In the quiet sunny flat Rebecca methodically cleared the table, loaded the dishwasher, emptied the percolator, dropped her napkin into the laundry basket, restored the kitchen to its gleaming order. A final clinging impulse made her want to leave something ready for her mother. Comfort or apology? How much did Esme really mind her going? Rebecca would never know, was the answer to that. But was there nothing that could be done to welcome her home? After her day at the yard she would swim at her club then put in a stint of remedial teaching at the centre in Craigmillar. She would dine at one of her series of favourite eating houses all over the city and come home late. Her competent productive disciplined life, its rough edges provided by the crises and difficulties of the business, the struggles and frustrations of her teaching, was on a personal level unruffled and smooth-running. Its dramas and battles had all taken place during her married years and if she had missed them since Francis was killed she gave no sign. Rebecca had been seventeen at the time and away at school. In the seventeen years since, it had seemed to her that outwardly little had changed in their lives, expect for the huge space left in it by her extrovert, energetic, pleasure-loving father. Esme, capable and self-sufficient, had taken charge and not then or since had burdened her daughter with her grief.

Rebecca found a card – UNICEF, field of poppies. One did not leave scrappy notes on the back of envelopes for Esme. She wrote, 'Thanks for not asking. Maybe I'll be able to tell you one day.' It's been so good, truly. I love you, R.' and propped the message against the slim vase that held the freesias. Her hand hovered. She had wanted to leave some sort of acknowledgement that Esme deserved to know what had happened but already longed to withdraw the half-promise. She left the card where it was.

Her bags were ready in the hall; she was taking very little. She no longer possessed the sort of clothes she would need at Ardlonach but could buy them in Fort William. Her mother had made room for her books and CDs and the possessions she did not want to part with, though these had turned out to be few. She had had no regrets about abandoning her furniture; it had belonged with the flat and she had made her decision about that. She raised her eyebrows wryly as she regarded the small huddle of waiting luggage. No one could call her a clinger.

How could walking down the steps and out to the car, as she had done every working day and most other days for the past seven years, feel so different today? Not just the luggage, not just the lingering ache of threatening tears after watching her mother walk so briskly away, but a whole interior sensation of being adrift, cut loose, superfluous to requirements.

She gave a little snort at the exaggeration of that as she fitted in her bags, locked the back from habit and went round to the driving side of her Ford Escort, innocuous-looking in spite of its flame-orange bodywork. Crocuses out in the black-railed garden, edge of sharp east wind lacing the sunlight; she would not see this as home again.

A couple of turns and she was heading for the Queensferry Road, dragged down by the clogged traffic, impatient suddenly to be away, have this over. Space and light opened at last over the bridge, the firth a flashing blue below, then finally came the chance to work her way through the heavy vehicles and surge away. It was not till she was well on the way to Perth that it struck her she needn't be forging on like this, need not have kept to the motorway at all. She could have cut westward, taken the slower road up through Glen Devon as they always used to do. She was far too much in the habit of being in a hurry. Also she loved driving and enjoyed her little car, an RS Turbo with more teeth to it than at first appeared. Well, she would enjoy this too, the escape achieved, the final step taken, the links broken. She settled herself in her seat and giving her whole concentration to the busy road vanished into the hills for the two days of absolute idleness which she had apportioned herself as a buffer between the life abandoned and the tentative return to the place she had once hoped would be hers.

Rebecca cruised slowly along the lochside road in the evening light, which seemed to linger later here than it had in the city only days before. On the face of the hill, across burnished water finely crinkled by the lightest of winds, delicate elongated shadows stretched with perfect definition from every tree and rock. Rebecca had always loved this kind of West Coast early spring evening and had chosen to arrive precisely at this time, nosing slowly along the well-known road with the sunset light filling the sky before her as the loch opened to the outer sound.

There were changes. Between road and loch on her left spread a picnic area with wooden tables and litter bins and paths artfully and meaninglessly coiling across open ground, where this year's weeds were doing better than this year's grass and trodden areas showed where human feet preferred more direct routes. Past this messy expanse was a caravan park, almost full of permanent trailer houses with their excrescences of gas cylinders, dustbins, locked tool boxes, water butts, concrete paths, even occasional flower beds and small bushes.

The line of houses spreading out from Luig began sooner than she had expected and where the hillside above used to be one great sweep of blazing yellow gorse there were now raw tracks gouged out and a scatter of log cabins on ugly breeze block foundations. Luig itself had changed little, she was thankful to see, its stone houses too tightly crammed round the narrow harbour to leave much room for invasive improvements. Some sheds and small shops near the pier had gone to make room for a big new carpark and there were the usual ravages of cheap wooden-faced loft extensions jutting out of slate roofs, plate-glass windows and crude fascias on the shops and a multiplicity of signs. However, it was still recognisably Luig, cherished part of childhood, and Rebecca wound down her window and breathed in its fumy, fishy, salty, workaday smell and was satisfied.

She went on, keeping to the now narrower and almost deserted road along the shore, at this time of year used only by local traffic. In summer most tourist cars and all coaches came as far as Luig, then went north over the moor and back to Fort William via Inverbuie, though a few cars took this longer loop round the peninsula. She would go round it herself tomorrow, Rebecca promised herself, get the map of all the well-known ground fixed in her head again.

'As if you need to, you idiot,' she said aloud, her spirits soaring. She should not have stayed away so long. Tony hadn't asked if he could inherit the place — had he? — and what would she have done with it, anyway? Well, skip that. It was good to be coming back under this flexible arrangement, to work her passage, stay as long as it suited her. Until she had decided what to do. But she dragged her thoughts hurriedly back. She would be part of the place and not just a guest. Or, since that had a different connotation now that the place was a hotel, not just visiting family. She had thought through, she believed, the idea of Ardlonach being full of strangers. She was prepared for the inevitable changes. She was ready to accept it as Tony and Una's home.

Una had first come to Ardlonach in her teens. Her father had been a shooting friend of Kenneth Urquhart's and had brought his daughter along 'to meet some young people' oblivious of the fact that the cousins were then in their early twenties and had seemed like a different generation to the shy sixteen-year-old. She had fallen there and then in love with Tony and had tenaciously clung to this devotion through his manifold affairs and two broken engagements.

Tony's three elder sisters and Rebecca, who grew very fond of Una through these fraught visits and felt protective towards her, had all assured her that he wasn't worth the agony and had advised her to forget about him, but they might as well have saved their breath. Una had hung in there with all the tenacity of the under-confident and she and Tony had been married while he was still in the Navy, eight years ago now. Tony had resigned his commission when Uncle Kenneth's will was finally thrashed out and they had opened Ardlonach as a hotel five years ago. Una was not only diffident and self-effacing but incurably messy and disorganised, the last person to be able to cope with the challenges and sheer drudgery of hotel life, Rebecca had thought when she had first heard of the plan. And Tony was never a stayer; it was hard to imagine him buckling down to them either. However, she had been proved wrong. By all accounts Ardlonach had been successful and was now about to open for its sixth season.

Three miles past Luig the road climbed along the flank of the hill and presently the familiar drive turned off towards the loch, winding down first through pines and birches then in the greater shelter of the steep south-facing slope through rhododendrons and azaleas and ornamental shrubs, to come out onto a gravel sweep behind the spreading, cream-painted, climber-smothered house.

'I love this place,' Rebecca thought, almost choking with

pure unexpected happiness as she got out of the car and stood for a moment in the golden light, the windless warmth and scented air which more than anything brought the nostalgic memories flooding back. 'Thank God I came.'

Where would Tony and Una be? No need to brace herself to face guests tonight; the place wasn't open yet. Would Una, a passionate gardener, be outside somewhere catching the last of the light and warmth? And would Tony, a considerably less dedicated worker, be in the drawing-room with his first gin of the evening?

Full of optimism and a tolerant affection for them both, Rebecca crossed with her quick buoyant step to the big glazed porch. Trapped warmth; smell of jackets in which people had fished, sailed, stalked. So good.

'Tony! Una!' she called in the silence, opening the inner door, 'I'm here.' At least she wouldn't be flown at by those damned pugs Una used to cart round everywhere with her. Her last two Christmas cards had contained no news except the demise of first one and then the other. Unless she'd replaced them of course. But no furious yaps arose, no dogs appeared. The door from the study opened and Una stood there, clinging to the door handle as though wounded, her small face drenched with tears, her dark eyes wide with despair.

'Una, what on earth has happened?' Rebecca leapt forward in consternation. 'What's the matter?'

Una rubbed at her face with a balled-up tissue, took a hiccupy breath and managed to get out, 'Oh, Rebecca, thank goodness you've come.'

'But what's wrong? Una, tell me, whatever's going on?'

'It's Tony, he's gone.'

'What do you mean, gone? Gone where?'

'To the Cayman Islands. With a Wren called Serena.'

Chapter Two

'But when did all this happen?'

The first wave of tears and concern was over and they had moved into what Rebecca remembered as her uncle's comfortable white-panelled book-filled study, now a chaotic office with a computer staring out of a raft of papers so rumpled they might have been its own nesting litter.

'Yesterday,' Una gulped, going to pluck another wodge of tissues out of a nearly empty box. The wastepaper basket was overflowing with a sodden mass. 'I tried to phone you but you'd already left. Your mother didn't know where you were.'

'But what did Tony say? What's it all about?'

In spite of Tony's track record her cousin and Una had always seemed to Rebecca, in the glimpses she had had of them since the wedding on their occasional visits to Edinburgh, to be remarkably happy together. But Tony had always been given to short-lived passions and it probably couldn't have been expected to last, she thought grimly, looking at Una's small vulnerable face and shaking hands.

'He'd been saying for ages he was bored by the punters and couldn't stand the thought of opening again and that he wished he'd never turned the place into a hotel at all,' Una poured out in a breathless stream, drawing back with both hands her mass of light-textured dark hair with a familiar and quite useless gesture, since it floated back at once to frame her thin face as before. 'But he says the same thing every spring so I didn't really take any notice, then he went off for a few days to drum up business, he said, then he came back and told me – he told me—'

But she couldn't go on and Rebecca with an angry exclamation stepped forward and wrapped her arms round her, noting as she did so that Una's slight frame, not built to withstand strife or shocks, seemed more fragile than ever. 'Oh, poor Una, that husband of yours always could be a bastard when he felt like it. But surely this affair can't be anything serious? It sounds terribly sudden.'

'No, no, they'd been writing to each other for ages, he told me so,' Una wailed. 'He told me everything. It was awful. He told me that he loathed people staying in the house and that since we'd been running the place as a hotel I'd changed, our relationship had changed. Well, of course it had, we're always so busy and I'm exhausted half the time and Tony gets terribly impatient with me when I'm late and everything, but I still feel exactly the same about him as I always did. I always shall, in spite of what he's done . . .' Sobbing, she rested her head against Rebecca's firm shoulder.

'But Una, Tony can't possibly mean to go for good. He's probably fed up, you know how he loses interest in things, but this is his home and his livelihood and you're his wife. He can't just walk out on the whole lot so lightly.' She wanted to ask brisk practical questions about what he had taken with him and what arrangements he had made about the business and cash and paying the bills but she knew that in general people found such matter-of-factness insensitive, and Una, if she had even thought about such matters yet, would certainly be incapable of discussing them in her present state.

'No, no, he loves her. They've known each other since he was in the Navy. They've always kept in touch apparently. She understands him.'

Rebecca's lips twisted involuntarily at the cliché, used so

sincerely by Una who obviously still accepted every word Tony uttered as meaningful and valuable.

'And she's rich. At least, her father is. He owns some sort of leisure complex, all very up-market, on the Cayman Islands and Tony is going to run it for him.'

It didn't seem to occur to her that it was precisely the sort of job he'd grown tired of here, Rebecca thought with disbelief, but resisted pointing it out. And Una was pretty well-off herself, or had Tony run through all her cash already? Surely not?

'It's such a nightmare,' Una went on desperately, 'we should be opening soon, Easter's so early this year, and now there's everyone to write to. Guests to put off and staff as well – will we be liable for some sort of compensation, do you think? Only the trouble is, so many of our guests feel they're special friends, they'll probably expect to come anyway. But that would be worse, because they know us, I mean. Then there are two new girls coming from Australia. They're on the way already and I don't even know how to get hold of them to stop them – and there are all the orders to cancel, only I'm not exactly sure what Tony had ordered already, and then should I tell Caroline and the twins, or will Tony have told them himself? And his mother, what should I do about his mother ... ?'

'Hold on. Wait a minute, never mind all that for the moment.' Rebecca realised that sounded impatient and hastily modified her tone. 'What are you saying about the hotel? Are you suggesting that you don't open up for Easter?'

'How can I open without Tony? How could I open ever? He organises things, he knows about everything, the accounts and the bar and wages and licences and fire regulations and all that sort of thing. How could I possibly do it without him? And how could I even think about all those things now ... ?'

'But you can't just shut.' To Rebecca's business-orientated mind this was much more important that what Tony might or might not have told his family. Let them sort that out among themselves. 'The place is doing well, isn't it? And what would you do then – just go on living here on your own?' Not phrased in the most consoling way, she realised, and in any case too large a question to be embarked on now. She hurried on. 'And if Tony comes back, which I'm damned sure he soon will, what are you going to say to him? That you've thrown up everything you've worked for together?' As he had just done. Rebecca knew what she would say if anyone put this to her in similar circumstances, but Una had a strange blind adoration for her flighty husband and this approach actually worked.

'Yes, it would be awful,' she agreed. 'I do see that.'

'Well, look, I can help you, if that's any use. I'm free for a while.' She was free indefinitely, though she thought it wiser not to say so and had no wish to be reminded of the reason just now. 'We can surely just carry on, can't we, for the time being? A lot of it must be routine for you by now.' Or was that hoping too much?

'But I can't fix things, do repairs. Everything's always breaking down, particularly when we're busy, you've no idea, boilers and hoovers and the ice-maker and all that sort of thing.'

'Then we get someone in to sort them. Don't be so wet.'

For a moment Una looked almost hopeful then her face crumpled again. 'No, Rebecca, you don't understand, it's not just the hotel, it's far worse than that.'

'What are you talking about?'

'It's this new plan of Tony's. He started it up last season, although it barely had time to take off then. But he's been doing a huge amount of marketing all winter and he's got dozens of courses set up. Oh, how can he have just walked away from it, he's been so excited about it – at least, I thought he was. But I haven't the first idea about all that side of things, it will all have to be cancelled.'

'Una, I shall shake you in a minute. What are you talk-ing about?'

'Tony's new courses. I should have started on those letters

first. Wherever are they?' Una made a helpless stirring motion among the curled and creased papers on the wide director's desk which made Rebecca groan and raise her eyes to the ceiling. 'How could I have forgotten about them? But I wasn't really involved, and it all sounded so daunting. Besides, I was far too busy with everything else. I didn't really pay much attention, it was all so much Tony's project. No, no, I'll explain,' she said hurriedly, seeing the growing fury in Rebecca's face. 'Tony was setting up an outdoor centre, you know the sort of thing, leadership training for managers and executives, throwing them out of boats and off cliffs and so on—' (she said this quite seriously, Rebecca noted with passing pleasure) '—and he's converted the farm buildings into accommodation for them and set up a sort of assault course, at least that's not finished yet, along in the next bay, and this year he wanted a new bar for the courses to use, where the coach-house used to be. He thought we might do bar suppers there, or anyway some kind of catering, though we'd never really worked out how, because the kitchen's at the other end of the house and we're a lot busier than we used to be in the dining-room now because of all the sailing people from the new marina they've opened in Luig—'

You bastard, Tony Urquhart, Rebecca thought, hardly listening any more. You've bitten off more than you can chew and you've taken the easy way out. An understanding Wren called Serena and her rich father turn up as an easy option and Ardlonach is tossed away. Too boring; too difficult; done that. And then what? Sell it? Let it go out of the family who four generations ago chose for it this perfect setting facing south over Loch Luig, who in the century since had created its profuse and varied garden falling in terraces to the little bay, and had loved the sprawling, comfortable, wide-windowed house? In that moment Rebecca knew that she wasn't going to let it happen.

'Una, listen to me. Calm down. We're not writing to anyone tonight. We're going to talk about this properly and see what we can work out. There's a lot to be taken into account, I can see that. This training scheme is a whole new issue. Perhaps that can be dumped, perhaps we could just keep the hotel ticking along, but for the moment we're doing nothing. Leave this lot exactly as it is and let's go and find some food. More importantly, some drink. Let's brace ourselves with a massive gin each to start with.'

One bright spot was that the pug era seemed to be over. It would probably be a bit brutal to express relief about it though, it occurred even to Rebecca, and anyway might provoke fresh cascades of tears which would delay dinner even more.

'Oh, Rebecca, I can't tell you how glad I am that you're here. It's the only thing that's kept me sane for the last twenty-four hours.'

'And even that seems debatable.'

A first wobbly smile appeared on Una's thin sad face. 'I wonder if you'll recognise your old room. I thought you'd like to have it, to start with anyway, but I'm afraid it's been done up a little. It's mainly used for children, though,' she offered, as though that would make the changes easier to accept. It didn't, though for a reason she couldn't possibly guess at, and Rebecca turned away to hide the stab of pain she couldn't dodge.

She knew she should show some interest in the work Tony and Una had put into the house but she was too honest to be enthusiastic about it. 'I'll fetch my things,' she said. 'No point in trekking all the way up there empty-handed.'

The little room on the top floor had not after all changed too much. Its rickety painted furniture with the cock-eyed transfers of Pooh and friends they had slapped all over it one wet afternoon had gone. The old rug with its deep blue edges and huge roses in the corners and threadbare beige centre had had its day even then. But Una had kept the colours the same – white paintwork, walls and carpet a soft smoky blue – and nothing could change the light off the loch which poured in through the high gable window, or the view down the steep fall of the garden, which even so early in the year was sufficiently protected to have the first lush look of spring. And there straight ahead lay the island. Their island. As she crossed to the window to gaze at it Rebecca was shaken by a great surge of nostalgia for the mingled scents of salt water and sun-baked turf, the feel of air cool on skin, familiar voices, seabirds' cries, childhood's time-scale of endless days. Why did I stay away so long, she wondered again in disbelief – while simultaneously the fierce resentment returned that Tony, the youngest of them all, should have been given all this as of right, a resentment sharpened by her new anger that he should take his ownership so lightly.

'We've managed a little bathroom up here too,' Una was saying. 'The water pressure's hopeless of course and there wasn't room for a bath, but we put a pump in and the shower works really well. It will save you going up and down, but of course if you want a bath the one at the bottom of the stairs doesn't belong to any of the rooms. Is this all right? Do you mind things being changed?'

'You've made it beautiful.' The appearance of rooms was not particularly important to Rebecca so long as they were uncluttered and more or less all of a piece. But she recognised the care Una had put into this small coom-ceilinged attic, she liked the crisp frills on the kidney-shaped dressing table and the new elegant brass bed – though that heavy white cotton counterpane must take some looking after if this room was used for children, as it surely must be. She pushed her mind on past that to the countless details that make up hotel-keeping, which for the time being were all down to Una, this waif-like gentle girl with her reddened eyes and bruised look of shock. In spite of herself, Rebecca felt her own brain leap to grapple with the problems ahead.

You're meant to be having a holiday, she reminded herself ironically. You're here for a rest. You've had several years in a stressful demanding job and this is meant to be a break.

She had spent two nights on the way here in a hotel in Lochearnhead, had made herself stay in bed late each morning and even have breakfast there, trying to persuade herself it was a luxury but actually longing to get up and get going. She had idled about for the intervening day feeling frustrated and wishing she hadn't decided to wait to get some outdoor kit till she reached Ardlonach. She had sat on a bar stool before lunch and dinner and failed to find rewarding company, had eaten a lot of uninspired food and begun to wonder what on earth she was doing there. In fact the two days of inactivity had been more than enough for her and she had been glad this morning to point the car north-west and sweep up the much improved road through Crianlarich and Tyndrum.

'Truly, I love it,' she said, turning to Una. 'It was nice of you to think of putting me up here.'

'Tony was sure you'd like it best—' Una began, then choked. That conversation had taken place so short a time ago.

'Come on,' Rebecca said gently, taking her arm and giving it a little shake. 'How about dinner? Do you think you can find us something? I didn't bother about lunch. I took a little side trip off to Loch Laggan. It was such a treat to hit the gap between winter conditions and no tourists that I couldn't resist the empty roads.'

'Goodness, you must be starving.' Rebecca had known the appeal for food would work. Cooking was Una's second equal passion with gardening. 'I'll go down and start. Your favourite, *brochettes* of pork. They have to sit for a while before grilling and anyway there's the barbecue sauce to make ...' Scatty as Una might be about almost every aspect of ordinary life, she had a phenomenal memory for people's food likes and dislikes.

Rebecca heard her running eagerly down the dangerous little stair and smiled affectionately. It was useful to have such instant therapy to hand. But a husband so callously, so carelessly, walking away would deal a wound whose impact she thought Una had as yet scarely realised.

*   *   *

Two days ago the mean pluck of Edinburgh's east wind lying in wait round street corners, flattening the crocuses in the squares, whipping at the early blossom; here the soft sweet air of the west, the quietness, and the unexpectedly powerful sense of homecoming. Rebecca had known this place meant a lot to her but she had not been prepared for her intense physical reaction to it, or for the fierce possessiveness which Tony's casual defection had renewed in her.

She went easily, letting her feet find the way instinctively down the twists and steps of the path to the bay. And pretty silly you'll look if they've been improving this too, she warned herself.

They had had dinner in the kitchen, Una deciding to open a good Margaux with a little spurt of defiance which Rebecca had been glad to see, though briefly irritated that defiance should be necessary, and in spite of all emotional stress the pork had been cooked to perfection. Rebecca had seen to it that Una's glass was well filled. Oblivious sleep would do her good, though how she would function in the morning when there was so much to be discussed and organised was another question. Una had lost some of her desperate tautness over dinner and Rebecca had let her talk and cry and once or twice even laugh a little hysterically at her own naïvety. Over the years they had established a good relationship and Rebecca knew that of all the family she was probably the best person to have turned up just now. Or had Tony deliberately timed his disappearance to coincide with her arrival? Because he couldn't face her, or because he knew he could off-load Una on to her, and even perhaps the plans which had got so far beyond his control?

Did Una have no friends nearby who could have helped her? But Rebecca could guess that she had been too devastated to think of turning to anyone. She had just sat alone in the house, weeping and helpless, knowing Rebecca would come.

Her eyes accustomed now to the tenuous darkness, Rebecca passed between the back of the long stone boathouse, black bulking shape against the paler water, and the small cliff which was the end of the protecting ridge which made Ardlonach the drowsy luxuriant enclave it was, and went out on to the jetty, solid under her feet. She avoided without conscious thought the spots where heavy ring-bolts were set into the stone, then realised what she had done and smiled. Cooler air off the water touched her cheek as she reached the end of the jetty. She turned up the collar of her long-skirted Musto riding coat. Odd how clothes which seemed casual in the city felt immediately so wrong here.

She could see the dark shape of the island across the silver-grey quiet water. In this light she could pick out no details but her memory produced them without effort. The seaward end was an eroded cliff, eaten away endlessly by the winds and pounding seas coming in from the west. The thin wind-scoured turf sloped down to a grassy central hollow with a white shingle bay in its curve, then the ground rose again at the eastern end, clothed with stunted birches and hazels and hollies. So familiar, so full of associations. Suddenly, most unwontedly, tears assailed her. Change, the simple fact of the passing of the years, Una's grief, her own resolute pulling up of roots and flight from the one thing she knew she could not face — it all added up to something unbearable, lonely, huge. She stood there shivering, looking through blurred eyes at the scattered lights across the loch, the high dark shapes of the hills, but she refused to let the tears come.

Chapter Three

It was clear from the beginning that this meeting was not going to produce very much of the positive planning Rebecca had hoped for. She thought she had rarely seen two more surly and uncooperative characters. They were wary and embarrassed with Una, whose strained unhappiness was all too evident, and resentfully dismissive of herself, making her sharply aware of how incongruous she looked, especially in the context of what they were here to discuss, in her emerald shirt and black wool skirt, her dark tights and high heels. She could understand their reservations. They had never set eyes on her till now, as far as they knew she had nothing whatsoever to do with Ardlonach, yet here she was plunging in with all these searching questions about their part of the operation. But what seemed to her a great deal more worrying than their watchful hostility and grudging replies was that they didn't even seem to be on the same side, seemed indeed as the round-the-table discussion she was trying to generate limped along with the minimum of input from either of them, to distrust and dislike each other profoundly.

That's all we need, Rebecca thought, surveying them with tight lips and eyes as truculently assessing as their own. The elder of the two, Innes Mann, head instructor of Tony's leadership school, was a wiry individual in his mid forties with the walnut skin of the outdoor man, the press-button aggression of the small man and, Rebecca suspected though he was being moderately careful about what he said, the sexist attitudes of the stupid man.

The younger, Dan McNee, was saying even less, his face expressionless but his whole body language proclaiming that he didn't like what had happened, didn't like being where he was and had no hopes of anything being resolved by all this bullshit. He was sitting in a late eighteenth-century satinwood armchair, his compact strongly-built body making it look dangerously fragile, his hefty thighs in tight washed-out clean jeans spread wide, arms folded across his well-developed chest. He was well back in the chair as though to distance himself from what was being said. His strong, smooth neck was revealed by the black T-shirt which was all he was wearing on a March morning a good deal cooler and windier than the last two days had been. His dark hair was short and smooth on his bullet head. (Good for head-butting, Rebecca thought detachedly.) His unusually light grey eyes were carefully blank. The impression he gave in the small cluttered office was of excessive tamped-down energy, and Rebecca marked him down as one of those P.E. instructor types who flaunt their fitness in perpetual challenge, usually because they have nothing else to offer. He should be bouncing aggressively on the balls of his feet in some gym, she decided with disfavour, wearing a vest and bawling at pale little wimps clinging to some impossible piece of apparatus like shot escapers impaled on the wire.

Where on earth had Tony found these two unfriendly bastards? But she knew because she'd checked. All the instructors (two more were due to arrive shortly) had been culled from ex-Service backgrounds. No surprise there; Tony in his heart had never left the Navy. In fact this whole enterprise of the training school she suspected to be an unacknowledged harking back to it.

She and Una had agreed to say that Tony was away temporarily but that everything would go forward as planned without him. It had been settled that Una would tell them this but when the moment came she had been unable to formulate the words, looking helplessly with filling eyes at Rebecca who had swiftly stepped in, dealt out the information succinctly and swept on at once to business.

'Naturally I'm more than capable of handling the course aspect,' Innes was saying patronisingly. 'That's what Tony employed me for and I have all the relevant qualifications and experience. But I must be sure that all necessary resources will be made available to me. So far we've got less than half the equipment we were promised, the accommodation leaves a lot to be desired and as you know we did find last season that there was a definite need for better facilities, a separate bar and so on, catering back-up, a larger drying room properly heated and ventilated, more storage space. I take it all that would be forthcoming?'

Pompous too, Rebecca noted dispassionately as Innes, clearly seizing his chance to up the ante, addressed all this to Una with a well-calculated degree of insistence. Rebecca was glad that she had stayed in the office till one this morning going through the relevant paperwork. She hadn't known what she would be up against when she did it, she was merely doing her homework from habit, but with this chancer she was obviously going to have to stay one step ahead of the game all the time. It would be a pleasure.

'The materials for the assault course are at the joiners in Luig, so that's not a problem and it will be the next job to be completed,' she stepped in smoothly, her tone a practised blend of authority and politic reasonableness as Una turned to her looking anxious. 'As for bringing the rest of the equipment up to requirement – boots, protective clothing, compasses, first-aid kit, maps, wetsuits, sailing gear and so on – we'll have to take stock to begin with and establish what's there.' She had been unable to find an inventory and didn't want to ask Innes for one. She suspected it didn't exist.

'Oh, here, that would take for ever,' Innes protested instantly and blusteringly. 'You've no idea how much we have to do. We can't go wasting time counting all that stuff if we've to finish the obstacles for the assault course and get everything else ready in time. Someone else will have to do it.'

'Well, you'll be able to work from your existing lists,' Rebecca said blandly. 'It's just a matter of checking that they're up to date. If you want deficiencies made up we'll have to know what's there – I don't know what the time-lag is for delivery but the first course arrives in two weeks so I should think confirming existing stock must be a priority.'

She felt rather than saw that she had gained the other man's full attention. He hadn't moved a muscle but he had definitely reacted to this – with antagonism? Would he and Innes simply walk out, considering it not worth their while to buckle down to sorting out the chaos Tony had left behind him? How badly did they need their jobs? Rebecca had been slightly startled at what they were paid; either Tony was being generous or they were greater assets than they looked.

'I'm sure we'll be able to get everything you need, though it may take some time,' Una put in worriedly and placatingly. 'I know Tony was very keen that the courses should be well equipped.'

Oh, Una, for God's sake, go back to your kitchen. The triumphant predatory gleam in Innes's little eyes had been unmistakable.

Tony had indeed been keen, which was why this meeting was about discussing the future of the courses and not about handing out P45s. Rebecca's researches had shown not only a terrifying outlay on marketing, building conversions and materials, but that the huge deposits paid up front by prestigious companies already seemed to have been gobbled up. She had not had time for a detailed trawl through the accounts, nor had she had access to all the information, most of which seemed to be with the auditors, but her hair had stood on end at what she had discovered and she was thankful that Una, trusting and innumerate, had no idea of it.

For some reason Tony had made the activities training a separate business in his name alone and it was already deeply in the red. Forward bookings were excellent, however, and with temporary help it might survive. The hotel showed an encouraging upward trend in turnover and it seemed to Rebecca that it was sound sense to go forward. Certainly the cash to return those deposits was not there. It seemed unbelievable, even for Tony, that he had swanned off making no financial arrangements of any kind. The hotel would have to subsidise the new enterprise for the time being but it had very little slack with which to do so, particularly in view of the big orders necessary to stock up for opening.

'But who's to be in charge?' Innes was demanding belligerently in his rather high voice, directing his fire at Una who though nominally his boss was a useless female, ignorant of his area of expertise and therefore easily bullied. The other woman, this black-haired bossy bitch who'd blown in from nowhere, would in any case soon be off back to the city where she belonged. 'What I'm saying is, Tony knew what it was all about and he intended to run a lot of the sea-survival side himself, so who's to take his place? And who'll handle the logistics?' It was clear he thought the word would alarm Una. 'I'll certainly be needing another instructor and someone to handle the equipment, clean the accommodation and so on.'

Good try, Rebecca thought. You do all the macho, ego-massaging instruction bit, dump the wet filthy kit for someone else to sort out and bog off to the bar which we obligingly provide for you.

'No extra instructor,' she said briefly. 'You've got two more coming next week. All maintenance and cleaning of the equipment will be done as before, by the people who use it.'

Innes swung a reddening face towards her. 'I'm still asking, who's to be in charge?' It was as near as he could go to demanding outright what any of this had to do with her. Those mean little eyes go round when he's angry, Rebecca noted. I must remember that. But he's quite right, I can't answer that, it has to be down to Una.

Dan still said nothing but Rebecca could feel his focused concentration, his waiting intentness.

Una didn't fail her this time. 'Oh, it's all right, Rebecca has agreed to help me out,' she rushed in eagerly, smiling with pleasure, oblivious of all undercurrents. 'Isn't it good of her? So we thought if we all agreed that we could try to carry on as before. At least, we can see how we get on, and then we don't have to write to everyone and tell them there's no holiday, or no course – or no job,' she wound up, innocently hitting the vital nail on the head, and looking at each antagonistic male in turn with a mixture of friendliness and appeal that Rebecca couldn't have achieved in a lifetime. Friendliness, directness, cards on the table she could cope with; appeal was an art she had never had much use for.

'Well, as I said, I can handle all the day-to-day running for you,' Innes repeated, having made a swift calculation of the pay, his comfortable self-contained cottage accommodation, the increase in control the new order would give him once the interfering cousin had disappeared and Una was on her own, and the relative lateness of the season for looking for another job with equal perks. He debated adding, 'But I shan't want anyone looking over my shoulder,' decided he couldn't hit a sufficiently uncontroversial note and left that for later.

Dan McNee merely nodded, without any relaxation of the set facial muscles. His winter job, in which he was still engaged, was based in a lodge over near Spean Bridge, instructing in snow and ice climbing. He had been delighted last season to achieve the perfect dovetail of summer and winter jobs in the area where he wanted to live and work. Unlike Innes, however, he had turned down Tony's offered accommodation, preferring independence in a rented slit of a cottage in Inshmore village, a tiny collection of dwellings half a mile westward along the shore. He craved its solitude after the months of crowded living in the climbing hut. And this development might, after all, be interesting. Tony had been a poncer, not even close to the tough man he liked to think himself, but Dan had been prepared to let him dream on since he was harmless on the whole and generous to the point of lunacy. Innes Mann, however, was another matter, dangerously conceited, carrying a permanent chip on his shoulder and one of those idiots who, unable to see their day is done, insist on pitting themselves against the younger, fitter men coming along at their heels. Innes could never leave it alone, making statements, picking fights, stretching himself fanatically. One of these days he'd blow a fuse – or someone would quietly drop him off something from a great height.

This girl Una, she'd been left with a lot on her plate. Dan had only been at Ardlonach for a couple of months at the end of last summer and had seen very little of her in the hassle of setting up the new courses adequately so that no one was actually killed at the outset, pruning Tony's over-ambitious plans, sorting out tackle, establishing some sort of assessment scale, even painting the bloody accommodation in spare moments. The hotel itself had been equally busy and he had known Una chiefly as a harried ghost, throwing him shy and lovely smiles as she passed, her cloudy dark hair ever wilder, her slim figure turning to skin and bone, her arms never free from oven burns, her fingers decked with the cook's regulation blue plasters.

What was the story about Tony? They were covering up, surely; they couldn't seriously expect to see him back. Then again, this bird Tony was always talking about, who it seemed he'd finally taken off with, had sounded definitely more than he would be able to handle so perhaps he would show up again sometime. When they'd got things up and running for him, probably, Dan thought sourly. It had been a shambles at the end of last season and it must have been pure luck that there'd been no comeback from any of the big companies.

But presumably whingeing about the course would hardly be good for the victim's image back at the ranch. Dan grinned inwardly.

And this other female, what was her interest in the place? She seemed to have a pretty good grasp of what went on and she'd given old Innes a couple of body blows he hadn't been expecting, but how long would she be around to keep Una straight? She could be trouble, Dan decided, his mind going back to one or two episodes last year which he knew they'd been lucky to get away with, but Una would need someone to help her and he suspected that the outdoor school would stand more chance of its needs being supplied in a methodical fashion with Rebecca around than it ever had till now. She looked as though she could lash things into shape. Executive trouble-shooter, he summed her up with ready contempt, taking in the well-defined cut of the glossy black hair, the square jaw, the uncompromising look in the dark blue eyes, the overall air of vigorous determination. She wasn't tall and she'd make two of Una but her body looked pleasantly firm and she carried herself well. He liked the way she went staight for the guts of a problem, clearly impatient with tap-dancing and waffle. She'd obviously be off back to the big city in due course, everything about her appearance was out of place here, but meanwhile she could probably keep Una on the rails. Only if she ever tried to give him the run around as she had just done to Innes she wouldn't know what had hit her. Still, all in all it would be worth taking a raincheck on the situation, Dan decided, and even if it turned out to be a total disaster it wouldn't be his head on the block.

'God, when did you ever meet such an arrogant and obstructive pair?' Rebecca broke out wrathfully when Innes and Dan had taken themselves off to the boathouse, supposedly to start taking stock but actually to make a brew and have their first head-to-head of the season. She had observed, however, that it had been Dan, not Innes, who had suggested taking with them a copy of the forward planner for the courses already booked. A pity that no such planner appeared to exist. Rebecca had told him she would prepare one, her heart sinking at the thought of producing it from scratch from Tony's disordered bulging folder with COURSES scrawled laconically across the front.

'Did you think so? Tony swore by them,' Una said in surprise. She thought everything had been settled most satisfactorily.

'Yes, well, they—' Rebecca checked herself heroically. It was no use saying she was certain that they would have had Tony exactly where they wanted him. One of the hardest things during the last two days had been to hold her tongue about him since any criticism reduced Una to instant tears and that interfered with the work. Rebecca found it hard to understand this loving protectiveness. Tony had behaved like a complete bastard, he was off halfway across the world with another woman, had left no means of contacting him and as far as she could see had not troubled himself to make practical arrangements of any kind for his wife or his property or even his personal belongings, yet all Una wanted was to have him back. She wanted Tony in charge, wanted his presence about the place, his casual passing hugs, the occasional kiss dropped on her hair, his laughter, his enthusiasm for new schemes, his airy capacity to fix what seemed to her enormous problems, but above all she wanted his arm under her neck and his familiar warm body close beside hers in the big empty bed.

'Well, unrewarding characters though they appear to me, they're both highly qualifed and one has to assume competent,' Rebecca conceded, but a doubt instantly rose in her mind. There had been a circled question mark with an explosion of asterisks around it against one section of Dan's CV. He had been a sergeant in the RAF Regiment (Rebecca wasn't sure what that was) but there seemed nothing in the brief resumé of his service career, from leaving school to four years ago at the age of twenty-eight, to raise that query in Tony's mind.

'They can presumably get on with the job under their own

steam,' she said, dismissing the niggling little uncertainty. Tony had decided to employ him, whatever that question mark had referred to. 'And do it safely, which is the crucial thing from our point of view.'

'I know Tony was very pleased when he took them on,' Una offered eagerly, only thankful that her cherished husband wasn't under fire again. Of course, Rebecca was family; she couldn't be expected to see him as Una did. 'In fact I think he thought they were both a bit overqualified.'

Rebecca grunted. 'Yes, well, I think they're going to be a pain in the butt. They've got us marked down as a couple of helpless tarts who wouldn't know a carabiner from a sheetbend – oh God, Una, don't ask – and they've probably made up their minds that they're going to take us for a ride. Don't look so worried, I shan't go picking any fights, believe me. We need those two and for a couple of moments there I thought we were going to lose them both.'

'Oh, no, I'm sure they wouldn't let us down, they thought the world of Tony,' Una protested.

She sincerely believes that, Rebecca realised with sardonic wonder. She actually thinks it's a consideration which would keep them here and she's prepared to like them because of it. Why can't I be a nice person like that?

Chapter Four

'Food orders, bar orders, wine stock. Glasses, china, silver, stationery, linen, kitchen equipment, cleaning stuff – how are you off for all those? And do you kit the staff out? What do they wear? How about oil and logs and Calor gas and that kind of thing?'

'Goodness,' said Una in simple admiration. 'You're an accountant, I don't know how you know so much about hotels.'

'Well, sometimes I eat, drink and sleep in them,' Rebecca reminded her. 'You don't need a four-year course to be able to work out that people are going to want sheets on their beds and salt in the salt cellars when they're expected to pay through the nose for the pleasure of staying here. You did take stock at the end of last season, I suppose? No, you didn't take stock.'

Had Tony just fudged up some figures for the auditor? She refrained from asking what he and Una had done with themselves since the hotel shut at the end of last season. Una, she knew, would have spent hours in her beloved garden which would always need far more attention than she could give it, though apparently she had part-time help for the heavy jobs. Tony had certainly done a good deal of work on the new bar for the survival courses, though he had not quite brought himself to finish it or of course equip or stock it, and much of his time this winter had been spent going off touting for business for his new enterprise, which he had done to some effect. But surely the pair of them hadn't intended to start the season on the remnants of stock left over from last year?

It was at moments like these that Rebecca regretted her rash confidence in deciding that the only thing to do was go ahead and open, trusting to Tony to see sense and reappear before long. She could believe that he was capable of leaving Una, brutal though that sounded, for Una in her own gentle well-meaning way could be maddening at times, but she could not bring herself to believe that he would abandon Ardlonach for good.

There had been times in the last couple of days when she had thought she would have to give up the plan anyway, those times when Una's despair overwhelmed her and she was unable to turn her mind to anything but her own grief and the tormented self-questioning as to where she had failed Tony, what she had done wrong. But Una had made valiant efforts to keep these agonies to herself, gathering up her determination each time to support Rebecca and tackle the formidable list of waiting jobs. It was rough therapy but it kept at bay the images of Tony plunging with fresh enthusiasm into yet another undertaking, Tony relaxing, sailing, drinking, talking and laughing in the Caribbean sun, Tony with Serena.

'I think we're all right for most things,' she answered Rebecca uncertainly, a worried frown appearing between her big gentle dark eyes. 'I mean, things won't have disappeared during the winter, will they? No one's been here,' she added reasonably.

Rebecca stared at her, swore, then laughed. 'What a nice relaxed way to run a pub,' she mocked. 'And I suppose when you look innocently at the punters and tell them very nicely that they'll have to drink their wine out of a tumbler or manage without soap they'll all pat you kindly on the head and assure you it doesn't matter a bit? Come on, woman, we've got things to do.'

In spite of her inborn zest for problem-solving it was a fraught period and Rebecca felt for most of the time that she was trying to run up a hill of sand. Except for the food side which Una looked after, though with a gay disregard for relative prices which Rebecca found distinctly scary, every order had to be made more or less from scratch, looking up the supplier from previous invoices (the most recent of which were at the auditors and should surely have been back long before this, another thing to chase up), laboriously checking references, quantities and phone numbers, many of which had changed and, on more occasions that she had ever told Una about, finding that an account had been closed. Starting up an order book was her first innovation.

Crushing Una's objections that it was too soon, she routed a couple of local staff out of their winter sloth and set them to work cleaning the house and even, though they were pointedly huffy about this, getting ready the staff quarters and the bunk accommodation for the course participants. At the west end of Ardlonach House the ground fell away before rising again to the low ridge which protected it from the Atlantic weather fronts. The basement area this created had originally housed the carriages of Victorian times and now, besides games room, cellar and various store-rooms, provided generous space for the new bar. Across the wide stretch of gravel outside staff bedrooms had been created above the garages in the ex-stables.

Rebecca could understand Donna and Aggie's resentment when she saw the state the accommodation was in, still just as it had been left after the end-of-season party, and she knew she would have to offer a sweetener. Fortunately it had been a lean winter and the two women were by now avid for the fat pickings of summer, so with a good deal of, 'This is the last time we'll do it, mind', and, 'It's no' our job, whichever way you look at it', they got grudgingly down to work.

Rebecca herself was discovering that no job could be started without doing at least two more to make way for it. Orders arriving couldn't be unpacked because the storage areas they were intended for had been used for painting or sand-blasting or were temporarily housing something quite different. There was a maddening lack of small but vital items like light bulbs, drawing pins, string, scissors, Sellotape, staples and stationery in general. Keys were missing, tools scattered, new purchases haphazardly piled on old stock, even sometimes on boxes that turned out to be empty, and every job anyone else started seemed to bring them within minutes to the office demanding equipment, materials or decisions.

Rebecca set her teeth and got down to it, trying to work out a logical sequence so that jobs didn't have to be done twice over, and to strike a level of ordering which would see them through the busy spell of Easter but not land them in immediate bankruptcy, much hampered by her unfamiliarity with the needs of the place, the suppliers, and half the items required. It appeared that last summer someone called Tina had dealt with most of this and Tony and Una had gladly abandoned the job to her. It had not been her problem to look ahead to the following season, indeed she had probably departed in utter relief that she would never have to worry about any of it again, but as a result there were some bizarre contradictions to juggle with. For example, Rebecca counted eighteen cases of spray polish but only two half-full toilet ducks in the entire building, four cartons of paper hand-towels which didn't fit the kitchen dispenser and one empty drum of powder for the dishwasher.

At least one thing which Rebecca had dreaded about coming back caused her none of the expected pain. She had thought it might sadden her unbearably to see this house, which she loved so much, not only in Tony's hands but pulled about and altered to meet the needs of a hotel. It had been changed of course, with new bathrooms wherever they could be fitted in, the kitchen wing gutted and redesigned, stairs and corridors chopped and divided by fire doors, and mandatory emergency signs marring Una's delicate colours and the air of solid old-fashioned comfort. But in the event Rebecca found herself far too busy to indulge in any morbid wanderings or attempts to recapture old memories and feelings. Work, more work than even her busy life had prepared her for, filled every second. Also in making the necessary alterations Una had done her job well, lovingly maintaining the style and even in some magical way the atmosphere of the house, with an eye for decor and an imaginativeness in furnishing which Rebecca knew she could never have matched. So the anticipated pain of returning in these new circumstances was simply by-passed, and when she had a moment to realise it she was thankful. She had been cowardly about coming back, putting it off with every kind of excuse. Now she had come at a moment when she was actually needed and that was good.

The run-up to opening had begun its inexorable process. The third instructor for the leadership courses arrived. He and the fourth man, due in a couple of days, were to share the other half of Innes's cottage at the old farm steading out of sight over the ridge. Rebecca decided the moment she saw him that here was Innes's runabout man, who would inevitably end up with all the tedious and disagreeable jobs and just as certainly wouldn't complain. Bernard was a big slow-moving, slow-speaking lad from Lancashire who called himself 'Bu-u-urn' in deep drawn-out syllables which no one could help imitating. He was huge and fair, enormously powerful and endlessly good-natured, a big relief after the unconcealed antagonism of Innes and Dan. Rebecca afterwards was convinced that without him and his willing help they would never have been ready to open in time.

Though Dan McNee had taken the chance when he came over for that edgy 'policy meeting' to shift most of his things into the Inshmore cottage, he still had another few days to work at the climbing lodge and wasn't on hand to make any contribution to the hectic preparations in the centre. How helpful he would in fact have been Rebecca wasn't certain, but she had an idea that he might value efficiency not only for its own sake but because in the long run it would serve his purpose. She didn't think he would have worked in Bern's unquestioning whole-hearted way, but he would probably have had enough sense to recognise that the centre could not function in complete isolation from the hotel.

Innes, on the other hand, though jealously demanding about his own requirements to the point of paranoia, took care not to be on hand for any job not directly connected with the school, and as far as Rebecca could see for very little that was. He seemed to make a great many trips to Luig and Fort William in the minibus, with no particular results that she could discover. Without comment she gave him all the rope he asked for. Hanging him would be a pleasure but the time was not yet.

Rebecca herself raced through the days with her mind leaping like a fish to a fly at all that had to be done, frustrated but not surprised at chaos and negligence, relishing the elimination of problems and crises one by one. Her spirits rose as they always did when she was stretched and involved, though she often wished she could go a couple of rounds with Tony during those whirling days. He had seen this coming, had let problems pile up to insurmountable heights and then basely run for cover. She longed to let him suffer the consequences but could not bring herself to inflict any more problems on Una, or more importantly to risk Ardlonach, that beloved, marvellous, rediscovered place.

Also she was not by nature a person to back away from challenges. Phoning to chat to Esme as she regularly did she had let rip about the frustration of it all in an eloquent tide and her mother had listened calmly and said when she drew breath, 'And you're loving it.'

Rebecca had laughed. 'Of course I'm loving it.' Bringing order out of chaos was meat and drink to her and as she put down the phone she thought, with the honesty which she always expected in others and rarely found, that it was the best thing she could have met with – unremitting work and demands thrown at her from every side on problems outside her normal field which forced her to concentrate her mind. There had been no time to think of the shock which had dislodged her from her home, her thriving career, the well-known and well-loved city, the carefully honed social life which filled her time, provided her with company when she wanted it and never touched the secret inner core of her being. Now she was here, faced with a single overriding requirement – to get this hotel and its attendant outdoor school equipped, staffed, cleaned and supplied in just over two weeks. And, if she could, to reduce the bruised look of shock and hurt in Una's eyes. Her own pain, the answer she had promised, must be put on hold.

'Why me? Why not Innes?'

He's nearly as direct as I am, Rebecca thought, suppressing a wry grin.

'It's Innes's day off.' Deliberately innocent, permitting herself the slightest touch of surprise at the question.

'Don't give me that.'

The Escort was threading fast up the curves of the moor road, heading for Fort William. Dan was not a man who liked to be driven by anyone, let alone some fancy female in a white silk shirt and some kind of woven peasant waistcoat in a lot of colours you wouldn't expect to see together. He had gone down fighting. They should take the minibus, particularly if there was stuff to collect. Bern could finish cleaning it later. Or it would only take him ten minutes to go down to his cottage and fetch his own car, an elderly two-litre Capri in racing green which he tenderly loved and nurtured.

'My car,' Rebecca had said.

He had gone out of the front door with her muttering, poxy Ford Escort, and screaming orange, for Christ's sake. Then he had taken in the model and the size of the exhaust. This was a racing car, just about, and he was wasn't about to put his life on the line.

'Look, do you want me to—?'

Rebecca had given him one upward look over her shoulder and said, 'I drive.' For dialogue he'd known better. But the way she had put the car up the switchback Ardlonach drive had made him raise his eyebrows and before they reached Luig along the blind corners and corkscrew bends of the loch road he had relaxed in his seat, face impassive but inwardly amused and impressed. This was an experience he hadn't expected.

Out of the tail of her eye Rebecca noted that deadpan face but could have told him to the second the point at which he had recognised and accepted her competence. All right, mate, don't give an inch, she thought without rancour, but I hope you're properly strapped in.

Dan hadn't enjoyed anything as much for a long time as that efficient traverse of the moor road. Anticipation, judgement, handling skills, she had them all, and she took no risks. Above all she knew her car; he wouldn't mind betting she could put it down to an inch. Keeping his admiration rigidly to himself however, he stuck strictly to business, repeating, 'But come on, why me, and what's this trip all about?'

He read the moment she made up her mind to tell him just as surely as she had pinpointed the moment when he had acknowledged that she could drive. 'We're short of funds,' she told him flatly. 'I need to be able to buy the bare minimum that the school will need to get us through the initial courses till some more cash starts coming in, and I can't do it without help.'

'All right, I'll ask you again. Why not bring Innes? It's his job.'

'Ego problem,' she said tersely. 'School versus hotel. Nobody's going to short-change him.'

Dan glanced at her assessingly, taking in the implications of this answer, observing the down-drawn brows, the firm jaw, the square hands in the optimum control position on the wheel, the concentration she never withdrew from the road. This woman didn't pull her punches and she had a lot of aggression in her, but she employed it with the sort of honesty he liked, and there was always a feeling of humour never far away.

'Do you think that's a good idea,' he asked, 'knocking the guy senior to me? I mean, you hardly know me, do you?'

Did he disapprove? Had she made a misjudgement by answering him honestly? Or was this just a bluntness equal to her own? 'I think you'll put the needs of the job first,' she said, without emphasis.

And she's leaving it at that, Dan realised with renewed admiration. She's not going hammering on, justifying herself, explaining, or running Innes down either. Well, well. 'No cash, no kit, no courses, no job,' he summed up, allowing the first faint signs of amusement to show in his face.

Rebecca nodded, with a quick sideways grin accepting a brevity that matched her own. 'Also from my own point of view I feel it would be unwise at this stage to ask Innes for advice. I'm in a fairly anomalous position here. I know little enough about the hotel but damn all about the survival school. And if I start scrapping with the man in charge none of us are going to get anywhere. Even by doing this when he's off and taking you with me I'm sure to offend him but that's something I decided I could live with.'

Glad she thinks I'll know what anomalous means, Dan thought sourly, but he knew he was gratified by what she had said. 'You won't get any cheap deals in Fort William,' he warned her, with an obscure instinct not to let that gratification show. 'All the shops are just into their main season.'

'Time factor,' Rebecca reminded him succinctly. 'It's no good trying the wholesalers at this late stage, though I certainly shall later.' She spoke merely as a person who has got her teeth into a job and sees it meantime as hers, but Dan registered the comment with interest. Was she settling in? Had they heard something definite from that shit Urquhart?

'We've got to get just enough gear today to meet safety standards,' Rebecca went on. 'Absolutely no compromise there. And we have to look professional. Image is going to matter because there's a lot of money involved and repeat business is there for the asking so long as we don't—'

'Fuck up,' Dan suggested obligingly.

'The very word.'

He laughed, his spirits unexpectedly rising. What did he have to gripe about anyway? He'd had a great send-off party from the lodge and his job was secure there next winter if he wanted it. He'd moved into his cottage and last night had savoured his own recaptured solitude, walking along the shore in the semi-dark with the cool sweep of the sea wind in his face, coming back to the quietness, the chosen freedom. And this job might work out after all, though he didn't look forward to being pushed around by 'the wee Mannie' with his vile temper and seriously inflated ego. But there was enough going for the job to hang onto it for the time being. Stuart, the fourth instructor, had now arrived and though keeping his own counsel so far with a shifty air that might need watching he had a reasonable level of experience and seemed keen enough. We'd better have a couple of instructors' play days on the hill and on the water, Dan thought, get our act together before the punters hit us. Had Innes allowed for that?

However, the immediate task was to collect up essential gear and not break the bank. That shouldn't be beyond the bounds of possibility. 'I know a couple of people,' he said brusquely. 'We'll be buying a fair amount. There may be some discounts going.'

'Good,' was all Rebecca said, keeping her voice purely practical. She knew the barriers would go up again at once if Dan thought for one moment that she felt she had scored. She didn't, she just wanted to get on with the job. But she was pleased and more encouraged than he could have guessed by this capitulation, and by the business-like way Dan tackled the task. For the first time in the busy days since she had arrived she felt she could rely totally on someone else's expert knowledge.

She used her own credit card to pay. Dan was taking stuff out to the car and she hoped he wouldn't notice. There was no point in letting anyone know the dire financial straits the survival school was in. And for the time being the less the hotel had to subsidise it the better. Cashflow would improve soon; till then Ardlonach could owe her.

With business completed they separated for an hour, each to do some shopping on their own account. Rebecca took the chance to get some more appropriate clothes and most of the time went on choosing boots, enjoying the look and feel of them, the smell of new leather, the wider choice that had become available during her city years. The clothes she grabbed up at the last moment, without even taking time to try them on. That wasn't her usual style, she thought contentedly, grinning at the contrast with her serious Edinburgh or London shopping, as she hurried along the footway to the carpark, sure Dan would not be late.

Driving home she reflected that she had been right in her decision to bring him with her today – he was a professional capable of putting personal prejudices aside in order to get a job done. More importantly she had the impression that, however reluctantly and with whatever reservations, he had decided for the time being to give her his support.

Chapter Five

'It's a relief to get out of the place. Do you realise, this is the first time we've taken a couple of hours off to do anything together since I came?'

Not on the hill or loch as Rebecca would have loved, just hotel business and the winding road to Luig once more, but at least she had persuaded Una, pale and hollow-eyed, to leave her kitchen for once.

'Oh, Rebecca, I feel so guilty about that. You were supposed to be here to rest, have a proper holiday. Instead you just got dragged into all this work and you've been flat out from the moment you arrived.'

'Probably did me more good than sitting about,' Rebecca grunted. She knew that it had. Though somewhere at the back of her mind the tug of pain was always there she had had no time during the flying days for agonising over it, or for the inner arguments and churning revived memories which had made the last weeks in the office so hard to get through. And even in the defenceless hours waiting for sleep, even as physically tired as she was here each night, or waking with a groan in the small hours, there had been the relief of realising that the exposure to more pain was over. She had removed herself from that danger and she had given herself time, as much time as she needed, to think about the astounding prospect that could be

45

hers. She was, as far as she had been able to make herself, free to decide.

Free! Rebecca laughed aloud as she drove and Una turned to her enquiringly. 'I used to think I worked hard in the world of finance,' Rebecca told her ironically.

'It won't be like this all the time,' Una promised her, instantly anxious.

Rebecca wondered with a lift of her brows just how far ahead Una was looking but decided as this was meant to be a little frivolous time off for them both it wasn't the moment to go into it.

'It was just the rush of getting everything ready,' Una hurried on placatingly. 'It's always quieter again after Easter for a few weeks – though this year the courses more or less go straight through, so of course that will be a little different. I can't believe how well Tony did on the marketing.' A wistful note crept into her voice which she couldn't help, though tears didn't overtake her as they would have done a few days ago. 'It's been so good of you to plunge into everything the way you have. I couldn't have faced opening without you and I certainly wouldn't have believed the new bar could have been ready in time. It was amazing the way everyone helped, wasn't it?'

She was always ready to be impressed by the general niceness of people in doing what she paid them to do, thrilled that the electrician had put in a lot of expensive overtime to finish work booked weeks ago, grateful to the fire officer for agreeing to provide a certificate (for which to give Tony his due the application had long ago been made), pleased that though Innes had absented himself on unspecified business the other instructors had turned to and between them finished the last of the decorating and laid the heavy rolls of coir matting waiting to go on the floor. Rebecca herself had been surprised that Dan had agreed to free Bern and Stuart for the job. Even more surprised that, while making his disapproval clear that other people's incompetence should have let him in for it, he had taken charge himself. In spite of his surliness Rebecca had been relieved that he had, since she didn't trust either of the others to cut a right angle or take an accurate measurement. He had seen the job through as well, mustering all available hands when the floor was finished to carry in stools and tables, settles and benches from the nearby games room where they had been stored, even, with a thoroughness which impressed Rebecca, setting up the table-tennis table when the room was cleared.

'That bar should have been finished weeks ago,' he had said shortly when Rebecca thanked him. 'Anyway, the instructors need somewhere to relax.' Making it clear he was doing her no favours.

This morning Donna and Aggie were in there cleaning windows and polishing everything in sight and hopefully they would go on to stock up shelves and wash glasses. Though perhaps not. They had definite ideas about work demarcation lines and Donna had said ungraciously, 'Well, we'll have to see how the time goes. I've my man's dinner to get, mind,' while Aggie had fretfully pointed out, 'Rightly, it's the barman should do the bar.'

The part-time gardener, an ex-fisherman from Lewis called Paddy, also it seemed looked after the bar when the hotel was open. Today he was occupied in cleaning and setting out the teak chairs and tables which occupied the top terrace in the summer. Rebecca had come across them by chance while looking for the old letter scales she remembered Uncle Kenneth using. (Una's method of doubling the postage on everything just in case, since the postman took mail away with him, had not impressed her.) Although Easter fell this year in the last weekend of March there had already been several days when it would have been pleasant to sit out, if ever there had been a moment to spare for such a luxury, and she had decided to get them ready before the demand arose.

She had quelled the grumblings of Aggie and Donna at being asked to do the bar by suggesting that they might prefer to clean last year's bird droppings off the garden furniture instead, and had earned herself some very black looks. It was obvious that Una didn't exert much authority over them, Rebecca thought, pulling out round a tractor. (Could the lad driving it possibly be that little shrimp once caught by the Ardlonach gardener under his strawberry nets and hauled howling to the study? The flaming head of curly hair looked right.) She must be careful not to push them into revolt. There would be plenty of seasonal jobs available in Luig from now till October and few local staff to go round. Another inducement to diplomatic handling was that the two Australian girls who were supposed to have arrived yesterday hadn't turned up and hadn't made contact. There was no way of establishing if they still intended to come and time was growing alarmingly short for trying to replace them.

However, hopefully all that would remain to complete the Coach-house Bar when they returned − Rebecca thought the name rather English and pretentious but Una clung to it because it had been Tony's choice − would be to put up the curtains which she and Una were now on their way to fetch.

'I'm so glad you're going to meet Trudy at last,' Una said. 'There just doesn't seem to have been a minute lately. And she's always busy herself, though I usually try to pop in when I'm in Luig. Actually I haven't seen her since before Tony . . .' Suddenly the prospect of meeting someone outside the enclosed hotel world in these new circumstances brought the reality of her situation sharply back. Her voice wavered dangerously and she turned her head to look out of the window.

Rebecca glanced at the clenched jaw-line which the fine flyaway hair did not hide and felt a quick anxiety. Una had been so good, valiantly trying to push aside her grief and shock about Tony, doing her best to apply her mind to the hundreds of questions they were obliged to ask her, and somehow scrambling through the food ordering and menu planning which were her own department. It was Una's magical cooking which had lifted Ardlonach out of the ruck of small 'country house' hotels which open in Scotland every year and in all too many cases disappear the year after that, and which after five seasons had given it a faithful following of returning guests. The opening of the marina in Luig, which had made it possible for Tony to add sailing to his courses, had also meant a brisk increase in chance business in the hotel dining-room and bar, as Rebecca had seen from the books. In practical terms it would have been madness to throw away this head start and all the hard work already put in, but sometimes she wondered if she had swept Una along too ruthlessly. The poor girl's marriage had just fallen apart and she had barely been given time to think about it, let alone talk about it. Rebecca knew she was hardly eating and from the look of her eyes in the mornings guessed that she wasn't doing much sleeping either.

Ardlonach wasn't hers to make decisions about, Rebecca reminded herself, it was Tony and Una's. Had she been right to push for what seemed to her the obvious course of action, to wade in with energy and conviction when Una was so completely without defences? But what had the alternative been? To tell all the customers to go somewhere else? Most would never return, love Ardlonach as they might.

'I think you'll like Trudy,' Una resumed, making a resolute effort to keep her voice ordinary, and Rebecca felt a rush of affectionate admiration for her courage. 'She's so casual and relaxed, just takes everything as it comes.'

Reluctant to upset her further but needing to know before they arrived, Rebecca asked gently, 'Have you told her about Tony?'

'Yes, when I phoned last night to see if the curtains were ready. I thought she'd better have time to get used to the idea. She can be pretty outspoken,' Una added with a sort of rueful resignation.

So it was fear of criticism of Tony that had prevented Una from turning to this friend during the devastated hours of the night and day before Rebecca had arrived. And probably an understandable reluctance to announce his departure as an accomplished fact, to let the world know what he had done to her.

'And I don't think she's very pro marriage,' Una went on in her fair way, as though wishing merely to be accurate. 'She and her husband came here about four years ago, or perhaps more, and he started up a pottery in the old mill, you'll remember it, up above the town. Trudy had a meal shop there. Then Ben wanted to go back south and she stayed on on her own,' – skate on quickly – 'and she bought one of those cottages by the harbour and moved her shop down there. You probably remember them being lived in but they've always been empty since I've known them. They're beauties and you should see what Trudy's done with hers.'

She had turned the whole of the ground floor into the shop, a low-ceilinged tempting aromatic colourful place, its wares offered up with as much simplicity as hygiene regulations would allow. Down the pillars which had been left to support the ceiling when dividing walls were stripped away hung baskets of various shapes and sizes, and a few leather bags and belts of a robust plainness of style. A tall girl with long brown hair, towering over both Una and Rebecca, wearing tan brushed-denim trousers and a patchwork smock in bright hexagons of velvet the size of fifty pence pieces, came beaming to meet them.

'Una, it's great to see you. How are you, love? Has it been hell, you poor duck, you should have rung me. Hi, you must be Rebecca. I suppose no one's going to let me sound off about Tony? No, I didn't think so. OK, then, I'll do my best to keep my mouth shut, but *honestly*—'

She folded Una into an enveloping hug which turned into a growl and shake of exasperation, directed at Tony Rebecca presumed. 'Anyway, so have you been madly busy getting everything ready? I could have given you a hand, you know. Still, the curtains are ready, which they might not have been if I'd been rushing back and forth to Ardlonach all the time.

Come on, you've timed it perfectly, I can shut for lunch as the tourist wave hasn't broken over us yet, though come the weekend I suppose that little luxury will be over for a while.'

She led them out of a door at the back of the shop and Rebecca exclaimed in pleasure.

'Like that?' Trudy asked, smiling at her.

'Hasn't she done it beautifully?' Una said with eager pride.

Each cottage in the row had a yard behind it divided from its neighbours by a single storey extension consisting originally of wash-house and store shed. In hers Trudy had made a freezer room for the locally smoked fish which had been so successful a part of her business, and had turned the rest into a work-room with its west-facing wall knocked into a huge window. Across the roughly cobbled yard she had planted climbers against the blank wall and had hanging baskets already blooming. Through a gap in the low white-washed wall at the far end steps led down to the harbour – at present straight into its briskly slapping waters as the tide was in.

'What a heavenly place,' Rebecca exclaimed, taking it in delightedly, the bright baskets against the stone, the trapped sunlight and shelter and privacy, yet the sense of light and space given by the openness to the harbour. 'And you make the baskets and leather things for the shop yourself, I see,' she added, looking with interest into the busy workroom.

'Bit of a joke, isn't it?' Trudy said cheerfully. 'Basket weaving cliché. For solitary females of moderate intelligence. But I like being busy and the things sell at an amazing rate. I mean, seriously, would you go on holiday and buy the sort of shopping basket grannie used to bring home two pounds of potatoes and a quarter of tea in? Anyway, I'll be glad to get rid of those. A job on that scale does rather take the place over.' She nodded to a neat pile of coffee-coloured rough-weave curtains which Rebecca instantly saw would be perfect in the new bar. Una knew what she was doing.

'Oh, Trudy, thank you so much. They look beautiful. Have you put the invoice in with them?' Una's glance at Rebecca showed what had prompted this afterthought.

Rebecca laughed.

'Invoice? 'Course not, haven't worked it out yet,' Trudy said carelessly. 'I'll post it sometime. Now, something much more important, why don't I go and fetch a bottle of plonk? You don't have to rush off, do you? And how about some food?'

'We didn't mean to land on you for lunch. We didn't even look at the time to be honest, just rushed out at the first gap between jobs.'

'Well, now you're here, take an hour off. Always plenty of past-its-sell-by date stuff to be eaten up in this house. Come on, Una, I've hardly seen you for weeks. No argument.'

'Could I give you a hand?' Rebecca suggested, making it not an offer but a request.

'Want to see the rest? Sure, come on,' Trudy said promptly. 'I always love nosing round people's houses myself. I took the original stairs out to make more room in the shop so I had to build these on. Not beautiful, but it did mean I could have a glazed door at the top. I love light. And beyond that I just went for simplicity, as you can see. One of the compensations of only having oneself to worry about.'

She must be good for Una, Rebecca thought, amused. The two were so different, and not only in physical type. This big outgoing smiling girl might give the appearance of being scatty but Rebecca guessed that she was actually very competent and she was obviously a worker. Not reconciled to living alone though, in spite of what Una had said or the impression Trudy herself imagined she conveyed. Did she still miss the vanished potting husband?

The former bedrooms under the sloping roof had been made into one attractive living area, tiny kitchen at one end, unmade bed at the other, its head pulled a couple of feet away from the wall presumably so that its occupant could look out of one of the new dormer windows that faced the loch. In between were some uncomfortable looking too-low wood and leather seats (had Trudy lashed those up herself as well?), and a general wall-to-wall wash of books, magazines, manuals, catalogues and brown envelopes. An open cash book revealed one entry and two coffee rings. The gable end had cheap cupboards built across it, most of which were gaping open. This room was evidently regarded as basic space for storage, cooking and sleeping, probably not even eating. Trudy's real life was spent in her shop and workroom.

'It's a wonderful set-up,' Rebecca said enviously, standing in one of the high windows and gazing out across busy harbour, sunlit loch and the too-sharply defined ridges of the hills beyond. It would be raining in two hours, she estimated, was pleased at how automatically she had registered the once familiar signs, then mockingly wondered why anyone should feel so proud of such a minor bit of cleverness.

'Must get a bench or something,' Trudy remarked, shifting her weight from one generous buttock to the other on the steps outside the workroom, where the stone had proved not so warm as she had expected.

'I'll get cushions,' Una said, hopping up.

Why doesn't Trudy bring down that weird sofa from upstairs and let it quietly rot out here, Rebecca wondered, without serious malice, head back to soak up the warmth of this sheltered corner, nice cool Moselle slipping agreeably down. It's the first time I've stopped running about like a headless chicken for days, she realised lazily. I've barely been down as far as the jetty since the first evening I arrived. Is stopping wise, though? Will I ever be able to get going again?

It was good to hear Una chattering away. She obviously felt comfortable with Trudy. They were catching up on local news and Rebecca let her mind drift as though she was a visitor in a strange place till names began to impinge and she remembered that this was, or had been, her world too.

'Have you seen Lilias lately?' Una was asking Trudy, scooping up some oozing Brie from round the edges of a wedge that looked as though it had been trodden on.

'I was over at Tigh Bhan at the weekend. She can't get about much now, her knees give her a lot of pain, but she's in tremendous form. Gave me a terrific going over for not keeping up with the current political scene. I told her I'd given up because the news is all so horrible but she said that was exactly why I should follow it. Didn't mince her words either. It's odd how so many widows seem to get a sort of second wind when they find themselves on their own after fifty years of marriage.'

Rebecca thought this not the most tactful of comments in the circumstances but Una appeared to make no connection with her own situation. 'It's so lucky it wasn't the other way round,' she said, looking as anxious as if even now the order of death could be reversed. 'Gerald would have been totally helpless without her.'

'Nonsense, he'd have paid some woman a fortune to do all the things his wife used to do for free,' Trudy scoffed, slopping wine generously round the glasses again. 'Men always do.'

'Gerald Markie has died? When was that?' Rebecca suddenly felt avid to be in touch with this place again, resentful of the demands of the hotel which had delayed her planned exploring and wandering and rediscovery. Apart from her mother the characters who had peopled the Edinburgh stage already seemed just that, figures with no substance, no continuity after the play was done. It had been one of the reasons she had opted for a complete uprooting. For a long time now she had felt unable to get near to anyone, at first defensive, fearing all encroachment into that private zone of grief and loss, then too self-contained, too successfully independent. But here, long ago, there had been friendships which had mattered and she had let them lapse unforgivably.

'I must go and see Lilias,' she said out of her thoughts.

'At least, would she like that, do you think?' with a sudden uncharacteristic doubt.

'She'd love it,' Una assured her with the eager warmth which made everyone cherish her. 'She often asks after you and wonders when you'll come back.'

'Thinks I should come back,' Rebecca amended with a grin. Lilias Markie was as bossy as she was herself. 'So where's Stephen nowadays? He hasn't been made redundant yet, has he?'

'No, he's still in the Army. He comes up with the children quite often. You heard Lucy had left him?'

'No, really? She saw sense at last?'

'Rebecca, that's so unfair. Stephen's one of the kindest people—'

'And the dullest.'

'It's a good job the military can find a use for him,' Trudy commented, not unkindly. 'Hard to think what he'd do otherwise.'

It was fun to gossip, Rebecca realised, to feel so immediately at home with this big slapdash girl, to relax for a while safe from all requests.

'It's lucky Catriona can pop in and out to keep an eye on Lilias,' Trudy was saying to Una. 'I'm going to be too busy soon to go over very often.'

'But would she be much use in a crisis?' Una wondered doubtfully.

'You're not talking about Catriona Finlay from Glen Righ? Is she old enough to look after Lilias?' Rebecca broke in, trying to work it out.

'Do you know Catriona? She's about twenty-two, isn't she, Una? Not that you'd think it. You'll probably know that Fergus died then, and she's been living on her own for the last eighteen months in that huge house with nothing to occupy her and not a bean to live on. We're quite worried about her, to be honest.'

'Twenty-two, goodness.' Rebecca's mind went back over the Finlay's tragic story, Catriona's parents killed in their light aircraft, her brother drowned in the deep pools of the gorge beside the house, Fergus, her grandfather, made mentally unstable by grief and Catriona herself a skinny, wildly untidy child, desperately shy, living a strange solitary existence up there at the head of the glen.

But another name drew Rebecca's mind from these memories. 'Clare Macrae? Is that Donald's new wife?' she asked with interest. Donald Macrae had often appeared at Ardlonach when she was a child, old enough to be something of a hero to all the cousins, renowned local shinty player, Highland dancer, excellent shot. Then he had married the dull daughter of a local farmer and had somehow disappeared, immersing himself in running his farm of Rhumore on the north shore of Loch Buie. Rebecca had heard that his wife had died three years ago and that he had married again.

Trudy and Una eagerly told her the story. Clare had left a glamorous lifestyle in the south to come and live in the Larach, a cottage on Loch Buie now owned by Stephen Markie, and for a time had helped Trudy in her shop at the old mill, and Una and Tony in the hotel office.

'She had to give it up when she had the baby,' Una explained regretfully. 'Tina wasn't half as useful.'

'I'm Robbie's godmother,' Trudy announced proudly. 'Only I hardly ever see him. Clare's happy as a pig in muck being a farmer's wife and never leaves Rhumore if she can help it.'

Suddenly, startlingly, Rebecca was swept by violent jealousy for this unknown girl. She had everything, Donald, the square solid house of Rhumore facing out into the westerly winds on its exposed headland, the established place in the glen, her baby.

'We must go out there one day,' Trudy was saying. 'You must meet her, Rebecca, she's great fun ...'

No, Rebecca thought, no, that I don't have to face. 'We must be getting back,' she cut across Trudy's well-meant words. 'Come on, Una, look at the time.'

'I suppose you'll take the order you phoned through?' Trudy asked with mild sarcasm as she unlocked the shop door.

'Oh, God,' Una exclaimed. 'All the dried fruit and flour and muesli and spices!'

'You're not going to bother with the cheese and the fish then?'

'Trudy, how awful, I'd have gone off without any of it. Everything to do with the hotel has just gone straight out of my mind.'

Mine too, Rebecca thought grimly, still oddly shaken by that vision of what Clare Macrae had found, something which, whatever choice she made, she knew could never be for her in quite that way.

She drove down to the main carpark and she and Una started on the list of vital odds and ends that had somehow been missed. There was unexpected pleasure in that too, as she found herself recognised and welcomed in many of the shops. She had dissociated herself so thoroughly from this place after Ardlonach had gone to Tony that she had supposed she too would have vanished from people's minds, but memories were long in this part of the world and the Urquharts had owned land on the Luig peninsula for nearly a century. The crowd of cousins who had spent their summers at Ardlonach for so many years had always been a popular part of the local scene. Over and over again she and Una had to drag themselves away from the easy flowing chat of people never in any hurry themselves, and she found it oddly warming.

'If we're not stocked up now we never will be,' she declared as they stuffed the last of the shopping into the car, using mopheads to separate water jugs and pushing a bag of darts' flights and ping-pong balls into a spare corner behind the seat. The car wasn't designed for this sort of work but hopefully in future most things would be delivered in sensible quantities and in good time.

Checking before getting in to make sure that Una hadn't left anything on the roof, a favourite trick of hers, Rebecca noticed a little spew of passengers getting off the bus by the pier and her concentration sharpened on two of them.

'Bet those are ours,' she said, bending to speak to Una who was already in the car. Straightening again she folded her arms on the warm roof and watched two blonde girls whose luggage consisted of backpacks and carrier bags look around to get their bearings.

'Do you know, I think you're right,' Una exclaimed, getting out again. 'Wouldn't that be marvellous?'

'We may be able to shanghai them even if they're someone else's,' Rebecca suggested.

'We couldn't do that, it wouldn't be fair,' Una protested seriously.

Rebecca laughed. 'Are we sure we really want them? Punctuality doesn't seem to be a strong point, or quality luggage, come to that.'

They went together across the newly created parking space. 'Are you for Ardlonach by any chance?' Rebecca called, as the two girls slung their packs over their shoulders and began to hook the limp handles of the carriers onto their fingers, assisted, as Rebecca observed without surprise, by a male bystander.

Two glowing brown faces swung towards her. 'That's right,' two voices chorused cheerfully. 'How d'you know?'

'Just guessed,' Rebecca said resignedly. What havoc were these two going to wreak among the survivors, especially when their resistance was lowered? Or among the instructors, come to that. Bern would fold; Stuart might be seen to smile. Dan – she found she did not know at all how Dan would react. Innes undoubtedly would sneer.

The tall long-legged one with the roughly cropped hair introduced herself as Thea; the little one with white-fair tendrils waving round a pointed face was Sylvie.

'We weren't sure you were still coming.'

'Oh, definitely. Twenty-seventh, wasn't it?'

'It was and this is the twenty-eighth, but never mind.'

'You're kidding?' Their delighted laughter could have been heard at Trudy's. 'Oh no, that's a good one. We were sure we were on schedule. Were you having hairy fits?'

Rebecca and Una laughed with them. Who could help it?

'How far's this Aardlownatch?'

'Three miles. But look, can you hang on here for a bit?' Rebecca asked. 'Would you mind? The car's stuffed full. You could dump your packs at a friend's — Trudy wouldn't mind, would she, Una? — and wander round or have coffee. I can be back for you in no time.'

'No worries. We can have a look round, can't we, Sylv? Great little place.'

'What a marvellous pair,' Una breathed, twisting round to watch them making for the meal shop as Rebecca headed for home. 'How could we have been that lucky?'

'They'll be fun,' Rebecca agreed, putting her foot down then wincing as she gauged the weight the car was carrying. Fun, and about as conducive to sober hard work as a couple of cases of champagne.

Chapter Six

Easter for Rebecca was like the seventh wave crashing onto her head and dragging her down into an undertow of demands from which she sometimes thought she would never fight clear.

It began with a clash with Dan. The play-day on the hill he had wanted for the instructors had been postponed by the work on the bar. Innes, returning from whatever it was he had been doing, never established, was furious to find that it hadn't taken place. Had he deliberately intended to avoid it, it occurred to Rebecca. Now it had to be fitted in on the last day before the courses began and she decided she would go too.

Partly she just wanted to be out of the hotel, away from the turmoil it seemed impossible to reduce to the order she was sure could be achieved but which no one else seemed interested in, but more importantly it went against the grain for her not to know exactly what was involved. 'The courses' was a phrase beginning to bug her with large vague implications and a worrying potential for problems she wouldn't be able to handle since she didn't know what went on. She had a feeling of her back being undefended which she was not accustomed to and didn't like. Though in fact, as she occasionally reminded herself, she had no responsibility for anything that happened in the hotel or outside it. The reminder never carried much weight. It was transparently clear that Una couldn't cope alone;

Rebecca herself had undertaken to help and now she had to get it right.

'What time are you setting off tomorrow?' she asked Dan when he came into the office to photocopy the fire instructions he had prepared for the bunk rooms in the farm buildings.

'Pretty sharp. It'll be a long day. Why?'

'Because I'll be coming with you.' Rebecca was tidying up the booking chart which had been altered and replanned so often that by now it was barely legible. She was terrified that in the end some guest would turn up who had been light-heartedly rubbed out and she was concentrating on what she was doing and didn't look up as she spoke. Dan's reaction as he slapped down the copier lid and swung round alerted her. She looked up at him with brows lifting but with determination instantly hardening to meet whatever objection he was going to make.

'No, you won't.'

It was a long time since anyone had used that flat and final tone to Rebecca and it was disconcerting for a second. Only for a second.

'I decide whether I'm coming or not.'

'Not a hope.' Danny's face was impassive, his stance implacable rather than aggressive, but she sensed his annoyance and hostility. She longed to tell him summarily that she would go out on the hill with them if she saw fit and that he'd just have to put up with it, but she had enough self-discipline to keep the objective view in mind, not only the needs of Ardlonach — and alienating a key member of staff was not one of them — but her own ambiguous position here.

'I'd like to see the ground the courses will cover and get some idea of what's expected of them,' she told him, keeping her voice business-like and without challenge.

It was more than Dan did. 'Why?'

Because I'm used to being in control, you smug muscle-bound bastard. And not used to explaining myself. And because I long to be back on to my beloved hill, but I wouldn't ever tell you that. 'Don't you think it would be a good idea to see what goes on?' A mocking note there she knew at once he wouldn't like. Her tongue always got her into trouble.

'There's no need. And we won't be hanging about, that's for sure. If you want to do a bit of exploring get Una to take you for a walk some time.'

The calculated put-down. Not bad, Rebecca thought with deliberate detachment. I bet I know more of this ground than you do. But she carefully resisted saying so. 'The point is to see what the people on the courses are up against.' Now that was sweetly reasonable, surely. But though her voice was level and her expression she thought under control, a gleam in her dark blue eyes betrayed her readiness for a scrap if he wanted one.

'Well, do it later. Come out with a Grade III one day. But tomorrow's definitely not for hangers-on. We intend to cover ground, OK?'

'Aren't you making a few assumptions here—?'

He rode her down. 'You're not coming.' His eyes were like bits of opaque glass, his voice uncompromising.

Rebecca had a rare, perhaps novel, sensation of meeting a will stronger than her own. Here was an object she could not lift, push, or affect in any way. One small part of her brain looked forward with interest to examining this phenomenon later. But for the moment good sense warned her not to waste her breath. She even felt a sort of reluctant admiration, the respect of a good fighter meeting a better one.

'Fine,' she said, reaching for her rubber again and going back to her chart.

Dan looked down at her with his mouth open, then shut it hastily. All his resources gathered for battle were suddenly redundant. That single word had not been petulant, nor did it have the ring of a threat of some later attack, of appealing to Una or perhaps Innes. This determined woman, obviously used to getting her own way, had simply backed down; yet that wasn't the right word. She had accepted his decision, and as far as he could see had accepted it with the utmost good nature. It was Dan's turn to recognise that he was up against something new to him. He had been sure he had had a fight on his hands and knew that verbally Rebecca carried heavy guns. For reasons of his own he was glad she had seen sense over this particular issue, yet he found himself uncertain as to where in the end the moral victory had lain. He suppressed a grin. Better get on with his copying.

Peace reigned in the office. Rebecca checked through a booking letter she had already read twice. Dan copied a couple of notices upside down onto the back of copies he had already made and, cursing inwardly, hoped Rebecca hadn't noticed. She didn't miss much.

But Rebecca wasn't looking. She might have achieved a tone of equable acceptance but she still had to get a fierce indignation under control. Though perhaps he did me a good turn, she thought, with her usual capacity to laugh at herself. For it was possible that she just might not be as fit as she believed. Squash and regular work-outs had made her comparatively fit in the environment she had just left but it wasn't necessarily the sort of fitness that would see her through a long day on the hill, particularly if Dan felt she had thrown down some sort of gauntlet.

Nevertheless her mind kept returning with astonishment to the fact that she had allowed him to tell her flatly what she could and could not do. All too often through the years uninspired and under-confident men had been attracted to her energy and exuberance. Now in her mid-thirties she was capable of looking back and understanding how they had been swept up into a similar mood, feeling suddenly larger than life, witty and lively, in the first heady glow of discovery and sexual attraction. But they had never been able to stand the pace. Soon their lack of originality, their dependence on her to maintain the momentum, were laid bare. Many had clung, not even recognising their own need for a partner stronger than themselves to take the lead and add spice to their unenterprising lives, and it had frequently been difficult and tedious to dislodge them.

Men in wine merchants' shirts, Rebecca summed them up now, slim elegant creatures who sold antiques or were vaguely connected with the arts. What did they see in me? But she knew; they had seen a confidence, determination and outspokenness which they lacked. Well, those were the nice words, the ones that came at the beginning. Arrogance, ruthlessness and acerbity, they would probably have said later, licking their wounds. If any of them knew what acerbity meant, she thought, with the irrepressible impulse to joke that was a large part of the trouble. She had often longed to meet someone stronger than she was, who wouldn't let her get away with everything so easily. And more seriously, who would be there, rock-solid, on those rare occasions when the batteries ran down and humour deserted her. Well, she had certainly run into some rock-like opposition from Dan McNee but she hadn't much relished the contempt that went with it.

Always ready with a story against herself she would have cheerfully told Una how thoroughly she had been flattened but, in the way she was rapidly becoming used to, the pressure of hotel exigencies made it first impossible then too trivial, simply swept aside.

New fire extinguishers were delivered but no trace could be found of the worksheet which said which ones they were meant to replace, nor indeed of any plan for fire points and alarms. This was something which Rebecca could only add to her ever-growing list till it could be looked into properly, though it went much against the grain to shelve such a serious deficiency.

Cases of wine were delivered to replenish the depleted cellar (Una candidly explained that Tony had always thought it silly to charge himself for anything they drank themselves) and only when she was putting it into the racks did Rebecca realise that scarcely a vintage corresponded to what was printed on the wine list. Then whenever they could snatch a moment together she and Una struggled with a duty roster whose constraints surprised Rebecca, who had supposed it to be a simple job. For one thing the two Australians, willing as they were to tackle any job that came along, still had everything to learn and couldn't be put on a shift alone. Donna and Aggie, having recklessly promised to be free for any extra hours required had by now received their first pay packets, plus their bonus for the horrible job they had faced in the staff quarters, and had both coincidentally discovered pressing commitments at home. While the schoolboy who was supposed to wash the pots had phoned to say he had cut his hand and wasn't allowed to put it into water.

It was a new experience for Rebecca, however, to discover how with the appearance of the first guests, ('Are we the very first of the whole year, how lovely!') the whole tempo and feeling of the house changed. Suddenly from a chaotic and cluttered place, half-heated and half-lit, with everything provisional and temporary and out of place, it emerged glowing and polished, calm and welcoming, with flowers everywhere, the drawing-room fire lit and Thea and Sylvie immaculate and almost unrecognisable in dark green skirts and cream shirts.

Although Una had warned her that many old friends from the past had found them, that Urquhart relatives to the nth degree of kinship regarded the place as still belonging to them, Rebecca had been too busy to think much about this aspect. But this first afternoon, working rapidly through the day's mail in the office while Una was in the hall improving on her flowers, on hand to greet people, she heard her exclaiming happily, 'Oh, but she's here! Yes, helping out for the start of the season, isn't it wonderful? I know she'd love to say hello. Rebecca, here's someone you haven't seen for ages . . .'

Christ, I hope she's going to brief me a bit more usefully than that, Rebecca thought as she got to her feet, her mind rapidly running over the names in the chart. But her initial reluctance, the result of the years of holding herself apart, of risking no emotional involvements, was swept aside by ordinary well-meaning friendliness, by the mingled greetings and reminders – 'You won't have seen us since Leonie's wedding. Of course you won't remember us, why ever should you, but what a nice surprise to find you here' – by taking up the luggage, by the Musgroves' praise of how the house looked, pleasure in their room, delight to be back.

'They'll all ask about Tony when he doesn't appear,' Una said miserably as she and Rebecca went downstairs. 'I shan't be able to bear it.'

'Just say what we decided, that he's away at the moment. You don't have to explain anything. The Musgroves are only here for four days, they won't know how long it's been.' Rebecca put an arm round the slight shoulders in a quick hug. Poor Una, she was right, the questions were inevitable and were going to hurt. At least for me the pain is private. Though chance reminders can never be avoided no well-meant questions can open wounds.

Then events caught them up, cars arriving, orders for tea, Thea rushing into the office in a pink-cheeked flurry, 'Quick, what the hell's Lapsang?', a log which Sylvie, who had never dealt with a fire in her life, had inexpertly propped on an unstable base, rolling onto the hearth and filling the drawing-room with acrid smoke as the first tray was carried in, and a surly carrier starting to bring ten boxes of loo rolls (thank goodness they'd come, though) into the hall just as more guests arrived.

'I don't think this is quite the best . . .' Una began anxiously and politely. The man, who had had trouble finding Ardlonach and didn't appreciate coming out to the backside of nowhere at this time of day, took no notice of her at all, pushing aside a bowl of pot pourri and slapping down his clipboard with a curt, 'Sign and print.'

'But I really think,' said Una helplessly over her shoulder as she went to the rescue of a couple, new to Ardlonach, who were politely hauling their suitcases out of the way in the porch.

Rebecca took a couple of swift steps and blocked the delivery man's exit to fetch the next box. 'Back door,' she said.

He decided to bluff it out. 'There was nothing in the delivery instructions—'

'Of course there wasn't. Back door.'

'Oh, here, I've the van open now—'

'Then shut it again. Round the end of the building, second door. I'll meet you there. Oh, and take this box out again as you go.' She hoped the polite apologies of the guests had prevented him from hearing Una's gasp. But he went.

Out of all the welter of events of that first hectic evening two stars emerged. One was Joanie, an anaemic looking wisp with sandy red hair and staring freckles who lived in Inshmore, had produced a huge now grown-up brood which had battened on her then abandoned her, and who was filled with a ferocious capacity for hard physical work which Rebecca had rarely seen matched. The other was Paddy, a figure hitherto glimpsed mainly in the distance, peacefully mowing the grass terraces or barrowing compost about. He was calm and quiet and though he tended to regard the panics and crises of the hotel with a tolerant resignation he was another person who ate up work with no visible effort.

It was Paddy who had suggested, when the roster patently wasn't going to come out, that after serving before-dinner drinks to residents in the small bar off the hall as usual, that they and the chance guests who had booked for dinner should be asked to go down to the Coach-house for the rest of the evening.

'That's the perfect answer,' Una cried. 'No one will mind a bit. In fact it's so nice down there now that everyone will probably prefer it. The hotel bar is so tiny and gloomy and north-facing.'

'Are you sure we haven't got any stuffy people who'll object to the rough element?' Rebecca asked doubtfully. 'And who'll want some padding for their backsides?'

'Oh no, they'll think it's fun,' Una promised trustfully. 'They're all terribly nice.'

Rebecca caught the look Paddy gave her, a glance of what could only be called wondering affection.

The question of the two bars solved itself just as he had suggested. Most of the hotel guests arrived that day and two full survival courses of ten apiece were also due, though they did things a little differently, Rebecca discovered. She had seen from their arrival instructions that they were to be in Fort William early and irrespective of how they chose to get there were to bring their own transport no further.

'But there's nothing here about lunch or their programme for the day,' she had said to Stuart when she was going through the meal requirements with him.

'They don't have any,' he replied with an evil grin she didn't much care for.

'What, they just fill in the day for themselves? Then what's the point of arriving early?'

'They have to get here, don't they?' he said, obviously enjoying himself.

'Well, what happens?' she demanded curtly. 'I haven't got all day to play guessing games.' Stuart allied himself too closely to Innes for her taste, treating Una and herself as though they were a pair of helpless females incapable of understanding arcane matters like reading a map or knowing one end of a boat from another.

'They have to work it out for themselves,' Stuart said, with a sort of automatic contempt which made no allowance for any individual qualities or abilities.

'What do you mean?' His tone and attitude were less than reassuring and Rebecca gave him a look which made him suddenly change his mind and explain.

'We chuck them out of the bus. Tell them to get on with it. It's their first task. Takes some of the – some of them – all day.'

Rebecca bit back the questions about kit and equipment which instantly occurred to her organising mind. That would almost certainly have been thought of, she mocked herself. And presumably not too many paying guests had been lost in this way. Not for the first time she felt handicapped by not having all this at her finger-tips, uncomfortably aware of openings for disaster. 'And what do they eat?'

'What they can scrounge. Focuses their minds when we go into all that later.'

They are paying for this, Rebecca thought. Had it been the way Tony had done things or was Innes enjoying a taste of power? It would have to be looked into but not now. The arrangement did mean, however, that the two groups, dropped off individually from the minibus at different points on the moor above Fort William, were allowed an evening of relaxation after the unexpected challenge to their resourcefulness and navigation and, though one or two went straight to bed after eating the evening meal they cooked for themselves, for the rest it was the Coach-house Bar without delay.

They were joined there by a mixed bag of hotel diners, some of whom seemed to feel they were taking part in a survival course themselves to venture down the stone stairs and sit on wooden settles in a public bar. The instructors had come in early, sitting at the bar in what Rebecca observed to be an incohesive and unrelaxed group.

How successfully are they going to operate together, she wondered with a frown. Innes was drinking mineral water, perched on a stool with one elbow would-be casually on the bar and the look of a man who disapproves of his surroundings. Stuart with ducked head and sour mouth watched the invasion of hotel guests with resentment. Dan sat in that hands-off stillness of his, his face unreadable. Seeing him beside Bern's relaxed bulk Rebecca thought how differently they gave an impression of strength. Bern was simply built on massive lines, with huge thighs and forearms like hams. Dan was superbly fit, muscles developed by weight training and hill running, and somehow, in spite of his apparent passivity, his power could be felt, a potent and almost threatening force. Like Innes, he didn't look too happy to be where he was. None of them, Rebecca noted with surprise, made any effort to welcome or join the members of their courses. If that was the accepted form she didn't much like it.

There also appeared a group of Tony's sailing chums who had been eagerly waiting for the new bar at Ardlonach to give them somewhere comfortable and convivial to drink where they no longer had to change to come in.

'Goodness, I hadn't expected them as well,' Una remarked in consternation, coming wearily down from the battleground of the kitchen to find the Coach-house twice as busy as she had bargained for.

'Has to be good, though, doesn't it?' Rebecca asked a bit breathlessly, after a trip to the cellar to bring up another bottle of Grouse and a case of tonic. 'Once we're geared up for it anyway,' she amended, seeing the number of people waiting to be served. 'I'd better try and give Paddy a hand, though I haven't a clue where anything is. How about you?'

Una looked terrified. 'Oh, I couldn't. I hardly even know which glass is which. Tony did all that. And people would ask for things I've never heard of.'

'Well, you've more than done your share today,' Rebecca conceded, remembering the stream of guests on their way to the drawing-room for coffee murmuring blissfully about the Camembert croquettes, the *tournedos provençale*, the peppered pineapple in toffee baskets. 'You shouldn't have to get dragged into this. I'll round up some glasses for a start, that should help.'

'You know what we should do,' Una exclaimed with sudden inspiration, catching Rebecca's arm before she could dash off. 'I'm sure Tony would have wanted it.'

Don't let that put you off, Rebecca told herself. 'What?' she demanded, wanting to get on.

71

'This should be an opening party. I should give everyone drinks on the house—'

'Hang on!' Rebecca checked Una firmly before she could swing round to the nearest people and tell them her brilliant idea. 'One round will do, not freebies for the rest of the evening. But it's a good idea – and I've had another one. If this is a party why don't you phone Trudy and ask her if she'd like to come along and admire her curtains?'

'Oh, Rebecca, she'd love it. And I ought to catch Megan and Joanie before they go home. They're having a brew in the staff room. They've both worked so hard this evening.' Megan was Una's silent, fat, slow assistant in the kitchen, with the lightest hand for pastry for miles around and a serious mistrust of anything that had herbs in it. 'Don't say anything till I get back.' Una whisked off with new vitality, as though she hadn't been on her feet virtually non-stop since seven that morning.

Trudy had invited friends for supper, John Irvine the doctor and his wife Jeanette, but that didn't prevent her from accepting Una's invitation without hesitation. They came in just as Thea and Sylvie, dressed up for the evening in flowery leggings and huge washed-out shirts and earrings came racing across from staff quarters, and Donna and Aggie, alerted by the bush telegraph and scenting handouts, turned up with their husbands.

It had been a good idea but the problem of serving had been compounded and even stoical Paddy was beginning to lose his cool. Rebecca did her best but she had to hunt for everything and knew she was really more hindrance than help. Feeling inadequate in a way she wasn't at all accustomed to, struggling with a cork that refused to budge and thinking crossly that this was ridiculous, one thing she could do was open a bottle of wine, hating to ask the embattled Paddy for help, she suddenly found the bottle taken from her hand.

'Christ, not surprised you couldn't shift that,' Dan remarked, big shoulders hunched as he imposed his will on the cork which gave way with an explosive pop. 'Get a glass.' In her hurry

Rebecca snatched up the first to hand, for red wine instead of white, but he made no comment. 'Keep the glasses coming, yes?' was all he said, then he was serving beside Paddy, falling at once into the barman's authoritative, 'Right, one at a time. Pint of lager, gin and tonic, tequila gold. Who's on tequila, that you, Sylvie, sure you can handle it . . . ?'

And diving under elbows and squeezing through the happily roaring crush Rebecca found herself suddenly exhilarated, exuberant, inwardly singing, 'We've done it, it's started, it's working . . .'

It was extraordinary, she thought, when she had time to look around her, how that round of free drinks had not only turned the evening into a party but had instantly welded the disparate groups. Before it there had been all those clean-cut, wary survivors, their apprehension of what lay ahead and their self-consciousness taking various forms of nervous loquacity or cautious taciturnity. There had been the aloof instructors, the slightly uncertain but willing hotel guests, more observers than participants, and there had been the noisy ease of the sailors, making it clear that they were very much at home, while the off-duty staff had naturally gravitated towards each other.

Now the bag had been shaken, Trudy and the Irvines were part of a big round at one survivors' table, Sylvie and Thea had been cut out by the rest. Mr Musgrove had taken drinks across to Joanie and Megan and then found himself obliged to go back for more for Donna and Aggie and their other halves, none of whom he had ever laid eyes on before. And the sailors had stopped showing off and shutting out the rest of the room with a circle of backs.

'We're going to run out of everything before the weekend even begins,' Rebecca said to Una, escaping briefly since there wasn't a used glass in sight, and watching with gratitude Dan and Paddy moving smoothly round each other as though they'd worked on the choreography for hours.

'Oh, Rebecca, no!' Una said in dismay. 'We won't be able to get any more, everywhere will be shut—'

'Calm down. We're stocked up to the eyeballs. It was only shorthand for aren't we doing well. Ought we to think about closing time though?'

'Closing time?' Una sounded as though it was a completely alien notion.

'I presume you do shut the bar sometime between now and October?'

'No, I mean, I don't know what Tony does—'

Give him his due, Rebecca thought as she had more than once lately, he did seem to have looked after a few things. Naval organisation. It was just the naval enterprise that had run away with him, and then been overtaken by his own lack of staying power. 'Well, what does the law require?' she asked Una gravely.

'Oh, God, I've no idea. We just shut when people go to bed, I think. Shouldn't we do that? Or is this bar different?' Una looked wildly round as though expecting a raid at any moment.

'Relax, just winding you up. This is still hotel premises, I checked. Though the non-residents probably ought to be moving soon.'

Dan, already getting twitchy about the fitness of his victims next morning, and agreeing privately with Paddy that it would be unwise to establish the new bar as a place where late drinking was the norm, at a nod from Rebecca swept the place clear in an impressively short time with most professional ease.

'Useful character to have around,' Trudy commented, as she and the Irvines joined an élite group heading upstairs for coffee in the kitchen, 'though I'm not sure I'd like to be stuck half way up a cliff with him shouting the odds at me.' But her tone was definitely admiring, Rebecca noted.

'Oh, heavens, I should have offered him and Paddy a

drink. Or asked them to come up for coffee,' Una remembered belatedly.

And made sure the till was put away and the door locked, Rebecca silently amended, with wine-mellowed forebearance. 'I'll go,' she said. She wanted to thank Dan for stepping in like that. But only Paddy was in the Coach-house, checking windows. He had helped himself to a dram, the usual custom in the past, and it stood half drunk on the bar. Beside it was an empty glass. Dan had already vanished into the night.

Chapter Seven

Though the welding effect of the impromptu party had been amazing and Rebecca had climbed wearily up to bed with a definite sense of satisfaction and success she much regretted the whole idea five hours later. Not a morning person, she had not seen much of the world before eight for several years and crawling shaky and grumbling out of bed she bitterly deplored having promised to be down to help with breakfast. There were only sixteen guests in the house, for God's sake, and Thea and Sylvie knew as much about serving them as she did. But the thought of Una rushing round alone in the big kitchen, after probably less sleep than she had had herself and certainly wanting to get ahead with preparations for thirty dinners and an unknown number of lunches, made her stifle her complaints and get on with it.

She was thankful she had when she found that Thea, on first shift, while in good spirits in spite of the nauseous amount of Baileys she had downed last night, was primarily concerned about the dining-room and blithely oblivious to other concerns. She had cleared the last of the glasses and coffee cups from the drawing-room, it was true, but had apparently not noticed that the curtains were still closed, cushions flattened, ashtrays dirty, magazines strewn about, fire dead. All down to management, Rebecca reminded herself, amused in spite of herself at this happy indifference, starting to create order with an unpractised hand. Pulling back the heavily lined damask curtains which had been there ever since she could remember she was suddenly caught between past and present. There before her was the familiar view down the tumbling fall of the terraces to the jetty and the U-shaped bay, thin early sunshine yellow on the budding trees of the promontory and the grassy tilt of the island while the hillside across the loch was patterned with sloping blue morning shadows. A view she had looked at a thousand times from this window (though rarely so dew-laden), yet today the room she had just crossed had been a completely different room. It had no longer been their shabby comfortable family meeting ground, the scene of endless games of Monopoly on wet days, riotous snap, mad gambling with matches at Newmarket and poker, noisy bagatelle and working at Uncle Kenneth's huge jigsaws which everyone added to in passing. Nor the room which had later witnessed the interval of yawning boredom when they had outgrown these pleasures and lolled about endlessly moaning that there was nothing to do, till at last they had entered the livelier era of drinks before lunch and dinner and uninformed arguments on large topics lasting into the small hours. The same friends had still been there. John Irvine already in practice in Luig, Stephen Markie appearing on leave, Donald Macrae occasionally coming over to shoot though marriage and fatherhood had made him markedly more dour by this time.

But in spite of all these memories, just now, a moment ago, discovering the mess Thea had so cheerfully ignored, this room had been simply hotel lounge, part of the new era, a job to be dealt with, its altered character accepted without conscious effort on her part to adapt. Odd how, for a second, its two phases had been so closely juxtaposed, each vivid and distinct, and she hadn't minded.

Interesting, only this wasn't the moment to mull over it and Rebecca whisked on. This weekend to get through, then there might be time to look about her, examine the new scene, relate the long-ago world to the present one. As to getting through the weekend, the anxious matter of the end-of-month accounts was looming large. Una hadn't so much as mentioned them. Was it really possible that she hadn't thought about them at all? Rebecca hadn't the faintest hope of anything reconciling and shuddered at the thought of the step-by-step struggle ahead to locate discrepancies. But she did find time to wonder as she put the faded firescreen in place (embroidered by Grannie with once-bright tulips, must have been hideous new) what she had done to her comfortable life.

However, she was glad that she had dragged herself out of bed to give Una some support when she walked in on the prima-donna performance pulled by Innes over the rations for the survivors. These had been indented for, allocated and set aside, and since the instructors had made it aggressively clear that their department was quite distinct from the hotel and under their exclusive control, Rebecca had given the matter no further thought. She should have done, she realised, as Innes began to create havoc about flasks and cold boxes and the way the stores should have been divided and packed. Also Thea had used the butter set aside for them for her tables (in generous rough lumps which Rebecca noted in passing she must do something about later) and Innes appeared to take this as a deliberate personal affront.

'There's masses of butter, what's your problem?' Rebecca demanded, finding him having a go at a startled Thea who was too conscious of the first guests arriving in her dining-room to defend herself.

'All this stuff should be ready for us to pick up,' Innes hissed furiously, already worked up into a surprising state of anger. 'We have a schedule to keep to in case you don't realise it and we can't afford to be messed about like this. I'd made it quite clear what the requirements were—'

'All right, just tell me what you want and we'll sort it

out,' Rebecca interrupted impatiently. Back-tracking achieved nothing; producing an answer was what mattered to her and she saw nothing here to get so worked up about.

'Oh goodness, I'd forgotten all that business about the separate groups and leaving food in odd places for them,' Una called guiltily over her shoulder, starting towards them for a moment then turning back to snatch her scrambled egg pan aside with an exclamation of dismay. 'And I hope no one asks for porridge in the next few minutes, I forgot all about it last night.'

There could be no help from her. Rebecca deliberately ironed irritation out of her voice as she said to Innes, 'Just tell me exactly what you need—'

A guest's head appeared through the swing door. Thea stood trapped with toast rack in one hand and tea and hot-water pots in the other.

'I wonder, I don't want to be a nuisance, but could someone possibly open the front door? I have to take poor Chummie out and I'm probably being perfectly idiotic but I can't seem to see how to unlock it – or if there's another door perhaps I could go out that way – only I think Chummie's in rather a hurry, poor old boy. I should have brought him down earlier, only then I suppose if the door wasn't open it wouldn't have made any difference ...'

At least I can still remember where to put the pressure to make the key turn, Rebecca reflected, with a small private sense of satisfaction. As she turned away from letting out the still-blethering woman and her fat spaniel and letting in a wave of pure cool scented air – wind was still from the north-west – another guest hovering in the hall caught her.

'How do I telephone Germany from here? Do you put a call through for me from the office?'

'There's a call-box along the corridor,' Rebecca told her, suppressing a giggle as she realised that from somewhere she had dredged up a bright helpful voice to mask her swift exasperation.

She knew she should have been more helpful but if she didn't get back to sort Innes out he'd be firing all his petulant demands at a frantically coping Una.

'Ah, then I shall need rather a lot of change.' And seeing from Rebecca's face that she was about to suggest waiting till after breakfast, which was exactly what she, a novice to the game, was thinking she might do, the guest went on smoothly, 'It is rather urgent. My daughter lives in Germany and she went into hospital last night to have her first baby. We're so excited ...'

Trapped. Key to the office. Open the safe. Get out the cash box. The change she herself had apportioned yesterday to its little compartments had been wiped out. Who by? For what? No time to worry about that now. Get some from the bar till; where had they hidden that for the night? Simpler after all to make the call on the office phone.

'This gives you a line—'

'Oh, could you just get through for me? I should be so grateful, I'm not very good at this sort of thing. So kind ...'

When Rebecca got back to the kitchen Innes had unpacked the entire allowance of survivors' rations for a day and a night for the Grade I group, and for a day only for Grade II, onto the central kitchen table. A member of each course, accoutred as for war, now hovered awkwardly in the background. Una looked as though she was about to weep. The porridge boiled over and the telephone rang.

It occurred to Rebecca later that though she could perhaps have given more thought to the question of how those rations should be packed up, Innes could have provided some clearer instructions. She recalled how during the last few days Dan had methodically put together the kit for which he was responsible, painstakingly tracking down every item casually scattered at the end of last season, checking and checking again. Innes was in charge of the catering side; had he deliberately let it be a shambles? Surely not, if he had any pride in his job. Could he be petty enough, spiteful enough, to let this kind of chaos arise? If it didn't reflect on him personally Rebecca was beginning to suspect that he could. He needed watching, she decided, wishing Dan had taken on the stores too, or patient lumbering helpful Bern.

I once had a quiet, high, sunny flat of spare lines and functional efficiency, a civilised timetable, an enviable social life and clothes that were always clean, she thought detachedly, brushing dust off her sleeve after a grubby search on top of a cupboard for a rucksack someone wanted to borrow. Even on the busiest day there had been time to renew her make-up and brush her hair and clean her teeth – go to the loo even. But though one part of her was ready to mutter in disgust she was surprised to find that there was something else in her which rose joyfully to meet the multiple demands of the day.

One thing she hadn't expected to have to contend with, however, was Una's sudden panic about her menu.

'Don't you think it seems all wrong to give them venison at this time of year? I mean, it must obviously be frozen and they might not like that. But then if I use the sirloin tonight what on earth can I give them tomorrow and the butcher may not be open on Monday though he doesn't always take the same holiday Mondays as other people, or you can phone him at home, he doesn't mind that, but if the shop's not open—'

'Una, for God's sake shut up. Of course use the venison.' Rebecca's brain reeled at the thought of redoing the whole sequence of carefully worked out menus. 'Everyone's perfectly used to eating it out of season. You're quite happy to give them pheasant and partridge. And what about fish? That's not exactly straight out of the sea every day.'

'But I do try to do as much fresh food as possible, I'm sure it's one of the reasons people come here.' Una sounded suddenly helpless, genuinely upset, and Rebecca saw that a dangerous mixture of tiredness, self-doubt and longing for Tony to be there to take his share of the load, was about to overcome her.

'Look, let's take a break for a few minutes. Yes, I know there's masses to do but you've been on your feet since heaven knows when. You were down before I was. And you haven't had anything to eat. Megan can get on here, she knows what she's doing. Come on.'

'I just feel so *lonely* all the time,' Una confessed, allowing Rebecca to lead her through to the office, agreeing to coffee but refusing food. 'I don't mean it isn't wonderful to have you here, of course you mustn't think I'm not grateful for that every minute of the day, but I always have this feeling that Tony's going to come walking in at the door at any moment, back from shooting or sailing or something, and then I remember he isn't, that he's gone ...'

We could do without this on Easter Saturday morning, Rebecca thought with a blunt practicality that cloaked a real ache of sympathy for Una, of whom she was very fond. And I'm fussing about getting my shirt sleeves dirty. 'Poor old thing, I know it's grim for you—'

'Could you tell me, how much are the postcards?' Jolly face at the door from the hall.

Oh, we don't mind selling them at the price marked on the rack right under your nose. Rebecca sold two postcards, pointed out on the map the walk along the headland to be told at the end of a detailed explanation, 'These aren't my reading glasses, I'm afraid, and I'm hopeless at maps but I'm sure my husband will manage to find it all right,' and turned back to find Una smiling waveringly, her lashes wet.

'It's always like this,' she said with a shaky little giggle. 'You can't have rows or anything without being interrupted. Someone always wants a postcard.'

Laughter seized them. A voice said, 'Are we too late to ask for packed lunches? Only the day looks so much more promising than the forecast ...'

The fine day was a mixed blessing. It lured most of the guests out for lunch but drew non-residents to the garden and the new bar, about which word had already spread. Paddy had luckily come in early and without reference to anyone had dealt with the clearing up and restocking. The only thing he had needed was change for the float. They had seriously underestimated this, Rebecca realised.

'Two more days before the bank's open,' she said, annoyed with herself. 'I really could have got that right.'

'No one could have expected last night to take off like that,' Paddy pointed out. 'Someone will be able to let us have some.'

'Trudy, do you think?'

'Good idea. Or she'd get some for you. We cleaned out the top bar till too. And at this rate we'll need a bigger stock of glasses.'

Rebecca added it to a list which was beginning to make her feel rather ashamed. She had imagined she had thought of most things. Then she reminded herself, as she had done more than once, that this operation had been running for five years. She and Una weren't actually opening the doors for the first time, though it often felt like it. And every problem wasn't down to her, though that often felt like it too.

She phoned Trudy, tore into Luig, bought some ugly and expensive glasses and several things Una had scrawled down at the last minute, found Trudy had made up a bag of change in spite of a busy shop, and was surprised by a lively and agreeable sensation of involvement as she wove home along the suddenly much busier road.

Additional refinements to having far more lunches than they had anticipated were the arrival of the last four guests in the middle of them with a mountain of luggage, an Afghan hound puppy, and a huge triangle of wilting florist's flowers for which they wanted a vase and scissors without a moment's delay, and of someone succintly announcing himself as 'Powercut'. Is that really a good name for a business, Rebecca wondered frivolously in passing.

It appeared that Tony had arranged for him to come and check all electrical appliances to see if any savings could be made, in itself not a bad plan. He had thought it would be nice to bring his wife and children and have lunch. 'Make a day of it,' he said, confident that he had had a brilliant idea. Rebecca hoped he wouldn't look for approbation for it from the hot and dishevelled cooks as he switched off their machines and examined the state of their plugs.

'Good job it was a fine day and people could eat outside,' Paddy remarked, for once appearing for staff lunch when by three o'clock the rush was finally over.

Did the presence of two smiling brown-limbed blondes in buoyant spirits after a morning's serving coffee, cleaning, setting up and scrambling through nearly forty lunches without Joanie have anything to do with it, Rebecca wondered, or was this routine now he was back in the barman role? Or did he simply like the grub, she amended as she watched Una give him a shy smile and a man-size helping of creamy seafood pie with Megan's golden melt-in-the-mouth flaky pastry on top.

'Any of that left?' she asked, suddenly realising that she was ravenous herself.

'Enough. Though this was really meant for tomorrow. Where on earth did they all come from?' Una asked, reaching for another plate.

'The news has travelled. What they really wanted was lunch in the Coach-house.'

'I don't think we can possibly manage that, it's at the other end of the house from the kitchen, it's miles back and forth,' Una looked as worried as if a queue had already formed.

'Give them soup and sandwiches down there,' Paddy suggested. 'I'd need a hand with it though, if we were as busy as today.'

Could we do it? Rebecca's mind jumped at the idea like a salmon up a fall. Custom just waiting for the taking. Anyone who wanted a proper bar menu could come into the main house and spill out into the drawing-room and onto the terrace as they had done today.

'Hey, what are we doing?' she demanded, her thoughts reaching this point. 'Why don't we take this outside ourselves? And can anyone see a fork that isn't in the wash-up?'

'Oh, good thinking,' said Thea eagerly. 'I'll go and get a few beers.'

'Here.' Paddy handed over the bar keys without hesitation. Their eyes met. One down, Rebecca thought. I hadn't even included Paddy in the raiding list.

'But what about the telephone?' Una demurred.

'Doors are all open,' Rebecca said. 'We'll hear it. We can take turns to run.'

As they went along the kitchen passage towards the beckoning sunlight she heard the dishwasher die as Mr Powercut reached it.

Chapter Eight

Rebecca had thought the shooting pain down the front of her shins was something that only afflicted other people, like the heavy reluctance of the thigh muscles to lift each tired leg in turn up a few more inches of sharply climbing stony path. But though the summit cairn was still invisible and the hoarse-breathing plodding men ahead of her, bent forward under their packs, probably no longer believed in its existence, she knew exactly where it was, and knew she would reach it. There had been moments this morning, in spite of her initial confidence that these hills were old friends who couldn't ever defeat her, when she had seriously doubted that, moments when she had profoundly wished she had done as Dan had told her and waited to go out for the first time with a Grade II or even a Grade III. It was partly because he'd been so dismissively curt about it that she had pitched herself into Grade I, she was ready to admit now, managing a brief grin, wiping back the damp curls from her forehead with her wrist in the single gesture she had the energy for, feeling with the utmost relish the first touch of cool wind coming over the ridge from the east.

Dan was at the cairn already, swinging his pack off as though it weighed no more than a handbag, standing first to sweep the sunlit crests of the inland hills stretching to the Ben itself, then turning with the wind pushing at his back to survey the bright reaches of Loch Luig and Loch Buie, the outer sound and its scattered islands. He looked as relaxed as if he'd done no more than come up the path from the jetty to the hotel, Rebecca thought with rueful admiration, sparing a glance from where she was putting her feet and seeing him standing there upright and easy, legs apart, breathing scarcely altered and still with that trim look he never seemed to lose with his compact build and close-cut hair and minimal body-clinging clothes. He was one fit man.

Though he had set a stiffish pace the group was well up together, Dan noted, turning his gaze to the toiling figures coming up below him, the first of whom had just wrestled off his pack, nearly borne down by its weight as its strap hit the crook of his arm, and thrown himself speechlessly face down onto the bare rock of the summit. Rebecca, whipping in, was coming up steadily, still maintaining the even pace of the experienced, though Dan could see the effort it was costing her now. She had done well, and he hadn't expected it.

He had done his best to prevent her coming.

'Out of the question,' he had said flatly. 'Everyone on a Grade I has had some experience.'

'I know,' she had agreed politely. She had done as much research into the background of the courses by now as the paperwork and a few chats with genial Bern could provide.

'I'm taking them out on my own so I won't have time to mess about with any delays or problems,' Dan had continued, assuming that was the end of the subject.

'Oh, we couldn't have that,' Rebecca had conceded respectfully, then had added, 'But I'm coming anyway.'

He had become aggressive, perhaps already suspecting the outcome. 'Listen, my job's to look after the safety of the group, you know that. If you can't keep up I'll be in deep – it'll be a problem.'

Rebecca too had changed what she had been about to say. An arrogant, 'I'll keep up,' had been circumspectly modified to,

'I'll come back on my own if necessary,' as it left her mouth. No point in making him feel he had to prove something.

'You can't split a group on the hill,' he had told her impatiently. 'Don't you know that?'

'Then don't count me as one of the group. I'll be independent, come with you as long as it suits me and peel off when I feel like it. I shan't get lost.' That much she could be certain of.

Dan had had to accept that, with her new standing at Ardlonach which had subtly altered after that busy Easter weekend, Rebecca could do just that and he wouldn't be able to stop her. The realisation that any arrangement so unprofessional, so outwith his control, could be forced upon him went badly against the grain but he had known he could do nothing about it. He certainly wasn't going to appeal to Innes for support.

'You'd have to get hold of the right kit,' he'd warned her grudgingly. 'I'm not taking anyone out on the hill who's not properly equipped.'

'There's a boathouse full of kit,' she had reminded him in a soothing tone which had annoyed him more than anything else in the entire argument.

'Not much that'll fit you, there isn't,' he had retorted, briefly hopeful. Neither Una nor Rebecca topped five four by his reckoning and there were certainly no boots in the store that would be anywhere near her size.

'I'll worry about that,' Rebecca had assured him with a lightness which had sounded very like mockery to him.

He had consoled himself with the thought that if she turned up with inadequate footwear he could legitimately refuse to take her, but he also knew he didn't fancy an up-and-downer with her in front of the group. He'd heard her give Aggie and Donna short shrift once or twice and had been surprised they hadn't sent their husbands in to sort her out.

He had spent a bad-tempered evening after this little clash, knowing he had been pushed into a corner, his mood not improved by discovering when he decided to do some soothing work on his treasured and cossetted Capri that it was going to need a new clutch before long.

He had been rather looking forward to this day before Rebecca had shoved herself in where she wasn't wanted. There was only one group in at present which always took the pressure off nicely and gave the instructors time to check gear, do some maint on the boats or minibus, and on the personal side catch up with the dhobi, get a haircut and take accumulated days off. A Grade I, though it meant more work in other ways, like night navigation and the island exercise, also meant that since a basic level of mountain experience was required straightforward terrain-covering days like this one needed only one instructor. Since Stuart didn't have his mountain leadership qualification that meant every third turn for the others but Dan didn't see that as much of a hardship.

He cast an eye round the panting, sprawling punters, all reaching for something to pour down their throats, all beginning to feel pleased with themselves that they'd made it so far. Nobody was in bad shape though that lad with the red hair looked as though yesterday's blisters might be giving him a bit of bother. Before they all got too comfortable Dan thought he would point out the route down and the nice little pull after it up the knife-edge of Stob Leacach. That should take the smiles off their faces. He grinned an evil instructor's grin.

Rebecca, having politely refused lukewarm Fanta and a limp Twix, was looking westwards down the long finger of the Luig peninsula. Dan could see that she was not just taking in the general view as the others were but was tracing the contours and details of a well-known landscape and he was struck by the look of deep contentment on her face.

His first surprise of the day had been when she had come along the path to the jetty to join them, walking out of the black rectangle of the boatshed's shade into the bright sunlight where the men had gathered while he checked their packs. There had been the cool flick of morning still in the air, the tang of salt water and seaweed, the faint scent of vegetation from the tree-clad bank above them brought out by the dew, the clean exhilarating freshness of a new day which could always stir him. She had come easily striding towards them, an entirely new Rebecca, and he had taken one startled look and bent to pick up his bergen snapping, 'Right lads, that's all we were waiting for, let's be having you,' thunderstruck.

He had only ever seen her in skirts and high heels, with a groomed look about her which had withstood even the ravages of hotel life since her clothes were well cut and expensive, her springing dark hair beautifully shaped and the colours she chose well suited to her vivid colouring. That was how he thought of her. The executive-style indoor Rebecca who it seemed had been a high-flyer in the financial world, who lived in some smart flat in Edinburgh, who drove a flashy little car and hadn't bothered to come to Ardlonach for years. The Rebecca who spent hours at the computer, tapping away with painted nails cursing as she tried to crack the puzzlers Tony had built into the accounts. The Rebecca it was rewarding to listen to as she laid uninhibitedly into some delinquent supplier, who with a natural authority which pre-empted any questions about what her precise role at Ardlonach was, laid down the law in emergencies and hauled poor little Una along by the scruff of the neck into making the decisions that kept the place functioning.

Now she was wearing neat blue-grey wind-proof trousers, blue-grey shirt, red bandana and hill boots which certainly hadn't come out of the store. Those, since they were evidently new, might give her trouble before the day was out but on the other hand were so obviously of superb quality she might get away with it. Was this what she'd had in the shopping bags that day they'd split up in Fort William? She wasn't carrying a pack but had a bum-bag strapped round her waist with a light jacket tied over it. A timely instinct had warned Dan that she probably had enough essential kit to pass for today's route and conditions and if he made a big issue of checking he'd probably end up with egg on his face.

She had looked good. Dan's mouth twitched sardonically as he remembered that moment of simple acknowledgement. He had admired her sturdy build and the way she carried herself since the first moment he saw her. He liked a bit of flesh on a woman (Una's skinniness was a definite turn-off), but although Rebecca hadn't looked flabby she could have been lashed in by a lot of webbing, you never could tell. Now the chunky body was revealed as gratifyingly firm, and she wasn't too hippy to look good in those trousers with their workmanlike zips and pockets. In fact they looked just right on her. Might she be fitter than he had given her credit for, he had wondered. And the grey-blue of the soft shirt brought out the colour of her dark blue eyes.

Oh Christ, McNee, what are you on about? Get the show on the road. How those eyes would light up with delighted mockery if she guessed one tenth of what had just flashed through his mind. And he had punished her by putting her at back-stop because she had rattled him by walking so freely, smiling, into the sunlight, looking so good. That was the hardest place for someone who had not been on the hill for a long time, burdened from the outset of a long day by the demoralising fear of being left behind if the pace became too tough, and by the psychological disadvantage of always having to keep up. If Dan had placed Rebecca directly behind him, with the rest of the group struggling behind her, the moral boost would have been incalculable. She knew it and had scarcely been able to believe he had done this to her as they had set off up the even slope of Luig Hill for the long walk-in.

Yet perhaps that placing wasn't as bad as it seemed, she had begun to reflect almost at once, her capacity for positive thinking never deserting her for long. The others in the party wouldn't know she was struggling. To them this order would seem quite natural since she was one of the establishment. Each preoccupied with his own perspective, unsure of his capacity, worrying about the rub of straps on shoulders already raw, a blister however carefully covered which was going to cause agony before the day was over, a queasy stomach, a weak ankle, an aching back, they would take for granted that she was fit and competent, even here as deputy leader.

And Dan, she knew, had done this with intent. He hadn't wanted her to come and he meant to teach her a lesson, which in itself braced her. Also she had a secure fall-back position. She was familiar with every inch of the route and could turn back if she had to. Humiliating perhaps, but comforting.

The deciding factor would be not the terrain or the distance but the pace. Everything hinged on the level of fitness and experience of the group members and that might be high. They were now well into their first week (Grade I courses lasted for two) and they had had time to hone a few muscles. But she had been challenged, and for Rebecca that was enough to pump up a bit of useful adrenalin. As they put behind them the taxing miles up a steady gradient which offered no change of demand on tiring muscles, she saw that she was at least as good as the slowest, then, with certainty, that she could match them all. And she still had in hand one telling advantage; she knew the route. For the others what lay ahead was unknown and daunting. They could not estimate how their resources would meet the task or at any point tell themselves, 'Right, that's behind me, I know I can hack it from here,' whereas Rebecca had an accurate picture in her mind of the points of peak demand, the chances there would be to husband resources, and the moment (unless of course Dan pulled any fiendish instructor's trick like, 'OK, so now we go round again,') when she would know she was home and dry.

Also she had been allowed one huge, inestimable advantage – she carried no pack. When she had walked self-consciously forward this morning to join the group, telling herself she was shivering because the dark shadow of the boathouse had struck ice-cold after the sun coming down through the fragrant garden, she had seen the raking look Dan had given her.

A professional assessment, she knew, making sure that she was properly equipped for the day, but as she had met the expressionless light eyes she had been conscious that all the rest were settling packs on their shoulders, humping them up to sit properly, adjusting straps. They were required to carry their entire personal kit on this exercise; would she be expected to carry the equivalent? She had known in a stomach-churning moment of apprehension that if that were the case then she'd better throw in the towel at once. But Dan had said nothing, not even, 'Good morning,' the miserable bastard, it occurred to her now, her spirits high again, and she had felt weak with relief as she had meekly taken up her allotted position. Perhaps it wasn't fair to the rest but if they regarded her as one of the staff anyway it shouldn't worry them. If she was in competition with anyone today it wasn't with them.

Now that they had all made the first summit – and if Dan hadn't been so perpetually tuned in to what went on around him Rebecca would have taken the chance to reassure the men that nothing to come would call for such sustained effort – they were much friendlier to her, accepting her into the group, finding her feminine presence a relief from the general atmosphere of testing and torture. Dan's face clamped into an expression if possible more dour as they offered her drinks and shared their mint cake with her and asked her, not him, the names of the hills.

Off the steep windward side Dan led them, descending fast down a slope of broken boulders and scree. After a little lurch of alarm, a tentative few steps picking her way like an old woman, feeling panic reach for her that after all she was going to fail, Rebecca shook herself angrily into sense. She had run down here a hundred times; she knew how to do this. Her muscles suddenly remembered the trick as she straightened up, let her knees do the work and began to descend in neat little zigzags, eyes picking out the line before her feet got there. Absorbed, enjoying herself, she threaded her way down, intent only on the steeply falling ground, the tempting stone slabs, the waist-high rocky lips which could be vaulted down. She came out onto the grassy level of the col at a run, laughing, and swung round to look back up the slope.

'I thought you were tail-end Charlie,' said a repressive voice beside her. Dan, boot-faced, was standing with his thumbs under the straps of his bergen, one foot up on a rock, watching his scattered flock bundle and lurch and stumble with varying success down the rock-strewn face.

Rebecca realised that she had outstripped them all. 'I can see them from here,' she said cheerfully, as the more expert came out at a run onto the saddle beside them.

'Humph,' said Dan. But he turned his head and gave her what passed for a smile, a brief concession to an unexpected degree of skill. He had underrated her and he was admitting it.

The serrated ridge beyond the saddle was pure pleasure. So much attention had to be given to hands and feet that height was won without pain. People were beginning to gain confidence and, except for the one or two with problems of their own, Rebecca was conscious of the mood lightening round her. It was marvellous to be out here at last, away from the confines of the hotel, the inescapable trivia that made up its days, the endless interruptions to every job. She had let herself become an indoor person, she realised with a slight sense of shock, not just in the weeks here, of course, but in the years in Edinburgh. She had never seen herself in that light. But she never need be again.

The thought leapt at her like a mugger from a dark doorway and there was nothing here to which to switch her mind to protect herself from it. She could live in the country; that life was on offer. Not this spacious light West Coast landscape it was true but a pleasant scene of smaller rounder hills and rich farmland.

'So who's doing your job while you're bloody day-dreaming?'

Shocked out of her thoughts Rebecca could hardly piece the scene together for a moment. The group halted ahead, Dan coming back at the trot, his face dark with anger, the defeated figure huddled down on a rock a hundred yards behind her which she must have walked past blindly.

She was horrified at what she had done but there was room too for swift thankfulness to have her mind dragged away so summarily from that area of pain and doubt. Dan was going to have something to say about this, though. With the others she stood, curious as a ring of cows and about as useful, while Dan deftly syringed and dressed a blister as big as a bantam's egg on the sole of a pallid foot, and restrapped the awful crater of yesterday's blister on its heel.

'Now for Christ's sake pay attention to what you're doing,' he said angrily to Rebecca as he fastened his pack again. But quite soon afterwards, when she had reached the stage of dully watching each boot toe swing forward in turn, with growing wonder that they continued to appear, he delegated the lanky sales analyst who had been first on the summit this morning, and who was a colleague of the blistered sufferer, to bring him down at his own pace and Rebecca was at last released from stumbling doggedly in the rear. This relief came not a moment too soon and was as restoring as a shot in the arm. Dan knew it, she was sure; had judged it to the second.

After that it was just a matter of holding on. She had been stretched to the limit by the gruelling route, even though Dan didn't pull any rabbits out of the hat and led them back as planned just after seven. She was only thankful she hadn't attempted any showing off while she still had the energy for it, as she was all too prone to do. If she had she would never have made it back. As it was she couldn't summon the determination to go down with the rest to the boathouse, though feeling obscurely that there was some sort of moral obligation to return to their starting point. But she knew if she did she would have to be carried up the terrace path.

When she checked at the top gate into the garden she barely had breath left to call to Dan, 'I'll break off here,' raising a hand in a formless gesture.

Dan merely turned and gave her one brusque nod, never checking his even pace.

Friendly bugger, Rebecca thought, weaving a weary course along a path shaded by mounds of rhododendrons, but the comment held no real animosity. Dan had been pretty even-handed today, apart from making her whip in and even that had focused her determination, and she had satisfied herself on a couple of points which she had needed to be sure of. He was an excellent hillman and an excellent leader, watchful, experienced, drawing out the last ounce of effort but accurately gauging each individual's needs and endurance. Towards the end of the day he had been encouraging, had even dealt out a few words of praise – though not to me, Rebecca thought wryly.

For once she actually took pleasure in the appearance of the messy eastern end of the hotel with its yard and outbuildings, gas tank and rubbish containers. But going in she felt a definite resistance, quite apart from her tiredness, to the idea that problems could reach out and engulf her. Hotel preoccupations had been wiped from her mind in the space and light and challenges of the day. She was glad to see that dinner preparations were well in hand, with still only eight in the hotel and no chance booked. It was bliss to sink down for an ice-clinking gin and tonic in the office with Una, decide the mail could wait till morning and luxuriate in the relief of tired muscles relaxing, mixed with the private satisfaction that she hadn't failed in what she knew had been a very touch-and-go affair.

Fortified, she made the aching effort to get upstairs but couldn't face the attic flight, turning instead into the big old-fashioned nursery bathroom on the first floor, peeling off her sweaty clothes and sliding with a groan of pleasure into a deep hot bath. She lay and let her mind go over the day, the sun and wind, the exciting sense of rediscovery of a place more important to her than anywhere else she had ever known. She was back, it was there, within reach, available to her for as long as she wanted it to be, and she need not think of that other landscape yet. How good the day had been, making demands, extending her. She smiled, going over the familiar sequence – separate silent effort from everyone to start with, the gradual relaxation of the mood as people realised they would make it, then the satisfying feeling of companionship as they hit the rhythmic homeward pace.

Una had insisted she wasn't to do a thing tonight. She could dress as she liked, snatch up something simple for supper, go down to the Coach-house and join the group to drink and chat and laugh about the day. She laughed now, recalling the moment when someone had let a polystyrene cup blow away. It had lodged in a crevice a hundred feet below them and Dan had roared with simulated rage and sent the offender down after it. Rebecca had hunkered down to enjoy the unexpected let-up and had been amused to see the others remain on their feet to watch their disgraced companion with all the silent round-eyed unease of children when somebody has gone too far. What on earth had Dan done to them, she wondered, intrigued. Perhaps he would permit himself to crack a smile about the incident this evening. On the whole he had seemed not dissatisfied with what they had achieved.

Dan, going inch by inch over Stuart's preparations for tomorrow's basic survival training, wished he had had the opportunity for a word with Rebecca, but she had taken him by surprise suddenly turning off like that. She'd done well today and he had wanted to say so. He'd given her the rough end of the stick, keeping her at tail-end Charlie, and she'd taken it without a murmur. He'd been hoping for the chance too to tell her why he had refused to take her out on that instructors' play day. Innes would have crucified her, simple as that. Well, he wouldn't be able to say anything tonight. He'd promised Aggie's husband he'd have a look at that clapped-out old van of his, though the best thing he could do with it in Dan's opinion would be run it off the end of Luig pier some dark night.

Chapter Nine

More acutely even than she had felt it in moments of nostalgia at Ardlonach, Rebecca found walking into the big kitchen at Tigh Bhan like walking back into childhood and she savoured with pleasure the sense of ease and certainty of welcome, the associations of special occasions, special clothes, special food, grown-ups on their best behaviour and a present to take home. How old had she been when she first came to Stephen Markie's wonderful parties? Five? Six? She and Tony had been the youngest by quite a gap but in a sparsely populated area like this everyone was gathered in. And now Stephen was a divorced colonel with two children older than he had been when his parents first bought this square white house looking down the length of Loch Buie.

And she herself was – what? Nothing. A thirty-four-year-old woman on her own. Who need not be on her own. No time for those thoughts to intrude now, thank God.

She was delighted to see Lilias Markie again, Lilias who had been one of the important figures in her world when she was growing up, filling almost the role of grandmother for Rebecca whose own grandmothers had both died when she was small. Active and energetic, warm and generous, a person of many interests, she had been a great provider of fun for the young. Rebecca had not seen her since Tony and Una's wedding and felt a pang to see her looking subtly reduced, vigour and colour leached away. Her bushy hair was thinning at last and now pure white; the gardening, sewing, cooking hands which used to be strong and positive, earthy and brown, had become pale freckle-blotched claws. But the faded blue eyes held an undiminished snap and sparkle and her tongue retained the well-remembered tartness.

Rebecca had come with Una and Trudy to tea, to proper lavish delicious tea, tea with their knees under the kitchen table, with two kinds of scones and honey in the comb and Lilias's special raspberry-and-redcurrant jam, with coffee walnut cake and a lemon sponge insubstantial as a breath of air. None of it, alas, made by Lilias now.

'From time to time I attempt to coerce Barbara Bailey into civilised ways,' Lilias said when they admired the table with murmurs of frank and happy greed. 'Left to herself she is the most unrewarding flinger-together of food. Of course the moment I've got her trained I shall be dead. No, Trudy, that tea must stand for at least three more minutes. You're as bad as Barbara.'

'That's a bit hard,' protested Trudy, helping Lilias with great tenderness as she made the journey to the table on two sticks, one ebony with an elegant silver head, its chasing rubbed almost smooth, the other looking as though she had cut it herself out of the plantation, uncouth and knobbly as a shillelagh.

The big warm wide-windowed kitchen was much as Rebecca remembered it, though if possible even more cluttered. It had clearly become the focal point of Lilias's life and to the high-seated wing-back chair by the window, the bird books and binoculars, the battered Bentham and Hooker, The Times and half a dozen books with ragged markers sticking out of them, there had been added a large television, a radio and a telephone. No dogs now. Whereas at Ardlonach Rebecca had been glad that the obnoxious pop-eyed pugs had been laid to rest – she passed their grave under the ilex hedge with the greatest satisfaction and agreed emphatically when Una said from time to time that she supposed she was too busy to train a puppy – the kitchen at Tigh Bhan seemed oddly empty without them.

Una must have felt the same for she said in her warm, well-meaning but unthinking way, 'Wouldn't you like a dog for company again, Lilias?'

Lilias snorted. 'Company? I have never found the conversation of dogs very inspiring, while their expectations for a suitable standard of living are quite outrageous.' Then, seeing Una flush she reached to prod her with a wavery stick and said in quite a different tone, 'Dear girl, I would give a dog a miserable life. Cursing every time I fell over it, no walks, no games. And you know in the end Topsy and Poppy drove me mad with love. They became so caring and attentive that apart from sending me my length a couple of times the silly creatures nearly broke my heart.'

Rebecca, with an unexpected lump in her throat, thought she had seldom heard a nicer apology.

'But aren't you alone an awful lot?' it encouraged Una to persist with a loving concern to which even robust Lilias could not object.

She grinned wickedly. 'How can I say, "Not nearly enough," when you have all so kindly come to tea? No, I am exceptionally well cared for. Clare and Catriona call whenever they can, such of my contemporaries as are still above ground and not irretrievably senile come and bring me plants I can't plant and food I can't eat, Ina Morrison pops in, as she calls it, in the intervals of filling the tourist population with fried food, and Barbara Bailey or a daughter with a mercifully lighter hand gets me up and puts me down. One long interfering stream really. And of course good kind Trudy often comes.' It was clear she loved it all and was grateful.

They laughed. 'Don't worry, it will be a long time till we're back,' Trudy promised. 'This will probably be the last early closing day I'll be able to take for months and Ardlonach is fast becoming the most popular pub in the whole Luig peninsula.'

'Yes, I had heard that the new bar is a huge success,' Lilias said enthusiastically.

'We're run off our feet at weekends,' Una admitted, looking pleased. 'Even now, though we're still in April. This time last year it was almost like being shut again. A lot of it is Tony's courses, they're well booked right through the season. He did so brilliantly with all the marketing.' That need still not only to mention his name but to proclaim loyalty.

Rebecca withheld a tart, But at what cost?

'Ah, now, Una dear, what *about* Tony?'

From Lilias the question was acceptable, Rebecca saw, as though Una too regarded her as a grown-up always known, always trusted.

'He's left me.' She said it honestly, and it seemed without effort, but her voice was strangely thin and Lilias pursed her lips in a little moue of sympathy and reached out again with her stick, this time to deliver a gentle little tap, the only contact at the moment available to her.

'Darling girl,' she said, 'that is so very hard for you. I can't tell you how sorry I am. But are you quite sure he won't come back?'

'Rebecca thinks he will.'

Lilias's shrewd blue gaze levelled on Rebecca and she nodded. 'Rebecca always had a lot of sense,' she said. 'And she has known Tony all his life.' She looked at Una again, her expression uncharacteristically gentle. 'You haven't heard from him at all?'

'Not a word. And he hasn't made any – arrangements – about, well about anything really.'

'Keeping the door open,' said Lilias. The comments she was suppressing could be felt in the air. 'Has he been in touch with his mother, or with any of the girls?'

Una shook her head mutely. She had resisted Rebecca's

urging to ask Tony's sisters if they had had any news of him, particularly dreading talking to Caroline, the eldest, whose autocratic capacity for interference had had a good deal to do with making Tony so irresponsible in the first place.

'If they knew anything they'd have been on the phone at once – or on the doorstep,' Una had argued.

Rebecca hadn't been so sure. She knew the intense Urquhart clan loyalty; she also knew, though she didn't say so, that it would be unlike Tony to make any major decision without their support. In the end it was she who had telephoned, choosing Caroline for exactly the same reason as Una had instinctively avoided her. If Tony had told anyone about his intentions he would have told this power base in the family.

Rebecca had asked no direct questions, letting it be understood that this was just a hello call as she was back at Ardlonach. The conversation had centred not on Tony, Una or the hotel, not on the twins, Leonie and Fran, or on their mother, not even on Caroline's children, and certainly not on Rebecca's own life, but on the horses. Caroline and her husband ran a training stables in that dedicated and holy ground north of Hungerford and it absorbed all their energy and interest, passion and aspirations. Clearly no anxiety about Tony's marriage, livelihood or future had come between Caroline and her concern with feed bills, vet's bills, insurance or the incredible and unwarrantable increase in the cost of hiring boxes.

The position remained as before. Tony had made no provision of any kind for Una or the continued running of the hotel. He hadn't closed any accounts and wasn't drawing on them – or paying anything into them – and seemed on the whole to have gone away with his rich and beautiful Serena much as he would have left for a fortnight's holiday. This absence of information was a form of torture for Una which Rebecca was sure he would be unable to imagine or believe he had inflicted.

'And Rebecca, how about your life? We hear so little of

you,' said Lilias. (Polite form for, 'You should have written'.) 'And how is Esme?'

Under that penetrating pale-blue gaze, conscious of Lilias's dagger-like perceptions, Rebecca had a most unexpected impulse to tell her everything. Briefly, in half a dozen terse sentences: the errors and misjudgements and her own failure to listen; the pain she had not realised would go on biting deep through the years; the promise broken, the question re-posed. Although plainly none of this could or would be said, the impulse brought her strangely nearer to one day being able to tell — who? Someone.

'Oh, mother's wonderful. She works so hard and is involved in so many things that I actually think she's becoming rather renowned in Edinburgh, though she'd hate to hear me say so. And her handicap's down to four ...' Easy to plunge into talk about Esme, whose activities always provided plenty to tell about.

And what are you not telling me, Lilias asked in silence, watching the vivid face, the arresting blue Urquhart eyes which just as they used to when Rebecca was a child would so often fill with laughter no matter how seriously a sentence had begun. How well Lilias herself knew that irresistible feeling of the joke taking over, the joke for its own sake, mordant words forming themselves and gone, mostly without ill intent but by no means always acceptable to their targets. Rebecca and Trudy would get on well together. They both knew what life was all about and they were both capable of surviving, though not immune to pain. They had learned lessons poor little Una was only just beginning to discover. Tony Urquhart should be shot — though that would hardly please her. He wouldn't stay long away from Ardlonach, Lilias decided. Rebecca was right.

There had been something lightweight about all the Urquharts. Kenneth of course had been a selfish old woman. Not the term that would be applied to him nowadays. And wild Francis, with his passion for sport in any shape or form, had been lucky to be able to indulge it, with Esme recognising the shape of things to come and calmly qualifying herself to run (or safeguard) the business she had inherited from her father. While William had simply been knocked down and trampled by the rush of dominant females he had first married then bred.

Rebecca seemed to have inherited a good deal of her mother's brains and sticking power, having by all accounts done exceptionally well in the modern battleground of the financial world. But had she now abandoned it? Was there something of Francis in her too? What precisely was she doing at Ardlonach? And what had produced that fleeting look of aching grief as she had answered Lilias's question with news not of her own life but of Esme's?

They asked after Stephen only in general and conventional terms, and though Lilias would have liked to share her sadness that he was still alone, that Lucy had vanished with a thoroughness they had finally had to accept, the disaster of a broken marriage was not a topic to inflict on Una just now.

Rebecca had made the right noises about Gerald's death. Briefed by Trudy, no doubt, Lilias thought sardonically. Really, now, she hardly missed him. At first there had been the extraordinary stretching out of silent empty spaces between meals which themselves seemed to take no time at all on one's own. She and Gerald had grown into such a habit of arguing that her brain had felt for a while it had no function without the endless familiar competing and chalking up of victories. But she had adjusted, and even to think of all that pointless contending exhausted her now. She would not have given up for anything the peace and simplicity she had by this time attained. There had been many happy things in the years with Gerald and they were good to remember, but she was content to have this final time alone, in her quiet warm house with its back to the hill and its face to the water, well looked after, with friends always on hand, with the young coming still to tea.

'Which reminds me,' she said, not bothering to explain

where her thoughts had carried her, 'John Irvine was here yesterday and he tells me he has finally decided on the new partner for the practice.' John too had been part of the childhood and adolescent group of Stephen's friends and he came to see her whenever he could, a level of care which Lilias appreciated and relied upon.

'Oh, which one did he choose?' Trudy asked with instant interest. 'If he's turned down the female because she's a female or taken her on to look after all his menopausal women I shall have something to say to him.'

Rebecca caught but did not understand the look of pleasure which Lilias darted at Trudy as she replied blandly, 'And how would you know, silly girl? John seems hardly likely to confess to either. However, I am able to tell you that the new partner is called Fitzroy Colquhoun.'

'*Fitzroy Colquhoun*? Seriously? Well, that has to be the Cheltenham one, used to coddling all the rich old geriatrics. Oops, sorry, Lilias. But I thought John was afraid he'd never stand the rigours of a West Highland practice?'

'He must have changed his mind,' Lilias said demurely.

'Fitzroy Colquhoun sounds rather grand,' Una commented, smiling in a way Lilias was glad to see.

'Not entirely unScottish.'

'What else do we know about him?'

'Marlborough. Cambridge.'

'You could call that pretty unScottish.'

'Thirties. Unmarried. Childless.'

'Lucky it's both if he's coming to Luig.'

'Oh, surely quite unimportant nowadays?' That was Lilias.

'The doctor still has to be above the law.'

'Well, he's looking for a house, so see what you can do, Trudy.'

'Certainly,' said Trudy, amused.

It occurred to Una as the talk rattled on how rarely in the last year she and Tony had done what she and Rebecca had done today, turned their backs on the hotel to spend an afternoon with friends. So simple, so ordinary, yet looking back she saw how a pattern had become established of Tony taking days off for his own pursuits while she stayed behind to hold the fort.

Major local event, new doctor arriving, Rebecca thought, amused and content. It felt good, the new face of the present imperceptibly merging with the past in this well-known room, the pleasure of being with people whose words could be received without decoding, whose laughter held no undertones. And there had been such a feeling of light-hearted escape as they had slammed the door of Trudy's shop and headed north out of Luig, not even the squally rain and buffeting wind on the exposed road able to spoil the sense of holiday which a mere couple of hours out of the hotel could give.

Sailing had been cancelled for the course and Dan and Bern had taken them instead over to Glencoe, not exactly a soft alternative. It had become automatic to Rebecca by now to have somewhere in the back of her mind the plot of where everyone was and what they were doing, a habit she knew Una had never acquired.

A propos of which, this problem Aggie and Donna had just come up with that their husbands didn't really like them working at weekends (starting this week) was a bit of a bummer. Were they really worth having, with all their moans and demands? But would it be possible to depend entirely on migrant Australians or similar? They had been so lucky in Thea and Sylvie – the hotel should be humming along peacefully at this moment in Thea's hands – but there was no guarantee they would find such a willing and hard-working pair again. The linen crisis had been funny though. She grinned at the thought of it. Donnie and Aggie, coming back after a day off (and why did they have to take them together?) had arrived squawking and self-righteous in the office. There were five rooms to change and no sheets, no towels, only six pillowslips, the laundry didn't come till Thursday and how could they be expected ...

'Yon lassies have no idea at all and it's us that has to suffer.'

Thea and Sylvie had said in unabashed surprise when questioned, 'Oh, yes, we change everything every day when we do the house. We thought that's what you did in posh hotels.'

But on the whole things had been a lot quieter in the last two weeks and Rebecca had dealt with most of the things she had been so exercised about before Easter cut across everything. She had gone as far as she could with the accounts and was seeing the accountant next week; she had set up systems for ordering supplies, for two-way communication with the survival school and for keeping track of bookings, something Tony had treated with a terrifying casualness. She had had her day on the hill, had gone along as observer while Bern put a Grade II through the first steps of survival techniques, and had had a private go at the assault course when everyone was busy elsewhere, not doing nearly as well as she had hoped.

Now all that remained on her list of question marks was the exercise on the island, the core and climax of the challenges the courses faced. And Innes. He was increasingly trying his strength, assuming an authority which the rest of the staff were not in a position to contest. Rebecca didn't trust him and was growing more and more concerned about his freedom to do just as he liked when out of sight.

The sound of a vehicle pulling up outside broke across the discussion Trudy was having with Lilias, which sounded like an argument but was just each trying to talk down the other in indignation over regulations which obliged Trudy to lay a new floor over the beautiful and ancient flagstones of her shop.

'Is it Clare?' Lilias asked eagerly. 'She said she would call if she could. You haven't met her, have you, Rebecca?'

'No, not yet.' Rebecca felt a terrible resistance grip her, then was angry with herself, knowing it was absurd to let the Macraes become in her mind some perfect family unit, or to imagine that if she had found someone like Donald everything would have been different.

'It's Catriona,' Trudy said from the window. 'And Braan of course.'

'Oh, darling Catriona. Well, that's lovely too.'

Rebecca hoped her relief didn't show. This was a face from the past she wanted to see again.

Catriona looked very much like the shy untidy teenager Rebecca remembered, her figure still childishly undeveloped in worn shapeless cords of a dull mustard colour much favoured in the sixties, and a grey-and-white flecked sweater which must have been very warm since it was washed to felt. She was followed in by a smiling long-coated retriever with a white muzzle who went with swinging tail to push his head under Lilias's hand with every confidence in his welcome. Catriona, after coming to kiss Lilias, hung against her shoulder like a wary child.

'You remember Rebecca?' Lilias asked. 'Dear Trudy, push the kettle back on again, would you?'

'You probably don't,' Rebecca was beginning, smiling, when Catriona burst out, 'Oh, but of course I do. I remember you terribly well, you and all your cousins. I used to think you were all so glamorous and grown-up.'

It was a gauche child's response but Rebecca saw the effort to overcome shyness which had prompted it.

'I'm not sure I'd call Caroline glamorous,' she remarked dubiously, and was pleased when Catriona laughed.

'Come along, Catriona, you must have tea. Yes, I insist. You're nothing but skin and bone. Una, cut her a large piece of cake. No, Braan, I do not remember extending any invitation to you . . .'

With three talkers present Catriona soon lost her shyness of Rebecca and even became quite amusing on her own account, telling them how she had had an unprecedented urge to clean the library curtains but when she had tried to spread out the first one to have a look at it the whole thing had come away in her hand and carried her to the ground in its heavy dusty folds.

'All that was left was a little rotting frill. You should have heard Watty. "If you'd never touched them in the first place they'd have been fine. These fancy ideas never get you anywhere."'

'So what did you do?' Trudy asked.

'Well, left it, of course,' Catriona said, sounding surprised. 'I don't think it could be mended,' she added nicely, realising she hadn't made herself clear.

'Who's Watty?' Rebecca asked as they laughed.

'He was sort of handyman/valet to Fergus,' Lilias explained. 'He lives in the house still but exactly what he does now it would be hard to say.'

Esme wouldn't be impressed by Catriona's situation, Rebecca thought, her own conscience stirring.

'I was sorry to hear about your grandfather,' she took the chance to say to her quietly as Trudy and Una were helping Lilias back to her chair, for she was looking tired now and the signal had gone round among them that it was time to go.

'Thank you,' said Catriona, with the smile that so altered her anxious little face. 'He'd grown very vague and didn't get up much towards the end. It was time, really.'

Rebecca had heard from Trudy what that 'very vague' had meant. 'It must be lonely for you now.'

'Not as lonely really as it used to be sometimes before grandfather died,' Catriona said honestly, and Rebecca thought that was one of the saddest things she'd ever heard. 'Trudy and Clare are here now – and I love little Robbie. I wonder, only not of course if you're too busy, but would you like to come up some time? I expect you remember the house. Or would that be terribly boring for you?'

'No, I'd love to come. Thank you. It's fun to revisit all the places I used to know.'

Rebecca missed the small nod of satisfaction which Lilias exchanged with Trudy on overhearing this invitation.

It could all close over my head, she thought, heading back towards Luig. There was a sense of belonging here which she had not even taken into account when she had decided to run for cover to Ardlonach. Could it be enough? Could she just go on hiding behind it, delaying a decision or even pretending she had never been given a second chance to make one?

Chapter Ten

Darkness and the huge weight of the water forcing her down. Flailing struggle of limbs that could do nothing against this vast relentless force. Pain in her chest, in her head. Fear.

Then the shock of light, blinding, wide and high. The rocky jut of the far headland in the sunshine, a boat coming in from the sound, white dots of cottages on the shore, bright, simple and ordinary like a page in some well-known book of childhood. Only one glimpse, a distant, unreachable vision, then fear turning to blind thrashing panic that she was being dragged under again, that the huge weight would this time press her down and down so that this sight of the sane, familiar world would be the last she would ever have, miniature, two-dimensional, unreal . . .

A dark shape came between her and the violence of the light as she came up for the second time, a hand grasped the collar of her shirt, a firm voice said, 'OK, steady on, I've got you.'

Dan's voice, Dan's powerful grip.

Rebecca choked up loch water, retched.

'Don't thrash about, you're all right, I've got you. Grab this.' His voice was close and quiet. Coarse wet feel of rope; tangible safety. Rebecca grasped it frantically, and at last remembered how to swim, kicking instinctively with her legs towards nothing, just away from the horror.

'It's OK, Rebecca. For Christ's sake calm down and I'll get

you into the dinghy.' One smooth heave and she was landed, flat on her face in the rubber-smelling wetness, and she felt her stomach swill and lurch as Dan turned sharply away from the launch.

'You all right?' His solid body was between her and the watching eyes, between her and Innes's eyes which would surely be gleaming with satisfaction to have witnessed her shameful panic. As she hauled herself laboriously round and up, to sit with knees apart and her head down between them, still choking up salt water, Rebecca managed to nod.

'Sorry, hate water,' she gasped, shivering and coughing and ashamed. 'Can swim though,' she added fairly, always accurate.

Dan gave a brief spurt of laughter. 'Glad you told me. Listen, we've got to get aboard right away. Can you handle that?'

She knew instantly that he wasn't asking if she was physically capable of getting back onto the launch, there were plenty of willing hands to help with that, but wanted to be sure that she could face Innes and find some adequate way to respond to what he'd just done to her. For Innes had thrown her in, hooked a vicious arm behind her knees and tipped her backwards into the greedy run of the tide halfway between Ardlonach jetty and the island. And it must have been planned beforehand because here was Dan on hand in the rescue dinghy and she knew that in spite of what had seemed nightmare aeons of time she had been fished out with the greatest promptitude.

Fished out by Dan who, aloof, wary, always making the point that he was his own man, always faintly contemptuous of her, had let her know even through her confusion and subsiding panic that this time he was on her side.

'I can do it,' she said, lifting her head and smoothing back her thick hair which bounced back at once under her hands into lively spikes. 'But that bastard, can you believe—?' She heard her voice shake as rage began to take the place of shock and mortification.

'Don't take him on now,' Dan warned. Though his voice

was quiet he was looking almost urgently into her face, assessing her condition but also, she felt, frowning as she attempted to pin down the thought, trying to tell her something. 'Are you listening to me? This isn't the time.' He had seen, often with secret enjoyment, Rebecca's up-front approach to everything, her capacity and even relish for wading into confrontations and rows with the utmost confidence and outspokenness. Even in this tense moment there flashed into his mind their exchange this morning.

He had seen a letter to Thea among the staff mail and with one of those automatic put-downs which he scarcely realised was a habit he had jeered, 'Legge? Thea Legge? What kind of a name is that?'

'That's rich from someone called McNee,' Rebecca had flashed back. 'Might as well be called McArse or McElbow.'

Though grinning inwardly at the memory, Dan knew her spectacular temper was very near the surface right now and that this was not the moment to unleash it. She had just been badly shaken up and Innes was a dirty fighter. She'd need eyes in the back of her head the day she took him on, and Dan fervently hoped he'd be there to see it, but it wouldn't be the best tactical move to wade in now. Though if she could resist going at Innes like a bull at a gate he'd be interested to see how she would play it instead.

I feel proud of her, he thought in astonishment a few minutes later. It wasn't a word he often used.

There had been plenty of assistance on offer to get Rebecca back aboard, assistance offered in mixed *schadenfreude*, guilty relief not to have been the victim and unease about whose turn it would be next. The men were accustomed to seeing Rebecca in the hotel in a position of authority, busy, effective, in charge and beautifully turned out. Here she now stood dripping on the deck before them, still coughing up loch water. What was going on? She was with them today as an observer, they had understood. Was some test being directed at them; how were they supposed to have reacted; were they meant to have jumped in after her?

As Rebecca came over the side she already had her shock and anger in hand, imposing control on herself with a stringent effort she thought no one would have noticed or understood. She looked around her, not specifically at Innes, who was watching her with eyes oddly bright, almost as though he had actually got off on this piece of vindictiveness it occurred to her with startled revulsion, and said with a good imitation of naturalness, 'So who else went in? Only me? Well, thanks, that's pretty friendly, I must say.'

Perfect, Dan thought in a relief which slightly disconcerted him, as he came nimbly over the side after her and saw that the dinghy had been properly made fast. She hasn't let that bastard get away with it, she's managed to get a laugh and she's been accepted into the group. And if she really is hydrophobic, in whatever degree, then she's done bloody well to pull herself out of her panic so quickly.

Innes stood rooted, that curious glitter still in his eyes, a little smile he couldn't control twisting his lips. He looked furtive and embarrassed, as though some anticipated pleasure had no way of expressing itself. He said nothing, but his eyes ran swiftly and greedily over Rebecca's soaking figure.

Dan had wanted to protest when Innes had given the orders for what was evidently a little exercise in personal spite but had restricted himself to the practical comment, 'Well, she's hardly part of the course, is she? We're not here to find out how she reacts and give her marks out of ten. Why waste the time?'

'She wants to see what goes on, doesn't she? Let's see how she likes it then.' There had been a vengefulness in Innes's voice which Dan had known better than to whip up by further opposition. Leave it at that, he had thought. Toss her over the side and get it over with. She grew up here, she's lived with boats all her life – he had been impressed by her handling of that relic Tony had been so devoted to, an elderly Firefly which must have been rebuilt at least twice since she was first put into the water – and he had made the natural assumption that Rebecca would be at home in as well as on the loch. Never assume, he thought now, angry with himself. Surely you've learned that lesson by now. He should have checked, prevented this somehow. But after that terror, and he would never forget the agonies of fear on her face as she surfaced, this girl he'd had down as a city career woman had shown remarkable guts to claw back self-discipline the way she had. Where had she learned that, he found himself wondering, as Stuart cut back the engine and the launch ran its nose gently up the shingle beach which curved into the low central section of the island.

So now she was here for the night, and she was the only one among them without dry kit. Often half a dozen victims could arrive in that state, it was all part of making it a bit unpleasant for them, but today Innes had reserved this exclusively for Rebecca, giving the other instructors nothing to say in the matter. Good job Bern was out running the beginners round the head of Glen Righ, Dan thought with a little grin; soft bastard would have been in tears.

Rebecca had seen the triumph as well as the excitement in Innes's eyes. Her distaste to realise that he had found some kind of kick in doing this had steadied her, just as Dan's professional calm had drawn her back to reality out of blind panic. Well, I shan't give him any more satisfaction, she thought with a defiance that had a certain returning zest in it, and though in spite of the sunshine the wind felt unpleasantly cold through her wet clothes she gave no sign of any discomfort other than to move to leeward of the knot of taller males as they came in to the shore. But it was war just the same; Innes had made a move she could not ignore.

Dan had drawn the long straw this time and was to return with the launch, to spend a quiet day sorting kit followed by an evening off. Innes and Stuart would stay on the island. Rebecca felt her jaw set at the prospect of the long hours ahead then smiled, recognising that she was spoiling for a scrap just as much as Innes was.

'A word.' Dan was suddenly beside her, close enough to nudge her apart from the rest of the group who were bringing the minimal permitted kit ashore, but looking away from her across the bay as though intent on something there.

'What?' Rebecca frowned, hating undercurrents and whispers, resisting the temptation to speak so loudly that everyone must hear and whatever Dan wanted to say had to be out in the open. She wasn't interested in any more silly games.

'You don't have to stay. Do it another time.'

She turned to look at him, surprised.

'It gets cold later on. You're not paying the fees, you don't have to take the aggro.' Dan didn't meet her eye, pulling up the zip of his smock, still looking away from her.

'I'll stay.' She said it after the slightest pause, making a calculated decision. He nodded, accepting that, and turned away at once, jerking his head at a couple of the men to come down and push off the launch. For such a powerfully-built man his movements were light and coordinated, Rebecca noted idly with one part of her brain, while the rest of it reassured her that she would have felt a miserable coward to be in that boat with him, curving away in the long sweep which would let the current bring him down into Ardlonach bay. But she couldn't help wishing that either Innes or Stuart had been in it instead.

She had not been able to establish to her satisfaction just exactly what went on in this particular exercise. She knew that the main objective was to put into practice the survival techniques which had been taught during the first part of the course and that arriving with every piece of kit soaking wet was a standard introduction. But the island was so limited in its scope, not a mile long overall and barely half a mile wide at its broadest point, that she could not understand just what they gained by being here. There was little available natural food and a group of ten men dumped here every couple of weeks or so throughout the season would soon strip the place. She knew they would be given a couple of live chickens or rabbits and that for most of them the reality of killing to eat would be a genuine challenge, though they habitually consumed slices and chunks of creatures two or three times a day every day of their lives, without a thought as to how this once living flesh so like their own had reached their plates. There was also the simple element of endurance, hours of inactivity and discomfort to get through when hungry, cold, wet and bored, with only a survival bag between them and earth and sky.

And there was the sense of being trapped. Rebecca had discounted that but found when the launch throbbed away that there was a definite awareness of loss of independent movement, a potent restriction to anyone used to ordering his own life, or believing that he ordered his own life. The distance to the tip of the promontory which sheltered the boathouse was not great but the currents that poured down the deep-gouged channel between it and the island would be a formidable challenge for the strongest swimmer and no one had yet shown any inclination to abandon the exercise before the end.

Was the comparative luxury of the instructors' camp also intended to point up the deprivations the victims suffered, Rebecca wondered cynically as she saw the one-man tents go up, and noted the amount of kit that went into them. She also found it strange to see them in the sheltered little enclave on the south shore, where four generations of Urquhart children had built their fires.

It was weird and disorientating to be here in these circumstances. For a moment she wished acutely that she had made the time to come back and re-explore this most beloved of all places alone or with Una. No, Una had not been there in those earliest years and even when she had started to come to Ardlonach her involvement in sailing and shooting and climbing had merely been part of her passion for Tony. Not in the calculated way many women employ, but in a genuine desire to do what he did, be where he was, in his world. By now, Rebecca knew,

Una hadn't the slightest inclination to do any of these things. Any spare moment she could grab outside the hotel was spent in absorbed contentment in her garden, oblivious of weather or the passing of time.

No, this rush of nostalgia, almost unbearable in its intensity, belonged to a long-ago period when the distance from the shore was enormous, the days sun-filled and endless, the mackerel which they caught and cooked over a driftwood fire a taste never to be matched. And now she was here with a dozen people she hardly knew, one of whom had just revealed a dangerous personal hostility towards her. She was on her own, in a way that not even the most apprehensive of the survivors could be.

During the couple of hours spent climbing and abseiling on the seaward cliffs Innes and Stuart made sure that every man got a ducking somehow. Rebecca, more and more repelled, didn't take part, preferring to be thought useless or even afraid than to demonstrate her knowledge of every ledge and hold on this unchanged playground of the past, and she observed the instructors more closely than the instructed. 'The victims' was the customary term for the members of the courses, used freely by everyone at Ardlonach as a convenient label. Now, watching Innes's face – and Stuart seemed to model himself blindly on the older man – Rebecca realised that the word had a real and unacceptable significance. That was how Innes saw them, men who in the conventional scale of things were superior to him in education, achievement, material possessions and future prospects, and who were now at his mercy. He hated and despised them, belittled and mocked them, and if the chance came to humiliate them physically he seized it with an almost savage pleasure.

What shook Rebecca most about this display was that he made no attempt to modify his attitude even though on this occasion he had an observer. Perhaps he was unaware of how obvious it was; he was stupid enough for that. More ego than brain, that was certain. But there was no doubt also that he felt secure. To him Una was a cypher, therefore Rebecca, here as it were to represent her, had no power either. In his view Tony had employed him, Tony presumably still paid him and Tony had never objected to his methods.

Rebecca felt slightly sick by the time the last drenched figure crawled off the wave-washed rocks and shaking with cold and fright forced himself up the streaming rock to the lip of salt-and-wind-scoured grass which it must seem like heaven to reach. Red wet hands clumsily coiled ropes and gathered gear. Breathing returned to normal, eyes began to meet other eyes in wry grins of shared relief that that nasty little episode was over. Digging-in time had come. They could sit it out now, they calculated. And in two days' time they would be on the way south, hopefully with the vital piece of paper which would assure their masters that they would one day be fit to take their places. Back to warm beds with wives or girlfriends in them, to food put in front of them by other hands, to endless sluicing hot showers, clean fresh shirts, long cold beers. Even their overheated offices seemed attractive, where every morning they switched themselves on with the computer and were safe.

First, they found, they had to run round the island a couple of times. Rebecca went with them. The mixture of wind and intermittent sun wasn't actually too unpleasant and her clothes were beginning to dry out patchily. Keeping up body temperature would be a good idea.

Making the circuit of the island emphasised the strange dichotomy of remembered time and present time. She knew every inch of this place, every tree and hollow, every cranny of its rocky sides where shelter could be found no matter where the wind was coming from. She knew it as private, a special family place, and the scenes poured back. Tony and the twins, she and Caroline, playing rounders on the flat grass above the bay, sleeping in their ancient tents (Urquharts didn't like new things) which always let in water somewhere, the smell of old groundsheets and sun through canvas, the stronger smell of vegetable decay, when they came to leave, from the rectangles of pale squashed grass where the dampness had drawn the worms. Waking to tree shadows swaying on the roof of the tent, the intoxicating sweetness of the air coming in through the tied-back door; running down the cold shingle into the shock of the still-shadowed morning water. Voluntarily, for fun.

Rebecca lifted her eyebrows sardonically as she dragged herself back to the new scenario. That dip in the loch hadn't been much fun today. Had she disgraced herself? Before Dan she had, certainly, but he had given no sign. What had the others seen? Well, none of the course mattered; she scarcely knew them. The day after tomorrow they would vanish, never to be seen again, though oddly enough more than one person going through this mangling had voiced a mad wish to return to Ardlonach one day as an ordinary guest. What she was asking herself, she knew, not allowing this thought to divert her, was what had Innes and Stuart seen of that flailing terror? No, get it right. Stuart was a nonentity, his opinion irrelevant; Innes was the one that mattered. He had declared himself an enemy, and it was not agreeable to think of having revealed such weakness to him. And how would he try to use the knowledge?

When the survivors began to make the best camp they could with their limited resources it was accepted as a matter of course that Rebecca was one of them. Now that we're all wet, she thought with amusement, but it was nice of them. They had been provided with mess tins and hexamine blocks for cooking and Stuart now appeared and chucked down a couple of hens who promptly legged it for the nearest bush. A tall fit-looking survivor whose expertise Rebecca had noted on the cliff, deciding that he was more competent than either of the instructors, dived with the promptitude of hunger on the nearest fugitive, capturing it by more or less flattening it under him then, as Rebecca heard with amusement as she dived past him after the second hen, apologising to it as he tucked it under his arm.

The other half of supper, unable in any case to make up its mind which way it wanted to go, was captured without too much trouble. Then came the question of dispatch. This turned into a bizarre struggle, reducing everyone to hysterical laughter mixed for most of them with shamed self-disgust. For these were live birds, desperately and vocally trying to escape, with warm bodies and thudding hearts and round panic-filled eyes. As their beating wings and darting beaks, combined with the ultimate reluctance of modern man to perform the act of killing, delayed the quietus yet again, Rebecca felt horror at the whole performance take over.

'For God's sake, get on with it,' she said to Magnus, the climber, who large and fit and strong as he might be was getting nowhere with his hen.

'It's no good,' he said, holding the angry wings away from him. 'I'm not going to be able to do this.'

'That means nothing to eat for about twenty hours.'

'It's no use,' he repeated helplessly. 'I've looked her in the eye. I know her.'

'Yes, well, she's food for five. Give her to somebody else.'

A small cleared space immediately formed around the flapping captive.

'Oh, give her to me.' Rebecca grasped the hen firmly, with a moment's anger as she took the soft feathered living neck in her hands that she should be forced into this. 'OK, hen,' she said briskly. 'Bet you wish we'd eaten you as an egg,' and with the practised stretch and jerk learned long ago for finishing off wounded game birds she put an end to its troubles.

Silently, respectfully, the second hen was handed over. Silently she put down its dead friend and broke its neck. Then she looked with raised eyebrows round the little group and suddenly they were all howling in a great release of laughter, reeling and doubling up and gasping at their own ineffectualness and relief to be let off the hook.

They would have left the plucking and drawing to Rebecca

too had she shown the slightest inclination to oblige. She didn't, merely stretching out on a survival bag on the grass with her hands behind her head and giving instructions if asked. Only when she saw the barbarous way in which they began to wrench the roughly plucked corpses apart did she sit up hastily, sharpen one of Innes's dulled knives on a stone and rapidly and neatly see to the dismembering. 'Useless lot you are,' she grumbled at them. They readily and meekly agreed.

It occurred belatedly to Rebecca, though she saw the men were too involved in this new experience to think of it, that if this was a test then who was doing the marking? Innes and Stuart were tucked up with all the comforts of home on the other side of the island, from where drifted irritatingly the faint beat of Radio One. Had they brought a television too, a gas cooker perhaps, a heater, lighting, Chinese take-aways?

But the real frustration and anger came when the survivors began to make their shelters for the night, following the training they'd been given. They each carefully chose a spot out of the wind, where water wouldn't run down if it rained, level enough to allow them to sleep; they shifted stones and twigs and scraped hollows for their hip-bones; then they began to cut or tear down branches to make rudimentary shelters.

Rebecca couldn't believe it was happening. They had split up after selecting their sleeping holes and she had climbed down to perch on a favourite rocky ledge to catch the last of the evening sunshine, hands and feet finding without hesitation the well-known notches and cracks.

Behind her there suddenly broke out a sound of thrashing branches, a rending noise. She thought someone had fallen and coming hastily to her feet went up the cliff with a speed she didn't even notice, to be confronted by a scene that roused her to instant heedless fury. The entire group of so-called civilised men were wrenching and tearing at the trees which in this wind-raked place had taken years to reach their present height. The hollies were the main victims, being likely to form the densest windbreak, but even the birches, not yet in leaf, were being subjected to the same unthinking devastation.

'What the hell are you doing?' Rebecca shouted, tearing down on them in disbelieving rage. 'You bloody vandals, what on earth are you thinking about? Stop that at once.'

They turned to her, startled, the damning branches sinking down round their knees as they let their arms fall. She could see in some of the faces a return of awareness of what they had done, put suddenly into the context of ordinary life. They had been deep in the scenario built up over the last couple of weeks and had been simply intent on doing as they had been told.

A few, however, still didn't see that it mattered. 'Building shelters,' one explained, taking both hands to a resistant branch and applying his full weight.

'Stop it! Let go!' Rebecca leapt forward, and Magnus for one thought his team-mate was in serious danger of being felled.

She was too late. Trailing a long raw tail of bark, the branch was off. Rebecca, cheeks scarlet, eyes flashing with a dangerous light, swung round on the group. 'Are you quite mad? These are living trees. They've taken years to grow. Don't any of you touch one more single branch. This is pure barbaric vandalism. I don't care what you were taught or told,' as one opened his mouth to argue, 'you stop this game right here. I'm going to talk to Innes.'

She looked challengingly round the circle, making sure she met every eye. She knew most were uncomfortable, resentful to have been put in this position, seeing what they had done with new eyes. None, even the most aggressive, would continue with the destruction when she had gone; she was sure of it.

Innes however simply outfaced her. That was the way it had always been done, it was what Tony had done, and this was Tony's island, wasn't it, not hers? A point that did nothing to improve her temper.

Rebecca knew Tony would have condoned no such behaviour but saw in time the futility of arguing about it. Stick to the main issue. 'Well, it can't go on,' she said flatly. 'The place will be a desert in no time. You haven't even run a full season's courses yet. How much will be left if every course tears down trees and bushes?'

'Not my problem.' Innes, shrugging, watched her with covert satisfaction. She could jump up and down all she liked but she couldn't do a thing.

And he was right. He actually went up to the group and told them to carry on as instructed, reminding them they were assessed on how they put their training into practice. Then with an open sneer in Rebecca's direction he went back to his warm nest.

She had rarely in all her life had to cope with such frustration. She had no authority, no recourse to anyone who would agree with her, and she was trapped here, in this place and in this situation, for a night and a large part of a day. Not that any of the men risked any more tree wrecking in spite of what Innes had said, but that wasn't the point. She had to get hold of her anger and sit this out, the last thing in the world she was accustomed to doing.

Chapter Eleven

◌◌◦◦

It was a long, restless night. Shiveringly cold, uncomfortable on the hard ground after so many years of soft living, gnawingly hungry, Rebecca found sleep almost impossible to achieve. When she dozed off she dreamed wild dreams of great waves battering her down, of the island stripped of growth and shelter, eroded, waterless, its bare rocks white with sea-birds' droppings, its precious beauty destroyed for ever. In the restless waking interludes she did her best to be realistic about a few branches torn down, the unspoiled richness of new grass and early wildflowers, but over and over again she would find herself in angry argument with Innes, see Stuart's sly eyes enjoying her defeat, and find herself back at the beginning again. What did Dan and Bern think of this devastation? Did they condone it too? But surely it went against all their training? Didn't a respect for conservation go hand in hand with the sort of field survival they taught? She could hear Innes's scoffing laughter at that idea.

The worrying question came, what did the courses do when they were up in Glen Righ, a large part of which was Donald Macrae's now, or on Luig ground? The whole westward jut of the peninsula had once belonged to Ardlonach itself. Gradually the few houses and cottages sprinkled along the shore road had been parcelled off and about twenty years ago Uncle Kenneth had sold most of the land to the Macleods of Luig estate, which stretched far inland beyond the Inverbuie-Fort William road. Tony had more recently let the rest of it to them as grazing, though keeping the shooting for himself. Was Ardlonach guilty now, Rebecca wondered anxiously, of sending out squads of vandals slashing and tearing and laying waste?

Back would come the jumbled tormented dreams, then awake again, exhausted, she found herself dangerously vulnerable to those treacherous thoughts always ready to pounce when her brain was not engaged. She need not be a person alone. The choice was hers. But she had made that choice more than seven years ago. Had never tried to alter it. Yes, but through those years the option of changing her mind had not been there and now it was.

To fend off the insidious images she tried to use the anger Innes had aroused to focus on what could be done about him, but it was hard to get beyond maddening reruns of their angry exchanges and her present helplessness to do anything about him.

As the darkness began almost imperceptibly to thin Rebecca came awake with a jerk to another thought that had been nagging at the back of her mind for hours and which she realised she hadn't wanted to face. No one on the launch yesterday had worn a life-jacket. When she had noticed this fact, as the boat swung away from the jetty, she had suppressed concern with the sort of facile justification that doesn't stand up to honest scrutiny. It couldn't matter, it was no distance to the island, it was harmless May weather and no local person using this type of boat on the loch would dream of using a life-jacket, would even possess one. It was an unusual piece of moral evasion for Rebecca but at that point she had not wanted to make waves about anything.

She had come racing down late to the jetty to find everyone hanging about ready to embark, exactly the sort of start she hadn't wanted, with Innes looking at his watch and calling sarcastically, 'Right, you lot, it looks as though we can go now.'

Rebecca had been held up by a guest who had caught his hand on the brass finger-plate of his bedroom door which had lost a screw at one corner. He had not only wanted antiseptic cream and Elastoplast and apologies, but had wanted the plate fixed at once. Confident of his rights since he was bleeding satisfactorily he had held his ground till Rebecca patched him up with an ungentle hand and found Paddy, who promised to have a look at the door with the repressive calm of a nanny taking the heat out of a nursery drama. In spite of her annoyance at being delayed Rebecca had been giggling about Paddy's total refusal to be hustled as she jumped down the loops of the path as recklessly as she used to when she was twelve years old.

Apart from having held them all up, she had also been conscious of being an onlooker, not only outside the scene but not wanted there. But now she could not avoid the cold, serious truth. Ardlonach was in the business of offering professional courses to the public, courses which involved physical danger, and the wearing of life-jackets had to be a basic safety requirement. Any accident would have them in court and no insurance would cover them. What provision had Tony made for this? What had his ruling been? With his service background surely he would have been punctilious on such a point? But what she had seen here in the last few hours seemed so pointless, so amateur, teaching nothing, achieving nothing, that she had to wonder what ground rules he had laid down for this exercise. If any? Oh, Tony Urquhart, damn you for all this. I'm getting dragged into it whether I like it or not.

Her tired mind turned up other niggling sources of irritation – the way Donna and Aggie continually bitched about the two Australian girls, with a prejudiced resentment nothing would ever root out. True, Thea and Sylvie had not spent their formative years in some novitiate for domestic cleaners and had by all the evidence never seen a skirting board or a bread knife or silver polish in their lives. They mixed up paprika and cayenne pepper, filled the pepper mills with cloves, buttered digestive biscuits to make them nicer for the guests and had a distinctly casual way with bed-making, but no two girls could have been more willing, smiling and friendly – or decorative, which probably had more to do with the problem than anything else.

Then how to break Una's deep-rooted habit of grabbing a handful of cash out of the bar till to meet contingencies? Oh God, what am I going over all this for, what on earth does it matter, Rebecca furiously asked herself, wincing as she tried a new spot for her shoulder. It seemed a long long time before the toneless light took on warmth, as the first long fingers of sunlight began to reach over the loch and touch the uneasy sleepers on the island.

Dan locked the boathouse door and tossed the key reflectively in his hand. It was now supposed to be left every night in the office. Rebecca had made a big fuss about that after one of those cock-ups when no one could get in one morning and someone had had to run up to the farm cottage to wake Innes on his day off, receiving a mega blast for his pains, and some other enterprising berk had had the bright idea of looking for a spare in the hotel office and had given Una a fright, while all the time Stuart, making his hungover way back after some gig in Fort William, had had both keys in his pocket.

Dan had planned a quiet evening tonight. He had got his anger under control and wound down a bit after coming back from the island, though sorting out muddled kit yet again for other lazy bastards wasn't the most calming of occupations. But from the moment the week's roster went up he had looked forward to this as pretty much a day off. Being alone, however mundane the job, was a pleasure, and then there would be the long hours of a spring evening with the light stretching every day, a walk out on the headland without a herd of panting anxious blistered no-hopers floundering at his heels, lambs everywhere, the feel in the air of summer at hand. He would come back along the shore, now alive with birds, each little bay leading enticingly to the next. The tide would just be right for walking along firm wet sand below the line of pale stones and dark ribbons of seaweed clogged with the dross of plastic bottles, plastic bags and other human rubbish.

And best of all, there would be that moment of coming back in the dusk with cold skin, cold hands, chilly enough to make it good to get in, opening the door to his own silent place, no voice raised at once in question or complaint, no ruined food angrily thrust at him, no scenes and no demands. Just objects exactly as he had left them, orderly, clean. Food simply and quickly prepared. A match to the ready-laid fire, a couple of beers, his own music, then bed without drama, tears, rows or sex.

No one was there to know if he took the damned key home or not. It wasn't something Una would notice, or care about if she did. It was only Rebecca who got excited about that sort of thing, he thought, grinning to remember some of the dustings-off he'd heard her give people. She didn't mince her words, but she did have a redeeming knack of making the outrageous things she threw at people quite funny. Perhaps it was because she was so completely open about everything. He had heard one or two of the locals who'd known her since she was a child comment admiringly, even affectionately, 'My, but she has a tongue on her, that one . . .'

He thought of her now on the island. It shouldn't be too bad out there tonight, wind had dropped, it looked as though the rain would hold off and she'd pretty well have dried out by now after being slung into the loch. That bastard Innes.

Dan shoved the key into the back pocket of his jeans. He'd be down before Bern in the morning anyway and it wasn't an early start, taking Grade III round to the Luig marina in the minibus by nine. Why couldn't the wimps walk there? That was a good idea, he must suggest it.

Nevertheless, when he came to the path which turned west

to the ex-farm buildings and was also a short-cut to Inshmore and his cottage, he found that he was continuing up towards the hotel. Now, who had decided that? But the rule about the key was a sensible one and he was a deeply practical – and thoroughly trained – man. Much as he might mock and mutter he knew that a lot of the things Rebecca had tried to straighten out at Ardlonach, against heavy odds of habit, sloth and Una's truly mind-blowing untidiness, were useful, logical and in many cases essential to health and safety. It was only a few hundred yards further for him to go round anyway. And if the key was on its appointed hook at least it wouldn't be his head Rebecca would be nipping if there was some crisis or other.

As he crossed the hall he caught the hint of a most alluring smell wafting from the kitchen, so delicate it was gone before he could pin down what it was. Tempting. Going into the deserted office he grinned again at the tale the small once-elegant room told. Una's desk was a mound of open recipe books sprouting fragments of markers grabbed from anywhere, notes in her huge childish writing on rough scraps of God knew what, jaggedly opened envelopes which had never reached the bin, unopened catalogues, the empty barrels of biros, stumps of pencils, dead flowers in a china vase. Rebecca's desk was bare except for an empty in-tray – she must have dealt with today's mail before she went to the island – and a small leather holder for neatly quartered scrap paper. Everything else she put by habit into drawers or filing cabinet whenever she finished work.

He saw that she had left a couple of letters held down by the hole-punch on what was now officially the instructors' desk. That had been her idea too, of course. Previously there had been a useless set-up with all the information they needed filed, or shoved at random, anywhere about the office, with invoices for school equipment in among bills for weedkiller and Twilight Mints and bathmats, personal details for survivors alongside Tony's correspondence with their companies from initial approach onwards, receipts for payments impaled on spikes, locked in the cash box, or any damned place anyone thought of putting them.

Now the school staff had a desk, their own supplies of stationery, a drawer in the filing cabinet, planner and status chart on the wall. Might as well be back in the Regiment, Dan thought now, and though there was an instant knee-jerk rejection of the association, he felt no rancour towards Rebecca for organising all this. Innes had demanded his own office down in the boatsheds and this had been her answer. No flies on her, Dan conceded; she wanted the operation where she could keep tabs on it as far as possible.

The memory, never far away all day, of her terrified face as she came up thrashing and choking into the air, tightened his mouth grimly. That had been totally out of order, and so had the way Innes had gloated so openly over her distress, as much of it as Dan had given him the chance to see anyway. Hopefully that first blind panic had been hidden from him. But she had come out of it fast, which took something pretty special in the way of self-discipline. Like all naturals in the training world, Dan accepted each individual's fears and limitations and felt none of Innes's contempt for them. What he looked for was effort, the giving of one's personal best. Rebecca, however she might upset tender egos by going in with both boots, gave one hundred per cent in terms of effort and he respected her for it.

What was that smell he kept catching, still so faint as to be indefinable? Worth a recce. He could eat up here perhaps, walk afterwards. He could do with an early night though. How would city-girl Rebecca sleep in the stony hollow of the island?

The kitchen was warm and messy and friendly and busy. No rules about who came and went here had as yet been accepted or imposed by Una, in spite of a big red folder full of hygiene regulations propped up on a shelf against a broken Magimix.

'What's the good smell?' Dan asked fulsomely, and could hear Rebecca jeering, Ho, very friendly all of a sudden.

Una only gave him one of her shy smiles and said, 'I think it must be the ginger for the crab cakes.'

'Sounds a bit special.' Creep.

'It's for the dinner party for the Stapletons, in-laws meeting in-laws. I thought I ought to do my best for them. But I made plenty, would you like to try one? Are you having dinner here? There's lamb *en croûte* if you'd like that.'

It would never cross Una's mind that he was paid a living-out salary and that food provided by the hotel was not part of the deal, particularly meals on this scale. She left such concerns to Rebecca. Una was a naturally generous person who liked to give pleasure; her wonderful cooking was part of it. That Wren must be some bird, Dan thought with a sudden angry protectiveness towards her, watching her add sauce to the crab cakes as carefully as if he were one of the opposing in-laws.

Sylvie was in the small staff dining-room, wearing only a sexy little camisole with her green skirt and distractedly picking dark fluff off her cream shirt.

'I never thought my new sweatshirt would do this,' she wailed, unconcerned about Dan's arrival. 'Can you believe it, just look at this shirt. What's the time, Dan? Twenty to? Oh, no it can't be, I'll never have the tables ready and there's that special party and everything. I'll just have to put this on as it is, it's the only clean one I've got. I'd pinch one of Thea's only it'd drown me and she'd kill me anyway.'

'Here, put it on. Turn round.' Dan dipped his fingers into the water jug, dampened the clothes-brush Sylvie had abandoned and rapidly began to remove the remnants of dark green from her shoulders while she did up the buttons. The soft curls on her brown neck were pale as silver-gilt, the neck as slender as a child's. Beats living in the climbing lodge, Dan thought, as she turned her head to smile gratefully up at him, unbuckling her kilt to tuck in her shirt. Be a pity to leave here really in some ways, when today's dramas blow sky-high as they surely will the moment Rebecca gets back.

'How do I look?' Sylvie asked.

'You look all right to me,' he assured her gravely, and as she raced off shouting back her thanks he set about his cooling but delicious crab cakes in sudden soaring good humour. He wished Sylvie had been able to hang around a bit; she'd put him in the mood for company. When he fetched his lamb from the now revving-up kitchen he decided that he might as well take it down to the Coach-house. Running down the stone stair he finally admitted to himself that this was what he'd been moving towards all along. He wasn't happy about what had gone on today; he wasn't happy about what might be going on right now on the island, he wasn't ready for the whole enterprise to fold and he didn't want to be alone with these thoughts.

Bern was already in the bar, clean and fresh-looking as a baby after its bath, his group gathered round him, boisterously cheerful after a good day. They always came back in excellent spirits when Bern took them out on his own, the sergeant's part of Dan's brain automatically noted. Paddy was peaceful behind his gleaming bar and in the last sunlight of a changeable May evening the scene looked burnished, spruce and welcoming.

'Where did you get that?' Bern asked, eying Dan's plate with open longing.

'Where do you think? Hands off. Anyway, you've eaten, haven't you?'

'Wouldn't mind starting again,' Bern said.

'Stop beefing and get one in for me.'

'My round,' said one of the course, too brightly.

'Good for you,' Dan replied without a smile. More money than sense.

Thea came in before Sylvie, having turned down beds and then done the pot-wash. Her smile at Paddy as she walked across the room roused disturbing memories in Dan. Those marvellous beginnings of relationships, full of trust and goodwill, hardly able to wait for the next session of the best contact sport in the world. Then what? Strife and possession, the unmeetable demands. His mind jibbed, turning hastily to a calculation of what these two might make of it. Paddy was nearly twice Thea's age and had been through a fair bit of stormy weather but he was a good bloke. Thea with her smiling face and sun-bleached nail-scissor haircut and endless brown legs would be off in a few weeks or months, and if Dan knew either of them the smile would still be in place. That was the way to do it. What was that corny line? 'Touch hands and part with laughter.' He didn't choose to remember the rest.

The sound of an engine sorely in need of sympathy and understanding coming gratefully to rest outside made him wince but sent his spirits up another notch. That had to be Trudy Thompson's decrepit old van. Another long-legged smiler to join the party and this time as far as he knew unattached. A hefty lass, he thought, watching her cross the room towards them, but as good-natured and outgoing as they came, and he'd never been much into bony women anyway.

'Hi, Trudy, what are you having?' Bern's natural generosity got him in first, in spite of Dan's intention to buy the drink for her.

'Dry white, thanks, Bern. That would be lovely. Don't let me forget I've brought some stuff for Una, though. I don't want to take it home with me.'

'Delivered to the bar? Oh, yes, good one, Trudy,' Paddy said. 'I suppose you'll be wanting someone to bring it in for you?'

'What a kind thought, Paddy.'

Trudy had adopted the Coach-house as her local and was by now a regular customer. Fond as she was of Una there had never been the instant rapport she had found with Rebecca, the sparring, the laughter and the frankness. With Una she had been protective and affectionate but impatient of the way Una let Tony treat her, longing for her to toughen up and fight back. Also Ardlonach in its previous form, with its rather smart residents' bar, had not lent itself to this slipping along just as she was whenever she felt inclined.

The big simple room with its wide high-arched west-facing windows appealed to her and she felt at home there, especially having been at its inauguration. Being able to come here, sure of finding friendly company, had filled a gap she had been increasingly aware of. Glad as she had been to end the tension and frustration of life with Ben she had minded very much being alone. The small exchanges of everyday life were important to her. She liked pottering about at the end of a busy day with someone to share the cooking, open a bottle of wine, sit for hours over dinner or cuddle up on the sofa to watch telly, and she liked above all going to bed with someone, friendly or amorous according to mood, lying close to drowse or talk, make love or sleep, enwrapped or merely touching, but together, safe.

She had got through the lonely aftermath of divorce, the busy determined filling of the empty spaces in days and evenings and long blank Sundays. She had done her basket-weaving. For a few months now she had been ready to meet people on new terms but though she knew most people by face and name for miles around she had been able to find no focal point where she felt at home.

Now she was drawn at once into the group in the bar, absorbed into its undemanding level of chat, the repetitive tales of the day's achievements, fresh for each course, the in-house jokes which the punters were so eager to pick up, the day's hotel dramas, nine kegs of beer for Inverbuie Hotel delivered here, the Ardlonach order still adrift somewhere; the couple who had arrived as dinner was starting and had announced not only that they were vegetarians but that they were allergic to feathers and didn't like duvets whatever they were made of, and the general consensus that it was a good thing Rebecca hadn't been around.

'Where is Rebecca?' Trudy asked. 'Will she be coming down or are they too busy up there tonight? It's the Stapleton engagement party, isn't it?'

'Rebecca's out with the victims,' Thea told her. 'Night on

the island, eating grass and worms. Rather her than me, I can tell you. She must be mad.'

'The instructors cheat with rations,' Paddy assured her, with a sidelong grin at Dan. 'She'll have looked after herself all right.'

'She's getting the same as the rest,' Dan said shortly, then wondered why the implication had annoyed him. 'Anyway, if she doesn't like it it's her lookout, she's there by her own choice.'

'She likes to get to the bottom of things,' Trudy said tolerantly. 'I think it's a good thing she turned up here when she did.'

'I'm not so sure about that,' Paddy remarked slyly. 'Things were a lot more peaceful without her.'

'They'd be even more peaceful if you were out of a job,' Trudy reminded him with her friendly grin.

That touched a nerve for Dan, and under cover of the increase in noise and laughter as Sylvie, finished in the dining-room at last, came flying in wearing a minuscule sea-green denim skirt and matching shirt open, all the men were pleased to see, over the little pin-tucked camisole, he let his mind examine the possibilities he had been trying to ignore.

Rebecca would not condone what she would by now have discovered. Being tossed into the loch, yes, perhaps, though Innes like a fool had let her see it was a matter of personal spite. Rebecca could deal with that, Dan was fairly sure, but unless Innes had the sense to alter radically what usually went on in the island exercise, leaving the guys to get on with it, instructors having a nice little rest, stuffing their faces, getting a good long kip, Rebecca was certainly going to blow her top. Had it happened already? Was it happening now? Or would she have sufficient grip on herself to let it wait till they were back and she could get her knees under her desk and use all the power props to back her? She'd have to include Una; he kept forgetting that. Odd how natural it seemed to them all that Rebecca was the one to reckon with.

And if she forced a showdown, and what else could someone of her temperament and integrity do, where did that leave the school, the courses, Stuart, Bern and himself? This was a pretty crappy show, what the punters paid for and what they got didn't add up, but still, it was a job. The set-up had many advantages – pay, duration, the cottage and apart from Innes no interference. Also this scene was good, he conceded, looking round with a pleasure his shut face was far from showing. The Aussies were a bit young for his taste and Sylvie too undeveloped – anyway old Bern would probably top himself if anyone else went after her now – but they were easy on the eye, always in good spirits. But Trudy, now Trudy he really fancied, a lot of woman there, with an equable nature he guessed it would take a good deal to rock.

To hell with worrying about the future. Let things take their course. This was this evening and the mood was good. He signalled to Paddy, who with ironically raised eyebrows filled a wine glass and passed it over. With it in one hand and his heavy bar stool carried easily in the other Dan made a circuit of the group to weasel in at Trudy's side.

Chapter Twelve

'All right, then, are you satisfied professionally with what goes on?'

'It's not my business to be satisfied or not. I'm paid to do a job and I do as I'm told.'

'But do you consider the night on the island actually achieves anything?'

'You'd better talk to Innes, he's in charge.'

'I'm talking to you,' Rebecca snapped more sharply than she had meant to.

Dan surveyed her across the few feet between the two desks, his face wiped clear of any expression beyond a warning that he didn't like this. She had taken him by surprise by firing her opening shots without warning but he thought he had his body language well under control. Hiding instant defensiveness he was leaning back easily in his chair, one hand holding his pen but not playing with it, his whole air as neutral as he could make it.

Rebecca on the other hand was leaning forward, elbows on her desk, fingers interlaced, shoulders hunched, those direct blue eyes with their dark depths intent on his — and not easy to meet. No worries about toning down body language for her, Dan acknowledged with reluctant admiration. Every bit of her was concentrated on what she hoped to achieve. She had even closed the office door to stem the endless interruptions.

Sorry, lady, you can shut as many doors as you like, you're not going to get anywhere this time.

'We can't risk some serious disaster,' Rebecca was insisting forcefully, frowning. At the problem and how to tackle it, not at him as Dan knew.

He said nothing.

'For the punters' sakes as well as our own,' she explained impatiently.

Dan didn't move a muscle, just gazed back at her with a stonewall expression which sent a clear and deliberate message.

Rebecca stared at him for one long moment more, challenge crackling in the air between them, and recognised yet again that here was someone she could not move or override. She mustered the control to abandon the attempt philosophically, managing not to make the little face-saving stabs few people can resist.

'Right,' she said calmly, with one brisk nod, and spinning her chair round pulled some checked-off statements and invoices towards her and went into the purchase ledger on the computer.

Had she watched him for one second longer she would have been rewarded by some revealing body language at last, Dan thought, conscious of how his muscles had relaxed in what – relief? No, anti-climax, even a sort of disappointment. He had been sure she was all set for a fight. He had been determined not to get embroiled in any evaluation of the way Innes ran the school but he had been hoping, expecting, that Rebecca would demand that they cleaned up their act. And more than that, he found he had been anticipating almost with relish a direct confrontation with her.

Was that to release some guilt? He knew she was disappointed in him. Well, not in him as a person, that wouldn't interest her, but disappointed because she had turned to him as a means of solving a problem which had to be dealt with urgently and he had blocked her. Now she had nowhere else to go. He wondered what she would do. He was concerned himself about a lot of the things that went on in the school but this time it wasn't going to be his head on the block; it never would be again. If this whole job went pear-shaped he could fill in the summer selling petrol or climbing gear – or lentils and birdseed come to that. Trudy had been saying that if this early part of the season was anything to go by she would hardly be able to manage alone in the shop later. His mind toyed momentarily with this tempting idea and its ramifications, then sheered away abruptly from the thought of the involvement it would bring.

Rebecca tapped away at the computer, knowing she would have to abort this entire batch but thankful to have something not only to occupy her hands but to keep her back turned to Dan. She had been so sure they would at least be able to talk about these increasingly worrying problems. Dan's refusal even to express an opinion, his obvious lack of concern about the whole issue, had discouraged her more than she would ever let him see.

Contrary to Dan's expectations, and Innes's, she had said nothing after the return from the island. Nothing in public, anyway. There had been no rows, no repercussions, no immediate changes. She had talked to Una, of course, and though Una was upset about what had happened she had been obliged to face facts which Rebecca had already accepted. Without Innes they could not run the survival school. If they sacked him – and that in itself might lead to difficulties since he would be sure to contest it and they didn't have the expertise to prove incompetence, and furthermore Tony was technically still his employer – then Stuart would go too and in all probability Dan as well. Bern might stay because of Sylvie, but he couldn't be left in charge of any but the most basic exercises. Una was frankly appalled at the thought of rocking the boat to this extent. The school to her was still sacrosanct as Tony's cherished project.

'What on earth would he say if he found we'd closed it down?'

'Say? He's saying remarkably little, remember,' Rebecca pointed out caustically. 'Not even where he is or what he plans to do. And how much did he care about it if he could abandon it overnight? Do you seriously think he expected you to keep it going? Don't forget you were about to write to everyone to cancel the day I arrived. We can't cope with the school with any degree of safety and we might as well face it, and even if Innes by some miracle left we wouldn't be able to select anyone better. We simply don't know enough.'

'Then we don't know for sure that Innes isn't doing things properly,' Una suggested hopefully.

'Una, don't be so futile!' Rebecca exploded, frustrated by such a facile dismissal of the pitfalls. 'We do know. It's not just this business of safety precautions or destroying a few bushes. It's the more or less complete autonomy Innes has. How can we tell what he does or doesn't do when he's away on his own? And his attitude to the people he's supposed to be instructing is truly frightening. You should see his face when he's watching them. What he really wanted to do during the cliff climbing was stamp on the fingers of anyone who made it to the top. He's dangerous because he's got no self-motivation. If he knows no one's checking on him, he'll go down and down to his own lowest level and you'll end up in prison for manslaughter.'

'Rebecca, don't exaggerate,' Una protested, looking thoroughly upset. 'He's got marvellous qualifications. Tony would never have—'

'Oh, *God*, don't be so ridiculous! All right, sorry, I know, let's not fight. But you've got to realise that Innes is a blind egotist, which makes him a high risk area, and we can't just do nothing about it.'

It was after this conversation that she had decided to appeal to Dan's professional integrity, and Dan had so infuriatingly and uncompromisingly backed off. Not his problem. She realised, tapping in some more rubbish that left the balance of the account for pest control at over five thousand pounds, that apart from being left with this major dilemma on her hands she was disillusioned about him personally. She had been wrong in her assessment of him. She had believed he had more intelligence, more sense of responsibility, more dedication to his job.

It was Dan, in spite of Innes being the one to make an issue about having a separate office where he could run centre affairs, who kept the paperwork under control, made sure reports were punctually written up and copies kept, who indented for stores and updated the status board. He didn't look the type, so essentially a physical man, but to Dan chaos caused by lack of organisation was time wasted which could be more valuably spent. He simply couldn't see the point of mess and confusion and, since Innes's inefficiency would affect his own work, he refused to let it take over. But, Rebecca now realised with dreary finality, that was as far as he was prepared to go.

Knowing that it was only scratching the surface of the problem she did take one or two precautions. With Una present and all the instructors gathered, Bern ill-at-ease and the others surly, she issued two straightforward orders. Life-jackets were to be worn without fail on the loch, whatever the boat in use, whatever the activity, whatever the conditions; and no damage must be done to the environment. She knew these two stipulations could not be enforced, but they had to be laid down.

The crunch came, and even tough Rebecca felt the adrenalin pump up, when she required each instructor to sign a statement to say that he had received orders to this effect. There was one highly disagreeable moment, charged with affront and hostility, when Innes stared at her with flaunting patches of colour in his cheeks and spittle at the corners of his mouth, his small eyes round currants of hatred and calculation. Rebecca, one hand flat on the page turned towards him for signature, the other holding the pen ready for him to take, kept her eyes on his, all her will concentrated on outfacing him without overt aggression. Even so, one tiny fragment of her brain wished that Una wouldn't gaze at him with such wide-eyed alarmed pleading.

The moment when Innes decided that this was a piece of nonsense, no one would ever know what went on anyway, this arrogant bitch had done her nosing around and wouldn't move out of her office again, was visible in his eyes, which slid away from Rebecca's with a sort of sneering bravado.

Rebecca saw how violently his hand was trembling as he flourished off a furious illegible signature. Dan stepped up next with a calm promptness that was reassuring, signed rapidly and gave her one quick unsmiling nod. Stuart gave a tell-tale glance of doubt at Innes before adding a backward-sloping left-handed signature, then Bern, cheerfully oblivious of undercurrents, obligingly and carefully wrote his name beneath theirs.

'I thought Innes was going to hit you,' Una confessed a little breathlessly when they had gone and the waves of belligerence and confrontation had ebbed a little. 'That was horrible.'

'And probably not much use,' Rebecca added grimly, rubbing her hands back through her hair, surprised to find how much energy she had just expended. 'There are probably pages of orders like that we should make them sign as having read – first aid, emergencies, safety procedures on the hill, even taking the damn minibus out. And the infuriating thing is that they, Innes and Dan anyway, know a damn sight better than I do what they should cover.'

'Let's go and have tea on the terrace—'

'Good idea.'

The phone rang and Rebecca picked it up.

'Hello, I speak from Iceland. My English is not good. I wish rooms for five persons, can you do it? And you meet us at the airport in Edinburgh or Glasgow? We wish castles and golf – hello, you ask what, the date? Ah, one moment, I will look now at the calendar . . .'

*　　*　　*

'How many years since you were out here?' Trudy shouted at the top of her voice.

'Ten at least,' Rebecca bawled back.

The van crashed and jounced with roaring engine over the bumps of the track. Lilias, padded with cushions and safely strapped into the passenger seat, beamed around her with every appearance of confidence and pleasure. Rebecca, in Lilias's wheelchair which was lashed to the side in the fish-smelling empty back, hung onto Trudy's seat and ducked her head to look at a jolting segment of hill and sound opening before them on a day of warm sunshine and lightest of breezes. It was hot in the back of the van, the view almost invisible, conversation only possible at full volume and there were at least two more miles to go but she felt exuberantly happy.

It was Sunday and she was out of the hotel, free, released. Soon at Ardlonach they would be drowning under waves of lunch-time drinkers in both bars. The terrace would be crowded; Paddy had already carried several of the tables from the Coach-house outside. The whirl and noise and heat and haste would mount in the kitchen. But everyone except Aggie and Donna was on duty, and even when it had been obvious that the day was going to be glorious Una had been adamant that she should stick to the plan of revisiting this best of all picnic places, Righ Bay.

'It may be your last chance to do anything with Trudy for ages. She won't be free except on Sundays from now on and that's when we're busiest. Anyway, why should you give up everything nice just because I'm stuck with a hotel to run? I shall feel really guilty if you don't go.'

So here she was, she who never let anyone drive her if she could help it, committed to this noisome rackety unreliable vehicle being swung along the rough track by Trudy's casual hands, and she didn't care. Today she would put, had already put, all worries about the survival school out of her mind. She could do nothing more about it for the time being and mulling over it gave grief to no one but herself. At this moment all should be calm anyway. Innes and Stuart had a Grade I over on Ben Nevis, Bern was hanging round the hotel where he would doubtless lend a hand wherever he could be near Sylvie, while with the IIs in tow Dan was running round the shore road. Tonight he would take them out on a night navigation exercise and in the interval would no doubt make sure he saw Trudy who was coming back to Ardlonach for supper.

That had been an unexpected development, Dan and Trudy, but on the whole Rebecca thought she liked it. Trudy was evidently enjoying it anyway, and Dan was a different person when she was there. At least he had stopped sitting with folded arms looking as though at any moment his lip would curl in scorn, Rebecca amended.

It would have been nice if he had relaxed a bit with her too, she thought with a moment's rare wistfulness. It would have eased the job along. Still, this thing with Trudy might, just might, be enough to influence him to stay when the inevitable crisis blew up with Innes. It didn't cross her mind that Dan might consider moving in with Trudy.

Another thing changing for the better was Una's attitude, whether she herself was aware of it or not. She had stopped dragging Tony's name in at every turn and had discovered that many things she had thought beyond her were quite simple to deal with after all. Obliged to take responsibility in areas where Rebecca had no experience or no authority to act, feeling guilty that Rebecca should have walked into so much work when she was supposed to be having a break from a stressful life of her own, Una had summoned her resolve and dealt with all sorts of things she had always believed only Tony could handle.

But best of all, as far as Rebecca was concerned, Esme was coming to stay for a few days, actually taking a holiday, unheard of in her crammed life, and Rebecca was greatly looking forward to seeing her. She often missed the talk and laughter they had shared, only at this distance appreciating the support her mother's understated love had given her through the long time of inheld pain, regret and doubt.

Una, no matter how bravely she had tackled the job dumped in her lap, was a girl whose husband had just walked out on her. That she had been too blind or too naïve to see it coming was hardly her fault. Though she could achieve a degree of cheerfulness in the contacts of the working day she was not sparkling company and, Rebecca summed up with an ironic grin, she was a bit too ready to see the good in everyone. It had been more rewarding to get to know Trudy who had a trenchant turn of phrase which Rebecca enjoyed, but now all Trudy's spare time and attention were taken up with Dan. Well, at least they had snatched this day together and could not have picked a more beautiful one.

What a good sport Lilias had been to come, Rebecca thought as she and Trudy settled her into her chair, Trudy having first sat on it to sink it into the sand as far as it was going to go.

'One of my favourite places in all the world,' Lilias had exclaimed when Trudy had suggested the plan. 'I tried to persuade Stephen to take me over last summer but he fobbed me off. Clearly thought I was far too decrepit, only he hadn't the courage to say so.'

So here they were on this deserted beach, long fingers of dark rock curving round it, the sun beating back from white sand, the great hills of the islands far away and blue across the sparkling loch and patterning the green slope behind them the tumbled grass-grown walls of an ancient township.

'Donald Macrae's ancestors lived here,' Lilias remarked. 'Only about three generations ago. Isn't it hard to imagine it was all so recent?'

Slight guilt stirred in Rebecca at the name. Trudy had originally suggested that they took Lilias out to Rhumore today and she had pleaded for Righ Bay. She had met Clare by now, finding her in Trudy's shop one day, and after all it had been easy because Clare had been on her own. About Rebecca's age or a little older, she was thin and fair, with a keen lively face, and Rebecca had liked her ready friendliness and quick humour. But to spend a day with her and Donald and their small son at Rhumore – that was a very different matter and Rebecca hadn't been ready to face it yet.

It will get easier, I'll go another time, she told herself, with the comfortable confidence born of something difficult being indefinitely postponed, beginning to unpack the sumptuous picnic which the resources of Ardlonach, Trudy's shop and Barbara Bailey's competitive spirt had combined to produce.

'I hope Catriona's got a good appetite,' she commented, surveying this spread.

'Though goodness knows when she'll turn up,' Trudy said, taking a bottle of Moselle out of the cold box.

'Or indeed if,' Lilias amended. 'Days mean very little to Catriona.'

'No, we're maligning her,' Trudy exclaimed, pointing with the corkscrew.

Turning Rebecca saw on the rim of the grassy bowl behind them, silhouetted against the cloudless sky, Catriona on a sturdy garron, long-maned and long-tailed, with Braan beside her, head up alertly, ears pricked. It was a moment of perfection. This is where I want to be, she found herself thinking passionately, watching the garron come down the slope with the easy swinging gait of the hill pony, Catriona slide off giving Trudy the reins while she bent to hug Lilias, then turn to Rebecca with her shy smile.

'Goodness, this looks marvellous,' Catriona exclaimed happily, surveying the picnic with much the same interest as Braan. It plainly hadn't occurred to her to bring a contribution of her own, Rebecca thought with amused affection, and knew from Trudy's grin that she was thinking the same. She hadn't made the opportunity to go up to Glen Righ yet. She must do that soon.

'Now I think today I shan't swim,' Lilias remarked, comatose after a lunch twice the size of her normal one, face up to the sun and eyes closed.

'Well, that's a relief,' Trudy said lazily.

Lilias gave a little huff of laughter. She felt happier than she could bear them to see, these kind girls who looked after her so well, for happiness was edged now, always, with the huge unanswerable question. What a relief it was to know that Catriona had this capable pair on hand.

They swam while Lilias napped quietly, or Trudy and Catriona swam while Rebecca carefully didn't, going out to the end of one rocky arm of the bay and dabbling about a bit in tiny sun-warmed pools. Then they dug Lilias's chair out and trundled her along the turf to look down into the next bay, while Rebecca took a turn on the garron to see if she could still ride and decided it was a pleasure she could live without.

Four females, she thought with amusement, when she and Trudy had seen Lilias, still insisting that she wasn't tired, into Barbara Bailey's tight-lipped care. What's happening to my life? But really, could any day have been more contented?

Chapter Thirteen

News at last came of Tony, indeed a message from Tony, impelled to communicate not from conscience or kindness but from exactly the reason Rebecca would have expected to prompt him – money. It was Caroline, portentous and solemn, who phoned Rebecca, speaking in a lowered voice as though all Berkshire was interested in her brother's financial and marital problems.

'I thought I'd phone at dinner-time as Una would be sure to be busy,' she said, her voice full of satisfaction that she had worked this out so cleverly.

Rebecca, dragged across the hall from the bar in the middle of taking a dinner order which she hoped Thea would now field, resisted pointing out that they all were. Caroline had always been able to take a concept so far and no further.

'Now look, the thing is,' (how that familiar opening brought this bossy cousin and her humourless intensity vividly back) 'Tony felt I was the only person he was able to talk to about this whole wretched business ...'

Oh please, do we have to have all that? Get on with it.

'... he's really been quite good about it all, if you think about it, leaving Una with everything.'

There was more than one way of interpreting that. Rebecca let Caroline rabbit on, glancing at her watch, one ear cocked to sounds of movement in the hall – table three going in, good, hopefully Joanie was in the dining-room to show them where to sit, and there was Thea on her way back to the bar. Had she remembered to put some Number 18 back in the fridge, the Dumonts had cleaned them out.

'. . . and of course as a hotel it will have increased in value enormously . . .'

'Caroline, were you phoning to tell me anything in particular? You've picked just about the busiest time of the day. What did Tony actually say?'

'You're always so impatient, Rebecca,' Caroline complained. 'This is surely more important than chatting to guests or whatever you were doing. After all, you're not involved in the hotel.'

God, I forgot to put 'salad, no dressing,' on the chit for the chance guests. Rebecca picked up the phone and crossed to where she could signal through the door to Thea on her next flight to the kitchen. 'Come on, Caroline, get on with it. Tony's bound to want something.'

He wanted to warn Una that he was clearing out and closing the survival school account, which was exclusively in his name. 'As it's really his money it's very decent of him to let her know,' Caroline insisted. 'He could have done it whenever he felt like it without saying a word.'

'Except that he left it overdrawn and it's now got something in it,' Rebecca pointed out bitterly, frustration spilling over. Without checking with Rebecca Una had gaily paid into it a couple of big cheques for the balance of fees from two of their biggest clients. Since nothing could be drawn out without Tony's signature this cash had been inaccessible for the school's formidable wages bill and other expenses. Later cheques made payable to the school had been returned for alteration and diverted into the hotel account, but this meant Tony could walk off with a comfortable sum he had done nothing whatsoever to earn. And she personally was still waiting to be reimbursed for several essential purchases.

'It is his money,' Caroline repeated huffily. 'He's not touching the hotel account, which I believe is a joint one so he easily could have been drawing on it all this time.'

'Of course he's not, you idiot. It's got nothing in it.'

'It's not necessary to take that tone, Rebecca. I'm merely passing on the message as Tony asked me to do.' Caroline's voice was going up, defensive and petulant, in a way Rebecca remembered well, reminding her there would be no hope of finding any useful meeting ground. Extract any available facts and keep the scrapping to a minimum.

'So Tony's staying with Serena?' she asked. In spite of the fact that she's obviously stopped his pocket money.

'He didn't discuss her with me, naturally,' snapped Caroline repressively, since Tony had successfully dodged all questions.

'But he's not coming back to Una?'

'I'm just passing on the message he gave me.'

'Then are you going to give me his address, phone number, fax number?'

'You know perfectly well I can't tell you anything of the sort. Tony trusted me.'

'Then the lawyers can send everything to him via you?'

'The lawyers?'

'Well, Una can't run this place on her own and it's far too big for her to live in by herself. They'll obviously have to sell so that everything can be split down the middle.' No point in letting Tony think everything would be simple, though there and then Rebecca decided that endangering Ardlonach would be the last thing in the world she would allow to happen.

'Sell Ardlonach?'

'How do you imagine Una could keep it on?'

'But that's out of the question. It is the family home, after all, where we all come for our holidays. We're managing three weeks this year though I may have to come down for a day or two in the second week. And Fran and Leonie are both coming, we even thought we might be able to persuade mother

. . .' Caroline floundered into silence, thrown out of her stride by this appalling idea.

Aunt Maida hated Ardlonach, Rebecca knew. She'd be delighted if it went and she never had to have another argument with Caroline on the subject.

'Then you'd all better start looking for somewhere else to spend your holidays.' Somewhere where you'll have to pay, she mentally added.

'But Tony would never allow Ardlonach to be sold. It's his home.'

'His and Una's. If he walks out and makes no proper financial provision, what else do you suggest? Anyway, sorry, must go and do some more chatting. Let me know if you hear anything useful from Tony.' If she didn't shift the last guests off their bar stools soon she and Una would find themselves alone in the kitchen serving out puddings at midnight.

'But Rebecca—'

'Keep it for Tony. And while you're at it ask him why he didn't have the guts to phone Una himself.'

'Rebecca, really, that's nothing—'

'Bye, Caroline.'

Rebecca could hear the agitated yapping continuing as she put the receiver down. Wearily she put her cool finger-tips to her closed eyelids for a moment. Sisterly love. Tony had genuinely managed to convince Caroline that he was doing the decent thing. What changed? And poor old Una, how would she take this? How much had she been banking on Tony's return? And the long-term prospect of keeping Ardlonach running would be very different from temporary fort-holding with Rebecca to back her up. And could it be done?

Thea stuck her head in at the office door. 'Oh, you're off the phone, thank goodness. Una says the second lot of avocados are like bullets, she can't use them, we've got to tell the last two tables.'

'How many people ordered them?'

'Four.'

'What's Una putting on instead?'

'She didn't say.'

'Oh, *Una!*'

But later that evening, when the house was quiet and she and Una, doing a final round of ashtray emptying and cushion bashing, curtain opening and window closing, had collapsed in united weariness in the big drawing-room and she took the chance to break the news, Una after the first bout of tears was surprisingly matter-of-fact, though with a desolate and defeated resignation that roused Rebecca's wrath with her cousin once more.

It wasn't an ideal time to talk as she was very much aware. They were both worn out, it was nearly one in the morning and Una would be in the kitchen again at seven thirty. But during the day there was never the slightest chance of being able to talk.

Rebecca had feared a return of the shattered grief of the first days after Tony's departure but Una had come a long way since then and, whatever she still felt about Tony, the practical aspect of coping without him no longer terrified her as it had.

'It was hopeless trying to go on together really,' she said. 'I see that now. The hotel had changed us, changed our whole relationship. I drove Tony mad with all my muddles, and I always look such a mess nowadays, there's never time for proper make-up and everything and you can't wear anything decent in the kitchen. And then he used to get so frustrated because he could never do the things he wanted to do, like going sailing when the wind was right, or accepting invitations to shoot and so on. And he got so tired of broken loos ...'

She giggled a little tearfully and took a big swig of the brandy Rebecca had fetched for them both. Rebecca suppressed the comment that Tony seemed to have done pretty much as he wanted anyway.

'Poor Tony,' Una went on sympathetically, 'of course he must need some money by now and it's been very good of him not to draw anything out of the main account, don't you think?'

Rebecca drew a deep breath and managed to contain the answers that came to mind. 'We'd have to operate the school as a joint business with the hotel,' she said after a second's severe struggle, sticking heroically to the practical. Its income from now till the end of the season would mainly be the balance of fees, the original deposits having long ago vanished. 'But the hotel's struggling itself. I think you'll really have to decide if you want to go on, Una,' she went on more gently. 'And if so, how to—'

'Oh, we'll have to go on!' That appalled response could have been instinctive dread of the alternative, a life abruptly stripped of occupation and aim and all familiar patterns, or it could have been Rebecca's own feeling, that the hotel was a functioning, living entity which was popular, thriving and full of promise.

'We'd have to look very carefully at how it could be done,' Rebecca warned dubiously. 'Everything would have to be put on a proper financial and legal footing for a start.' No more blithe emptying of accounts whenever Tony found himself strapped for cash.

'But you'd stay? I couldn't do it without you.'

Decision time. Rebecca felt her stomach clench and hastily reached for her brandy. But really it was simple. She was no nearer to resolving her personal crisis than she had been when she came, still unable to convince herself that she should seize what she wanted and disregard all the warning bells. She knew she was simply using immediate day-to-day demands to hide behind but one thing was certain; there was nowhere else she could face living at present. Here there was acceptance and company, work to be done and problems to solve. Just as she had guessed Una had felt a moment ago, a new start somewhere else looked blank and frightening and pointless. She could spend the summer here, by which time Una's affairs must surely be sorted out one way or the other. Though the possibility that

Tony would one day turn up, oblivious and confident, could never be discounted.

'I'm not going anywhere at present,' she told Una gently, and to say the words aloud brought an odd sense of peace. She could set a date for giving Ivor her answer, months ahead. That would give her time to think everything through properly, safeguarding a happiness more precious than her own.

'Oh, Rebecca, that's marvellous,' Una cried, getting up to give her a hug. 'It would be so awful just to give up now. It's a good thing there's plenty of money,' she added happily.

Rebecca stared at her, mouth open. Had they been holding different conversations? 'Plenty of money?' she repeated. 'What are you talking about? Where?'

'In my account, of course. The account Daddy opened for me.'

'But Una—' Rebecca's mind floundered helplessly. 'Are you saying—? Do you mean to say that while we've been scraping the barrel to pay the bills and the wages, nip and tuck with every order we've made, while I've been tearing my hair out wondering how to squeak by without another bank loan, you've had money in another account? Money you had access to? You can't possibly mean that! What on earth are you talking about? What did you think I've been panicking about all this time?'

'Well, I know how you like to keep costs down,' Una said reasonably, 'and I do tend to be a bit extravagant sometimes. And then the books were in rather a mess. I thought you were just frustrated about the way we'd done things. And the hotel has to be able to make a profit without always drawing on capital, I understand that.'

'Oh, good, I'm glad we've got that bit straight.' Laughter, as ever, was beginning to overtake Rebecca. 'Now just tell me what the hell you're talking about.'

'Well, Tony was always very good about not using my money for the business, except of course for the amounts we both put in at the beginning. He sold some of his shares to start up the school, that was his own special enterprise so naturally it's always been kept separate from the hotel.' She still spoke as though Tony had done something very clever here, as no doubt he had impressed upon her he had, and it had clearly never struck her that the hotel subsidised the new company with food, accommodation, light and heating.

'But he took out a loan for the hotel,' Rebecca reminded her, with that feeling of the goalposts not having been moved but taken away which business discussions with Una frequently produced. 'He, you, are paying so much interest that the hotel can barely break even on present turnover.'

'I think he was told that if my capital was left where it was it would make more than the loan would cost,' Una said doubtfully. 'Could that be right?'

'But the interest on the capital wasn't coming into the business, was it?' Rebecca reminded her with careful moderation.

'No, I don't think so. No, of course it wasn't, it was accruing!' Una brought out the word like a child producing the answer to a riddle for some obligingly stumped adult.

Rebecca pressed a cushion to her face and began to laugh wildly.

'You're not crying, are you?' Una asked in horror, getting up again, this time to pat her anxiously.

'Not quite, though I'm not sure why not,' Rebecca told her, lifting a red face with tear-filled eyes and pitching the cushion into a corner of the sofa. 'Tomorrow, Mrs Urquhart, you and I are going to do some serious talking.'

If Una's fit for it by then, she thought with sudden compunction, for the implications of Tony's callous message had hardly had time to sink in yet. Thank goodness, really, that the hotel would be there to bowl them forward to the next job and the next, no matter what misery or loneliness lay beneath.

Her last thought before sleep rolled over her was that when the survival school situation blew up, as it surely must do soon, they would at least have the means to repay all those deposits, though it would cause her real pain to do so.

Esme, composed and immaculate as always, with her air of being a woman very much in control of her life, drove almost as fast as her daughter westward on the A86 by lovely Loch Laggan. She had had an excellent lunch at Killiecrankie; she was looking forward (she assured herself) to the first holiday she had taken in years, and she was most certainly looking forward to seeing Rebecca, whose inconoclastic humour and sharp tongue she had acutely missed during these past weeks. But her stomach was quivering with nerves and, though she swept on smoothly, a large part of her longed passionately to turn and go back to the gleaming, safe, exactly ordered perfection of her flat.

This was ridiculous, she had been back to Ardlonach since Francis died. Yes, and the brief visit remained a dark muddled memory of the agony of warding off associations and grief. She had gone because she had been determined that the loved place would not change for Rebecca but then had realised that Rebecca was old enough to go without her, perhaps even to prefer that, and she had thankfully spared herself the pain a second time. But that was years ago and everything had changed. The three Urquhart brothers were dead; William's wife Maida had long ago admitted to having suffered the worst boredom of her life at Ardlonach and nowadays never left a busy social round in Shaftesbury if she could help it, and of the cousins who had so adored the place in childhood only Rebecca was now there. And in any case, how different it would be, busy, full of hotel guests. Or would that make the sense of loss worse?

Seventeen years since Francis had been killed; the memories should have lost their power to hurt by now. But recently, inevitably, they had flocked back, and coming to Ardlonach was a bid to acknowledge and hopefully say goodbye to them, as much as to see Rebecca. Would there be the chance to talk to her about this? Or was it too soon? And in what state would she find her daughter? Would that look of a blow received, of pain renewed, still be so clearly visible?

How vast and high the lines of this landscape; how empty and splendid and exciting. As Rebecca had felt, she found it hard to believe that she had stayed away so long. How indecently profuse by contrast was the blossoming dip of ground where Ardlonach lay. All kinds of words she never used, like embowered and verdant, came to Esme's mind. Displacement thinking, she recognised with a perception very like her daughter's, swinging the car round to park on the gravel space at the back of the house.

Rebecca must have been watching for out she came, running, brimming with pleasure and welcome, seizing her mother in a no-quarter hug, standing back to look at her and coming in for another one. She looked wonderful, Esme thought, the skin that tanned so easily dark against a cream shirt, her gleaming hair less severely cut, a couple of inches trimmed off hips which looked good in terracotta jeans, but above all the bruised look she had feared to see gone from her eyes.

'I never thought you'd actually do it,' Rebecca exclaimed. 'Five whole days off, I can't believe it! Great pile of luggage? Oh no, not too bad, I think we can manage that between us. Una got caught on the phone, a guest who left a jar with a smear of some disgusting vitamin product in it on the breakfast table and actually wants us to post it to her. I'd already binned it, so that sorts that out. Oh, here she is.'

They've been good for each other, was Esme's instant relieved assessment, they're a team, as, like the chattering children the house brought so vividly back to mind, they led her up to the top floor.

'You're quite sure you don't mind being up here? Only we're so busy this weekend. We've put a spare bed for Rebecca into my room. Or would you rather share with her and I could come up here? Whatever you prefer ...'

The little room with its dusky blue walls and white paint brought back a rush of memories, memories so rich and good they knifed through Esme's well-defended heart. Most clearly came the image of reading to a clean, pyjama'd Rebecca in bed, the solid strong little body, the brown face and hands, the shining hair, the glowing look of health and happiness, with the window open then as now to the sweet flow of air, the gleam on the loch as the wind dropped at evening, the island golden in the last of the sunshine.

The years had swung round. Not now for her the big bedroom on the first floor, the big bed, Francis's arms, nor the established place in the family, wife of the second son. Instead this child's top-floor room, the bathroom at the foot of the stairs, the hotel guests who now had priority.

And that was fine, Esme discovered. It was just moving on; a sensible and acceptable answer to all the changes life had produced. And would produce. But now that she was actually here, with Rebecca, listening to the two girls' eager voices, her own concerns seemed very far away and she could no longer imagine arbitrarily introducing them.

'I shall be perfectly happy up here,' she told them, turning back from the window to the two enquiring faces so clearly wanting her to be satisfied. 'Truly. And I'm thrilled to be back again.'

Delighted as Rebecca was to have her mother there the weekend created an exhausting two-way tug between hotel and personal demands. After resenting when she first arrived that one thing after another had prevented her from the wandering and looking and revisiting of old haunts which she had promised herself, she had grown too absorbed in the new calls upon her attention and energies to think about it. Hotel matters had been too urgent, unfamiliar and in the end too interesting to leave time to repine over solitary walks over the headland or twilight meditations on some rock along the shore. And being always occupied had had its advantages.

Now she was continually trying to make time to be with Esme during these few precious days, longing to recapture memories of Ardlonach which no one else could share. She wanted to follow well-known tracks, spend lazy hours on hidden beaches, above all go across to the island and listen there to the voices of the past, letting them obliterate more recent associations of rage and frustration.

There was never time for any of it. Aggie had by now developed that invaluable stand-by of the unwilling worker, a back, and came and went with a high-handed approach to the roster that made Rebecca tear her hair.

'Why on earth does she do domestic work if she has back trouble?' she complained bitterly to Esme as they found themselves making beds together.

'Perhaps she has back trouble because she does domestic work,' Esme suggested calmly, with a few deft touches achieving a look of neatness in the big sketchily cleaned room which made Rebecca give her a thumbs up of mocking approval before they went on to the next.

'Making beds and cleaning baths wasn't one of the things I was looking forward to our doing together while you were here,' she remarked apologetically as they shut the last door behind them. 'You really are good to help.'

'Well, it makes more sense than you doing the rooms on your own and me sitting waiting for you. At least this way we can chat as we go.' But not talk, Esme amended to herself. But perhaps after all it had been too soon to do any telling. As for asking about Rebecca's life, Esme was sure that whatever the violent emotional shock had been which had impelled her to tear it apart, it was submerged for the time being under the protective layers of more pressing practical concerns.

'And take a quarter of the time Aggie and Donna need,' Rebecca observed, checking her watch. 'What on earth do they *do* up here all morning? Anyway, let's vanish for a bit now. I want to walk over to Inshmore to see if Joanie can come in a bit earlier tonight, and ask her if she knows of anyone who might do a few hours a week in the bar. It's such a drag covering Paddy's days off. It may rain a bit,' she added, glancing out of the stair window, 'but it won't be much.'

'It won't matter. Odd how rain is so much friendlier here than on the east coast,' Esme was observing as they reached the hall, only to find Sylvie coming to fetch Rebecca as departing guests wanted to pay their bill and Una was checking in a dry goods order.

It was after lunch when they finally made their way to Inshmore and then they had to hurry, heads butting into a rising rain-laden wind, in order to be back in time to do teas as Una was on her own and more arrivals were due.

The tiny place had hardly changed over the years, except that most of the cottages were now used for holiday letting, and one or two, with glued-on conservatories and breeze-block garages, concrete drives and tormented gardens, had been bought by retired English couples.

Rebecca caught sight of Dan's Capri parked at the far end of the row of terraced cottages which lay at right angles to the loch. They were definitely paying him too much if he could afford that one, double-fronted and the most substantial of the entire row. Had Trudy been down there? Of course she has, she told herself crossly. Dan might make a big thing of keeping this retreat entirely private but the ban wouldn't include the current woman in his life and neither of them made any secret of what kind of relationship theirs was. Dan certainly looked more cheerful – some of the time – and Trudy had said quite openly that it was marvellous having a bloke in her life again.

In the end Esme went by herself to see Lilias, to call on the Macleods and visit frail Urquhart acquaintances of another generation still living in Luig, where she was given an infinitely slow lunch of immense formality and tiny helpings of potted shrimps, beef olives and jam roly-poly. Once she set off for a long walk along the shore alone and came back very soon, shaken by tears for the past and doubts about the future, but resigned by now to the fact that she must drive away again with none of them shared.

However, one thing that Una and Rebecca were both determined on, each apologising separately and guiltily for neglecting her, was that the dinner party planned for her last evening was going to take place whatever happened, and that they were going to be part of it.

Chapter Fourteen

Trudy was only half looking forward to the party. For one thing it was to be dinner in the dining-room and that meant some sort of skirt, and she had noticed that her sandals were looking a lot more jaded than she had realised. Then she'd never met Rebecca's mother, and kind though it was to include her, she couldn't see why Rebecca's mother should in the least want to meet her.

Worst though was that her wretched van was playing up. Dan had said he'd have a look at it on his next day off but had also warned her without much sympathy that it was almost certainly due for the knacker's yard and she'd better start thinking about what to get next. She had known this was coming but had hoped to scrape through the season with it and get a new one when the bank account was looking a bit healthier.

Another thing that was putting her off the evening was that because of the van's state of health the Irvines had helpfully made the kind of arrangement she least liked. They themselves were going over to Inverbuie to fetch Lilias, who was to stay the night at Ardlonach, and had organised John's new partner to collect Trudy. He had only just arrived and she hadn't even met him, and disliked extremely after the years of solo living the thought of going anywhere without her own wheels to take her home whenever it suited her. Also, finally admitting it, she didn't much want to go to Ardlonach for an evening in which Dan would have no part. She might not even see him, almost certainly wouldn't see him, and there would be no chance of slipping away from the party to go and look for him. Not that he'd suggested that she should. When she had told him she was invited to the dinner party he had made no comment at all. It was one of the small rebuffs she was learning to get used to from him.

She didn't even know what he would be doing this evening. He was always very cagey about the programme, giving the vaguest of answers when she tried to sort it out in her head. And if she did see him and they could escape together would he suggest going down to that cottage of his? She had never seen and the fact was beginning to get to her slightly. He always came here, turning up when it suited him, and she knew, scraping through to another layer of honesty, that this was what really lay at the root of her disgruntled mood this evening.

The fact was that matters with Dan seemed to stand more or less where they had stood after their first evening together. Well, he had been perfectly up front about it; company, sex and fun were what he was looking for, with no commitment of any kind. That's what she had thought she wanted too, but the sheer almost-forgotten pleasure of being involved with someone again had begun to enmesh her. And physically, or should that be physique-ly, she amended, grinning wryly as she lifted trails of pink geranium with the back of her hand and inserted the spout of the watering can among the foliage, he was tremendously attractive. But there was a coldness in him you could never quite forget, a deep, fiercely guarded reserve under the laughter and teasing, an almost deliberate matter-of-factness in his vigorous expert love-making, which though it didn't prevent it being marvellous at the time could leave a chill afterwards. At the least suggestion of any emotional response from her, as she had learned by now, the shutters would immediately slam down. He would say something facetious, tell her some outrageous story, get up and forage for a couple of beers or make coffee, but his eyes would warn her, that's it, come no closer.

Well, she wasn't looking for a profound and meaningful relationship either, she thought, sighing, but some progression would have seemed natural, some developing mutual trust.

Still, she reminded herself more briskly, going to fill her can at the freezer room sink and deliberately turning her mind to something positive, it would be fun to see Clare tonight. Their opportunities to meet were all too rare these days. And Clare and Donald were bringing Catriona with them. Trudy had been delighted to hear she'd agreed to come because every so often in the background of her busy life the worry nagged that she wasn't doing enough to help Catriona, though it was hard to see what it could be. And dear Lilias agreeing to come over for the night, she had lots of guts. She wouldn't be with them for ever, hard though that was to take in, and every glimpse of her was precious.

From her little yard Trudy heard someone come into the shop. She had been watering the hanging baskets, resisting the temptation to tidy them up a little since she was clean and ready to go in a droopy Indian cotton skirt and orange T-shirt, with a leather waistcoat over it to blur the full impact of her breasts through the thin stretched cotton. She often kept the shop door open if she was around in the evenings since a sale was a sale and at this time of year a lot of tourists drifted round the town with nothing much to occupy them after high tea in the guest houses.

Coming in from the light of a pleasant evening she saw across the shadowy shop, where only half the lights were on, the back of an unusually long and narrow male shape. It nearly reached the ceiling, was clad in a silvery-grey beautifully-fitting suit and appeared to have no head. Her brain not quite computing what her eyes were seeing, Trudy peered uncertainly into the gloom as her customer turned towards her, still headless.

'Perhaps I should smile,' said a deep, rich, amused, enormously cultured English voice. 'You look seriously alarmed.' A white smile flashed as her eyes sorted out the image of a lean face of grape-bloom black and stunning handsomeness.

'Goodness,' said Trudy, beginning to laugh. 'It really did look as though your suit had walked in on its own. Can I help you or were you just looking?'

'For you, I believe,' said the marvellous voice, and for one dizzy moment it seemed to Trudy that something like 'all my life' should follow these courteous words. 'Fitzroy Colquhoun, John Irvine's new partner, and may I say how delighted I am to find myself not only asked to a dinner party so soon but to be commissioned to call for you as well.'

John Irvine, I shall have something to say to you very shortly, Trudy vowed, but it was an excellent joke and by his expression Fitzroy Colquhoun was enjoying it too. His eyes were snapping and his whole stance and expression were those of a man who loved to laugh.

'Do we have to lock some doors?' he suggested, reading the expressions flitting across Trudy's face with the greatest amusement. 'Though of course I am in no hurry if there are things you have to do.'

'Oh, the doors.' Trudy had been quite ready to walk away with him there and then. She was sure he'd known that too, and she laughed as she ran up the outer stair to her living quarters, found she had already locked the door at the top, checked the workroom door which she was sure she had locked and found it open, told herself that no one would row across the harbour to rob her anyway and then reminded herself as she had done a hundred times that there was no reason why they shouldn't. But it was all surface froth, under which bubbled a new and cheerful anticipation of the evening ahead.

Fitzroy arched his bean-pole length of what, six foot three, six four, to open the door of a gleaming MG for her. Of course an MG. Trudy's spirits shot up another few notches.

What had she been feeling so grouchy about? She couldn't even remember.

'Blimey,' said Rebecca in astonishment. 'I didn't realise Colquhoun was Scottish for Coon.'

Dan let out the involuntary laugh which Rebecca could frequently draw from him as he too looked out of the office window and saw the immensely long-legged and elegant black man in expensive shades coming round to help – shit, that was Trudy – out of an immaculately kept MG. Two years old, less; a beauty.

'That was a bit racist, wasn't it?' he asked, pulling himself together enough to make a show of putting Rebecca down.

'Quite good, I thought,' she said blithely, rapidly sorting the day's mail, some of which she had hoped to get rid of before dinner, into its appropriate piles. 'John Irvine's clearly been enjoying himself keeping that a secret. What on earth will Luig have to say? Dan, look, I'd better get going but these two are yours, one about equipment, one with a query about the kit list. Just scribble the answers on them, I'll do them tomorrow.'

Dan was watching Trudy and her escort crossing the gravel sweep with a strange expression on his face. He took no notice of what Rebecca had just said.

He's jealous, she thought with a little stab of – what? Irritation, she decided, always hating to be held up for as much as a second when her mind was bent on work.

'I'll leave them for you,' she said, slightly more emphatically. 'I'll have to go, party seems to be starting.'

Dan put the stapler on the letters without looking at them. 'See you,' he said, picking up the neatly wrapped parcel of baked trout Una had given him and walking out.

She shouldn't do that, Rebecca thought crossly. If they're paid to live out they should feed themselves. But she knew perfectly well this was only a minor irritant which it was convenient to clutch at.

I must talk to her, Dan thought, taking a route along the kitchen corridor and down below the terrace to make sure he didn't run into anyone from this damned dinner party they were making such a fuss about. He could nip into the Coach-house and get another six-pack. No he couldn't; he still had a couple of cans in the fridge, he'd make do with those. He'd had enough of people for one day. Bloody Innes, he'd have them all in the proverbial soon. But when was there ever going to be the chance to talk to Rebecca? Her mother had been here for the best part of a week. He was out on the two-day exercise tomorrow and the next day, then Bern and Stuart were both on day off after that. And trying to get hold of her in that damned office was impossible; every time you opened your mouth the phone rang or some guest came barging in with the usual bleat, 'Now, I know you're busy but I just wanted . . .'

He'd promised Trudy he'd have a look at that van of hers and he'd never got round to it. Had it packed up altogether? Was that why she'd needed a lift tonight? A look – it would need a month's work done on it at least. He'd be better off spending the time hunting for something else for her but when was he going to get the chance to do that? Well, perhaps he'd have all the time in the world soon. He couldn't see them limping through an entire season the way they were doing at present. Something would have to give.

So that was the new doc. Rebecca's comment came back to him and he grinned, jogging and twisting down the steep slope above his cottage. That tongue of hers would get her into trouble one of these days.

As he went into the quiet cottage he found his spirits had somehow improved. The little hiss as he opened the first lager can, the highly promising look of the trout he unwrapped – Una had given him enough for two, what a doll – made him feel better still. It wasn't seeing Trudy with that tailor's dummy that got to you, you stupid bastard, it's just the same old story all over again. You've started something you want out of. She says she's not looking for anything either but she's getting keener all the time. She's been on her own too long and you've got in there and woken up the appetites again and now she's going to want more than you can give. Is it time to get out after all, get clear of the whole place? Would a major blow-up be quite useful? June to October, I can cruise that, he calculated, knowing there's a winter job for certain at the end of it. But do I want to leave this cottage? Well, there are other cottages. He tipped his head back and the chill pale amber stream flowed soothingly down his throat.

'Isn't it wonderful, no chance dinners, no extra residents turning up, just those two two's and they came in early,' Una said with the greatest satisfaction, looking down the long table in the centre of the otherwise deserted dining-room. Her first party without Tony there to look after everything, a small bleak voice reminded her, and was resolutely ignored.

'Aren't you supposed to want customers?' Jeanette Irvine teased her.

'Not tonight. Even Rebecca doesn't want them tonight,' Una assured her with mock gravity.

'Ah, well, it must be all right then.'

How truly involved is Rebecca in all this, Esme wondered, listening to the chatter and laughter. I can see how easy it must be to rush from job to job, and from day to day which becomes week to week almost without noticing it. I have to go back tomorrow and in all these days there hasn't been a single moment to talk. It seems hard to credit but one just does get rolled along. Is she contented here or is she just making do with surface busyness? She looks happy enough now at any rate, laughing, protesting at the teasing.

The long table with eleven faces smiling round it brought

back with a sudden pang the family gatherings of other years, children's voices, Francis's flashing smile, his dark good looks, his blue eyes alight with laughter just as Rebecca's were now.

It was good to have the links rewoven tonight, especially to see Lilias here, Lilias who had been so central to all the friendships of the past. And Donald Macrae with his delightful little fair-haired wife who was such an improvement on unsociable Ishbel. Even shy Catriona Finlay, looking still so much the untidy farouche child Esme remembered. She clearly needed help of some kind; would Rebecca take her on as well? And there was steady old John Irvine, always somewhere in the background of the group of cousins and friends, blandly producing this dazzling charmer of a new partner, whose own amusement at himself, as it were, made the looks and the charm totally acceptable.

How good of the girls to arrange all this for her – and how good of their nice staff to see to it that nothing should break in on this rare evening off. Catching Una's eye, opposite her at the other end of the table, Esme raised her glass, smiling. There could have been twelve faces, the thought came without warning. Next time perhaps she would be braver.

'... are you sure Cheltenham will have prepared you for this?'

'We had to go out to Eilean Raidh this morning,' John put in.

'Bit choppy?' Donald asked, with that straight-faced expression of his which Esme remembered well.

'I had my moments of doubt.' Fitzroy's laugh was a huge melodious boom that made not only everyone at the table laugh and Thea smile as she slid a plate between two bobbing heads, but made even Joanie, who normally let nothing distract her from her concentrated whipping round the dining-room, allow herself a brief grin.

'His face had a sort of subcutaneous green glow,' John was saying. 'Most unusual.'

'And this is summer,' Jeanette pointed out.

'Go out sailing,' Lilias advised. 'Nothing like taking the tiller to settle the queasiest stomach.'

'Would that be the occupied mind or the sense of control?' Clare wondered with interest.

With relief and pleasure Una suddenly realised that she was enjoying this. She was holding a party, in her own house, without Tony, and it was the greatest possible fun. She didn't have to worry about whether he thought she was doing everything right, what she looked like, whether he approved of the food. There wasn't a soul at this table who would criticise anything. And no party could flag with Fitzroy's flashing smile and courtly manner and big deep laugh and obvious relish of the absurd.

'Could it just be Fitz,' he was pleading. 'Fitzroy always sounds a bit Edwardian to me.'

'How on earth did you come by a name like that anyway?'

Already they were were confident no question would give offence.

'Fitzroy's a good Jamaican name, as you must all know,' he began, laughing as they all clearly wondered with varying degrees of doubt if they did, while Jeanette and Una even obediently nodded. 'Colquhoun was the name of the people who adopted me as a baby and brought me to England. The family has been involved for years out there in the extraction of bauxite and my father had died working for them so they took me on.'

'What's bauxite?' Rebecca asked. 'And don't all pretend you knew the moment he's told me.'

'The chief ore of aluminium. Used in making abrasives, insulating materials, cement, chemicals, and in the oil and steel industries.'

'Thank you, Fitz.'

Trudy wondered where Dan was. He would have disdained the frivolous tone of this gathering, she knew. But why was she so sure of that? Conversation with the instructors and survivors in the Coach-house certainly wasn't pitched at any higher intellectual level. She felt elated by the laughter and wine and good food and knew what would be good after an evening like this – going home with someone. Not going home alone. Not going to bed alone. That sounded as though anyone would do, which certainly wasn't true. Then, as always when her thoughts turned to Dan in this context, there was the check, the admission which honesty forced her to make, that it wasn't all as wonderful with him as she had thought it would be. Yet in this mood, at this moment, she wanted him, wanted the muscular arms, the fit and adept body, the warm solidity of him. She took another swig of wine. Good job you're not driving home, she told herself repressively.

Catriona Finlay, safe between John and Trudy, contributed very little. She could never understand how everyone found so much to say. She loved listening to it all and, after a flurry of nerves as she had arrived with Donald and Clare, had by now realised she had nothing to fear in this gathering, but when she struggled to produce some offering herself invention failed. Absolutely nothing ever happened in her life, that was the truth of it.

When her grandfather had been alive and she had felt tied to Glen Righ House and to looking after him she had rarely examined or questioned this. It was just the way things were and it suited her deep shyness, her natural preference for solitude. Clare and Trudy had provided the friendships she had lacked and Lilias, known since childhood, had definitely become a mother figure in recent years, particularly as these days Lilias herself needed help and care. But now, nearly two years after Fergus's death, the need to do something about her empty life, about the near-derelict house and neglected estate, was beginning to torment her.

Still, for this evening she could forget it all and enjoy herself. Rebecca's mother had greeted her with a friendly warmth that had removed any doubts about whether she was really wanted at the party, and even this new doctor, this amazing tubular creature in his elegant grey suit and gleaming white shirt, with his booming laugh and instant air of being at home, was quite unalarming.

Too many women, Rebecca thought dispassionately. Was Trudy wishing Dan was here? She'd had her chance to ask him but had said at once that he'd hate it. Then she'd rushed into all sorts of rubbish about how it would create waves with the other instructors, which had made Rebecca wonder what the real answer was. Certainly Dan glowering round the table might not have improved the general mood, though Fitz didn't look as though he would let much subdue him. On the other hand Dan could be very good company when he chose; he just didn't choose very often.

Esme looked wonderful in that tunic, Rebecca decided. Classic lines always suited her. And she looked happy, well looked after by Donald and John on either side of her. Would the reminiscing bring back too many memories for her, though? In spite of Father giving her such a rough time did she ever miss him, still, after all these years?

It was a shame that she had to go back tomorrow now that the weekend rush had died down and there were a couple of quiet days coming up, but it was a miracle that she had agreed to leave the yard at all. Perhaps if she had enjoyed herself she would come back and they would manage more time alone. She had asked no questions; she was so good about that.

And if she had asked? Rebecca felt the instant mental equivalent of drawing in sensitive horns. The reason for that panicked flight from Edinburgh seemed too remote from this room and this gathering even to think of. Flight had worked then? Perhaps this was all she needed to do – bury herself in the minutiae of the moment, let the anguish fade and die. And never give an answer? No, she would never take that way out.

Anyway, she was committed for the season now, and that decision meant many things must be sorted out. More important than anything had to be defusing the time-bomb that was the survival school. As always the thought of it made her shiver. They couldn't let it go on operating in its present way, out of their control. Could Una move on from seeing it as something to be preserved at all costs exactly as Tony had created it?

'A grim face for a party,' Lilias murmured beside her.

'Lilias, I'm sorry, have I been neglecting you?'

'I'm afraid I was unable to keep Donald's attention away from your mother. How young and slim and elegant she looks, I do admire her.'

That conversation with Una must not be put off any longer, Rebecca vowed as she brought her attention back to the party.

Chapter Fifteen

The house was asleep and in the quiet office Rebecca lifted her head to relish the silence. It had been a rare early night. Even the Coach-house had been unusually empty, most of the survivors apparently sleeping off the island exercise, the rest seeming subdued when she had gone down to fetch a bottle of vodka for the top bar. Four of the guests had gone out for dinner and taken a key since they intended to be back late. Una had cooked for the others as it was Megan's day off, then had confessed to being very tired and had taken herself thankfully off to bed as soon as the kitchen closed. There was a cooling pan of soup to be put in the fridge as late as possible and that was all.

'Must remember to do that,' Rebecca said aloud, writing herself a note and putting it with the chit for morning teas to be pinned up on the kitchen board.

She swung her chair away from her desk and looked at the window. With the light on in here it seemed dark outside but even though it was nearly eleven she knew that once out of the house it would be light enough to see easily. Nearly midsummer. On nights like this in the past they hardly used to go to bed at all, often coming home from the hill or the loch in broad daylight, which felt very dissipated till you remembered it was only about two.

The window was open, three or four moths batting round

the lamp on the desk. An owl called somewhere up over the ridge. Behind the garden scents she caught again the background sweetness of newly cut hay which she had been pleasantly aware of all day. Strange how that particular scent never seemed to stand alone but was always interwoven with nostalgia. It was tempting to go out and wander through the garden and breathe it in and remember, but she must do something now, tonight, while she had the chance, about this problem of staff. And I thought I worked hard in Edinburgh, she thought wryly, as she often did. God, I had evenings off, *weekends*.

She swivelled back to the desk and began to go through the small pile of letters. She must do this; it really was down to her. She was the one who had driven Aggie to flounce out, though she had not bargained for Donna instantly downing tools and following her.

It had been bound to come. In fact Joanie said Aggie had already been offered a job in a new tea-room opening virtually next door to her house, offering lower pay it was true but also inducements like late starts, no evenings, and handouts in the form of meals for the family which would keep everything nicely below tax and insurance levels. A serious point of contention had been Rebecca's insistence on doing everything by the book which Tony had never troubled himself about.

This morning's preliminary round about punctuality played back irritatingly in Rebecca's mind. Her impatient comment that even with a bad back you could just as easily be early as late had not been well received. Should she have been more diplomatic? It was Una's pub, after all, not hers. She made a small sound of exasperation, automatically squaring up the waiting letters, letters it would almost certainly be fruitless to follow up as these possibles wanting jobs a few weeks ago would either be employed by now or would have decided it was less hassle to stay on the dole.

But discovering Aggie leaving yesterday's duvet cover on for new arrivals, that she couldn't have let go. She had heard the exchange clearly.

Sylvie: 'Hey, don't put that back, I haven't changed the cover yet, here's the clean one.'

Aggie, contemptuous, 'Oh, Christ, dinna' be bothering with that. This lot were only in the one night. I just turn them over . . .'

Even so, what had it had to do with Donna? Did she have a more attractive job on offer too?

'It's the petrol,' Joanie had explained succinctly. 'She'll no' be wanting to come in every time on her own.'

'Petrol? It's only three miles.'

Joanie had made a significant gesture with her finger-tips in her palm.

'Well, she could come on her bike.'

'That one!' Joanie had hooted. 'And if Aggie wasna' here, who'd she have to moan to? Ach, you're better off shot of the pair of them.'

Almost certainly, but—

A step in the hall. Not the returning guests, no car had come down the drive. Someone who couldn't sleep? Una fretting about her soup?

Dan stood in the doorway and across the shadowy office, lit only by the desk lamp, his heavy body and truculent stance against the dim light from the hall seemed for one scary moment actually threatening. Certainly his appearance here at this time of night was startling and Rebecca felt her heartbeat quicken in apprehension.

She forced her brain to take over. 'Some problem with the survivors?' she asked, her mind going to illness or accident. She half rose with an instinct to meet the emergency, whatever it was, and Dan lifted a hand in a brusque signal to her to stay where she was, taking a couple of strides into the room and watching her with an unreadable expression on his face. He had a look of being poised for action and, though not afraid of him, Rebecca did feel conscious that something was coming which she wasn't going to like.

With her eyes fixed on his face and unconsciously narrowing, she sank back into her chair. This looked like some sort of fight. Her mind searched rapidly for a cause and found none. She knew that because she didn't mince her words she frequently gave greater offence than she intended, rushing off to the next thing leaving thin-skinned egos feeling raw, but she didn't think anything she could say would have much effect on Dan. He was giving notice then; it couldn't be anything else.

'There's something you should know,' he announced abruptly.

'Yes?' She wished he wouldn't stand there in the middle of the floor like a dangerous device ready to explode, dark in his dark clothes, hostility in every line of him. She resisted loosing a flood of questions to ease her sense of being menaced.

'Someone was slung over the side yesterday. He hit his head as he went over, was out of it for a couple of minutes. He wasn't wearing a life-jacket. No one was.'

Rebecca stared at him. The light didn't reach his face. He had made sure of that. In those few terse sentences there were enough disturbing facts to trigger a dozen horrified responses. Yesterday! And this was the first she had heard of it. No life-jackets, when she had made that an absolute proviso, the hair's-breadth closeness to the sort of tragedy she had done her best to guard against. That damned Innes pulling his vicious tricks again, she thought in fury, but taking a firm grip on control she made a swift mental triage of the facts.

'He's all right? There's no immediate action we need to take about the victim?' How uncomfortably apt the habitual term had suddenly become.

Though she couldn't read his expression Dan could read hers and in spite of his fierce anger, nearly at erupting point that he should have been forced into this position, through the boil of resentment which encompassed Innes, Tony Urquhart and everyone at Ardlonach, above all through the reawakening of associations he had wanted to erase from his mind for ever, he felt a grudging approval for the way Rebecca had reacted. She had assessed the information he had given her, broken it down into its component parts and pinpointed the vital issue.

'He's OK.'

'Thank God for that. Sit down, Dan, I want to hear more about this.'

'Well, you're not going to hear it from me,' he told her flatly, not moving, arms folded across his chest. 'You know what's going on now. That's it.'

'But has this been going on ever since—?'

'That's all I'm saying, right? You can make something of it or not, it's up to you.'

'But I'll need—'

'You're not listening to me, are you?' He leaned suddenly towards her, loosing some of his anger on her. 'I've told you what you have to know. And you didn't hear it from me, either, have you got that?'

Rebecca held hard to calm. For once in her life the prospect of a fight looked unattractive. 'But this is serious stuff. Anything could happen. We must talk about it.'

'Talk about it!' He wilfully misunderstood her. 'Yeah, that'll be right.'

'We must talk about what action to take, then.' She managed to keep her voice even. Why was he so antagonistic? He had come here specifically to warn her about what was going on. Surely he would be prepared to discuss what could be done about it?

'Listen, I don't give a shit what you do,' he was saying roughly. 'That's your problem. I've told you what the score is and that's all I'm interested in. The rest's down to you. I'm out of here.'

Did he mean now, tonight, or for good? She shoved the question aside. 'But Dan—' All the vague worries about the survival school, that area of potential disaster so disturbingly outwith her control, her dislike of the undercurrents of contempt and hostility associated with it, poured back. She needed support here and, though Dan had rebuffed her once before when she had asked for his help, they were up against something not potentially dangerous but actually life-threatening this time.

He gave her one long look, full of implacable resistance and something more which her mind for the moment refused to register, then he turned and with his light athlete's stride was gone. So strong was her feeling of helplessness that Rebecca actually leapt to her feet to go after him but common sense checked her. Dan was a million miles from giving her any help tonight, even from listening to her.

Bastard, she thought, oddly shaky, walking to the window to subdue the physical reaction not only to what he had told her but also to that sense of real enmity he had projected. That was what she had seen in his face and had hardly been able to bring herself to recognise. Hatred. But instantly she rode past the thought. She couldn't do anything about it, horrible as it was to discover. What she could and must do was deal with this new situation.

How to confront Innes without being able to quote Dan? How to persuade Una to get rid of him, which patently must be done without delay? And then how to continue to run the school, if indeed that could be done? Was that part of Dan's antagonism? Had he realised he was putting himself out of a job? But he had come; he had, however grudgingly, given her this essential information. Or was he merely trying to save his skin? If all this came out and he was found to have done and said nothing, was he afraid that he would be in trouble?

Rebecca remembered suddenly, unwillingly, that ominous question mark scrawled by Tony against the brief resumé of Dan's service career. What had happened? Had Tony had doubts about employing him? Dan would be capable of pretty well anything, Rebecca decided grimly, turning back to her desk. Well, tomorrow this must be faced. The obvious approach was to speak to the survivor involved. Easy enough to discover which.

For tonight, she must write these letters, pin down her brain to the mundane task. Jesus, she thought, switching on the computer, even now unable to suppress a grin, have I just wiped out six of Una's employees in one day, not two? And then there's the soup to put away.

In frowsty early morning squalor and bitter argument as to what should or should not be said, the members of the long course were eating breakfast, getting kit together or snatching a last few cosy moments in their bunks in the barrack-like room which had once been the barn.

Rebecca stalked in, indifferent to the half-dressed or less than half-dressed, and simply said, 'Good morning. The person who was involved in the accident – a word please.'

No one even noticed that she didn't have a name. The event was pre-eminent in all their minds. Her tone of authority did the rest. Without a word the man concerned laid down his mess-tin and followed her out into the steading yard.

'I'd decided not to say anything,' he said, on the defensive at once. It wasn't true. He had decided to say nothing here, since he didn't think there was anyone to appeal to whose powers exceeded Innes's. He had however every intention of saying a great deal when back in the safe territory of his powerful company, with its legal team ready and waiting to flex their muscles and snap their jaws.

Rebecca, reading the slight evasiveness in his eyes and the patching of red along his cheekbones, guessed as much. She decided she'd turn Una on to him for the smoothing down of feathers. That wasn't her forte.

'Innes will be sacked, as of today,' she stated crisply. Dan had not needed to tell her who had been involved. 'But perhaps you'd like to come over to the hotel now and give us your version of events. And I interrupted your breakfast; you'd better have some with us.' Not as conciliatory in tone as it could have been perhaps, always a weak point with her, but breakfast for some reason always seemed to be a potent buzz word for males, and seeing him brighten up at once she knew with contemptuous disbelief that he would be easily dealt with.

'Do you want Innes to be present while we talk?' she offered, as they came down the path to the courtyard and crossed to go up by the stone stairs. Safe suggestion; Innes too had made sure he was picking a wimp.

'No, that won't be necessary,' her victim hurriedly replied. 'I'd just like to be sure you know exactly what happened.'

Porridge and cream, bacon, eggs, mushrooms, tomatoes, freshly baked croissants and coffee, with Una gazing at him with huge concerned and sympathetic eyes, with Rebecca showing him standing instructions for safety requirements, promising that no repetition of such outrageous behaviour would ever be permitted, and in particular making notes of all he said and briskly taking it for granted that he would be prepared to appear in court, polished him off without too much trouble. He signed a statement to the effect that he had decided to take matters no further – after all any damages won wouldn't go into his pocket – but he did say he thought it would be better if he went back to Doncaster that day, without seeing 'anyone' again. He wouldn't mind a bit having to hang around Fort William if there wasn't a train right away.

Una, who had forgotten to order cheese and in whose mind a list of other vital items instantly formed, murmured that she would be very happy to take him in whenever it suited him.

That was the easy part. Rebecca knew that she must now face Innes. She had to be seen to take action without delay. Neither she nor Una debated for a second which of them would do so. Innes would be down in the equipment store on the jetty, preparing to take Grade I out on their penultimate test known as the Fast Slog, a round of the Munros east of Glen Righ taken at a punishing pace, before the finale of the assault course. Bern had already left with the sailing group in the minibus and Rebecca, feeling a flurried mixture of wishing he was on hand and relief that there would be fewer witnesses to whatever ugly scene was about to erupt, realised she was desperately nervous.

The thick-walled, small-windowed store seemed dark and crowded. Rebecca was sharply conscious of the watchful stillness which fell as she walked in, men turning with kit in their hands, a boot up on the slatted seat to fasten on gaiters, someone down on one knee beside a gaping pack. Innes, leaning over the grubby book where kit was signed in and out, raised his head without straightening up and stared at her with sharp wariness. Stuart was beside him, his quick glance from Innes to Rebecca and back a clear giveaway. Dan appeared silently in the doorway of the partitioned-off cubby-hole where the instructors kept their own gear.

'Innes, I should like to talk to you.' Rebecca couldn't quite manage a please but was gratified to find that her tone was acceptably level in spite of her thumping heart. 'Perhaps if the course could give us a few minutes?' She turned with a small enquiring lift of her brows to the watching men, but even as they began to make the small gestures of putting down what they were holding, turning towards the door, a quick movement of Innes's hand halted them.

'No way, we've got a schedule to keep to,' he objected aggressively. 'I'm not doing any talking. Get on with it,' he ordered the men, who hesitated, hating the position they were in, uncomfortable at the prospect of a row, resenting the whole situation.

'You're not taking this exercise,' Rebecca said quietly to Innes, knowing she couldn't afford to enter into an argument about when or where they talked. 'You're suspended as of now.'

'Says who?' jeered Innes, but he took a quick glance to reassure himself that Stuart was beside him, and Dan too,

Rebecca noted with a sick dismay. So they were both going to support him. Dan really had come to tell her about the accident only to save himself from being implicated if things got nasty.

Rebecca felt very much alone. The crowded shed seemed dark and threatening, the familiar smell of cagoules and wool socks and damp boots overpowering, the waiting silence after Innes's jeer uniformly inimical. Well, she'd been on her own before. She'd come through a lot worse than this. If Innes wanted a fight he could have one, here in front of everyone if that was the way he preferred it. He was finished here and he wasn't putting one more person at risk on loch or hill.

'There will be an enquiry into the incident which took place two days ago,' she told Innes, her voice firm, her tone final. 'You disobeyed safety orders and you will take no further part in any school activities.'

'Just who the hell do you think you are?' Innes spat at her in fury. 'This school is none of your bloody business, or had you forgotten that? You don't employ me, you useless tart, and nor does that other one up there in the hotel. Urquhart's my boss. He took me on and he pays me. So get your ass out of here and let me get on with what I'm supposed to be doing.'

Rebecca caught the sharp jerk of Dan's head and was aware of the room emptying behind her. She faced the three instructors, head up, jaw set. The chips were down.

'You neglected to comply with basic regulations to safeguard the clients. You're not fit to be in charge. Contrary to what you may assume, you are no longer paid by the survival school but by the hotel and Una's decision, which I am relaying to you, is final until the court hearing. You can of course get in touch with Tony and tell him whatever you like.'

'That creep, I should have let him drown. As it is I'll break his bloody neck. Don't think you can get rid of me that easily. Court, you tell me? I'll take the whole boiling of you to court and you'll see where it'll land you.' Innes was shaking violently, gripping the scarred table where kit was checked. His eyes were hot round dots, flecks of saliva spraying from his mouth. 'I'll have this place closed down. If I go all the lads'll go, you hadn't thought of that, had you? And then how long do you think your fucking hotel would last? I'll have everyone on to you, taxman, health inspector, the lot. That kitchen, it's a joke—'

He broke off as the door opened, One of the course members came in, a dark well-set-up man, rather older than the rest, with an air of authority. 'We just wanted to make an input,' he said curtly to Rebecca, then turned to Innes. 'The group agrees, we wouldn't go out on exercise with you again. Two or three of us are prepared to go on record as saying that,' he added to Rebecca and departed as abruptly as he had come.

'You bitch!' Innes's fury centred illogically and uncontrollably on Rebecca and he actually lunged at her, his face pale except for the red patches on his leathery cheeks. Out of the tail of her eye Rebecca saw Stuart smiling, before Dan's hand shot out to catch Innes's arm and swing him round.

'You stupid bastard, what do you think you're doing?'

'She's done this deliberately. She's turned them against me—'

'They saw you toss their mate over the side and haul him back unconscious, you mean.'

'Well, they're all hers now, and all the rest of the cretins coming after them. You want me out of here,' Innes shouted at Rebecca, 'you'll have the rest out too. Then where will your precious school be? Come on,' he said to Stuart and Dan, 'leave her to it. Let her sort it out. She wants them, she's got them.'

'Suits me,' said Stuart, speaking for the first time now that he didn't have to make any decisions. 'I can't stand this crappy place anyway.' He slung a belay length threaded through half a dozen carabiners violently across the room. 'Let's go and spend the day getting pissed. Coming, Dan?'

Dan had released Innes but had remained between him and

Rebecca. Now he stared at her, his dark face unreadable, and she remembered the look in his eyes last night which she had interpreted as hatred. He would go. How absurd she had been to think his relationship with Trudy would keep him here. He would be able to see more of her doing almost any other job.

So, rightly or wrongly, she had destroyed Tony's once cherished project. They would have to send everyone home, cancel the rest of the bookings, refund deposits and see if Ardlonach could survive as hotel alone. Instead of relief Rebecca felt a huge sense of failure. As Innes had said, what business was it of hers? She had whipped this up into a head-on collision where compromise was no longer possible and she had finished off something which had had great potential and had just begun to take off. Una would back her loyally but she would be distressed that Tony's pet scheme had been so ruthlessly wrecked. Well, Tony hadn't been keen enough on it to stick to it himself, Rebecca reminded herself, but that was meagre comfort.

'I'll get the P45s ready,' she said and turned away.

She felt a touch on her arm and with a lurch of fear thought for a second that Innes was actually hitting out at her and she swung round with the adrenalin charging up to meet whatever was coming. It was Dan's hand which had halted her, Dan's eyes that met hers. Stuart and Innes, fuming and vindictive in the background, suddenly seemed as incidental to the story as the two ugly sisters.

'I'll take the course out,' Dan said quietly.

Chapter Sixteen

This brisk wind would be ideal to take the Firefly right in to Trudy's harbour steps but it would also bring out all the evening sailors, making the harbour tricky to negotiate single-handed. But as Rebecca rounded the point of Ardlonach bay she caught the flash of spinnakers away up the loch. Good, they were racing, that should keep most of them out of her way. The wind might not last to let her tack home, that was the only problem with coming out at this time of day, but she had needed to be out of the hotel, alone however briefly to assimilate the events and developments of the last few days.

The most amazing thing had been and still was Dan's decision to stay, and not only that but the way in which he had quietly and effectively pulled everything together on that eventful morning, impervious to Innes's abusive rage and Stuart's covert sneers. The whole mood of the school, and therefore of the hotel, had changed in the few days since and, though Rebecca had thought at first it was because Innes had gone, by now she had had time to see that it was because Dan had taken over in such an unexpectedly positive way.

Naturally Innes had not made his exit without a lot of ranting, threats and unpleasantness, and by that time Dan had been pushing his group hard along the Glen Righ skyline and wasn't there to protect them from it. Innes had come up to the office and bawled and stormed about being sacked illegally, about redundancy payment and compensation and about not getting rid of him as easily as that. He had also repeated what he had said about Tony being his boss, but with less conviction, and Rebecca knew her momentary suspicion that he might be in touch with Tony was unfounded.

Una had been wonderful, looking faintly panicky once or twice but, as instructed by Rebecca, steadily refusing to enter into discussion. She had in fact revealed an unexpectedly tough attitude, Rebecca thought not for the first time as, with the dinghy running briskly before the wind, sail well out, she savoured with pleasure the touch of the air on her cheek, cool in spite of the evening sunshine, and felt tension seep away.

There had been no repining over what Tony would have said or wanted. 'You did absolutely the right thing,' Una had said definitely. 'Even if it had meant the school shutting down I'd have totally agreed with you. Even if we still have to shut it down.'

'Yes, we'll have to talk to Dan and Bern,' Rebecca had agreed. 'Dan says completing the present courses with just the two of them will be no problem but of course we'll have to work out as soon as possible what we're going to do after that.'

Stuart and Innes had packed up and gone on the day of the row, Innes leaving his dishes in the sink and mess everywhere. There was also a large hole in the bedroom wall of his cottage where he had apparently put his foot through it and about this too Una had been phlegmatic. 'How petty and horrible. How on earth did we put up with him for so long? But I'm sure Paddy will be able to patch this, then we'll get the whole place cleaned up.'

'Una, we've hardly had time yet to decide about replacing Donna and Aggie,' Rebecca had said guiltily. 'I don't think there'll be much hope of replies to those letters I sent. Where could we bung an ad in quickly?'

'Oh, something always turns up, it's quite astonishing,' Una assured her, speaking from five years of harried experience. 'For one thing, Joanie says her daughter Mona has left her boyfriend and turned up on the doorstep again. She needs money, I'm sure she'd help out for a week or two.'

'Do we want someone called Moaner?'

Una had laughed. 'Scowler would actually be more apt, but she's not bad really. She's worked here before, doesn't mind what she does, races round just like Joanie, but just remember never to speak to her before ten in the morning.'

'Well, we could live with that as a stop-gap, I suppose.'

'*The Lady* would take too long, but Thea and Sylvie suggested the *New Zealand News*. Apparently it's very popular with all the new arrivals in London.'

But on Saturday Leonie had phoned, primarily to make sure her August booking was safe, and Fran's too, since the only time the twins had ever gone away separately was on their honeymoons, from which each had returned early. She had exerted some pressure to get Uncle Kenneth's big south-facing room, in spite of being told it was promised to a paying customer, then, in a brisk dismissive way which indicated she wasn't very pleased about that, had said the daughter of a friend, plus boyfriend, was looking for a summer job before going up to university.

They were on the way up today. Una had been right, something always did seem to turn up, and how good it was going to be to have no Aggie and Donna flouncing petulantly about stirring up trouble.

Bern, returning with his sailing group to find Innes and Stuart gone and hearing the story from the staff, had been appalled. Rebecca grinned, remembering. She had assumed he was worried about the disintegration of the school set-up, and his own job. But what had upset him was the idea of her taking on Innes and Stuart without him there to thump them for her. The original incident of the victim being pulled unconscious from the water had made much less impression on him than the thought of a fight where he hadn't been on hand to help and protect. The possibility of his job being in jeopardy didn't seem to have entered his head. In fact it had become clear that he intended to stay at Ardlonach in any capacity even if the school had to close. Because of Sylvie? Not entirely, Rebecca decided with affection.

Another surprise had been the straightforward good fun of the final day of the two courses. With only Bern and himself left Dan had decided that the Grade III programme should be abandoned. Everyone had spent the morning climbing on the western cliffs of the promontory then, divided into four teams picked out of a hat, had competed in a run over the headland followed by two circuits of the assault course. Dan had also surprisingly suggested that the hotel guests might like to go down and watch, and since no one wanted to miss the fun Joanie and Megan had agreed to field arriving guests and answer the phone, so long as they could take numbers for Rebecca to phone back and didn't have to make bookings.

What an extraordinary mood had overtaken them all, Rebecca marvelled, still thrilled by it. It had been so good to be out of doors, everyone together, the uneasy division between survival school and hotel forgotten, good to shake off the memory of Innes, to shout and yell as the competition hotted up, and pack into the Coach-house afterwards in a great roaring crowd to go over the glories and disasters of the race.

It had been hard, and she knew Una had felt the same, to drag herself away from the party, change hastily, serve before-dinner drinks, explain what a seafood timbale was to a man with more money than he was accustomed to who was secretly yearning for the steak and chips his wife wasn't going to let him have, then dive down to the laundry to search for the washing of a guest who wanted to pack, praying someone had done it in the absence of Aggie and Donna, and return to deal with an enquiry for a party of twenty for Hogmanay.

God, where shall I be anyway by Hogmanay, she had wondered, putting the receiver down.

It had been good of Dan to leave the tremendous party that was developing in the Coach-house, particularly as he was the focus of it and Trudy had now arrived, and come up to the office after dinner to discuss what should be done about the survival school.

Rebecca, with one eye on the bright cloud of sails wheeling with the precision of a flock of gannets at the end of the long tack which had taken them to the southern shore, sailed on past the entrance to Luig harbour to give herself time to go over that discussion, the memory of which could still surprise her.

It had become clear immediately that Dan, having arrived at his decision in that crucial moment in the boathouse store, had moved there and then from a watchful, almost disdainful reserve to vigorous whole-hearted involvement, his mind instantly going to work on problem-solving and planning. It was Dan who had infused that spirit of cheerful enthusiasm into the day's activities, which he had organised with a professional efficiency that had been balm to Rebecca after the weeks of worry about the whole operation of the school.

He had agreed without hesitation to hold the fort till someone could be found to replace Innes. Una had suggested to Rebecca that they should ask him to take over as head instructor and while Rebecca had agreed it was probably the obvious solution she still had at the back of her mind that unexplained query against his record. She had temporised by saying they could see how he got on, reminding Una that his change of heart might be short-lived. She didn't want to worry Una unnecessarily but was uncomfortably aware that she must find out soon, even if he didn't remain in charge, what that question mark, so ominously starred, had meant. If they really intended to keep the school going they would have to have someone to run it who could be relied on utterly. But Tony had hired Dan, he must have thought he was all right. Yes and he took on Innes and Stuart as well, she had told herself disgustedly, laughing at her own idiocy.

'One thing I'd better point out,' Dan had said at once, looking uncomfortable. 'You realise that we don't need four instructors to cover what we do?'

They had gaped at him.

He had smiled dourly. 'Christ, why am I saying this? I could have stuck to the cushy life. But if you go through the timetables, even with three courses in together which isn't always the case, you can cover all the elements with three instructors. Look at Bern with the sailing course yesterday, he only went along because he had nothing better to do. Usually we just deliver them. Taking the Fast Slog you only need one person out. The punters have been here two weeks by then, and have to have had some experience to be on the course in the first place. You can amalgamate groups for runs, survival technique training, first-aid lectures, all that stuff.'

He had patently been raring to get down to the programme and rework it on this new basis, see it start to coalesce, put his own stamp on it. He had become a different man. And he had been sure he could find a third instructor with the right level of competence and experience, something they certainly wouldn't be able to do for themselves.

How busy was the harbour? Damn, quite a lot of tourists still flailing about in rowing boats, but good, there was Trudy sitting out in the last triangle of sunlight to reach her sea-wall. That would help. Suddenly, out of the blue, Rebecca felt a pang of acute sexual envy for Trudy. This new focused and positive and happier Dan was hers; there had to be some spin-off, lucky woman.

'Wine's not as cold as it was, sorry. I've been tippling away while I was waiting.'

'I came along gently,' Rebecca admitted.

'Thinking time?'

How good it was to be with Trudy. 'Just that. It's been a lively weekend with staff so thin on the ground.'

'How did you get on about your new pair?'

'On their way up. They may be a bit grand for us, but they sounded keen so we'll see.'

'And this week's courses have settled in?'

'Oh, Trudy, I can't tell you how different all that feels. Complete confidence that it will work.'

'And is in safe hands.'

'Exactly. And no having to tread carefully—'

'Which you're so good at.'

'How kind of you to say so. Una took me by surprise, though. No fuss about Tony's special baby. If the whole thing had blown sky-high she would have accepted it.'

'She's changed,' Trudy agreed thoughtfully. 'And though she must be shattered by what Tony did to her, and it must always be there in her mind, hurting, she talks about it remarkably little.'

'Hotel life,' grunted Rebecca cryptically. 'When does anyone ever talk about anything? But I did wonder if perhaps she had transferred her dependence from Tony to me, or if I take over too much.'

'Oh, perish the thought,' said Trudy mildly. 'No, I don't think she has. Well, to a certain extent of course, but I think she's discovered there are a lot of things she can cope with on her own and that's been really good for her.'

'She was certainly very laid-back about the staff crisis I provoked, not a word of complaint, and she never seems to question that we can keep things going for the season at least.'

'Have you had the chance to discuss what might happen after that?' Trudy enquired, topping up Rebecca's glass, then squinting up at the vanishing sun and trying to pull the cushion she was sitting on along the wall without swinging in her legs and getting down.

'No,' said Rebecca, and threw a handful of Bombay mix into her mouth.

And she says Dan's unforthcoming, Trudy thought with amusement. 'Sun'll be gone from here in ten minutes,' she remarked, obligingly letting the question go. 'It's the one serious disadvantage of this place.'

'The wind's dropping too, I knew it would,' Rebecca responded, grateful Trudy hadn't persisted. 'They'll have just enough wind to get back,' she added, nodding to the sails visible through the harbour mouth. 'But it's going to be horrible trying to tack home when it's gone completely.'

'Do you want to go now? I could come too and we can go on talking.'

'How about getting home? I'll have to dive into dinner and conversation.'

'I should think I might get home one way or another,' Trudy said gravely. 'It would be nice to get out on the water for a change.'

'We could go to the island,' Rebecca suggested with sudden eagerness. 'Even if the wind dies altogether we could row back from there.'

'Great idea,' Trudy agreed enthusiastically. 'Hang on, I'll fetch another bottle of wine.'

'And a jacket,' Rebecca shouted after her.

Wish it could be a toothbrush, Trudy thought regretfully as she slapped flat-footedly up the outside stair. Still, now that Dan was feeling so on top of the world perhaps he would feel able to drop his guard a little and might take her back to that cottage of his at last. Perhaps the lift home would be given in the morning. How lovely that would be. Full of ready optimism Trudy leapt down again.

'Have you heard the latest about Fitz?' she asked as they cleared the harbour wall and found enough wind outside to tack comfortably down to the island.

'No, what? He hasn't been in for a couple of days.' Fitz

had become a Coach-house regular and his laughter and huge enjoyment of life always stepped up the mood the moment he appeared. 'What's he done now?'

'You know he's been making all these hello visits, trying to get round the patients he's taking over from John, so as Clare's pregnant he ran over to Rhumore on Saturday, as in *ran* over to Rhumore—'

'Clare's pregnant?'

'Oh, sorry, hadn't I told you that?' Trudy apologised, slightly taken aback by the sharpness of Rebecca's tone. 'Anyway, so Fitz—'

With an effort Rebecca dragged her mind back. 'Fitz ran to Rhumore? From Luig?'

'Well, he took his car over to Inverbuie and left it on the glen road, but he ran the rest of the way over the headland.'

On those first mornings when Fitz's immensely long black legs had been seen flashing up and down the hilly roads and tracks around Luig the town had been afroth with outrage, mirth and derisive comment. One or two patients had absolutely refused to leave John Irvine's calm tweedy care but on the whole people had been more intrigued than damning.

'But that's miles.' Just concentrate on this.

'I know, but it's not the best Fitz joke.'

'What else?'

'You know old Kitty McBain, stuck up by herself in that cottage at the top of Glen a' Chorvie? She can't move for arthritis nowadays, I really miss seeing her in the shop. Anyway, yesterday morning Fitz was running up there and he saw the name on the gate. He's got a mind like a photocopier, takes in whole pages of patients' records at a glance, so he promptly clicked up Kitty's name and details and thought he'd call. He remembered she lives alone and knew she couldn't come to the door so he was going to tap on the window, then thought she might have a cardiac arrest if this black face suddenly looked in. So he went to the door and knocked, then opened it a crack and called to her, "It's Fitz

Colquhoun, your new doctor. Can I come in and have a chat?"
"Aye, come away in," Kitty shouted. Fitz still thought he ought
to warn her so he called, "I think I ought to tell you that I'm
black." "Ach, never worry about that, laddie," Kitty said, "you
can wash it off at the kitchen sink the same as I do myself."'

'What did Fitz do?' Rebecca asked laughing.

'Can't you just imagine it? Hopping about on the step, "But
I'm a black man, I don't want you to be frightened . . ." Anyway,
Kitty thought it was the biggest hoot possible, nearly fell out
of her chair laughing, made him make tea, kept him there for
over an hour and told him she expects regular house calls from
now on.'

'He seems to have settled in at remarkable speed.'

'Oh, I think Fitz would settle in anywhere.'

'I think you're right. But isn't that good news about Clare.
When's the baby due?' Rebecca made herself ask as they
grounded on the island, pulled the boat up and taking the
wine and a supply of prawn crackers headed for a sheltered
spot still bathed in sunset light.

'End of January. Donald's sure they'll be snowed in, he's
flapping already.'

'I can't imagine Donald flapping about anything.'

'Flapping in silence. Actually Clare had quite a bad time
with Robbie. And that's another thing that's slightly worrying
me.' (Have I heard about the first? Rebecca wondered.) 'She
wasn't very fit during her pregnancy either. If she isn't well this
time she'll be doing a lot less.'

'Why will that matter? Donald's the type to cope if anyone
is.' Would any woman be better looked after?

'Oh, definitely. No, I was thinking more about Catriona.
I'm worried about her. She's just getting to the point of wanting
to dig herself out of that trap she's in and she's really up against
the fact that she has no training, no qualifications, barely any
education. She's having a serious confidence crisis and Clare's
her great stand-by. I half thought of asking her to help in the

shop but I really can't afford it, especially now Dan's condemned the van, says it would be a total waste of cash to do anything to it and I'd better get something else, as of yesterday.'

'It's hard to imagine what Catriona could do,' Rebecca mused. 'Though qualifications needn't always matter if you're switched on and competent. I shouldn't think Sylvie and Thea have passed two exams between them but they're tacklers, loads of enthusiasm and enough common sense to get them through most things.'

'And smiling. Yes, I know, and Catriona just drifts about. The poor girl has never been expected to do anything else. I always come up against a brick wall when I try to think of something she could do. Oh, and by the way, that was another thing I meant to say about Clare. She doesn't think she can cope with their shooting people staying in the house this year, or more accurately Donald won't let her attempt it, so she was wondering about booking them in with you. I think she's going to phone you about it.'

'That should be fine. Any bookings after the summer blitz would be good . . . God, is that the time? Come on Trudy, we'd better make a move.'

'We need a longer gap between closing the shop and hotel dinner time,' Trudy grumbled, hauling herself to her feet reluctantly. They had found this was the only window when they could both snatch a free hour and even then only on nights when Ardlonach wasn't busy.

Still, this had been good, Rebecca thought, pulling easily for the jetty helped by the making tide. She laughed again as she thought of Fitz on Kitty McBain's doorstep. Wish I were Trudy, though, she couldn't help thinking. Work over for the day, relaxing in the bar, Dan coming in from the hill, his dourness shed as though it had never been, going to bed together when the evening was over. She had a sudden precise vision of being driven in Dan's Capri along the loch road back to Luig in the sweet June dawn.

Chapter Seventeen

Coming up the steep stone stairs two at a time Dan registered his own mood with ironic surprise. 'You daft git, you're happy in your work,' he mocked himself, pulling open the heavy door at the top. It was true. He was actually looking forward to going into the office, to sitting at a desk and dealing with petty cash chits and correspondence. The surge of high spirits that had carried them through the weekend after Innes and Stuart had gone had not died on them, and everyone in the place (well, perhaps not that toffee-nosed bastard, Felix, just imported, who seemed to be some sort of Urquhart connection) appeared determined to prove they could get on just as well without them. He'd been lucky to find Geoff Marshall at a loose end and willing to fill in for a couple of weeks. He wasn't exactly lively, in fact after two minutes of his company you remembered just how turgidly boring he could be, but he was safe, knew his stuff and would do an adequate job till a new instructor could be brought in.

Dan found Rebecca bogged down with four Dutch guests wanting to book last minute golf for the husbands and pony-trekking for the wives, who also needed to fit in some shopping and get their hair done. Dan grinned privately. Rebecca must be loving this. It wasn't eight o'clock yet and peace at this time of day was vital for doing the tills, entering last night's charges and preparing bills. Her desk was covered with bags of change and little piles of counted money and her tone was ultra polite. The phone rang; someone altering an August booking.

The Dutch finally took themselves off, promising to come back as soon as they had had breakfast to see what Rebecca had arranged.

'Please, please, have a long slow breakfast,' she begged their well-fleshed backs, rapidly flicking five-pence pieces into her palm. 'How did you get on last night?' she asked Dan eagerly. 'Did you get hold of—?'

'Oh, Rebecca, I'm so glad I've caught you, I'm afraid we've had a little accident in our room.'

That could be anything from a broken ashtray to a fire. Rebecca waited calmly, her face courteously enquiring, hands suspended over the cash, and Dan recognised with almost affectionate admiration her readiness to cope with whatever was coming, just so long as she was given the facts promptly and concisely.

'It's not what you'd imagine, and I don't want the girls to worry and think it was Timmie and I'm sure it won't hurt the carpet though it does look rather awful, but it was only the bowl that was tipped up. It was Bob who kicked it over, not Timmie, he didn't know I'd put it there, but I've mopped it up as best I could with the bath mat and I don't think it will matter, only I didn't want the girls thinking they had to disinfect it or anything and Bob's very sorry . . .'

Rebecca decided it wasn't worth working out whether the culprit was canine or human, got rid of Mrs Hume with assurances that she'd write it down on the housekeeping list and that it didn't matter a bit, and started counting again. Una buzzed from the kitchen to ask her to catch Paddy and see if he could bring some extra cream in with him. Mr Palmer, room three, looked in to see if his bill was ready.

'Just about to do it,' Rebecca said brightly. If anyone will give me the chance. 'Would you like to have breakfast first, Mr Palmer?'

'Well, if you could bring it to the table as soon as it's ready,' said Mr Palmer, not liking his planned sequence spoiled. 'I'd like to look through it. And if you could add half a dozen of your whisky miniatures I'd be grateful.'

'Just what I wanted,' Rebecca remarked to Dan as she reached for her keys. 'A trip to the wine cellar at this time of day.'

When she came back Dan had counted out the rest of the change and taken both tills to the bars.

'Oh, Dan, that was nice of you. It's such a pain when the money's lying around and you can't get at it. Now, better see if room three's got anything in the bar book, God, he must have been drinking all night.' She rattled through the entries, entered the total and the charges for the miniatures, switched on the printer. 'So tell me, did you find him?'

'Eventually, up at the top of Glen Etive. He was in his kip by that time.'

How anyone found one man in a tent somewhere in a glen at least ten miles long was beyond Rebecca but she didn't waste time on that. 'And?'

'He can be free by the end of next week.'

'Oh, Dan, that's marvellous. You're pleased, aren't you? He's the one you really wanted?'

A week ago she wouldn't have dreamed of asking him such a question with such enthusiasm, and would have expected to be put down automatically if she had.

'He's just the man we need.' Dan allowed himself one of his rare smiles which so startlingly lit the pale watchful eyes. Rebecca was delighted to see it but nevertheless could not quite quell a small lurch of apprehension. It was good news that Dan had located this Irishman who had worked at the lodge with him during the winter and was filling in the summer with labouring jobs, taking time off to climb as it suited him, but now, without time to draw breath, the question had to be decided as to who would be in charge of the school. How could it be this new man, taken on in this hand-to-mouth way, with nothing on paper, no references except Dan's say-so. How could he then be put over Dan's head?

Rebecca knew that whatever the problem was that Tony had highlighted in Dan's CV it could no longer be ignored. They couldn't risk blindly putting themselves into the Innes situation all over again. The irony was, of course, that she couldn't ask anyone who was the better qualified except Dan himself.

'Dan, could we—?'

'Pardon me, but do you have stamps for the the US of A here? And do you have facilities for weighing letters, I think these may be a little over the allowance. And those blue airmail stickers? Oh, you do, well, isn't that neat? Also, what do we do about dry-cleaning? Do we give that to you? It's just two pairs of my husband's pants . . .'

Mr Palmer came back to check the price of a bottle of wine on his bill. 'And we were thinking about next year. Not quite the same dates but of course the same room . . .'

Dan was bringing the status board up to date from the letters in his hand. As Rebecca pulled out next year's booking chart she glanced at the well-developed shoulders in the smoothly fitting navy T-shirt, the muscular brown arms, the dark bullet head, and her mind skidded away in alarm from the idea of questioning this formidable touchy man about anything remotely private.

It wasn't a reassuring prospect. And in the last few days Dan had taken on the whole operation of the school with so much zest, eating up the work, smoothing difficulties, clearly delighted to sort out at last anomalies which had been bugging him, even spending a couple of hours on Saturday evening, traditional meet-and-greet time in the bar for new arrivals, in tidying up the mouse's nest of Innes's paperwork.

'Yes, of course I'll put it in provisionally for you, Mr Palmer. Room three, August the third, leaving on the tenth . . .' She and

Una had agreed that the only thing to do was accept forward bookings and not worry about long-term plans for now.

'And my mother-in-law will probably join us. Do you have a single room also with private facilities, close to ours and not too far from the stairs, with a view over the loch of course?'

Dan was pushing letters into their appropriate slots, rolling shut the filing cabinet drawer. 'Dan — excuse me a moment, Mr Palmer — Dan, could we have a talk this evening? Probably after dinner would be best. Would you mind?'

'OK by me,' Dan said easily. Management chats were part and parcel of running the school. 'I'll look in after dinner.'

He thought no more about it but the prospect loomed uncomfortably at the back of Rebecca's mind all day, and she was forced to realise that Dan had created in her a healthy respect for his toughness and independence which she had rarely if ever experienced before. Driving over the Luig moor on her way to see Catriona gave her too much time to ponder the matter and it was a relief to have her mind distracted by the extraordinary set-up at Glen Righ House. She only vaguely remembered it; couldn't have been there more than two or three times in her life, she worked out. Fergus had never entertained and Catriona had been too young to be part of the childhood group of Urquhart friends.

How could an occupied house look so uninhabited? It was more than the weedy terrace, the spread of untended rhododendrons and rank bushes which reached out over the unmown lawn. The blank windows might have been empty of glass, the door boarded up, for all the impression the big building gave of being lived in. Cracked downpipes showed spreading stains of rust, twigs and leaves fringed the gutters, tufts of grass and weeds grew from unpointed walls and chimneys, and planks roughly filled a gap in the terrace balustrade. On this grey, chilly day which threatened rain at any moment there was an unnerving stillness about the place, a heaviness of dereliction and defeat.

Rebecca hated it all. She liked order, things working, practical answers, energy, efficiency. Was it really such a good idea to suggest that Catriona came to help at Ardlonach if she had let Glen Righ get into this state? But Trudy was so worried about her, to the point of declaring she must take her on in the shop no matter how hard it would be to find the wages, that Una and Rebecca had decided to step in.

Rebecca had found herself increasingly tied by mundane routine tasks and the ceaseless demands of telephone and guests which cut across every other job. When she tried to go round the house to check the rooms she was hauled down half a dozen times, when she went out to cut flowers a head would invariably appear at a window bawling some question at her, and when she went into Luig or Fort William, always with a list as long as her arm, either Una had to deal with the phone in the middle of cooking or some very strange messages were recorded by the staff. She had resorted to doing the accounts after eleven at night in sheer desperation, and even then wasn't safe from people who noticed the office light was on and popped in with requests that could have waited till morning, or merely for friendly chats. These were the hardest to object to since old acquaintances were always turning up and somehow here it was easy and natural to be sociable, the carefully preserved and self-protective isolation of the past few years feeling far away and unreal.

Across the weedy terrace Braan the retriever came padding to welcome her, tail gently swinging, too old to bother with the silly business of barking. Catriona came hurrying after him, shy and nervous, looking very much as though she regretted letting Rebecca come, or indeed disliked the whole idea behind this visit, which Clare had been deputed to float past her a couple of days ago.

Well, if she hates the thought of it that might solve the problem neatly, Rebecca reflected. Chat, have a cup of tea, go home, forget the whole idea. But in spite of herself, Catriona's strange plight moved her. Her upbringing here had been so extraordinary, the loss of her parents and brother, the lonely years looking after her grandfather who, in the kindly glen phrase, had been 'away with the fairies' since his beloved grandson had drowned in the ravine below the terrace wall. Catriona had been away at school briefly, then there had been governesses, none of whom had lasted long. The very word, in the nineties, said it all, Rebecca thought. What would you call them these days? Private tutors? And now Fergus was dead and here Catriona stayed with only Braan for company, unoccupied, unmotivated, the house by the look of it rotting around her.

Why doesn't she knock it down, build herself something smaller, move into one of her own cottages, Rebecca wondered impatiently as she waited in the dusty, drably-faded and penetratingly cold drawing-room for Catriona to produce tea. Then she caught herself up. What thoughtless bossiness. It would cost a fortune to demolish a house this size. And why should living in something smaller be better for Catriona? Why not do just as she was doing, use this up till it became literally uninhabitable? It was her home; she was no doubt accustomed to its spartan style.

But to have something useful or interesting to do, that was another matter altogether. Trudy was right, they couldn't just leave her to fester here alone. It must damage her development as a balanced adult and might even affect her brain in the end, a possibility not at all outlandish when you took into account Fergus's mental history. At the very least it would gradually undermine all initiative, all confidence in herself. But would having her at Ardlonach, instead of lessening the work load, just add one more job to the rest?

'Watty made scones,' Catriona announced, coming in with her narrow back arched against the weight of a laden tray, whose carved wooden sides and solid base must have weighed a couple of kilos on their own.

'Watty did?' Rebecca asked, leaping up to shift several books and a tin of saddle soap holding a brown stiffened saucer shape of rag. (What's she reading? Gide, *The Immoralist*. Wasn't that about abandoning society and its morals or something? *Goodness*, thought Rebecca, who only happened to know this much since one of her boyfriends had read a paper on Gide to a literary club which he had failed to make Rebecca join.)

'Yes, Watty the handyman,' Catriona said, without apparently feeling the need for further explanation.

The scones were still warm, perfectly risen, lightly dusted with flour. The butter had been kept in a room a lot warmer than this one. The jam, a brownish-red opaque jelly full of pale seeds, had almost certainly come from the Inverbuie Stores. Yet somewhere behind the house lay, Rebecca was sure she remembered, the traditional walled garden with its ranks of currant bushes and raspberry canes, its gooseberries and rhubarb, its plum and apple trees at the very least even if anything more exotic had long ago succumbed to neglect.

'So would the idea of coming to help us at Ardlonach appeal to you?' Rebecca asked, getting down to business as soon as the preliminaries of tea pouring and butter and jam passing had been dealt with.

Catriona's knife clattered onto her plate, rocked and fell to the carpet, and she stared in speechless misery at Rebecca while Braan's tongue came out very delicately to lick off the butter and fluff. 'I'm sorry, I should have phoned and not let you come all the way up here. Not that I didn't want to see you, of course it's lovely, but I just don't think I can come to Ardlonach. I know it was really Trudy's idea and it was very kind of her – and of you and Una – but you see, I'm actually quite useless. No one could possibly employ me.' Her eyes under the rough fringe of dark hair, which she obviously cut herself and not often enough by the look of it, Rebecca thought in passing, were huge, tragic, full of guilt. 'I really, literally, can't do a thing.'

Rebecca's intolerant impatience at all the evidence of indolence and indifference around her was instantly forgotten. Here was someone who needed help. She thought of Esme's 'disadvantaged' pupils. Though at a casual glance Catriona might have advantages beyond their dreams, hers in fact was a need just as immediate and imperative.

'You can learn, though,' she said, leaning forward, holding Catriona's eyes with her own. 'It's just ordinary, day-to-day dealing with people. Just helping. Una or I would always be on hand. Look on it as a first step, something to take you out of the house, something to tackle, to make you feel braver.'

'Clare thinks I should do it.'

'And Lilias?' Rebecca asked with a grin.

'And Lilias.' Catriona's small face broke up into the most engaging smile. Um, thought Rebecca, I was thinking in terms of developing her confidence, teaching her a few skills, but what about all those virile young males about the place? I hadn't thought about them.

'You could learn basic office practice,' she said briskly, putting that consideration onto the back burner for the time being. 'All very noddy. You could get your hand in on a computer, that's always useful. We have a really simple front office programme. Would that appeal to you at all?'

To her great surprise, for she had expected panic at the mere mention of the word, Catriona said diffidently, 'Well, we did have a word processor here for a while, before Grandfather died. It was Clare's, really. She showed me a few of the basics. I don't remember much but I wouldn't be utterly terrified. I don't think I could put it much higher than that, though,' she summed up judiciously and Rebecca, laughing, thought with relief and rising optimism that a sense of humour tucked away under all the nervousness was going to be a help.

'But it's no good,' Catriona cried suddenly. 'I should have said at the very beginning. I really can't come, I don't have any clothes.'

I think I agree with that statement, Rebecca conceded, looking at the baggy fawn sweater with both elbows out, the drooping grey cord skirt, the canvas shoes with fraying sides. 'We'll kit you out,' she said. She would not have chosen to dress an assistant for Una and herself in what the staff wore, but it was the obvious solution here.

What have I done, she found herself wailing as she headed down Glen Righ, turning up the heater and putting on the fan. Catriona and Una, what a scatty pair to be landed with. But no, that was unfair, Una had changed a lot in the past few weeks. The helpless stricken girl Rebecca had found weeping and distraught on that March evening had taken huge strides forward. She made decisions, had discovered that people appreciated what she offered them and had stopped agitating about every minor detail, and her whole manner to guests and staff was much more outgoing and confident these days.

Would Tony come back? Rebecca had been so sure he would, and guessed that deep down Una had always expected it too. But there had been no further word of him, no news via the family, no more holes in the bank accounts; more importantly, no indication for Una of what he intended to do about his marriage. Like all other personal concerns, large or small, that question could be buried under more immediate preoccupations, but if nothing had changed by the end of the season they really would have to sort it all out properly, to establish a secure future for Una if nothing else.

There would be just time to call in on Lilias and get thoroughly thawed out. And this was June, for God's sake. She would be pleased to hear that Catriona had agreed at least to try the new plan for a week or two.

Rebecca hadn't told Una that she was going to talk to Dan. An uncomfortable instinct warned her that something disturbing might be uncovered here. Fortunately this evening Una was involved in a duty chat with some guests who had been sent to Ardlonach by her father. They had wanted her to have dinner with them and though that had been easy to duck a drink afterwards was unavoidable.

Thea and Rachel had finished in the dining-room. As soon as they went down to the Coach-house Rebecca knew

Dan would appear. Rachel and Felix, the pair Leonie had sent, were marginally more use than she had thought they were going to be. She grinned to think how horrified Leonie would have been at the disarming way Rachel had announced, 'Oh, we only need one room thanks.' She was a delightful, smiling, smooth-skinned sixth-former with a lot of straight glossy brown hair which she was always wiping off her face with her fingers, a tendency to wear very skimpy clothes in a very innocent way, and an artless, helpless approach to cleaning which made the two Australians look like pros. Felix was arrogant and, Rebecca suspected, would turn out to be indolent when the first keenness had worn off, but he was fairly practical, with an unperturbed public-school approach to basic living conditions which was useful.

I'm trying not to think about what I'm going to say to Dan, Rebecca realised with that odd lurch of fear catching her by surprise again. Why am I dreading this so much? Because you don't want to make an enemy of him, the answer came promptly and definitely. Because you are about to infringe his personal space and he's going to hate it.

And here was Dan, his light swift step bringing him across the hall without her hearing him come even though her nerves were stretching.

'OK, so what's it all about?' he asked with that new easy assurance, that air of being ready to gobble up work, take problems by the throat. He clearly expected some fine-tuning on management points, some re-organisation of catering, accommodation or schedules.

'Dan, look—' Rebecca came to her feet, flustered and awkward, feeling absurdly caught at a disadvantage though she had been waiting here for some minutes. 'Do you mind if we go along to the library? People are always bursting in here no matter what time of the day or night it is. And the library's empty. At least, it was when I looked a few minutes ago, unless someone's gone in there since of course . . .'

Shut up, she told herself furiously, seeing his look of mild surprise.

'Fine by me,' he said, though with a half glance at his desk as though his brain was protesting that any information they might need was there. However, he stood aside to let her go through the door and followed her without comment. The flow of petty requests which besieged anyone in the office, half of them concocted he reckoned simply to get attention, always maddened him and he was more than happy to be free of it.

The library was empty and quiet, with the dead air and colourless look that rooms acquire at the end of the day. The fire had been lit, perhaps by a guest as the day had been so depressing, but allowed to go out during dinner as no one was geared to checking on it in the middle of summer. Rebecca felt a quick irritation that she hadn't thought of it herself, marked down the point for future reference then pushed the red herring firmly away.

'Dan, look, there's something I need to ask you.' In her apprehension and determination to tackle this at last she didn't even bother to sit down but swung round and faced him in the middle of the room, quite unaware that she was frowning and that her whole pose looked vigorously aggressive.

'What the hell is this about?' Dan looked down at her in frowning surprise, speaking in the blank tone of someone who has had no suspicion that anything unpleasant might be coming.

How differently, how defensively, Innes would have asked the question, Rebecca thought – or Dan himself a few days ago, come to that. The thought of how he'd changed steadied her. There had been doubts and concern about the school ever since she had arrived. They had the chance to start again with a clean slate now but what a fool she had been to leap in in this challenging way. What had happened to all her training and skills?

'Sorry, let's sit down.'

Dan, without taking his eyes off her face, settled back into one of the deep leather armchairs as though proclaiming he could handle anything she threw at him, but nevertheless with a look of being ready to bounce out of it like a squash ball if he didn't like what came. Rebecca perched sideways on the edge of another deep chair, knowing if she sank into it her chin would be on her chest, her legs stuck out in front of her, and this crucial interview conducted with no dignity at all.

'There's something I have to ask you about,' she plunged desperately. 'We didn't really decide if you were to take over the running of the school, and we've never had time to talk about it again, but I shouldn't think if we sign on your friend Liam you'd really want him put in charge, would you?'

Dan didn't answer directly. 'Isn't that Una's decision?' he asked after a fractional pause, and his eyes were once more lightless and inimical.

Prevarication, conciliation, would not do with this man. 'I haven't discussed this with Una, I didn't want to worry her. We're both aware that we're very much in the hands of whoever runs the school — we don't have the knowledge for that to be otherwise. We've had one near disaster and only escaped a court case by the skin of our teeth.' It was becoming difficult to meet Dan's eyes. His face was wiped clear of expression but his very stillness held a threat. Rebecca had a sudden primitive fear that it had been unwise to come to this deserted part of the big house, then wrathfully told herself to calm down.

With a conscious effort to subdue the charge of adrenalin this momentary panic had produced she made herself go on steadily. 'I saw that Tony had put a question mark against your service record. I wanted to ask you if there's anything we should know about your time in the Air Force or whatever that query referred to.'

In a crawling moment of silence after she had finished speaking Rebecca was clinically aware that her heart was thumping and a pulse beating in her temple.

Then Dan came to his feet in one explosive movement, his face dark with anger. 'You interfering sanctimonious little bitch,' he said with a controlled venom that was more frightening than violence. 'What does any of this have to do with you? Tony took me on and that should be good enough. I don't have to justify myself to you, particularly as you're nothing to do with this place anyway, or had you forgotten that?'

A barb from quite another time.

'Dan, all I need to be sure of is that there's nothing important Una should know. If you can tell me there isn't that's all that needs to be said.' She had stayed sitting where she was, deliberately not leaping up in her turn to confront him, and she kept her voice level and reasonable, though it cost some effort.

'You bitch, you're not going to let it go, are you?' Dan seemed to have difficulty in getting the words out and to Rebecca his rising anger seemed out of proportion to the question she had asked. There must be something serious involved here. Her heart sank. If there was, then they couldn't go on as they were. Even so, for the space of half a minute she wished passionately that she had left well alone.

'All right, you've got what you wanted,' Dan snarled in sudden bitter frustration. 'I'm out of here. You can get whoever you like to run your bloody school.' With black despair settling on him he said goodbye to that enticing new challenge which he'd been so happily geared up to meet. He had had plenty of responsibility in the past but never the chance to run the show. It had looked so good, the hotel and the centre at last in tandem, Bern so easy-going and willing, great to work with, Liam coming in with his mad Irish humour and his incredible rock gymnastics and his love of a drink and a crack — and now this, the fell hand of the past reaching out once more, never to free him.

'Jesus Christ, Rebecca, I'd like to wring your neck,' he said in a choked voice, and swung round to the door.

Chapter Eighteen

Rebecca stood stunned for a moment by what she had done, bitterly regretting her interference, her arrogance in being so sure she was doing the right thing. Then anger began to burn. All she had done, in cold fact, was to ask a perfectly legitimate question. Her right to put it, as opposed to Una doing so, might be technically dubious but Dan knew she was involved in running the place if only temporarily so that was a mere quibble. If he really had something to hide then he shouldn't be here. And if he wanted to be here, in charge, then he must see as clearly as she did that such a point had to be checked out.

With a furious exclamation she leapt for the door on Dan's heels, expecting as she opened it to hear the whoosh and thud of the heavy door that cut off the basement stairs, which would take him either to the Coach-house or out to the short cut to Inshmore. Nothing. She paused for a second, frowning, tense with anger, head on one side to listen. He must have gone the other way, through the main part of the house. Back to the office? No, fool, he'd brought his car, it was raining.

Without a second's hesitation Rebecca was across the library, up onto the window seat to release the catch, down again to grip the brass handles and haul up the huge sash, and over the sill. Even in her anger she pulled the window as far down as she could behind her to prevent the thin rain from drifting in on the cushions. As she crossed the narrow strip of lawn which divided the gravel sweep from the house she saw against the lights Dan come out of the front door reaching into his back pocket for his keys.

'Dan!' Nothing conciliatory about that as she went towards him, just anger that he'd gone up like a rocket when an ordinary explanation or refusal to explain would have done; and anger that he had walked out on her.

If Dan heard her he gave no sign. She came up to him as he put the key into the lock.

'You touchy short-fused so-and-so, do you realise what you're throwing away?' A vision of the different person he had been during the last week fuelled her rage – a man eager for a new challenge, his abilities and energy no longer on hold, a man who had looked at peace with himself for the first time since she had known him.

The image impelled her to fierce attack. 'Look, you fool, think for a moment. Put yourself in our position. Would you have been happy to take on an instructor with some query against his name without finding out what it was about? These courses aren't oil-painting classes, people can get hurt, and you know that better than anyone. We've nearly had one disaster and it was you who had the sense to avert it, so what's your problem now? I wasn't prying into your personal life, which is a matter of supreme indifference to me, I was merely trying to find out if there was anything we needed to know on a professional level. Though, come to think of it, if you need that spelling out you'd probably not have been much use in a management role anyway.'

'Then why the hell have you rushed out here after me to chew my head off?' Dan snarled at her, yanking open the door between them, reaching one foot into the car. 'Why didn't you leave it alone?'

'Because you'd have been marvellous, that's why,' Rebecca blazed at him. 'Because I hate waste.'

He stared at her in the dimness at the furthest reach of the house lights, mixed with the grey light of the end of a dreich summer day, getting outside his own anger to take in the exasperation in her voice, the face tilted up to his so undauntedly, the silvery fuzz of rain on her hair and on her dark blue silk shirt, which he suspected she hadn't even noticed. A hundred per cent every time; he had thought it of her often. And this meant something to her, meant enough to make her come after him, head him off, have another go at him.

'You're getting soaked,' he said brusquely. 'Get in.'

Rebecca, intent only on thrashing things out, wasted no time arguing. She nipped round the front of the car and was in the moment Dan released the catch, starting in again without delay. 'You could have told me to mind my own business, or that there was nothing I needed to know. You didn't have to blow your top and walk out.'

Suddenly Dan felt tension released, amusement taking over. 'God, you're like a terrier down a foxhole,' he said. 'Won't bloody let go.' He knew he admired her for it, liked her for refusing to be walked out on, jumping out of the window, squaring up to him indifferent to rain or cold, hanging in there. She must think this mattered. 'You're pretty wet,' he said. 'Are you getting cold?'

Rebecca looked at him blankly for a moment and then began to laugh. 'I thought we were having a row,' she protested.

'Done that,' Dan said. 'Here, there's a jacket in the back. Want that?'

There's a fundamental comfort in a man wrapping his jacket round you that it takes a hard woman not to accept, Rebecca thought. Corny, obvious and worked to death as it might be, nevertheless it was good to feel the unfamiliar weight and bulk cut off the chilly air. She had never thought it a particularly fair deal, though.

'What about you? You're just as wet as I am.' Wetter; his neck and arms were bare.

'I'm never cold.'

She could believe it. Active, fit, his solid body was exiguously clad in all weathers yet he always looked perfectly comfortable. Even now she imagined she could feel a warmth coming from him. She had an instant's vision of how good it would be to pluck out that black singlet from the belt of his jeans and put her cold hands on the warm barrel of his chest. She grinned in the half light; she didn't think he'd appreciate it.

'I didn't want to have a row with you, you know,' she said, turning to look at him.

He was staring straight ahead out of the rain-streaked windscreen which was rapidly misting up with their breath. He was silent, his face a grim mask again. Rebecca wished with all her heart that she could leave matters there but that would be a bit inconsistent.

She let a few moments slip by, then said quietly, 'Dan, I just—'

'I know,' he snapped. The silence stretched again.

Don't hassle him, Rebecca warned herself. There's something here that matters deeply to him. Give him time.

Dan turned his head towards her and she caught a white flash of something approaching a smile before he turned away again. 'Quite a clever lady, aren't you?' he taunted, but there was no real malice in his voice. He didn't elaborate.

Rebecca waited, but she couldn't pretend she was calm.

'What you need to know is whether my record's good enough to be trusted as boss of some tin-pot little outfit like your precious survival school. Well, it isn't.'

Rebecca was sitting slightly turned towards him and she kept very still. If that flat statement meant the dashing of her hopes and Una's for keeping the centre going then so be it. It was no longer the most important issue here.

'No questions? No big flap?' Dan's voice was sardonic. 'You're some woman, you know that?'

'You don't need to tell me anything more. We can leave it at that.'

He hesitated, drumming his fingers on the dash, looking away from her to where the drive curved down towards the Coach-house. His was the only car parked ready to drive away. 'I was responsible for a man getting killed. Live firing exercise.' He announced this in a harsh, dismissive, almost jeering tone which discomforted Rebecca. There seemed something about the bald statement which didn't ring true.

'Tell me,' she said, and Dan knew quite certainly that the request was nothing to do with his employment here, present or future. She was saying get it off your chest, out into the open, talk about it. He also divined instinctively that Rebecca felt no morbid curiosity about it, and would not judge him.

'I was in the Regiment, as you'll know if you've been poking through my file.'

She let that go. 'What exactly is the Regiment?'

'Jesus,' he swore quietly to himself then informed her briskly, 'RAF Regiment. Soldiers of the Air Force if you like. Called Gunners. Raised in the Second World War to guard airfields and vital installations and so on.'

'What do they do nowadays?' In spite of the impatient terseness Rebecca could tell from his tone that this was a subject on which he would be capable of talking his heart out.

'Well, there's the Air Defence Squadron, that's to operate and deploy the Rapier missile, still defending airfields. Then there's the Field Squadron, that's more a combat role, in peacetime intended to counter terrorist attacks on dispersed sites, stuff like that. We handle most infantry weapons, a lot of us are parachute trained, some are employed on helicopter squadrons – and you'll have seen the Colour Squadron on telly, everyone has, the old continuity drill and guards of honour and all that bullshit.'

Had he noticed he had slipped into the present tense, Rebecca wondered.

'So what happened?'

He found it almost impossible to begin, now that it came to it. When he did his voice was so hard and hostile that even though this had nothing to do with her Rebecca found it daunting.

'We were out on the range at Otterburn. Some silly bugger got himself killed. I was the sergeant. I was responsible.'

'Do you mean you caused his death, or you were responsible because you were in charge?'

'Got to hand it to you, Rebecca,' he commented, with a mockery she didn't much like, 'you don't mess about, do you? Pick the flesh off the bones.'

He had never used her name till this week. 'Go on,' she said.

'Yes, I was held responsible because I was i/c.'

'You mean that was normal procedure?'

'Everything by the book,' he said, with a sort of savage acceptance. 'Just as I'd done everything by the book. Only that didn't count.'

'You weren't to blame?'

'Blame.' He spoke the word as though it was a pebble he was turning in his mouth. 'Blame,' he repeated consideringly, as though after all this time he could not arrive at any answer to that conundrum. 'Well, I was a very good sergeant, if that's what you're asking. Only this cretin thought he knew better, didn't he, disobeyed orders, lost his head.'

'But surely that couldn't be your fault?'

'I was due to be made up, ACRs always excellent, no clouds on the horizon.' The rancour in his tone made Rebecca let pass references that meant nothing to her. There was no need for her to speak now anyway, she realised.

'Fourteen fucking years. Nothing on my record. Recommended for a commission. And none of it counted. Man dead, court-martial, cheers, thanks.'

'You were court-martialled for it?'

'Oh, cleared, of course. But yes, they had to take it that far. All the years of work and service went for nothing, all the evidence that the exercise was correctly run and that orders had been directly disobeyed. They could have stopped it, someone could have, but no, they had to go through the whole performance.'

At last she understood the source of his pain. Exonerated or not, the dedicated, efficient NCO, proud of his regiment and his place in it, proud of his service career, could never shake off the stigma of court-martial, the disbelieving shame that they had done this to him.

'You left of your own accord?'

'Came out, yes.' He was still there, his mind back in that welter of anger and resentment, the sense of injustice burning all over again.

'But if you were found not guilty then this can have no bearing on anything you do now, surely? I don't understand why Tony even bothered to mark your CV.'

'That's just it,' Dan burst out in sudden rage. 'That's what really set me off. I told him about this because I thought he ought to know; he was ex-service himself, he knew the score. And he was all matey and reassuring, all that's in the past, blah, blah, blah, no need ever to think of it again, and then the shit marks my card. It's as though I can never be clear of it, it'll be there for the rest of my life, dragging me down. And now, when everything seemed all set to go well, that wanker Innes out of the way at last, the chance to get my teeth into this job, being really needed because you and Una haven't a clue, you come waltzing in and ask me what this question mark is all about. Bloody hell . . .'

He sounded shaken, words not there to express his profound chagrin and dismay.

It doesn't matter, Rebecca wanted to assure him, concerned and remorseful that she had triggered all this. But the words could only be infuriating; it did matter, deeply.

'It won't hound you,' she said definitely, 'because it stops right here. Una knows nothing about it, I know what really happened and Tony's out of it. Whatever you do next it need never be mentioned in your life again.'

'Next?' His tone was full of contemptuous sarcasm and Rebecca felt her cheeks go hot at what he had believed her to mean.

'I mean, whatever you do in future. After this season, after your job here ends.'

'You want me to stay? After what I said?'

She could hardly work out what he meant for a moment. The hot words directed at her personally had seemed unimportant. 'Yes.'

'Well, don't wrap it up, will you?' But the relief and amusement were clear in Dan's voice. 'And that's in spite of my being — what was it, a touchy so-and-so with a short fuse?'

'I'll rephrase that if you like. You've got a tender ego and a foul temper.'

'And you're full of sweetness and light.'

'Glad you've got that right.'

A car that had been parked down by the Coach-house came up the slope and turned into the drive. Other people came walking up to their cars.

We could be seen here, thought Dan, with a glance at Rebecca to see if she was conscious of it. He gave a thought to Trudy if tongues wagged, but pushed that away irritably, not wanting it to intrude just now. But Rebecca seemed oblivious, other than putting up a hand to shield her eyes from the dazzle of swinging lights. 'So tell me more about the Regiment,' she said, 'I've never heard about it before.'

Dan smiled, aware of relaxing. The terrier still had its teeth sunk in. He began to talk, off-handedly at first, not sure she was really interested, but gradually drawn on by her occasional questions to tell her of tours in Belize and Cyprus, with the Colour Squadron, in Northern Ireland. When he backtracked to describe his trade training she realised how superlatively well qualified he was for the job here.

'Did Innes have all this background stuff too?'

Dan noted how involved in the subject she was, putting the question in a purely practical tone. He snorted. 'P.Ed. training, a lot of climbing experience, that's all that joker had.'

'Why did Tony put him in charge?'

'Ex-Navy. Both fishheads. Knew each other from somewhere.'

The more I discover about the way you handled all this, Tony Urquhart, the more convinced I am you are a useless, brainless fool. The hotel lights had all gone out by now, except the one over the front door. Paddy's rusty old Datsun hadn't come by. Doubtless he was already tucked up with Thea; Rebecca didn't want to think about that. She did want to suggest to Dan that they went in and opened up the bar, had a drink and went on talking somewhere warm and comfortable, but she knew it would break the mood, make too definite an arrangement. So drawing his big jacket round her, warm, intimately his, his faint scent about it, she listened as he talked on, free to voice again after the long silence his commitment and pleasure in the service which he felt had failed him in trust. Privately Rebecca thought he had jumped the gun by resigning, but didn't imagine this would be an opinion she would ever air.

'Damned woman, three more enormous faxes to send. And just look at these bids for Sotheby's. J.C. Harrison *Eagle*, £3000. Oh, here's a nice one, bronze cock, £1600, must be a bit chilly.'

Though Dan, making out invoices for equipment hire, grinned, Una only enquired, 'Who's that for?' dragging back her hair in a messy clump in one hand as she searched haphazardly through a couple of cook books for the right spelling for *topinambours*, which Rebecca denied all knowledge of and recommended not putting on the menu in the first place.

'Room seven, Mrs Constable.'

'I think she likes it to be pronounced Cunstable,' Una remarked absently.

'And I suppose she reads *The Cunt of Monte Cristo*,' retorted Rebecca, crossly punching in the fax number.

Dan let out an involuntary snort of laughter.

'No, it would be *The Count of Munte Cristo*,' Una pointed out equably and this time Rebecca laughed. Una would never have come back so neatly three months ago; she seemed to be developing as a person all the time, steadying down after the first shock of finding herself alone, ready to meet people on her own terms as an individual, not as half, the inferior half, of a couple.

Dan scribbled rapidly on, still looking amused. He enjoyed coming into the office these days, sharing it with Una and Rebecca on an equal footing, busy, rushing through the work, but always with time for passing chat and jokes. He particularly relished Rebecca's mordant style as she muttered about the guests with uninhibited vigour. They were all mentally subnormal if you listened to her, incapable of understanding the simplest piece of information, of sticking on a stamp or finding a loo.

'God, who wrote her lines, Alan Bennett?' she would ask in disgust, barely lowering her voice as some complacent chatterer departed. Or in a hurry, impatiently describing someone to Una, 'You know, that woman with no top to her head, well with her face very high up then, daughter's called Saponaria or Pulmonaria or something. Oh, Jasmine is it, well then, there you are, knew it was a flower of some kind.'

But Dan also observed the way she rose to meet every request like one of those people who actually like turning over exam papers. He watched her welcome newcomers, making them feel relaxed in seconds by the sheer warmth of her own personality. She was a people person in a way Una could never be and the hurly-burly of hotel life with its multifarious demands suited her ideally. He didn't realise, making these observations, how much his own changed mood had affected the working atmosphere of Ardlonach, or how good it felt to Rebecca to know that she had his support.

Catriona's arrival in the office introduced a new element which affected them all. Almost speechless with nerves, ill at ease and untidy, the dark green skirt and cream shirt which looked so good on Thea, Sylvie and Rachel hanging off her scrawny little body, she was so completely incapable of taking in any instructions on her first day that Rebecca's heart sank. She had obviously taken on an extra liability here. They would never be able to leave the office in Catriona's hands, she would need nursing every step of the way.

In her bath that evening Rebecca actually decided they must cut their losses and say at once that the idea would never work, then she had a sudden vivid image of Catriona driving back alone up Glen Righ, going into that gaunt desolate shell of a house knowing she had failed, thinking in despair that if she couldn't do this then she would never be able to do anything. Rebecca, ashamed of herself, was all ready to leap out of the bath and phone to reassure the poor girl, then realised that would point up the very inadequacy she wanted to console her about. No, she must see if Catriona was brave enough to come back, then start carefully from the beginning again.

In fact, like many intolerant people, Rebecca only became irritated when she thought someone wasn't doing his or her best. Psyched-up determined struggles like Catriona's with the computer, the booking charts and the complexities of the courses brought out all her patience and care and she was rewarded by seeing Catriona's panic subside, her very adequate brain take over and her confidence and interest grow.

The most helpful factor was that everyone in the place immediately took her under their collective wing, even Rachel and Felix who had only been there a couple of weeks themselves, and Liam the new instructor, who though he had just arrived had all an Irishman's outgoing readiness to be instantly part of any new scene.

The temporary instructor, Geoff, had done an adequate job. He was proficient and reliable and Dan had put down a marker to bring him back in August when they would be running at maximum level for a few weeks. But Geoff had no sense of humour that anyone had been able to discover, made no voluntary input and if persuaded into conversation was unutterably dull and long-winded. He had emptied the bar on more than one occasion, with the action moving to staff quarters or the old steading.

Liam on the other hand could hype up the level of laughter and enjoyment just by joining a group, in the same way that Fitz could with his great rolling laugh and his jokes against himself. Fitz was very much a feature of Ardlonach life by now and Rebecca seized the chance to talk to him whenever she could. He had a zest for knowledge and involvement she had rarely seen matched. Apart from finding his way around the whole vast area of the practice, he was already deeply into its history and archaeology, areas Rebecca had never bothered her head about, though Uncle Kenneth had a mass of stuff about it in the library, where Fitz was often to be found till the small hours of the morning after a lively evening on quite another mental level in the bar. He was keen to acquire a rudimentary grasp of Gaelic, and even waded through the obscurities of Scots poetry. Rebecca didn't know which was worse. More understandably he wanted to learn to sail, had settled with Dan that at the first opportunity he would go out on the hill with the courses and he continued to lope about to see patients in a way people had now grown used to, though they still laughed about it.

With a satisfying sense of the tempo quickening, of immediate objectives clear, enjoying the welding of these friendships and a growing sense of fitting in to the new character of the place, Rebecca was still honest with herself on two points. She knew she had shelved the decision about her own future which, though the first shock and pain had lessened and she had given herself a breathing space, still lay in wait. And she knew she was a great deal more drawn to Dan than she had ever imagined she could be. At least, she would comfort herself wryly, the second problem could have no bearing on the first. If it had been anyone but Dan it might have, but with him she had to accept that she would never be any closer than she was now. For one thing he was involved with Trudy, though through that very affair Rebecca had learned one essential fact about him. He implacably refused personal commitment.

'He's an emotional retard, he told me so himself,' Trudy had confessed bleakly one evening when the long course was sleeping out. This exercise didn't take place on the island now, but up on the moor where the survivors were supposed to put their fieldcraft skills into practice and were closely monitored. 'He's always been completely up-front about it. No involvement. He's a loner and prefers it that way. Trust me to get too keen. I try not to let him see it but it's hard not to when I just want to be with him as much as possible. He can be really moody sometimes, though.'

That was as far as she would go to describe those frustrating evenings when she was happy and ready for sex and Dan would rattle down the shutters, fob her off with some jokey excuse or simply relapse into dour silence.

'That's such a shame,' Rebecca said sympathetically and genuinely. Trudy was the warmest-hearted person in the world, this was the first time she had felt real sexual attraction for anyone since her dismal-sounding husband had left her, and it was sad that she should be rebuffed by a man incapable of loving feelings.

Dan was unexpectedly kind to Catriona though, probably because she was too immature and physically undeveloped to be regarded as permissible prey, Rebecca surmised correctly. And he had the true trainer's awareness of the problems of a frightened beginner. He's marvellous with her, Rebecca would think with wonder, watching them together, he protective, reassuring, teasing and encouraging, Catriona smiling and unwinding. And I'm jealous. Oh, not seriously, not pettily, and I can be amused about it, but honestly, yes, I'm jealous of that warmth and kindness which he lavishes on her.

Chapter Nineteen

Paddy had been in his element arranging the barbecue. In spite of the obvious convenience of having it outside the Coach-house, where they had plenty of room and chairs and tables and a few other useful props on hand, there had been a strong lobby for holding it down on the jetty. However, the deciding factor on the West Coast on a summer evening is not the weather but the midges and Rebecca absolutely refused to cart everything down to the bay only to have everyone running for cover from the inevitable torment. The return of fine weather had sparked the idea — she had suddenly been sharply aware that midsummer was past, that these amazing long light evenings would not last for ever, that autumn and reality and the end of this temporary, unlooked-for phase in her life were not far away.

The day had been bright but breezy and by evening the wind was quite cool, but they were sheltered in the hollow here and no one had as yet chosen to go inside. They were quite a crowd. All the guests were here, not surprisingly perhaps since this was the only form of dinner on offer. None of them had raised any objection to the idea, however, and there they all were in a ragbag collection of clothes, particularly the anti-midge headgear which ranged from deerstalkers to baseball caps. Rebecca was pleased to see that some of the Macleods of Luig had come down; her general invitation had been very much a last-minute idea.

There was Mariotta with a toothsome Italian husband who had somehow become involved in the cooking, and her pretty cousin Gillian who had been deaf from birth and was smilingly lip-reading some earnest speech from Jeanette Irvine. They were both involved in the local Highland dancing group and Jeanette was no doubt getting a little business done.

Donald and Clare were at Donald's mother's celebrating her eightieth birthday tonight, and Lilias had said frankly that being eaten alive on a chilly evening and eating half-burned food in her fingers no longer attracted her, but Fitz was there, laughing at something Liam had just told him, and he had brought Jeanette and Trudy as John was on call. Had Dan still not found a van for Trudy; how was she managing? And by the look of it half the Luig sailing club had turned up.

When Una produced a barbecue you could forget hanging about for hours waiting to receive a buckling paper plate holding a couple of blackened sausages, a potato cold as a stone in the middle and a chop cooked on one side. The meat had been basted in its marinades for hours, the leg of lamb baked beforehand, the devilled turkey legs were tender and spicy, the liver and sage kebabs delicately flavoured, the duck with its orange and chilli sauce rich and tangy. Paddy, having left the bar to Bern, was stylishly flipping over gammon steaks and curried chicken drumsticks, with Thea beside him (paying undue attention to Mariotta's handsome Italian, Rebecca considered) dishing out the gooseberry devil sauce and the creamy mushroom and horseradish dip and all the other glories Una had produced.

All the staff were here except Mona, who never spoke to a guest if she could help it. If they ventured into the kitchen in search of their packed lunches she would walk out of the other door, leaving them hovering, uncertain whether she had gone to fetch them or not. Felix and Sylvie had drawn the short straws and were on duty, but Rebecca saw that Rachel had swapped with Sylvie and was going round collecting glasses and plates, while Felix explained to the courteous headmaster of Oundle that a lot of idiots thought when you said you were going up to Exeter you meant Exeter University.

He would need watching, Rebecca thought. He was producing less and less while Rachel was rushing willingly into the trap of doing everything for him. What possessed these eager besotted subservient females, now, still, today?

She stood back mentally from the crowded, noisy, cheerful courtyard. Paddy had brought his Corries tapes, though he'd doubtless move on to Capercaillie and Runrig later. That was fine. She was aware of a fleeting and unprecedented wish that Tony could have stuck to what he had started and seen his plan work out, the Coach-house taking shape exactly as he had conceived it, a comfortable, popular gathering place for courses and locals alike. And this new, still tentative but very promising integration between the hotel and the school; surely that was what he had hoped for. Then she felt the little niggle of uncertainty which the thought of Tony always brought. The joker in the pack. What would he do? He had the power to destroy all this. He was so unpredictable, so prone to act on the whim of the moment. If things didn't work out with Serena, how would he react? What would he decide about his marriage, about Ardlonach? It was outrageous that so much should hinge on him.

She looked round the eating, drinking, gabbling crowd for Una and discovered her talking to three guests who had arrived today. She was flushed, smiling, her dark hair in light straggles round her face, relaxing at last because it was obvious that even with this mob the food would meet demand. If they'd done this a few weeks ago, Rebecca reflected, Una would have been hiding behind the table serving it out.

In contrast Bern didn't look happy. Rebecca smiled at his heavy gloom, there for all the world to see as he carried a tray of pints to a party of sailors, but she felt affectionate sympathy for him. One of the Grade II course this week had fallen hopelessly, openly, disintegratingly in love with Sylvie, following her round as though attached by a piece of elastic like a child's mitten, indifferent to his mates' barracking. Poor lumbering kind-hearted Bern was stricken, helpless, baffled. He and Sylvie had never slept together, Rebecca was certain. Perhaps Sylvie was growing restless. Was she simply enjoying being chatted up by someone more articulate or did she think it might implant an idea or two in Bern's slow brain? Good job it hadn't been Dan she had tried that trick on. There would have been one less survivor to send home.

Rebecca's eyes found him. She had known where he was all the time, talking to that little redhead with the startlingly white face and the emphatic curves. The wall had finally been breached; there were three females on the Grade II this week. In what was supposed to be an era of sexual equality it had been exasperating to watch the effect of this quite ordinary event, the anticipation, the jokes, the arguments about the duty list, the surreptitious checking of booking forms. It could all have belonged to any decade in the last fifty years, Rebecca had decided with scorn. And now that the girls were here even Dan, obdurate as he had been about their being treated exactly the same as the men, was behaving differently towards them in subtle ways he was probably not even aware of. In theory Rebecca applauded this change, in practice she was jealous, in a simple, straightforward way she couldn't hide from herself. She wanted to be the one setting off up the hill in the morning; she wanted to excel and impress in the tests they would meet. And I'm annoyed with the way the men are behaving, she was at least able to taunt herself cheerfully.

Her eyes went to Trudy, catching her for a moment alone as she turned from talking to Joanie and Megan, who always hung together on these occasions as though they were joined at the hip. Trudy's eyes, without looking, took in Dan's smooth dark head bent to the flaming red one, and after a moment of almost panicky search thankfully found

Catriona. In that moment Rebecca saw her pain, and her resignation to it.

She's given up hope, Rebecca thought, now, in this exact instant. Oh, Trudy. And oh, Dan, you heartless wretch, don't do this to her. Not like this. Talk to her, tell her. She's too good to be hurt so callously.

Trudy, smiling, had reached Catriona, who turned to her with the eager smile that so altered her anxious shrouded little face. It was good that she had agreed to stay tonight, Rebecca thought, beginning to make her way towards them. Catriona had of course resisted the idea, but there was literally nothing to take her home. Braan was here with her, as he always was, stationed now at the end of the long serving table where everyone stopped to speak to him, and where a gratifying stream of offerings came his way. He thought Una's sauces slightly over the top but otherwise was a happy dog.

Catriona, off-duty, was back in her own depressing clothes, culled from the various drawers and wardrobes of Glen Righ House and none, it would appear, ever bought, new, with money, for her. Rebecca assumed the quilted waistcoat hanging on her to mid-thigh had probably once been green; did she realise it could be washed?

Since the hotel was full (which couldn't be bad for the end of June, Rebecca thought with a new complacency), Catriona was bunking in with Sylvie and Thea. Their idea. Would that include Paddy? And the lovelorn survivor? Was Catriona's education about to begin?

She was turning out to be surprisingly useful in the office, struggling still with the computer because she was nervous of it, but perfect with guests and telephone queries and calm in a way that had amazed Rebecca about one-off problems, like the plausible caller who just happened to have the exact amount of material left over from another job to tarmac the drive, or a child stuck in the linen lift, or the library chimney going up. Life at Glen Righ must be peppered with dramatic episodes, Rebecca supposed, as slates slid off roofs, plumbing and wiring gave up the ghost, wildlife invaded a building increasingly undefended and the weather took its toll.

Certainly Catriona's help had released Rebecca from the humdrum daily chores efficiently enough to make life much more enjoyable, and had freed Una from the double duty of cooking and front of house cover which it was so difficult to combine. Rebecca was now available to take on such jobs as driving survivors round to the Luig marina, or picking them up at some designated spot after an exercise, or taking out kit to set up an accident or test scenario. This meant that the school would be able to get by with three instructors in July and again in September till the end of the season, a useful saving in wages. It also meant that Rebecca was out and about more, doing the things she had looked forward to doing here and increasingly involved in this new part of the scene which she enjoyed.

Yesterday she had had a whole day on the hill, out with Liam and the IIs on Bidean. It was the first time since she came back that she had been over to Glencoe and it had been magnificent, the sharp curved ridge, the long views, the descent through the Lost Valley, a day of pure pleasure and holiday, with no feeling of being tested or assessed. Liam was a great acquisition for the school and he had given them an excellent day, which he saw as the object, not belittling, hounding or driving them into the ground. The only thing that had marred the day had been Dan's surliness when they came back. Some argument about equipment. Rebecca hadn't been interested, irritated that he had reverted to his churlish mood. He hadn't appeared at all in the evening. He was still living in his cottage in Inshmore. Una had offered him Innes's cottage, financially a better deal and still allowing him to be on his own. Dan had refused curtly, clinging fiercely to his privacy.

Trudy and Catriona turned to welcome Rebecca as she reached them. 'Do you think the evening's going to end with a punch-up?' Trudy asked cheerfully. 'We're just laying odds.'

'A punch-up?' Rebecca's mind swung instantly to Dan as the likeliest source of trouble. Or because Dan was uppermost in her thoughts so much of the time? She managed not to turn her head in his direction.

'Have you seen the sailors? And that tidy little all-Jaeger lady they're chatting up? Isn't that her husband all puffed up and highly coloured over there?'

How did I miss that, Rebecca thought, one quick glance taking in the picture. But she knew exactly how she had missed it. The guest in question, a faded-fair little woman of around fifty, was surrounded by a bluff crowd of mariners, telling sailing-club jokes if the huge regular roars of laughter were anything to go by, filling Mrs Chalgrove's glass assiduously. Her husband, somebody senior in IBM and a Lloyds name who was mysteriously richer than ever, had given up all pretence of discussing the regrettable increase of insider dealing, once an élite sport, with the owner of a large shipping company, and was planted feet apart and jaw thrust out, watching the noisy group, swishing brandy round a huge balloon in a violent swirl which had nothing to do with warming it up.

Paddy had put on Runrig now and the pace was hotting up. Felix was head down in the cleavage of a stalwart female survivor who for relaxation after a day's exercise did a couple of flips round the assault course. This was strictly forbidden unsupervised but Rebecca hadn't heard much being delivered by way of reprimand. Rachel tottered by under a pile of plates with bones sprouting out between them.

'Why are men such bastards?' Rebecca enquired dispassionately.

'Because we let them be,' Trudy said. 'I think I need a refill.'

'So do I,' said Catriona.

We're like a pair of bossy big sisters, Rebecca thought amusedly, realising that she and Trudy had both turned to look at Catriona's glass with exactly the same checking look. It was fortunate that it never seemed to have occurred to Catriona to solace her loneliness with alcohol since, according to Clare, Fergus had downed gin by the case. Tonight after a couple of glasses of white wine she was pink-cheeked and engagingly giggly, and it was just as well she wasn't going to set out over Luig moor in her filthy little Fiat with only Braan to look after her.

Agreeably on cue, Fitz appeared beside them with a bottle of wine in each hand. 'Red or white? Good or bad?' His smile was brilliant in the gathering dusk, his enjoyment of the party lifting their mood at once. God, are we eternally dependent on them, Rebecca asked herself resignedly. Yet Trudy and I believe ourselves to be self-reliant, self-motivated mature individuals. And I'd like to shake the teeth out of Dan's head for what he's doing tonight.

The trouble began when a move inside was made, tables were pushed back and people began to dance. One after another the sailors scooped up Mrs Chalgrove, to toss her about or lean on her for support, or grope her according to temperament or alcohol intake. Mr Chalgrove was picketed by other members of the group in what they believed to be a subtle fashion. Most of the other guests had by now disappeared, hoping they would be able to sleep if they closed their windows. Dan and the redhead had also vanished. Trudy and Rebecca ordered Una up onto a bar stool and told her to stay there while they set about clearing away the last of the food, helped by Bern who by now looked on the point of tears.

'Where's your lift?' Rebecca asked Trudy, polishing off the last of some tiny almond tarts and for the first time that evening thinking of her figure, then remembering with pleasure that she needn't. Racing round this place every day saw to that.

Trudy didn't answer at once and glancing up at her as she piled sauce bowls on a tray Rebecca saw that she was reddening in embarrassment. 'Gone. Jeanette wanted to get back.'

'Oh, Trudy.' Rebecca put a hand on her arm, and their eyes met in wry understanding. 'I'll run you back.'

'I didn't think he'd stay with her for the entire evening,' Trudy confessed, the words bursting out almost involuntarily. Had he taken her to the Inshmore cottage, where Trudy had still never been? She couldn't bear to think of it.

At this moment Mr Chalgrove decided enough was enough. With a wordless roar he broke out of the circle of singing sailors, now swaying and pithless as men of straw, and lunged for the one who had his chin sunk on Mrs Chalgrove's shoulder and his hand spread over her neat camel-skirted buttock. Everyone joyously leaped into the fray. Paddy actually vaulted over the bar, helped by putting his foot on the draining board, but looking impressive just the same. The sailors, laughing, swayed forwards; the survivors, in much better shape since they had not been allowed to forget they had an early start in the morning, swarmed in with enthusiasm. Mrs Chalgrove disappeared.

'We'd better get her out of there,' Trudy shouted to Rebecca, suddenly looking lively again. 'Let the rest do what they like.'

'Makes sense,' Rebecca agreed, as the first punch landed in the wrong place.

They had just withdrawn Mrs Chalgrove, squeaking and tousled, from a mêlée in which no one had the slightest interest in her any more, and looking round for somewhere to put her had begun to laugh helplessly at the sight of Una, Catriona, Thea and Sylvie up on the bar in a happy row cheering and brandishing bottles, when a bellow of wrath dispersed the warring factions like chaff.

'What the hell is going on?' Dan, belligerent, disbelieving and disgusted, was among them. 'Get out of here, the lot of you,' he roared at the sheepish survivors. 'Seven thirty start, and be there. And it's time you were on your way,' he went on, swinging round on the shambling sailors. 'Who's your driver? You? Don't piss me about, you couldn't drive a supermarket trolley. Liam, it looks like a minibus run, I'll toss you for it. And who've you got there?'

Bern and Paddy each had Mr Chalgrove by an arm, and Mr Chalgrove looked seriously like a candidate for a heart attack, reddish-purple, wheezing, his eyes popping.

'We're leaving now,' he spluttered at his wife, whooping for breath. 'Pack at once. I shall need my bill.' He teetered alarmingly as he turned in search of Rebecca or Una.

'Evening seems to be over,' Rebecca remarked to Trudy. 'Quite good fun really.' She had seen the light returning to Trudy's face as she realised that Dan had come in alone and guessed she would not be needing a lift to Luig now. She was also delighted to see Bern lifting Sylvie down from the bar and the two of them starting to pick up chairs and retrieve glasses together.

Why am I glad, she thought crossly, unlocking the office and going to switch on the computer. All these happy couples – except of course for Mr and Mrs Chalgrove. Can I be nicer than I thought I was? The fact that remained in her mind was that one voice, one presence, had been capable of stilling that uproar. As she failed to persuade Mr Chalgrove that it would be more sensible to leave in the morning, as she saw to his bill and his luggage and finally waved him away (Mrs Chalgrove seemed to have decided on quiet humming as her best defence), she had some muzzy thoughts about what constituted natural authority.

Dan watched the stretcher in its cradle of ropes being lowered smoothly down the rock face. Liam and Bern knew what they were doing. But black depression, the deepest he had known for a long time, had taken over and he felt powerless to shake it off. This was not the mood of contempt for Innes, the deliberate holding back from the job, the automatic readiness to find fault and put everyone down from which he had so recently and thankfully emerged. This was dark, personal misery, guilt and failure combined, bringing a frightening renewal of that sense of having no aim or focus which mattered to him.

First and foremost, of course, there was today's accident, bringing back the associations he had thought at last put behind him. He'd been in charge and a man had come off, could have broken his neck not his leg. But all precautions had been observed, the man leading had been correctly belayed and had held him. It was just bad luck that he had caught his foot on that jutting boss of rock so that in the second as the slack was taken up it had taken the whole weight of his falling body.

And Fitz when he came had been perfectly satisfied with what they had done, had merely given the bloke a shot and told them to start the descent, saying the ambulance was on its way. The terrain was too rough and too steep to bring in a Land Rover but luckily it wasn't a long walk in to these practice cliffs. In fact there were cars beside Fitz's on the road whose occupants had been watching the climbers through binoculars. A reluctant grin twisted Dan's lips as he recalled the way Fitz had attacked the slope and the near vertical gully beside the face. He was a natural and his reach was phenomenal. As always, Dan found himself wanting to like the man, held back by an obscure sense of being threatened. Fitz established relationships with an ease which Dan knew could never be his, and it irked him unreasonably.

This afternoon's incident shouldn't be bothering him like this. Everything had been straightforward, all eventualities covered. There could be no comeback from the man's company, no possible repercussions. But would Una – no, you stupid bastard, it's not Una you're worrying about – feel he had been negligent, begin to question his competence?

Oh, get to the point, Dan told himself wearily. You know what's behind it all. You behaved like a shit to Trudy. No good protesting that she had known the score all along. He had used her, had hurt her, and hadn't had the courage to come out with it directly and tell her it was over. He had had to go through all that business of chatting up another bird under her nose like a teenager, giving her the message in the way least difficult for himself. Then when he had driven her home he hadn't even had the decency to wrap it up a bit, had barely been able to talk to her, feeling trapped and helpless and in the end irrationally angry with her for taking it so well.

And all for what? It took him no nearer his goal. It had just removed from his life a cheerful agreeable relationship, female company he enjoyed, quiet evenings with supper for two, music, talk, good sex. Wrecked, gone; alone again.

'Where's Dan?'

Liam and Bern, looking into the office to pick up their mail, barely glanced up, Liam turning a postcard over and back again as though in search of more information than it was giving him, Bern with his mouth open plodding through the single lined page his mother sent every week to thank him in three unvarying lines for the money Rebecca forwarded for him.

'Checking kit,' Liam said, examining the blurred date stamp.

Why? Why were these two free, finished, and Dan still down in the boathouse? Rebecca frowned.

They had called in on Fitz's mobile; she knew every detail of the accident. The injured man was in hospital in Fort William having his leg put in plaster; she had contacted his firm, who had undertaken to tell his wife. Liam and Bern both seemed to regard the whole thing as routine, only chatting now about peripheral aspects.

'You should have seen old Fitz legging it up the mountain,' Liam was saying. 'He's fit as a goat, that one.'

Why hadn't Dan come in at once to report? Not that Rebecca felt he had any obligation to do so, not to her anyway, but she would have thought he would see it as a priority.

On an impulse she was up and away, Liam glancing after her in surprise, Bern re-reading his letter.

The jetty was deserted, the door to the boathouse standing open. Rebecca felt a flicker of reluctance, reminded unwillingly of the unpleasant confrontation with Innes which had taken place here. The main store was empty, equipment neatly ranked, its characteristic redolence bringing back more forcibly than anything that disagreeable scene.

'Dan?'

He came out of the partitioned section at the far end, and in spite of all his efforts looked defensive and unwelcoming. He had deliberately let the others go on ahead up to the hotel. Let them spill out all the news, drop him in it if they liked, let them get all that out of the way. Then he'd go up and Una could have a go, Rebecca could have a go, who the fuck liked could have a go.

'That was bad luck, Dan,' Rebecca said quietly. 'Thank goodness it was you and not Innes in charge.'

'What do you mean?' he asked blankly, all his aggression suddenly having nowhere to go.

'Because we can be certain everything was being done properly. Anyway, I just came down to tell you that I got in touch with the man's firm and they're grateful he's being looked after so well. They sounded quite resigned about it, seemed to regard it as the equivalent of a skiing accident, except that they felt more responsible because they'd sent him on the course. They're letting his wife know.'

'Oh, right.' Dan could feel his defensiveness and truculence trickling away.

Well, that was probably about all the reaction one could expect from him, Rebecca thought resignedly, but quite good-humouredly. 'Fitz said you did a great job with the splinting,' she called back from the door.

Dan jerked his head in acknowledgement, still caught on the hop.

Rebecca raised a hand in farewell and turned to go out. Curmudgeonly so-and-so.

Dan took a quick step forward. 'Rebecca.'

She stuck her head back in enquiringly.

'Thanks.' He literally could find no other words.

She grinned, gave him an ironic thumbs up and vanished.

He wanted to call after her, wanted there to be more than that. But what more did he need, he asked himself, his black depression lifting like morning mist off the loch. She had known what he was feeling; had come down specially to signal to him that this was routine, unfortunate but straightforward, no one's fault. She had understood.

She could have waited. He could have asked her to wait, to take the key up with her. He'd have to go up himself now. He knew he didn't mind. Company, a lazy jar or two, suddenly looked good.

Chapter Twenty

Luig Hall was packed and hot, its rickety structure swaying to the pounding of feet and the beat of a Highland Schottische, smelling of the dust which rose from the interstices of its pitted, stained, unvarnished floorboards.

This annual ceilidh in the week of the Luig Games seemed to Rebecca less changed than anything she had encountered this summer, bar the loch and the hills themselves. There were so many faces she recognised, a strong contingent of Macleods with their house party, people from Inverbuie, Glen Righ, Inshmore, the whole of the Luig peninsula, and the townsfolk of Luig itself. There were a lot of visitors, and Ardlonach guests were present *en masse* since, as she and Una had learned from the barbecue, it was the only way to get a night off. Too many Urquharts in evidence perhaps, since Leonie and Fran plus husbands and families were up, and how exhausting that was proving to be. Though they weren't quite as demanding as Caroline and her mob had been, Rebecca had to concede, unrepentantly thankful that they had had to go back early because of some drama about one of their most valuable young horses casting itself, whatever that might mean. But essentially this was a party for the locals and she was glad to find that it had retained that character through the years. There was no disco, just the same trio of little men in dark suits (the jackets would be dispensed with before long) who had played for these events as long as she could remember, accordion, fiddle and piano.

She was dancing with Donald Macrae. She used to long and yearn for him to ask her up as a child and he had usually been kind enough to remember. His timing and footwork were as good as ever, though she doubted if these days he would be persuaded to get up and dance across the swords as he used to do. Thank goodness Esme had brought her country dance slippers for her, not the elaborately laced ones of the serious dancers, but light practice pumps which made you feel you could dance all night and the day after. She hadn't worn them for ages but it would have been misery trying to do these dances in heels.

Esme was dancing with Fitz, who only needed to see a figure once to grasp it, but who danced with an excess of leaping energy which the purists would certainly frown upon. Esme looked as though she was trying to hold down a kite in a high wind. It had been a surprise when she had agreed to Rebecca's urging to come over for this traditional rite, and a surprise too to see her looking – what? – more alive somehow, less contained and separate. Had she grown used to Rebecca's absence, accepted it as permanent? There was a tiny feeling of rebuff in that. I haven't decided yet, Rebecca found herself protesting, familiar panic swooping, even here. I'll go home for a couple of days once we've battled our way through August, she promised herself, feeling suddenly too out of touch with her mother. It's hopeless even to think of finding time to talk now, especially with all the family around. We're just being hurtled along a millrace at present, but I want to find out what's been happening in her life, and perhaps, just perhaps, begin to talk about my own.

Dan, leaning against the back wall near the door, his face unreadable, watched Rebecca. She was a beautiful dancer, amazingly light on her feet as people of her build often were. Though she'd shed a few pounds this summer, he allowed, studying her shapely body with pleasure. She looked happy, laughing up at Donald as the dance ended, arching back against his arm in a final swing. Where did she get her energy from? She was on her feet virtually all day. And how ruthlessly she had dragooned the guests into coming tonight, even persuading them that they'd like it, overriding doubts with her usual sweeping firmness.

It looked as though the tea interval was coming up. Had he time to get across to her? No, there was Trudy joining her after a rough birl with one of the lads from the Inverbuie Hotel, her brown hair all over the place, her face scarlet. Foiled in his impulse to reach Rebecca Dan checked, looking at Trudy objectively, conscious that he still felt guilty about her. She didn't raise the faintest spark of attraction in him now. He could grant objectively that she was a kind and smiling girl with a big generous body, and he knew she had a big and generous heart, but the feeling had gone, killed for ever when she had wept. He hadn't wanted to make her weep; the memory still stirred him with a helpless savage resentment, not solely directed at her. To give her her due she hadn't made a big scene, hadn't made any demands, but she had shown her hurt, had not been able to hide her tears.

Rebecca now, there was a woman who was free and independent in the way he admired. She was as tough as he was himself and had a completeness about her, a confidence in herself, which drew him powerfully. She had pulled amateurish muddled Ardlonach around virtually single-handed in the last few months, changing its atmosphere completely. She could be arrogant, forceful and dismissive, infuriatingly sure of herself, but she had the redeeming qualities of always admitting her mistakes and never taking herself too seriously. In all the good things that had come his way in the past few weeks, all of which if you came down to it were because of her, he knew that what he had valued most and would always remember was Rebecca's laughter.

Yet the qualities that drew him to her were the very ones that made her inaccessible, he reminded himself, watching her being re-absorbed into that big family crowd. She didn't need him. Well, isn't that what you're always looking for, he jeered at himself, a woman who doesn't get dependent and start the same old emotional dragging down process? But Rebecca, he knew, was in any case out of his league, an educated up-market well-heeled woman with her own career to go back to. She was just marking time at Ardlonach. And she gets on far too damned well with Liam, he growled inwardly with a little spurt of anger, returning to more immediate concerns, tongue finding the sore tooth. He'd really resented that day they'd spent in Glencoe together. And she's too pally with Fitz who, good value though he was, appeared at Ardlonach a good deal too often in Dan's opinion.

He jumped, scowling automatically, as someone touched his arm offering him a limp sandwich oozing pale egg and Heinz salad cream.

'I do believe it's the very same urn,' Rebecca was saying joyfully to Trudy, as all the busy tea ladies around it disappeared in a cloud of steam. 'Oh, and look, nothing's changed, here's the teapot coming along before the cups.' She leaned forward to look along the row to catch Esme's eye, pointing and raising her eyebrows. It was the same teapot too, in all probability, the grip on the front bound with soggy grey string, being passed meekly from hand to hand since there was nothing anyone could do with it.

Rebecca wasn't having any of that. She captured it and put it on the floor at her feet. 'Hey, where are the cups?' she shouted towards the steam-shrouded business end of the room. An appreciative grin momentarily lightened Dan's dour face.

A grinning child with a huge basket came running and jingling across the empty floor, ending up in front of Rebecca with a sideways slide.

'Right, one for me, one for Trudy, then off you go, *that* way.'

'God, I'm glad you're so bossy,' commented Trudy contentedly, as the milk and sugar arrived and went on their way and she took her first gulp of tea.

'I've seen it all before, everything going round and round the room and everyone gossiping and laughing and taking not a blind bit of notice and the tea half cold by the time you finally get it. Um, good scones though. Jailor Bailey's do you think?'

'Or Watty Duff's?'

'Oh, look, there is Watty, getting up on the platform. What's his speciality?'

'Scott. Reams of it.'

'Oh, well, at least we've got something to sustain us.'

Watty's extracts – Rebecca supposed they were extracts – from 'The Lay of the Last Minstrel' went down well, Watty enjoying them most of all, then the call for cups went out and apart from the few missed under benches among the sleeping babies the hall was scoured clean. Half a dozen women disappeared to wash up, the men came in from downing drams beside the dyke to mass darkly round the door and the band, wiping their mouths with the backs of their hands, hurried back to their posts to get the second half of the evening going with a Duke of Perth.

'Oh, Broon's Reel, can't miss that,' exclaimed Rebecca, looking round for a likely partner in the manner of someone entirely at home. Stephen Markie was already heading towards her. Well, that was all right. Uninspired but he'd get it right. He was up at the Larach for the shooting, having parked his son and daughter at Tigh Bhan with Lilias, and had made his number at Ardlonach without delay. He hadn't improved with the years, Rebecca decided coolly. The leggy height of his 'children', Oliver and Libby, jolted her though. What must it be like coping alone with two teenagers? She jerked her mind away from the thought sharply.

The irresistible music swept them on. Jeanette Irvine's dancers, Macleods, Urquharts and most of the older generation knew what they were doing, the odd visitor who belonged to a Scottish country dance group in Brighton or Manchester over-egged it, and one or two hapless innocents who should never have got up at all were pushed into place, while the younger locals preferred a less inhibited version with nothing fancy about it at all and a lot of hooching and double clapping and extra swings wherever they could be squeezed in.

A quarrelsome father and son duo, unsteady on their feet after the interval, clambered precariously onto the platform. The son seated himself at the piano and went into a long flourishing introduction. His father settled his violin then lowered it again, glowering. As his son played a chord and turned for his father to begin the old man thrust out a pugnacious white-bristled chin at him and demanded angrily, 'What the hell's that you're playing?' Roars of laughter from the audience.

Dan, who had never moved from the position he'd taken up when he arrived, watched the top set of an Eightsome Reel with grudging pleasure but also with a feeling of exclusion which was rare for him and which he restlessly resented. Una, Esme, Rebecca and one of those bossy cousins; Donald Macrae, Fitz, Liam and that poncy colonel who'd recently appeared on the scene. Who wound him up in the morning? Another berk to hang round Rebecca, the sort of plonker with no guts or go of his own who'd always be drawn by someone as alive and outspoken as she was. Old Fitz was giving it his best shot though, Jeanette must have been at work there. Liam was in the centre now, producing a crackling succession of precise and intricate steps without moving a muscle of his upper body or his long saturnine face, drawing riotous applause from the rest of the set.

Why the hell am I here, Dan wondered with sudden tired anger. Watching; outside it all. I could dance half these idiots off their feet but I haven't moved from this spot since I came. If I bogged off no one would even notice. And I'm not exactly enjoying myself. But some pull he couldn't analyse kept him there, reluctant to make such a blatant admission of rejection.

Then the MC, the Luig butcher, face pink and smooth as a newly scraped pig, was bustling up the splintered wooden steps at the side of the platform. 'We're very pleased to see the party from Ardlonach here tonight,' he began in the unadorned forthright way which was the tone of the evening. 'And for old time's sake we hope Rebecca will give us a wee song.'

Dan, sharply alert, turned his head to where she was standing, still in the group that had danced the Eightsome. Surely she wouldn't agree. He wasn't sure why he thought that; perhaps because it would have been his own reaction, perhaps because he had never heard her sing or heard anyone suggest that she could.

But Rebecca, raising a hand to the MC, was obediently threading her way through the dancers who had not yet dispersed, and there was an approving ripple of clapping from those who knew her. With the least possible fuss, in true ceilidh style, she had a quick word with the white-haired lady who worked in the chemist's and who had come up to play for her, faced the audience and began to sing.

'The Mingulay Boat Song'. Dan, riveted, almost forgetting to breathe, felt the hair rise on the back of his neck. Her voice was beautiful, true and strong. Somewhere along the line she must have had lessons. But he was hardly aware of these thoughts in that first astonished moment. He was simply caught up by the beauty of it. She looked marvellous, her black hair gleaming under the stage lighting, her face vivid and happy, her stance relaxed and unself-conscious. She belongs here, Dan found himself thinking, belongs to this whole friendly, easy-going roomful of people. And she's lovely. And casting a spell on me with this pure simple singing, with her courage and openness, her smile.

As the applause broke out after an encore Dan moved, cutting swiftly through the ranks of the men to fetch up at Liam's side as Rebecca made her way back down the hall, smiling at friendly calls of, 'Better than ever you were, lassie', and, 'It's grand to have you back, Rebecca'. The next dance was for him.

When Hamilton House was called he had a moment's blind panic, unable to remember a thing about it. But if they weren't first couple he'd be all right. Liam was turning to Rebecca. Not this time, Dan thought, high on his draught of beauty and music and enchantment. His hand reached past Liam for her arm.

'Dan! I thought you were glued to that wall for ever, definitely a non-dancer.'

Though earlier in the evening she had hoped as every dance was announced that Dan would come over, now she wailed inwardly, 'Oh, no, not Hamilton House,' one of her great favourites.

Dan said nothing, leading her onto the floor, intent on finding a good set, and once in it combating an instant move to send Rebecca to the top no matter who her partner was. The second the music began his brain cleared, and when their turn came he saw Rebecca's eyebrows go up in a look of mocking approving acknowledgement.

He danced in the way of so many Scotsmen, not having much truck with the smart footwork, but absolutely on the beat, his hands ready and sure, his weight perfectly balanced against hers, and also he danced with a vigour and enjoyment that took Rebecca by surprise.

'I love it,' she said, when they had danced down the set. 'You sit out all the Gay Gordons baby stuff then launch into this. What a waste of an evening.'

'Not quite.' His grin was sardonic, but he could not remember ever in his life feeling this soaring explosion of pleasure and heady satisfaction.

Don't go away, Rebecca found herself wanting to plead as the final chord came. He was the best dancer in the room; the one who suited her best anyway, she amended. Liam was a brilliant dancer but there was something of the solo performer in him, a view confirmed before the next dance began when he was persuaded to give them an Irish jig. He gave them the traditional rigid style first, Jeanette Irvine nodding in professional approbation. Then he broke into the Riverdance version and the audience went wild with delight.

Rebecca needn't have worried. Dan wasn't going to leave her now. He felt elated, recklessly possessive, dismissing all inner warnings about the pitfalls of involvement or hard lessons learned. When a Dashing White Sergeant was called he hastily scooped up Catriona to dance with them before Stephen Markie could attach himself as their third.

Esme, herself in great demand, nevertheless found time to watch Rebecca with love and relief. She was so different from the self-sufficient curt girl slicing through her busy days with daunting competence, or more importantly from the stunned silent person who had fled from home in March. The pell-mell ruthless tyranny of hotel life seemed to suit her, and she seemed surprisingly well integrated with this new circle she found herself in. Tonight she looked brilliantly happy, bringing back for Esme tugging memories of the irrepressible ebullient child, so like Francis with his flashing smile, his charged-up energy. But without his heedlessness and irresponsibility, she added, her thoughts moving on with a little secret smile.

At the next lull between dances there were unexpected calls for Fitz. Apparently John Irvine had given him away, saying he sang all the time, you could never damn well stop him singing, a statement feelingly corroborated by a fisherman who'd drunk enough whisky to call out, 'Aye, yon lad was humming like a bloody skep of bees all the time he was stitching me up the other day. I could have seen him far enough, I can tell you.'

'Give us some rock gospel, mate,' shouted one of his cronies, as Fitz sprang up onto the platform without bothering with the steps. A joke cheerfully racist, received with laughter entirely affectionate.

Fitz delighted them with 'Daddy Sang Bass'. He'll never go back to Cheltenham now, Rebecca thought, cheering with the rest, not attempting to pretend she wasn't happy to have Dan beside her at last, positively, definitely with her, warning off all intruders.

Fitz, laughing, white smile splitting his lean handsome face, hands up in refusal to sing again after two encores, headed back to the group and observing them from the outside as he came caught the pain behind Trudy's careful I-am-enjoying-myself expression. She still minded about Dan, he knew, and she would mind still more if Dan now turned his attention to Rebecca. Turned his attention. Fitz gave a little ironic snort at the feeble phrase; the man was locked on like a missile. Fitz bowed like the handle of a ladle over Trudy and swept her into a Scottish waltz.

I can't bear it, Rebecca thought wildly, having to ferry all the damned family home, making hot drinks, opening up the bar to serve nightcaps. It's three in the morning, for Christ's sake. Why can't they all just go to bed? Who do they think I am? They don't own me.

Oh, grow up, she told herself, quelling fresh exasperation to discover that the Grouse on the optic was finished, crouching with a groan to find another bottle on the rack. You're not some besotted teenager. You are in that mature stage of development known as the mid thirities, which apparently go on till your fortieth birthday. And don't imagine Dan's even thinking of you. He'll have his head down by now and be out to the world. And he's made his rules clear enough; you have the way he treated poor old Trudy as a clear warning in front of your eyes. But she was still caught up in the magic of the evening, the welcome and the friendship, the beat of the music, Dan's strong arm around her, the exhilarating feeling of lightness which dancing with someone so exactly suited to her style bestowed, and the heightened awareness of the senses that always followed singing.

How hard it was to wind down, to pay attention to an

order for someone's hill lunch tomorrow (today), to fetch keys for those who had ignored advice to take them with them, to go to the kitchen for ice to put in a Glenmorangie for Leonie of all people. It struck her that for the twins this was a nostalgic recreation of what they always used to do after the Luig ceilidh, come home and drink and chat, make sandwiches, sometimes even go on dancing. It would not occur to Fran or Leonie that she was out of tune with their mood, longed only to see the last of them for the day.

At last the house was quiet. Una had gone trailing wearily up to bed soon after they had come in. Rebecca felt a restless reluctance to follow her. They were sharing again so that Esme could have the little room on the upper floor and tonight Rebecca wanted to be alone. She felt flat, filled with an obscure unease which she traced with surprise to a rare threat of tears. Must be exhaustion, she told herself prosaically, but the sense of anticlimax, of having expected too much, dragged at her and once she had checked doors and put out lights and locked up the cash drawer in the safe she sank down in the chair behind her desk, too unmotivated to go or stay.

A light tap on the window startled her, but before she had time to be frightened she knew for certain who it was.

'Come out for a second,' Dan said quietly when she pulled up the window.

Without the slightest hesitation her foot was on the sill and she heard him laugh as he swung her down beside him. (It's nice to feel that light, she observed with detached gratification.)

'It was a good evening,' Dan said, his hands still on her waist, firm but not making any statement or demand.

She nodded, looking into his face in the light from the office window. 'It was,' she said.

He laughed again softly. She sounded positive to the point of brusqueness but he knew her now, understood this instinct not to wrap things up.

'I just wanted to say goodnight.'

He had known she would come in here last of all, had waited while everyone fussed about with their endless trivial demands.

'That was good of you.'

They stood for a long moment, searching each other's faces. Those few bald words seemed enough. Quietness encompassed them, an absence of questioning. Ending the evening together, Rebecca thought. That was what I needed.

'Goodnight.' Dan didn't kiss her but put up a hand to touch her cheek with the tips of his fingers. It felt so right at the time that it was only later, as she curled into a tired ball in the small divan bed, that she thought what a delicate gesture it was from such a man.

Chapter Twenty-One

She hadn't chosen the best of times to be madly attracted to someone for the first time in years, Rebecca decided ruefully as August came swiftly to the boil, but it certainly added an extra happiness to that busy month. Having the family there was more fun than she had expected, and very useful in terms of extra hands for driving, bar-tending and chatting to guests, though she and Una sometimes felt exhaustingly pulled two ways when they tried to make time to join them for picnics or fishing trips or even dinner.

Rebecca thought that even when they were all growing up there had never been so much laughter. She was glad to catch up with Fran and Leonie, easily her favourites of the cousins, and with their husbands who had both been part of that early scene. She had barely seen Leonie's daughter and Fran's two sons and liked the way they cheerfully did their share.

Beneath the growing relief that it was working, they were coping, there was the new satisfaction of knowing Dan was in control of the school. He had taken on the job with a whole-heartedness which impressed her, in tremendous form as he juggled with roster and programme, transport and supplies. Liam's buoyant spirits and lively humour had made a big difference, but the new sense of purpose and unity came from Dan.

For the victims these were changed days. Pitting themselves against a variety of disagreeable challenges, subject to humiliation and scorn if they failed, was no longer the form. As a result they extended themselves further than their predecessors ever had, willingly pushing back the thresholds of pain and endurance, inspired by an atmosphere of challenge, trusting in the training they were given and repaying encouragement. Feedback from the companies who sent them was more positive and a flurry of provisional repeat bookings for next year was one more consideration which had to be pushed onto the back burner for now. The words 'We'll think about that in November' had become a subsong daily heard.

Rebecca, gratefully aware of the new temper of the centre, only wished she could have more part in it herself. Happily as she rose to meet the exigencies of the hotel she longed to be outside more, hating to be barred from hill or loch when they were at their most beautiful, but even with Catriona coming in more often, and more and more useful as her self-confidence grew, they were still pushed to the limit.

Rebecca took every chance she could to see Dan. Even a glimpse or a word was good. It surprised and thrilled her (in a diffident unfamiliar way which she identified with astonishment as shyness) that he evidently felt the same. He always looked into the office before going out on an exercise, came in the moment he could when he got back, and the brief exchanges of laughter, gossip, in-jokes and day-to-day trivia acted like a shot in the arm for Rebecca. We're on the same side, she would think with jubilant satisfaction when Dan had looked at his watch, sworn and reluctantly taken himself off, sometimes merely with a hand lifted in farewell, sometimes with a crushing offhand hug, occasionally with a quick kiss.

'Come and meet us when we come in,' he would say, and she would nod, beaming, absurdly happy. If the timing was feasible she would take the path up onto the moor in the late afternoon, or run down to the boathouse when she saw the straggle of victims heading over the ridge to the steading, and walk back up the garden with Dan to have tea in the office, or on the terrace if there weren't too many family or punters about to butt in.

Rebecca was even more sharply conscious these days of Dan's easy teasing affection for Catriona, finding herself bristling when he reached to rough up the already shaggy hair with a brown hand, or put a casual arm round her as he thanked her for typing some letter for him or fishing out an address he'd needed.

That's fine though, Rebecca recognised with cheerful pragmatism. That's good honest sexual jealousy, with no trace of resentment for Catriona in it. She felt the same when Dan, always fond of Una but now relaxed enough to express the feeling, showed her open affection, and she growled and hissed about any females who appeared on the courses. But she knew it was all quite unimportant, part of her awakened feelings and as such to be welcomed.

Una of course was often present when Dan appeared in the office, their only sitting-room and private retreat with the house so busy. Dan could not have put into words the happiness that would seize him as he came in to find Rebecca there or, almost as acceptably, the two of them smiling a greeting. Matt and Gloss, he called them, seeing the two dark heads, Una's light flyaway hair dusky, Rebecca's gleaming and vigorously bouncy, lift as he came in. It was coming home; he acknowledged the feeling without prevarication. Home to welcoming acceptance, without complications. Here, hang on, he would protest with irony, without complications? When you are jumping into a new affair with both feet? But part of his elation these days was his conviction that with Rebecca there would be no complications. She was too independent, too realistic and she had the permanent framework of her own life to go back to, the career which was a bit more demanding than writing letters that began, 'Thank you for your letter. We have reserved for you one double-bedded room from ...' With her there would be no dragging emotional entanglements, no pressure to be something he could never be. He could enjoy the anticipation of an exciting new relationship without worrying about his own failures in patience or concern.

On evenings when Rebecca could free herself from family gatherings, when the last round to refill coffee cups had been made, charges entered on bills, tomorrow's arrangements for shooting parties settled, she would run down the stone steps to the Coach-house with happy anticipation fizzing up. There the big cheerful group would open to let her in, Dan would make a space on the bench seat beside him and she would be instantly absorbed. Not very long ago, she would sometimes deliberately remind herself to keep things in perspective, this had been Trudy's place.

Trudy appeared much less now and when she did it was more likely to be for dinner with the family or with the Irvines and Fitz than to look in on her own for a drink and company. She had come for lunch one Sunday with Stephen Markie and his teenage son and daughter, but heavy-going Stephen was no substitute for Dan. In any case, to Trudy's mild annoyance, he had been far more attentive to Rebecca than to her. But then she and Stephen had long ago recognised the limits of their interest in each other; not extensive. She was far fonder of Lilias and of Oliver and Libby, and was quite often at Tigh Bhan while they were there. They left the simple living at the Larach to their father, preferring to keep Grannie company with the benefits of telephone, television and access to the Fort William bus.

Trudy was very busy at present anyway, on her feet for long days in the shop, still without help, and quiet evenings alone in workroom or flat had their attraction. Rebecca had gone to see her a couple of days after the ceilidh, calling in on the way back from a hot and frustrating afternoon of trying to shop through, over and round the ambling tourists in Fort William, though noting with detached honesty that she would have preferred to be back at Ardlonach when Dan came in. But Trudy was important to her too.

Rebecca had been searching for words to begin, settled in the workroom on a dingy old chair from the Luig saleroom which had been awaiting renovation for so long that no one noticed it any more, when Trudy, hand-hemming a curtain at ferocious speed, bit off a thread, spat out the end and said, 'Dan's chatting you up.'

Her tone was prosaic. She was threading her needle, squinting as she held it up against the light. Rebecca could not immediately read her reaction and for a moment felt her heart bump uncomfortably. She would hate this to be a source of conflict between them.

'Yes,' was all she said, her whole character rejecting excuses or any attempt at justification. To her immense relief Trudy pitched aside the curtain, needle, thread and all, and leaning back in her chair let out a whoop of laughter.

'I love the way you let me down lightly,' she said. 'But it was nice of you to come to tell me.'

'How did you know I was going to?' Rebecca very reasonably asked.

'A certain to-the-guillotine expression. And a slightly upgraded offering.' Grinning, she gestured at the Cabernet Sauvignon Rebecca had brought.

'Are you going to mind?'

'Not about you. About him a bit. Or about the way I blew it, more like. He'd made it quite clear he wasn't out for any kind of meaningful relationship, as they say. I suppose I'd just been a bit too lonely for a bit too long.'

'Oh, Trudy.' On a rare impulse Rebecca got up to give her a quick hug. 'I'm sorry it worked out like that for you.'

'Yes, well, be warned. He's got some serious hang-ups about anyone encroaching on his life, especially pathetic women who need reassurance or comfort. But you should be all right, you're tough, and you don't need anyone, that's the vital thing.'

So sitting where Trudy had sat, close to Dan but not touching him, in an accepted place beside him but only there as part of the larger circle, Rebecca would remember this and be grateful that such a cogent warning had been there for her. She only wished it had not been at Trudy's expense.

With the safety net of the crowd in place, with the waiting for Rebecca over, fired up by Liam and his jokes and laughter, conscious of a personal popularity he couldn't recall since he'd left the Regiment, Dan would savour again the unfamiliar tide of warm happiness which seemed to reach every part of his being. He also, which was another new experience, felt proud. Proud that Rebecca would come smiling with her rapid step across the room and slip into a place at his side; proud that she made no bones about being with him, openly, easily, with no self-consciousness that he could see, leaving her own family party to come down here and seek him out.

That was good, but what was even better was the quiet end of the populated, strenuous days, when together they put the house to bed and settled down for a final drink or mug of coffee together, at the big kitchen table, in the office, in the softly-lit hotel bar or in any of the big deserted rooms with the lingering warmth and smells of the evening still about them.

In these quiet hours, the knowledge that the whole round would start again in a few hours and that they should be getting some sleep having no reality or importance, they would talk greedily, urgently, at last beginning the process of getting to know each other. Not all about each other; they were very far from that, each clinging fiercely to private areas of pain, but learning peripheral unimportant things, sharing the trivia of the day's doings, arguing over personalities and events, doling out occasional anecdotes which gave glimpses of each other's outlook and make-up, humour and beliefs.

Rebecca even managed to extract a few facts about Dan's life before the Regiment, though they were delivered with a dismissive terseness which didn't put much flesh on the bones.

He had grown up in Comrie, she discovered. I came through it on the way up, we've driven through it a hundred times coming to Ardlonach through the years, she thought, snatching at the link. I might actually have passed him. Then she gave a splutter of laughter at this adolescent reaction.

'What's so funny?' Dan demanded, instantly on the defensive, as absurd as she had just been.

'Nothing. Me. Just a thought. Go on.'

But he was less forthcoming now and she had to work hard to extract the information that his father had worked in the Royal Bank, his mother had died when he was fourteen, and that he'd joined the Air Force out of sheer boredom.

'Don't you believe everyone joins up because they're rebels or dropouts or have been in trouble with the law. It's far more likely to be boredom or the dole. After all, what was there to do in Comrie on a Saturday night? I was fairly lucky because I was always involved in sport, but other than that – the pits.'

'Did you do any climbing then?'

He grinned. 'Go up all those boring lumps of earth and rock? Never occurred to me.'

'Does your father still live in Comrie?'

'No, he lives with my sister. She's a librarian in Paisley.'

'Married?'

'No, likes to do her own thing.'

Rebecca carefully substituted, 'Do you see them much?' for an ironic, 'You surprise me.'

'As little as possible. Oh, Pat's all right but Dad's a gloomy bugger, never speaks unless it's to tell me all over again about doing his national service. Take him out to the pub, buy him a pint and you're back on Christmas Island again with the land crabs crawling all over you, painting pictures on coconuts to send home.'

Well, now I know, thought Rebecca. It all sounded monumentally dull but at least it gave some shape to the early years.

And now, at a slower pace than Rebecca would ever have

expected Dan to set, they began to learn each other's bodies too, savouring the infinite pleasures of comfortable closeness, of first touch and exploratory caress. For there was no question that here it was Dan who set the pace. That was the sort of man he was, and Rebecca, bossy, confident Rebecca, barely asked herself why she wanted it to be that way. It just seemed natural and good. She would have felt uncomfortable and dissatisfied with herself if she had tried to take the initiative as she had so often in the past, bored with some unenterprising or undersexed male. Now Dan was in charge, and she floated blissfully on the unfamiliar sensation of being willingly in someone else's hands, moving at someone else's pace, embarking on something which would be kept finite both by inclination and the constraints of time, November the known horizon here just as it was in prosaic decisions about shampooing a carpet or reprinting the brochure.

Though she wouldn't have admitted it, Rebecca welcomed the discipline imposed by the busy days. She couldn't do as she liked, couldn't have what she wanted. She had to wait, exercise patience, and she valued the moments alone with Dan more because of it.

Trudy sat idle in her workroom, a mess of leather pieces and a punch and half-finished bag at her feet. More revealing to anyone who knew her well even than the tears on her brown cheeks was that defeated inactivity.

She was just tired, she told herself. Another few weeks and the pace would let up. She had opened the shop yesterday for a few hours as it was a holiday weekend, and with the extra stocking up it had been an effort to get the basic domestic chores done. Also she needed more bags and baskets, she was almost cleaned out. In theory this was a peaceful way to spend the evening, productive and satisfying. In practice she wouldn't care if she never sold a single thing to a single person ever again in her life. And her depression was not mere tiredness. The end of summer was approaching fast, followed by the drab weeks of November and December when the town was dead, local customers came in at long intervals, silence was like a weight, dark came early and the cold of winter lay in wait like a threat. This was the time to go to step classes with lots of panting women in leggings and bulging T-shirts, to scrape around for some latent creativity to expend on defenceless materials, to fill the time, to make the best of things. This winter and every winter. And in the intervening summers to sell things to droves of strangers in hideous holiday clothes examining price tags and whispering to each other that they could get the same things cheaper somewhere else.

She didn't at first relate the calling voice to herself. Only Rebecca appeared from the harbour steps and this was a man's voice. Somebody lost? Aground on the submerged steps? Let them rot there, Trudy decided with a vengefulness quite foreign to her, sniffing and gulping and wiping her nose with the back of her hand. A movement at the top of the steps startled her, then she recognised a beaming Fitz dressed for ocean travel in long tubes of white trousers, navy-and-white striped shirt and yachting cap.

'Come along, dry your tears,' he ordered, apparently not at all surprised or concerned by them. 'I am taking you on a voyage for your health.'

He stooped to sweep away the clutter round her feet, reached a hand to draw her down the steps, and Trudy found herself quite unable to mind being discovered in this state. No one could be more matter-of-fact than Fitz and there is something reassuring about a medical man who is accustomed to seeing humanity in all its humiliation and weakness and indignity.

'Where are we going? Not to Ardlonach?'

'Not to Ardlonach. Perhaps not anywhere,' Fitz added with a touch less calm as the bows swung back in to the steps when he thought he had directed them elsewhere. 'Not without your help anyway.' His big laugh bounced back from the water and Trudy put gloom and foreboding behind her, smiling with her face still tear-stained, her nose red and shining.

'I know of no other woman in the world,' Fitz observed with admiration, once their course was more or less established for the head of the loch, 'who would be found weeping, make no apologies, give no explanations, and get into a boat and sail away without having to fetch a bag or a jacket – or a box of tissues,' he wound up, handing over a white handkerchief of impeccable provenance.

'And I don't know anyone else in the world who wouldn't ask why I'd been crying,' Trudy retorted, blowing her nose and pushing back her hair.

'Ah, but you'll tell me. Not just yet, as I am going to talk now, but quite soon.'

With a big sigh, interrupted by a final hiccup, Trudy relaxed, letting misery seep away, opening her eyes to the gold glimmer of evening light on the calm water, on the flanks of the hills across the loch and accentuating the first hint of yellow of the trees along the shore. Ten minutes ago this would have been a sight to deepen her despair; now it was beautiful.

They didn't go far, just beyond the straggling line of houses and gardens, caravan site and picnic area. Then Fitz headed into a shallow bay where a small burn spilled out from a tree-filled gorge.

'There's someone here, I think,' Trudy warned him, seeing a small spread of objects on the narrow strip of sand above the stones. 'Rugs and stuff. Do you want to try somewhere else?'

Fitz was too busy making sure he didn't run hard aground to answer but managed to cut the engine at almost the right moment, and casual Trudy was quite happy to kick off her sandals and plunge into the water, her long skirt dipping, to haul the boat up with one powerful heave.

Fitz was too pleased about his success so far and too eager for the next surprise to worry about the boat, which Trudy secured with raised eyebrows and loud lack of comment. He took her hand and led her across to the spread rugs, the hamper, the filled ice-bucket.

'I was so glad you didn't waste any time. I hardly hoped to find any of this still here,' he admitted, 'but I had this burning desire to do it this way, like the ads. Such a marvellous cliché, don't you think? And it's actually worked!'

He was so happy, he had planned all this with such enthusiasm that Trudy thought no one could have been churlish enough to refuse to enter into the spirit of it. Certainly not she, a pushover for romance and fun.

'And now to the celebration,' Fitz announced, easing the cork out of the champagne, glasses propped ready in the sand.

'Birthday?'

'Partnership.' His smile was dazzling, elated, full of the delight of imparting a secret.

'Fitz! You're staying? It's definite? Oh, I'm so pleased.' Trudy reached to hug him delightedly, and he hugged her back with vigour and didn't let her go. 'But what about the others, John and Jeanette, shouldn't we be having a party?'

'We'll organise one. This is just for you and me. I wanted you to be the first to know. And I wanted to dry your tears.' Serious suddenly, they looked into each other's eyes.

'You mind about Dan?' he asked, gently, but with an intent gravity she could not mistake.

She looked away from him, their arms still loosely round each other. 'Not really about Dan,' she said after a moment. 'Or Dan only because he represents something.'

'You mind about Dan and Rebecca?'

'No.' She shook her head definitely. 'That's quite separate.'

'Tell me about the tears. Come, sit down, help yourself to anti-midge cream and smoked salmon and brown bread from your own shop, and talk to me. Here's a jacket for you and one for me. And you'll be in charge of getting us home.'

Delighted by Fitz's brand of laughter and comfort which cut

through the layers of reticence and convention and tongue-tied uncertainty, Trudy took a big light-hearted swig of champagne. She knew she would be able to tell him exactly why she had been crying and that he would exactly understand.

Chapter Twenty-Two

This is Ardlonach at its perfect best, Rebecca thought lazily, squinting up at a pale blue sky lightly marled with white curls of high cirrus soft as goose down. Across the loch bracken patterned the lower slopes with that range of colour from green through yellow to bright caramel which means the first ground frosts have come. Above it the heather glowed strong tan in the sun; under rain it would be a heavy dark brown. Everywhere berries hung thick, leaves mottled and changed, long grass was pale. In the mornings there was a gold scatter of birch leaves across the still-green mown grass of the terraces. But the geese haven't gone south yet, Rebecca found herself arguing with something or someone, and rolled over on her stomach again, amused at what that protest had just told her.

Everywhere around them the unmistakable, inexorable signs. Summer over. And for her, and she suspected for others in this lazy gathering, sprawled in the September sun on the grass or on the big flags round the stone seat, there was a strong wish for none of this to end.

Their all being together was in itself a sign of things changing, having time on a Sunday afternoon to idle here leaving only Mona on duty in the hotel and Bern out on a run with a Grade I, the only course in this week. They had barely noticed the winding down process begin. First the Scottish schools had gone back and there had been a slackening off of morning coffees and lunches and teas; then as term began for the English and public schools Stephen Markie had come over with Oliver and Libby to say goodbye, Urquharts and hangers-on had gathered up their scattered possessions – or most of them – and departed, Fran and Leonie both promising as Caroline had done to be back for Christmas. From the problem of working out how to join up tables for big parties in the dining-room they were suddenly struggling to find enough two's for all the retired couples who now came out of hiding. Half bottles of wine were in short supply, the bar shut early after evenings of soporific conversation, and the long list of morning teas forced the early person, swearing, to get up on time, flying feet coming across the gravel in the crisp mornings with the mist curling up from the loch to rise through the trees like smoke, sparkling nets of spiders' webs jewelling the cotoneaster and roses against the cream walls.

Then had come a moment of realising that orders could be reduced by half, two menus were enough, there was time to iron more than just the shirt you needed to put on, have conversations which lasted longer than two minutes. Mixed with relief, nostalgia was already making itself felt, an odd sense of loss, and Rebecca for one looked ahead with trepidation to November which rose like a blank wall across the landscape of her life.

How much worse must this sense of things ending, of decisions waiting like some dreaded exam, be for Una, she thought now. It seemed incredible that there had never been time to discuss the future, to gain some idea of what she intended to do about Tony, the hotel, the whole enterprise, but that was literally the case. They had long ago decided that they must accept forward bookings; there was no alternative. If in the end Ardlonach was to be sold there was every likelihood that it would continue as a hotel, and a chart like theirs, well filled with repeat bookings, would be an important factor. But beyond that obvious piece of common sense other, more personal, more painful decisions waited unresolved.

And how would this end of season be for the others, her mind roamed on, deliberately shutting out her own dread. For Thea and Sylvie, who had come for three months, had been here for six and had now agreed to see out the season? Sylvie would probably have been ready to move on long ago but she was an easy-going little soul and Rebecca guessed she had agreed to stay for Thea's sake. Had Bern's devotion touched her at all, or had it been merely a source of comfort since Thea had become so involved with Paddy? And would *that* affair end in tears? The two had been an item virtually since the day Thea and Sylvie had arrived but Paddy's life was nomadic, irresponsible, futureless. He had no ties that he had ever admitted to, spent everything he earned before next pay-day, appeared to want no other lifestyle and could be quite content alone. For Thea there was an affluent background, father a well-to-do sugar cane planter, a university place waiting, the sun and the long Queensland beaches north of Cairns which she and Sylvie so much missed.

Rachel and Felix were off tomorrow. Felix had been on the whole as lazy as he looked and it was surprising he'd stayed this long, but Rachel had pulled her weight. Would they need to replace them for the last few weeks of the season? Well, if so there would be plenty of local school-leavers available who had treated themselves to a nice long summer holiday and would now be penniless and urgently looking for jobs.

Liam was laughing with Trudy who looked marvellously relaxed and happy today, her fall of brown hair shining in the sun, the warmth of a tomato-coloured denim shirt reflected in her cheeks. In spite of the slight edge to the air her sleeves were rolled up, her big brown feet still in sandals. She had plenty of inner warmth to keep her going, Rebecca decided with affection. It was good that with her new confidence about Fitz she had slid easily back into the group. She came with him and when he was busy she came without him. Today he had been called out just as they were leaving but she seemed to accept that placidly. It was good too that Dan had finally found her a van and had done some work on it for her. Why is that good, Rebecca paused to query with detached interest. Because indirectly it makes my own conscience easier? Because Dan had thereby made up a little for hurting her? How ridiculous and devious our minds are, how could two such issues possibly be related, she ridiculed herself in lazy disgust, pulling a cushion under her face and lying flat, luxuriating in idleness, consciously content, the sun warm on her shoulders.

Softly, across the circle, Dan's guitar picked out '*Macpherson's Rant*'. So surprising and satisfying that they both liked the traditional songs so much. No one, not even Liam, had known Dan possessed a guitar till that evening when they had begun singing in the Coach-house after all the guests had gone and he had vanished for a while, coming back in looking oddly shy, and had played for her to sing. And later, the evening they had gone to the island, he told her he had done it because her singing had so moved him at the ceilidh.

'It's so naff,' he had said with a shrug, 'some poser always turning up with a guitar. But I wanted to share music with you.'

The island, back in her hands as a special, precious place. They had managed to seize a whole day together, taking out the Firefly and beating slowly up against a head wind as far as Righ Bay, then going ashore on one of the rocky dots of islands reaching out from the Rhumore headland, to lie baked by the sun, a cool wind coursing over them, feeling as though the black sea-pitted wind-worn rocks themselves were sailing free, carrying them away. Then suddenly they had been shivering, a big cauliflower-head of cumulus engulfing the sun, the wind icy, the sound turned from blue to an unfriendly pewter, and numb and goose-pimpled they had grabbed up sweaters and jackets and pushed off and sailed down to the island, where Rebecca had taken Dan to the sheltered nook among the rocks that faced the sunset, and they had lit a fire and drunk the last of the wine and carried on the conversation that had flowed between them all day.

Only now Dan had held her close, comfortably drawn in against him, and the warmth of his barrel of a chest had spread through her like the output of a radiant heater. Their voices had been lower, their talk more intimate, against the quiet shadows and utter privacy of the island, which Rebecca knew to be hers again, theirs, unspoiled.

Dan's kisses had been slow, most unexpectedly sensuous. She had felt she could float away on them as she had felt adrift and free on that tiny exposed knob of rock an hour ago. She had responded with complete luxurious abandonment to the moment, all questions suspended.

'You know that I want you,' Dan had said softly, his lips barely withdrawn from hers.

'I know,' she said, and had felt his smile.

'And you?'

'I want you.'

'You know it will be – just this?'

'I know,' she had said again.

'You feel the same? That's what you want?'

'That's what I want.' That was the way it had to be. Time was pouring away; she had given her word, promised an answer once the summer was over. That fact was quite clear, alarmingly clear, but the answer itself and everything connected with it seemed some faraway phantasy, the options open to her as unreal as the plot of a novel she had read somewhere, sometime, long ago.

'Only I don't want to hurt you,' Dan had said roughly, and Trudy was in both their minds. 'I want you to understand, I'm not a person who likes getting too involved. It just doesn't work for me.' She had known from his voice that he hadn't been satisfied with the way he had put it.

'You won't hurt me.' There would be a simplicity about all lack of expectation which she imagined would be rather comforting. There could be no disillusionment, no weighing and measuring, no fighting down resentment and disappointment, no ultimate return to loneliness. Just the single acknowledged fact of a mutual physical attraction which she felt certain she could trust in. For to her surprise Dan had told her how he felt on that score, had described very explicitly the tingling moment when she had started to sing on the night of the ceilidh and his senses had been enraptured. He had used that word.

'And you make me laugh,' he had added prosaically, and Rebecca knew that mattered to her even more than the fleeting moment of attraction he had just told her about. 'Those bloody awful things you say about people, but always with that little gleam in your eye. And you don't sit about, you get on with things, you have a go, and I like that.'

And he had told her, tightening his hold in a quick hug, 'And I like a woman with a bit of substance to her. Oh, come on, Rebecca, don't let me down, you've got more sense than to start squawking about a remark like that. I mean what I say, you're a wonderful shape, and you're fit and firm. I want to see this beautiful body naked, I want to make love to it.'

To her body; not to her. Well, that had been precise enough. 'Here?' she had asked with a practical readiness which had made him laugh.

'I want you right now,' he had assured her, 'no question about that, but I think it might be a wee thing spartan right here and now, and neither of us are exactly in our teens, are we?'

In fact, and this he hadn't quite been able to bring himself to say, he wanted their loving to be perfect for her. It mattered to him in a way he didn't analyse but he did catch himself thinking, 'this first time,' revealing enough in itself. And he was conscious that Rebecca's life was a lot more sophisticated than that of most of the women with whom he embarked on one of these casual non-relationships. Or was he just worried that if the whole experience was less than satisfactory Rebecca would be quite ready to tell him to get lost next time he tried it on? That was much more like it.

'And your bum would freeze and mine would probably bear the imprint of these stones for ever,' Rebecca had added helpfully.

He had laughed aloud, hugging her again. 'So take me home to your house,' he had said against her ear, then drawn his head back to look into her face, needing to see her reaction.

She had smiled at him, her face blurred and pale in the last of the light. The fire had died to a faint glow among the insubstantial flakes of white-grey wood ash, the shadows of the bushes and small trees behind them were ink black and seemed to have drawn closer.

'With pleasure,' she had said.

She had taken him up to her little room, passing with serene nonchalance through the evening activity of the hotel where a few people were still in the dining-room, where they had met Sylvie scurrying across the hall with the coffee jug in her hand, and been held up behind an elderly couple who were hobbling arguing up the stairs. Rebecca had chatted to them, fielding a dropped stick, opening their bedroom door.

Dan had kept his mouth shut, disconcerted by this casual openness which seemed to him as blatant as running up a flag, then had found he rather liked it, then realised, relaxing, that he could have expected nothing else. It also made a statement about Rebecca's feelings which had oddly moved him and as he followed her up the attic flight where he had never been he had vowed to himself, almost with anger, not to do her any harm if he could help it.

Practised and experienced lover, emotionally uncommitted as he professed himself to be, always in control, always setting the pace, always escaping unscathed, Dan had been startled and reluctantly amused to find that when the blue curtains had swung across the black eye of the gable window, when only the bedside lamp spread a soft light on the white painted bed and white cover, and shadows softened the outlines of the small room, his heart had been beating with a most unaccustomed excitement and anticipation.

Rebecca had not started flinging off her clothes in the matter-of-fact manner he had half feared, but had turned to him with a gesture of simple readiness, of awaiting his pleasure, which had caught him by the throat. To hide from her what his face might show, he had taken her in his arms and drawn her against him, his hand cupping her head into the hollow of his shoulder. She was such an authoritative character you forgot she was so small, he'd thought. Her breasts were firm and beautiful. He had pulled back the jackets they were still wearing so that he could feel them against his chest. Her hair under his hand was crisp and still cool from the frosty air on the water. They had stood together in a long moment of pure, absorbed sensation, a moment Dan would always remember, one of the best moments of his life.

His love-making had surprised Rebecca. She had been careful to remind herself, as he tossed her jacket across the room onto a chair and drew her sweater over her head, that this was an exercise in simple physical pleasure. Dan would not be a man to go in for refinements like worrying about what was happening to her. He was here for gratification, for fun. The whole thing must be kept light, cool, a finite act to be enjoyed here and now, with no significance beyond the moment. Her body hadn't felt in the least calm, however; it had waited a long time for this.

But for Dan, that first time, Rebecca's pleasure had been paramount. He could hardly believe yet the gift he was being given. This marvellous woman, with all her looks, brains, ability and vigorous independence, her abrasive humour, was openly happy with him, wanted his company and now, unbelievably, was ready to welcome his body.

He had slowly, slowly caressed and stroked and kissed her, sending her the message that time was theirs, endless, pleasurable time. Ready to satisfy his urgent demands and deal with her own feelings as best she could, Rebecca had been hazily aware of the dangers of this leisurely, delectable arousal. I shall give myself away, she had thought, trying to remember why it mattered that she shouldn't. What she did give away was her absolute delight in him, her body telling him beyond any possible doubt how completely he had satisfied it.

Coming dazedly back to reality Rebecca had remembered with a sort of dim alarm that she mustn't say any of the things she felt. Had she already? She vaguely seemed to have heard somewhere in the background a voice which could only have been her own crying out in pleasure.

'Some lover,' she had managed to say, making a big effort to strike a note of judicious approval which had jarred Dan out of his sensuous drifting delight. Well, that was what he had wanted, someone who took it all in her stride, who didn't perpetually demand those three worn-out words of mindless reassurance, who didn't cling or measure or compare or use sex as a weapon.

'You're not so bad yourself,' he had said cheerfully, turning on his side and pulling her against him. 'I reckon today's been one of the best days I've ever had.' Putting this loving, whose perfection had taken him by storm, into the context of the whole, equating it with sun and wind and sunset and woodsmoke and wine, and Una's lobster salad and poppyseed rolls.

'Here's Fitz,' said someone, and Rebecca turned her head to see a huge smile spread across Trudy's face as she watched him leap like a jumping Jack over borders bright with asters and Michaelmas daisies and chrysanthemums and down stone-faced banks, carrying a big basket. He dumped it down and pulled Trudy to her feet, whirled her round like a boy, giving her a hug and a smacking kiss which could have been heard on the jetty.

'Una's coming with the cake. Wouldn't trust me with it,' he announced.

'And who could blame her?'

'What's the cake for?'

'Did you see Bern? He must have been letting them walk it if they're not back by this time.'

'Does Una need a hand?'

'Catriona's here, she's bringing the rest.'

'But who's the cake for?'

'Rachel and Felix, of course. Farewell party.'

Even arrogant Felix had the grace to look pleased as Una and Catriona, taking a less direct route than Fitz, carefully carried down a beautifully decorated cake, Braan coming ahead of them with his plumy tail high and a big grin on his face. He never let Catriona leave Glen Righ without him these days; any car journey might lead to this delectable place full of friends and food and conversation of a complimentary kind.

This can't be as good as it seems, Rebecca thought, trying to rationalise a giddy sense of euphoria. I've nothing whatsoever in common with at least half these people. They're transients or youngsters, welded into a unit by the summer, the place, the shared work. Outside Ardlonach what would I ever find to talk about to Sylvie, to Paddy, to Bern who was now coming at a lumbering run up from the boathouse, anxious in case he'd missed the best bit of the party.

So why are you missing out Dan, Rebecca teased herself promptly, but she knew quite well it was because she hadn't yet sorted out her thoughts about what she and Dan had in common beyond the magical pleasure of sex, of touch, of simply being together. That in itself was so compelling and overwhelming that balanced realistic judgement was still impossible for her.

Though she might objectively recognise the separate elements of this group as incohesive, not her style, yet she knew she was happy in it, happier than she had ever been among the so-called friends of the Edinburgh years, which in retrospect had taken on a grey uniformity without peaks or landmarks, depressing to contemplate. This contentment is real, she thought, suddenly angry with herself. Why diminish it by analysing and questioning? Barring Felix I like everyone here. I shall be sorry to say goodbye to Rachel tomorrow and truly sad when Thea and Sylvie set off for the other side of the world and Liam wanders off to pick up the next job.

Still dodging about Dan, I see. All right, it will be unbearable when he goes back to the lodge and I – but the unknown ahead for her made her shiver, and she pushed her face into the sun-warmed cushion again in an instinctive gesture of evasion.

Voices above them roused her at once. Joanie and Megan, each carrying little fancy-wrapped gifts of the tartan variety, each wearing lipstick and a pleated skirt. It was good of them to come in their time off. People are so nice, thought critical, sarcastic Rebecca. God, and I haven't even been drinking.

'What's the joke?' Dan demanded, holding level a plate where two large moist wedges of carrot cake were glued together by creamy icing as he sank with perfect control cross-legged onto the rug beside her.

'Me. I think I'm turning into a nice person.'

'No chance,' he assured her, licking icing off his finger and holding out the plate. 'Yours is the little piece.'

She put a hand on his thigh, briefly aware of the hard muscle, and of the tiny coil of inner fire which that contact instantly lit, smiled into his light smiling eyes and took her hand away again. It was so good to have him there.

Later he said, 'Sing for us.'

When Rachel chose 'The Bonnie Earl of Murray' an unbearably elegiac mood took hold of them all so that Rebecca, standing in the slanting sunlight looking out over the gilded shimmer of the loch, could barely keep her voice steady.

Chapter Twenty-Three

This sense of things ending, of time fleeing, spiced the whole mood of those early autumn weeks. Everywhere Rebecca looked the clichés were there, swallows gathering, field mice coming in from the cold, tall heads of willow-herb silver in the sunlight, a thousand thousand pinhead seeds dotting the floating down, blazing clusters of rowan-berries bending the slender boughs.

'Aye, it'll be a hard winter,' Megan would warn portentously over her tea and custard creams.

'Or it's been a fine summer,' Rebecca would suggest, knowing Megan would say it every autumn anyway.

The hotel wasn't as quiet as it had threatened to be, or promised to be according to viewpoint, as there appeared a trickle of Belgian, French, American and even English one-nighters touring the West Coast and booking on spec. Each week there were three or four booted, tweed-or-loden-clad Danes or Germans stalking on Luig, early to bed and sharp into breakfast, grimly unforgiving if their packed lunches weren't ready ten minutes ahead of time, marching into the office each morning, cased rifle on shoulder, to change £50 notes into pocket money for the day. Every evening before dinner one Dane explained why yet again he had missed his stag. Rebecca said she'd had enough of the foresight saga and refused to go into the bar.

This was a good time for her though. She and Una knew by

now that the back of the season was broken. Worries about the survival school were a thing of the past, now it was one facet of the whole, ticking along successfully and providing an element of variety which enlivened ordinary hotel routine.

There was time now to go up the hill with Dan's group, or better still go alone with him for walks along the shore or over the headland, time to go sailing occasionally, field a hotel team for the assault course or spend a couple of hours on the playground of the practice climbs.

'You're a natural,' Dan told her, as Rebecca negotiated the delicate final moves on one of the harder routes which brought her up beside him. 'How about coming with me some evening to the climbing wall in Fort William?'

'Great,' she said without hesitation. It might prove beyond her capacity but it would be fun to try and Dan would be there. Anything shared with him, anything that took them away on their own, was precious. She knew too that anything which took her into his world was important to her, a need she did her best to keep in perspective but which was an inevitable and natural part of her feelings for him.

Dan gave her something else. One evening when she thought they were going to the climbing wall again he took her instead to the swimming pool.

'What's going on?' she demanded, resistance and apprehension instantly aroused.

'We're going swimming.'

'Swimming? We most certainly are not.'

'Come on, don't argue,' Dan said, reaching over to the back seat for a sports bag, getting out of the car and locking his door while Rebecca was still protesting.

She pitched herself out and confronted him across the roof. 'Dan, I'm not coming swimming with you. There's nothing I'd loathe more. If that was the plan why didn't you say so and I could have stayed at home.'

'Tonight we're swimming.'

'Don't keep saying that. I haven't got any kit anyway,' she added and was instantly annoyed with herself for the prevarication.

Dan lifted the bag. 'Una got your things for me.'

Rebecca stared at him, her face tight with indignation. 'You're pushing me.'

'I want you to do this.' His tone made no attempt to be conciliatory, his face was expressionless.

Rebecca's mind began to marshall all the excellent reasons why she should refuse, then rejected them angrily. She didn't need reasons. She stooped to reach into the car for her bag. She should have brought her own car; she should always bring her own car, she had learned that long ago. If she had, Dan would be standing in the middle of the carpark right now with a long walk home. He moved fast round the bonnet and blocked her way as she turned. He didn't touch her. 'Just do as you're told,' he said quietly, his eyes on hers.

She stared back at him, jaw clenched, mouth set, bitterly resenting being made to face this very private terror so unexpectedly, here, like this, by him.

Dan didn't attempt to reason or browbeat, he simply waited, compelling her with his will alone, it seemed to her, to take this step. And suddenly she knew it would be possible. She could hand over to him this deep-seated irrational fear, give him the chance to resolve it for her if he could, and if he didn't succeed it wouldn't matter. Only the two of them would ever know. And she had also discovered that she didn't want to fight with him, she who loved a good fight. She liked him too much.

She said nothing but leaned her forehead for an instant against him, then straightened to look up into his still watchful face, letting him read her capitulation but also her vulnerability. He said nothing, nodding, but dropped the bag he was carrying at his feet and for one moment took her with bracing comfort into his arms.

In that one session Rebecca made herself float with her head back letting the water lap over her face, opened her eyes under water, swam under water, and finally steeled herself to dive, something she had never been able to bring herself to do. Dan treated her with an impersonal professionalism, part of which was a most unexpected gentleness as well as a matter-of-fact acceptance of her phobia. Only when she had dived in at the deep end and swum a steady length without dragging her head up awkwardly between strokes like some idiot female panicking about her hair did he abandon the instructor's detachment, hugging her as she came up out of the water, grinning like a boy, repeating, 'Good for you, love, good for you. I never thought you'd do it, God, I'm so proud of you.'

Happiness bounded by time and agreed rules. Within those limits Rebecca knew she was totally caught up in it. When the reckoning came it would not be easy.

The Irvines gave a dinner party to celebrate Fitz joining the partnership and Rebecca enjoyed the almost forgotten experience of willingly, pleasurably being one of a couple. They couldn't all be off duty to go but Catriona insisted that if Megan and Mona did dinner she could handle the rest and would join the party later, staying at Ardlonach for the night.

So though Dan and Rebecca took Una to the party Catriona brought her home, and they came later, purring along the loch road in the relaxed peace that follows an evening of good company and good food, with before them the prospect of sleep wrapped in each other's arms, in a narrow bed which had never seemed too small to them yet. It was good to share lazy comments, laugh at Fitz's buoyant delight in the new prospects before him, exchange jokes and gossip garnered separately, comment without constraint on how happy Trudy looked. Though one piece of information Rebecca did keep to herself. Fitz had come to talk to her after dinner and told her his decision to stay in Luig had been dependent on Trudy. He had made no secret of his hopes and intentions. The news gave Rebecca huge pleasure, but behind the pleasure a knife twisted.

Immediate happiness, finite and contained. And the alternative, holding all she had thought for so long that she wanted, so nearly perfect, so irredeemably flawed.

It was fun to go one afternoon, the four of them, Trudy and Fitz, she and Dan, to tea with Lilias, who daily more frail and vague was a growing concern to everyone. Rebecca had hardly thought Dan would want to go but he agreed at once with perfect readiness. He took no notice at all of the arguments about who would drive and which car they would take. He would drive his car and Rebecca would come with him.

A few weeks ago I'd have put up a fight about that, Rebecca realised, amused. Her car was oddly unimportant nowadays, receiving no attention, barely even cleaned. It had become a mere workhorse, and one not particularly suited to the job it had to do.

For Dan, time spent with Rebecca was quality time and opportunities to talk to her alone were rare. He knew her apprehension about the future and wanted to understand it and help her if he could. In spite of their agreement that their affair belonged only to this time and place, again and again he found himself hankering to know where she would be, what shape her life would take, what it was she dreaded.

It was pure pleasure to be swept by Dan over the Luig moor in the autumn afternoon sunshine, Loch Buie bright below them, Rhumore headland a glorious sweep from its white frill of shell beaches, through the green of grazed grass and the yellow of bent patched with heather, to grey summit rock.

Lilias welcomed them lovingly, a sign of growing frailty which Rebecca thought more poignant even than her slow struggle to reach the table, the rattle of her cup in the saucer. She enjoyed Fitz, whom she already knew well, and watched him and Trudy together with open benevolent pleasure, but it was to Rebecca she said, with a fierce clutching farewell hug, as though not ready yet to leave love and laughter, 'Dear girl, it's so good to see you happy. You've been on your own far too long.'

It was fortunate, Rebecca thought, that Dan would see nothing strange in her blinking away tears as they drove away. Though his hand drawing hers to his thigh and holding it there almost made them flow in earnest.

Tony came back on the last night of September, in a mood of self-satisfaction and apparent confidence which suggested he was unaware of any grief dealt out and expecting no disapprobation. Only Rebecca noticed his eyes slide away as he seized Una in an embrace that looked planned if not actually rehearsed. Even so as he came bounding into the office he was more at ease for a couple of minutes than any of them, Una, Rebecca and even Dan feeling roughly jolted out of an accepted pattern, questions and instinctive objections buzzing up in a disordered swarm like wasps from a disturbed bike.

It was Rebecca who was the first to realise that Tony's outward assumption that everything would at once be back to normal now that he was home was in reality dread of admitting any other possibility. He simply didn't know how else to deal with it. He hadn't been able to find the sort of courage it would take either to make contact first and prepare the ground, or to come in with an honest apology, or even a question as to whether his appearance was acceptable or not.

'Thought I'd give you a surprise. Meant to get here a bit earlier only I've had a hellish journey up, car's been playing up all the way, loose fan belt, radiator leaking, God knows what. You're looking fantastic, darling. And how are you, Rebecca?'

Don't you bloody touch me, Rebecca silently warned, feeling anger rise in a hot tide as she saw the rigidity of Una's slight body, the pallor of her face, the shock in every line of her. Out of the tail of her eye she caught Dan's quick protective look towards Una, and knew the hostility in his face reflected her own. He had risen to his feet as Tony burst jovially in, and his stance said all too clearly that if anyone wanted him to smash him straight back into the hall again he would be happy to oblige.

In that startled, arrested second everything hung on Una's reaction. Rebecca found her heart beating quite painfully as she realised this, as though the whole summer's effort and achievement could be wiped out, brought to nothing, in the next tick of the clock.

Una stepped back and her face, though the colour had drained from it dramatically, was surprisingly calm. 'Hello, Tony, we're all well, thank you. But I think it would have been considerate to let us know you were coming.'

She couldn't have done it better, Rebecca thought in startled admiration and relief. So courteous, but oh so cool, so damning; and 'us' not 'me', establishing solidarity. She felt Dan's threatening pose relax marginally.

And then, in the way of hotels, the phone rang and at the same moment Joanie came in with her determined flapping rapid walk and began, 'Megan says are the menus written yet because she doesna' think she's enough damsons for the sauce to go with the venison and should she – oh, my, is it you Tony? I never thought we'd be seeing *you* here again. Had a good holiday, have you? So shall I say to Megan you'll be through just now?' she asked, turning back to Una with a single-minded sticking to the main issue which neatly reduced Tony's presence to the level of importance Rebecca thought it deserved.

Megan was preparing for a dinner party the Macleods were giving for their stalking guests, keepers and wives. As this was yet again a holiday weekend the house was full. There was no time for emotional reunions or renunciations, barely time to change and certainly no time to wonder where Tony might sleep tonight.

He was shoved to the sidelines in the most ruthless fashion, though Una cooked in a trembling daze of shock and distress,

Megan in a tight-lipped supportive silence which promised trouble for anyone who upset her precious boss any further, and the rest of the staff flew about raising their eyebrows at each other in awed enjoyable speculation about this sudden reappearance of the absent husband, and the storm which looked likely to burst once dinner was safely over.

Rebecca, changing rapidly for the evening, felt breathless and choked with anger. She longed to have a blazing row with Tony, wanted to phone and tell Esme what had happened and get rid of some of her rage and frustration, and she wanted to establish, now, without delay, what Una would do. Above all, she longed to let rip to Dan, who she was certain would feel as she did.

What she had to do instead was hurry downstairs, chat to guests, pour drinks, take dinner and wine orders, deal with requests for needle and thread, sleeper reservations, a supper tray upstairs for someone's grannie, a leather bootlace. The next day's butcher's order was delivered by car just as the first main courses were going out, with the excuse that they had two vans off the road, and Ellie, the local farmer's daughter Trudy had found for them to replace Rachel and Felix, spilled red wine over a pile of starched and folded napkins.

Rebecca tried to stand back and put into perspective her burning impatience for some kind of confrontation and resolution, slightly startled by a violent feeling of possessiveness for Ardlonach, Ardlonach in its new form, and all they had made of it this summer. It was a nightmare to have to accept that any decision about it precipitated by Tony's arrival was out of her hands. All her resentment at his inheriting the place, submerged during these busy months, came back with new force. She comforted herself with the prospect of pouring all this out to Dan, but as the evening dragged frustratingly by she had time to remember that he was not the man to welcome hysterical outbursts. That steadied her. She was used to self-discipline, she could get this under control, though it was a new experience to find she had to measure up to standards even stricter than her own. She had been so used to trampling over the men she was involved with that to find she valued someone's respect sufficiently to modify her behaviour was salutary but oddly satisfying.

It was not an easy evening but during its busy course she did force herself to move from blind rebellious anger to an acceptance that this really had very little to do with her. She had stepped in to help Una because Tony had gone; now he was back. This was their life, their home. Indeed Tony's behaviour rammed that point home all too clearly. Of course he knew most of the guests and they welcomed him eagerly, with the instinct of their kind to enjoy being close to the core of power, owner not family, even husband not wife. And of course their noses were whiffling to the scent of drama. Tony, easy, sociable, gregarious, was at his best in such a situation and Rebecca, working flat out, ground her teeth as he made the rounds of all the flattered groups, getting the names right, pulling the appropriate reminiscences out of the hat and, with a casualness which reduced her to speechless rage, giving them drinks which he didn't write down.

His summer's truancy, she gathered from snippets overheard, had been a business undertaking that hadn't quite come off.

'Had a wonderful time, though, marvellous part of the world,' she heard him say, neatly cutting across more searching questions, moving on to the next table.

He came back from a visit to the Coach-house full of pride in how brilliantly his plan had worked out. 'Can't think why you let Innes go, though,' he commented. 'He was a damn good bloke. And Dan seems to have turned a bit surly.'

He appeared with a loaded plate before dinner was half over and ate it at the bar, a piece of informality which Rebecca hotly resented. He joined the Macleod party for coffee as of right, chatting up Thea when she took in the liqueurs.

You complete bastard, Rebecca thought helplessly, watching

him. We're working our butts off here and you're completely unconcerned. And he had gone up to shower and change. Where? What assumptions had he made about that? What had Una permitted? Poor Una, how infinitely worse all this was for her. And what would she do? Rebecca, hope as she might, simply could not imagine her turning Tony out again. And then what? Would he get up in the morning to carry on as before, secure, impregnable, a man back in his own house? With sick consternation she saw how close this would bring a decision about her own life.

'. . . as we shall be leaving early tomorrow, I wondered if you could let me have my bill tonight . . . ?'

Oh, go away, go away. Rebecca smiled, went to the pantry board for the chits, switched on the computer.

'Now I see you've charged me for morning tea for two for five days but I think you'll find my wife had orange juice the first morning . . .'

Rebecca put in a credit, made out the sales voucher, filled in the authorisation number.

'Oh, I should perhaps have added something for the staff. Could I do that, do you think?'

It doesn't really matter, Rebecca thought calmly, tearing up the voucher and starting again. Three more minutes of my life spent making squiggles on paper for this idiot cannot affect anything very much. But please let it all be over soon, let things be settled one way or the other. As she sold a postcard, made a note to order a newspaper, she realised with a dull sense of anticlimax that although they had successfully got through the evening and things were winding down, the Macleod party settled in the drawing-room with even the junior keeper's wife smiling at last, there would not necessarily be any answers tonight. If it had been down to her there would have been, she thought grimly, but Una was a very different person. And this was between Una and Tony; they might not talk tonight, they might, ultimate frustration, never talk at all. They might simply slide uneasily into some compromise; and they had every right to do so.

Oh, Dan, I want you. Had he waited? He didn't always. She had had to learn not to be hurt when she found he had gone off to his cottage without telling her. Once she had tried to tell him that she minded this and he had given her short shrift. 'I'm not answerable to you,' he had said brusquely. 'I thought you understood that. I don't have to tell anyone where I'm going or what I'm doing, OK?'

Just as Trudy had told her had happened with her, he had never taken Rebecca down to his cottage. That at least she had had the sense not to suggest, divining something of his deep need for a private place, a lair to be guarded.

Tonight he would have seen how shaken and disorientated Tony's appearance had made her feel, might realise she needed him. But with Dan you never could tell; the very fact of her need could be enough to make him walk away.

Una, coming wearily from the kitchen, dread clear in her face, found Tony and Rebecca in the top bar. Not bothering to answer, perhaps not even hearing, well-meant questions about whether she had eaten, refusing a drink with a single shake of her head, she said, 'Would you both come upstairs with me, please?'

They looked at her in surprise, uncomprehending.

'We can't talk without interruptions anywhere down here,' Una went on, and Rebecca saw that she was desperately holding down frustration at this need to explain. 'We'll talk in my room. Rebecca, would you come too, please.'

'Oh, look here,' Tony started to protest.

Una faced him, her small face exhausted, her voice thin. 'If Rebecca's not there I shan't talk to you at all.'

Rebecca felt a first small stir of hope. This was a Una she had not seen before. With an odd self-consciousness she and Tony followed her upstairs. Una herself seemed unaware of any strangeness in the situation, her whole spirit focused on what was coming. She walked into her room, littered with the day's working clothes tossed down when she came to change into fresh ones before dinner. It had been light then; the curtains weren't drawn. The long windows reflected the stiff little scene brightly in their big blank panes.

'Una, come on, this is nothing to do with anyone but ourselves—' Tony began in an uneasy mixture of bluster and cajolery. Her look stopped him dead, a look of resolve wound up to an unshakable pitch.

'Tony, either you leave Ardlonach now, tonight, and agree never to come back, or I see my lawyer and file for divorce, dividing everything we own between us.'

Rebecca thought she had probably gasped audibly. Certainly she found her mouth was open and hastily shut it. She had no place in this discussion – if Una was going to allow discussion. She was here as a witness and for once in her life she must keep quiet.

Tony threw an angry glance in her direction. He was still sure he could get round Una if he was given the chance. 'That's ridiculous,' he said, in the tone of a man who still thinks wheedling will serve him. 'Anyway, it's far too late at night to get into all that heavy stuff. I've had a long day and you must have had a strenuous evening, I know only too well what it's like—'

You fatuous creep, you haven't the faintest idea, Rebecca thought with searing contempt.

'—but in the morning everything will seem different—'

'Because we'll have slept together?' Una's voice was not quite as steady now but her eyes met Tony's with an unaltered resolution. 'It's no good Tony, you're not going to sleep here. Not in this bed, not in this room, not in this house. If you do, it's the end of Ardlonach. I mean it.'

'Rebecca, get out,' Tony snarled, suddenly furiously angry at the situation he had been forced into. 'For Christ's sake, this is our bedroom.'

'I'll go when Una asks me to,' Rebecca said quietly.

'You're so bloody obstinate,' he shouted, needing a target and strangely unsure of how to deal with Una. 'You always did do just what suited you.'

He had not bargained for the affection and strong feeling of trust and support which had grown between these two so different women in their months together. Now Una was angry, now she was prepared to fly at him.

'Having Rebecca here was the one thing that kept me going when you walked out. Just walked away without explanation, without telling me what you intended to do, without helping me or making any plans for me. Just walked off with some woman who had the time to look after you and make herself beautiful for you and share the things you like to do. Rebecca has worked ten times harder for this place than you ever did. She's organised it and got the accounts straight—'

'I had a look during dinner. Well, good for Rebecca, we can certainly do with the cash—'

'We!' Una moved forward sharply and for a second it looked as though she was going to hit him. 'We! If there's any "we" here it's Rebecca and I. You have nothing to do with this place any more, or if you do it will be on your own.'

She looked tiny, frail in her kitchen whites, the long tendrils of her light-textured hair straggling wildly, but there was a burning determination in her eyes Rebecca had never seen there before and which she suddenly recognised as the product of a transformation she had been too close to or too busy to appreciate. Una had tasted the pleasures of being valued in her own right, of achieving, of having a creative talent praised and recognised. She had learned that responsibility need not be terrifying, that working in harmony with someone instead of always being pushed into the role of the less efficient, the less able, can be not only rewarding but fun. And here confronting her in the room they had shared together and where he had abandoned her to lonely aching weeping nights was the husband who had just spent six months with another woman. No doubts shook Una at this crucial turning point.

Opening the baize-lined door at the head of the stone stairs relief filled Rebecca to see the light still on. Perhaps after all Dan was there.

In the Coach-house the wall lights were off, the big room empty and shadowy except for the rectangle of light gleaming back from bottles and glasses. Paddy was still there, though no longer behind the bar. Thea, bless her, had done as much of the locking up as she could and had the house keys in front of her. Liam and Bern were there. Dan was there. Rebecca didn't mind that he wasn't alone. In fact, crossing the big room to them she felt an odd weakening affection, the surprising sting of tears. Like a family, she thought, needing them, sure of them, grateful. As she reached them Dan curved an arm to receive her and she leant against him, letting emotions deflate in relief.

'Brandy,' said Paddy, getting off his stool.

'I think it's going to be all right,' said Rebecca, nodding her acceptance.

'We're off then,' they said promptly, smiling at her, seeing her exhaustion, asking no questions. Liam patted her as he went by. Dan held her quietly as she sipped the welcome brandy.

'Come on,' he said. 'I'm taking you out of here.'

Chapter Twenty-Four

Dan didn't even live in the cottage Rebecca had thought was his. So much for the fantasies she had indulged in, imagining herself walking up the path and into the door of the double-fronted end house to find him. Instead, leaving the car on the disused quay, he led her along a path at the side of it, opening a door in the wall which extended unexpectedly far at its back, a door leading straight into a poorly lit, cheaply fitted kitchen-living room.

Guitar propped in the angle of wall and cupboard, fishing rod in a corner, a scatter of tapes and videos, a surprising number of books stacked on a small side table covered with a grubby green-check seersucker cloth. There was a pile of logs on a modern tiled hearth, the grey remains of a fire in the grate. There were plates and a couple of mugs on the draining rack, washing-up bowl tilted to drain in the sink, a J-cloth draped over its rim. No obsessive tidiness here, no careless squalor either, but something to be discovered of Dan, his private self, and Rebecca wanted to pause, have time to absorb the room's messages. But Dan had seen her immense tiredness, which Rebecca herself had scarcely realised, after the shock and stress of the evening, and he wanted first and foremost to look after her, to offer her warmth and peace and comfort. He took her hand and drew her with him into a dark cupboard-like hall and up a narrow steep-pitched wooden staircase. It gave onto a landing with a single bed buried under an orderly array of climbing and skiing and subaqua kit. Dan took her through this into a coom-ceilinged bedroom with a double divan bed, looking oddly low with its flimsy legs unscrewed and slung into a corner, its plywood headboard propped against the wall. On it a rumpled duvet was tossed back. There was a junk-room wardrobe and matching dressing table with its top at shin height and a mirror like a leprechaun's ear and two 'jewellery' drawers jammed crooked and minus handles.

Dan made no apologies, leaving Rebecca only to cross the room to slide the flimsy curtains along their plastic-covered wire, coming back to kiss her gently and in silence begin to undress her.

It was true, she had not known how tired she was. She barely helped Dan but stood passive, sighing in blissful relief when he swung her up and laid her on the surprisingly comfortable mattress. 'All evening I was hoping against hope you'd still be there,' she confessed, turning to him thankfully as he joined her a couple of seconds later, closing her eyes, pressing her face against his chest. 'Thanks for waiting.'

'That bastard,' Dan said angrily, sparing a hand to punch the pillow so that it didn't rise up between their heads. 'Turning up like that as though nothing had happened. How's poor old Una?' He guessed that Rebecca would want to talk. There had been nothing in the way she turned to him that spoke of sexual need, though his own body had responded with instant urgency.

'She was incredible,' Rebecca told him. 'I was so impressed. She'd evidently made her mind up at some point during the evening and she was absolutely unflinching. I'd never have believed she had it in her to be so determined.'

'He's really gone?' From the Coach-house they had heard a car leaving and had looked at each other in hopeful surmise. Apart from their sympathy for Una none of them wanted some dickhead crashing in and throwing his weight about at this stage of the game.

'Una flatly refused to have him in the house. And he's so weak, he just went to pieces when he realised that she meant it.' It had not been an attractive sight and she would willingly have slipped away at that point but Una had refused to let her go, showing the first signs of suppressed panic. 'Then luckily he started whingeing about how badly Serena had treated him. Stupid berk didn't seem to realise that would hardly help him.'

'Is Una all right on her own? Do you think she'll sleep?'

'I doubt it, but once she was sure Tony had gone she only wanted to be left alone. The poor girl will have to be up at seven as well for those early breakfasts.'

'Surely someone else could do them for her? I'll do them, come to that.'

'She won't hear of it. To be honest I think it's something to cling to, a familiar piece of routine which will just roll her along into the day.'

'As though nothing has happened. Well, maybe you're right. And you don't think Tony will come back?'

'Tonight? I don't think he has the guts, frankly. Whether he'll try to weasel his way in tomorrow to re-open the whole discussion is another matter. He's got a lot to lose, particularly now he's seen how nicely his pub's doing,' Rebecca added bitterly. That sly examination of the books had really rankled.

She tried to push it out of her mind, knowing the thought would make her too angry. It was good to talk, to indulge in a moan about how she'd hated the evening, have Dan remind her what Una must have been going through and tell her not to be so pathetic, and speculate together about what Una would do if she finally did end up with Ardlonach as hers.

In their comfortable warmth and closeness, oblivious to the utilitarian meagreness of their surroundings, for the first time free of the sense of the big house around them with its people and sounds and overriding demands, Dan saw his chance to draw Rebecca for once into talk of the future, to get some idea of what she planned to do when this situation which bound them all together so closely was ended, as it so soon would be. This need was new for him and he was wary of it, reminding himself whenever it surfaced that it hadn't been part of the deal. Still, he told himself now, he had a gap of a few weeks before the lodge job started up again and Rebecca might easily stay on for a while after the hotel shut, for a bit of a break or to keep Una company, particularly now all this business with Tony had blown up. He had thought of going up to the north-west for some climbing with Liam but could keep the cottage on for a while perhaps, or even from Spean Bridge could still easily get over to see her. So long as they both knew what it was all about.

'Do you think Una would run the place on her own?' he asked. 'Open up next season?'

His job would be in the balance, Rebecca realised. It was hardly likely that anyone taking on Ardlonach as a hotel, if it did change hands, would be interested in the survival school too.

'I don't know,' she said thoughtfully. 'She seemed tough enough for anything tonight. I truly think she's begun to enjoy it all, and to realise what she's capable of.'

'But she'd need you to help her. I mean, her cooking's brilliant and it brings the punters in, but she'd never handle all the admin side by herself.'

'Easy enough to find someone who could,' Rebecca observed, beginning to sound drowsy as warmth reached every part of her and her body began to relax at last.

'So what will you do when the place closes?' Dan asked, letting that one pass. It seemed extraordinary, even as he put the question, that close as they had been in these past few weeks they had never talked of this, rigorously avoiding all reference to the future.

'I shall have to go back,' Rebecca said, after a fractional pause. Her immediate instinct had been to say casually, 'Oh, this and that,' a form of saying, 'That's none of your business,' which Dan would have understood. But all at once she knew that she could talk about this. It was a piece of her past, conceivably of her future, which was completely dissociated from him. She trusted his perception and good sense; trusted him to understand.

'Yes?' Dan was querying. The 'have to' had surprised him.

'I promised someone an answer.' Rebecca was very tired or she would have realised what Dan would instantly infer from this. But she was seeing only her own point of view, her mind already locked onto the deep, agonising doubt as to what that answer must be. Dan was merely the recipient of her thoughts.

'Tell me about it.' There was latent anger there already, but she missed it.

'Oh, back in the spring I had a – an unexpected encounter – ran into someone I never expected to see. It was why I came here, well, why I got out of Edinburgh anyway—' No, this was still too difficult to say, the astounded heart-stopping certainty in that brief glimpse too painful to describe. She couldn't begin that way. She tried again. 'I'd had a boyfriend, years ago. Well, we were engaged actually only it didn't work out. Then he'd reappeared at a time when I needed help, much later. He did help me.' God, she was saying nothing, explaining nothing. After the years of rigid silence, of being unable to talk of this even to Esme, she might just as well have been struggling with a foreign language.

'He wants you back?' Jesus, I might have known it. Women like Rebecca don't come without baggage, without some man in the background. She's just been pissing me about. Then Dan caught himself up angrily; she had been doing exactly what he had wanted and demanded, sharing with him an affair which had no past, no future and created no ties.

'He's offered – well, he's suggested that we get married but he—'

'And what are you going to say?' Dan cut harshly across her hesitant voice, failing to hide the anger in his own. It sounded like a taunt, giving away a great deal more than he had intended, but Rebecca hardly seemed to notice, didn't even reply, faced at last with the unanswerable, besieged by all the enormous consequences of this choice.

'So you ran into this bloke, yes, and it all started up again?' Dan knew he was hectoring her but he couldn't bear her silence. He wanted all this out in the open, furious with himself for not having guessed all along that something of the sort existed, even more so for caring so much now that he knew it did.

'Oh, no,' Rebecca exclaimed, sounding surprised, 'it wasn't Ivor that I saw. At least, of course he was there but that wasn't the shock, though he had promised he would never come back, that he would never let it happen. No, I saw – I saw – the child—'

It was the only phrase she found she could use. The child who should have been unrecognisable, anonymous, handed over as a baby like a limb torn away, now seven years old, living in another part of the country, gone, inaccessible. And suddenly there coming towards her through the pedestrians in Rose Street had been the small girl with her own face, exactly as the photos of childhood showed it, the bright cheeks and crisp black hair, the laughter in the dark blue eyes. And even as she had clutched at common sense – it cannot be, it cannot possibly be, it's just like all those torturing moments of believing I saw her in her pram, as a toddler, everywhere about the city for those first desolate years – there had been Ivor behind her, in his face a mixture of spontaneous pleasure and fearful appalled guilt to see her drenching helpless tears.

'What child?' Dan's voice rasped out the words he would have paid even as he said them to have held back.

'My daughter, my baby. I gave her up for adoption, only I refused to take advice. Everyone warned me not to let her go to anyone I knew, never to let there be any links. But I ignored them, I let Ivor have her. He and his wife couldn't have a child and I thought it would be better than knowing she was with strangers, and he promised me faithfully that he would take her away and never bring her back anywhere where I would ever see her. He promised me, and suddenly there she was, quite close to where I lived, somewhere I would often go, looking just like me, coming towards me laughing . . .'

With a violent wrench Dan dragged his arm from under her neck, rolled free and was on his feet. 'I don't want to hear this,' he shouted roughly. 'All this emotional crap. It's your problem, right? You bloody women, you're all the same, like some choking weed that tries to grow all over a man and strangle the life out of him.'

In furious anger he was dragging on his clothes, ignoring Rebecca who, her eyes full of tears, shattered and dumbfounded by his explosion of anger, had struggled up dazedly onto one elbow.

'Dan—'

'And don't fucking cry, that's all I need. Don't bring me your problems, do you hear? Can't you stupid bitches ever, ever just be content with a simple straightforward relationship? But no, as soon as anyone's half decent to you you're all the same, you start in with the messy problems, demanding, depending, clinging . . .'

'Dan, no, it wasn't like that—' She hadn't even been thinking of him, it was nothing to do with him, with them. But trying to speak released the tears and that whipped up his anger even more.

'Oh, for Christ's sake, I've had enough of this, I'm out of here.'

'Dan, don't go, please listen—'

'Listen! Is that all you can think of? Dan, listen, Dan, help me, Dan, give me. Well, not you too, Rebecca, not you. I thought you understood. I thought you had more brains and courage and self-respect, but you're just like all the rest. I knew you'd had enough to cope with tonight and I just wanted to—' To hold back from making love to you because that wasn't what you needed, to comfort and look after you. He couldn't bring himself to use the words, feeling that protective instinct yet again hopelessly betrayed.

He stamped his feet into his boots, scooped up the jacket he'd dropped on the floor, turned to the door.

'Dan, then I'll go, this is your house,' Rebecca cried, shaken and distressed, not understanding the source of his anger but sufficiently aware of this place as his refuge not to want to drive him from it. But he had gone, rattling thunderously down the stairs, and she heard the slam of the outer door. Sobbing, dismayed by this storm which had burst upon her from nowhere, drained by the events of the evening and by the feelings she had finally allowed herself to uncover, she curled up in a tight ball of misery on the no longer welcoming bed.

The consciousness that Dan might be prowling somewhere near at hand, waiting for her to go, stirred her at last, and with pithless limbs she swayed and stumbled into her clothes, even clumsily straightened the bed, telling herself that it was ridiculous to bother but dimly wanting Dan to come back to some sort of comfort. She went awkwardly down the stairs, her legs stiff and heavy, her head throbbing. Should she leave him a note?

'Oh please, don't be a total idiot,' she exclaimed aloud. What on earth was there to say to him? And what made her think for a moment that he would read anything she wrote? She took one look round the small unappealing room with its temporary surface skin of his belongings, and crossed to the door. Dan had warned her and she had in tiredness and weakness let down the barriers. He would never forgive her. It was over.

She waited for a few minutes, letting her eyes accustom themselves to the darkness, shivering as the lovely warmth receded, shivering with a new loneliness, till the sky became grey not black, the line of the water's edge emerged down the slope at her feet, the wooded shape of Ardlonach point was visible against the sky, and she could set off past the row of silent cottages, cross the road and find the just discernible path over the ridge.

*   *   *

She came down with unfortunate timing just as the early departures were in the hall. ('I wonder if you could look for a sock for me. White, oiled wool, rather a good one. You have my address, don't you? Only my wife had hung it over the towel rail to dry and she thinks it may have got mixed up in the laundry. I should be so grateful . . .')

In the kitchen Una, her eyes dark, red-veined caverns in the unhealthy pallor of her face, was draping bacon across a baking tray.

'Hi,' said Rebecca gently, putting a quick arm round her, her own troubles receding into a truer perspective. 'How are you feeling?'

Una leaned her head for a second against Rebecca's, her lips quivering, but said nothing.

'Did you sleep at all?'

'Not really,' Una admitted, pulling another tray towards her and starting on the sausages.

That makes two of us. 'I'll make some coffee.'

'Rebecca, you don't think he'll come back today, do you, and start fighting about it all?'

He. Tony. 'He may. But I don't think that would matter, if you could bear it. You could thrash out a few details, if you're certain you know what you want.'

'I'm certain. I've done a lot of thinking lately, and I was nearly sure what I was going to do. Seeing Tony come waltzing in like that, so sure of himself, so completely insensitive to how anyone else—' Her voice wavered and Rebecca dropped the pouch of coffee filters and turned quickly back towards her.

'No, I'm all right.' Una pulled a couple of green paper towels out of the dispenser and mopped at her eyes with their unfriendly woody roughness. 'I'm honestly all right. The tears just seem to come on their own. I'm not really crying over him.'

'You were marvellous last night—'

'Hi, there. You OK, sweetheart?' Liam came in at the end door. 'Nice one, Dan,' he added in quite a different tone, propping the bergens he was carrying against the steel legs of the worktop where the survivors' food was usually set out.

'What about Dan?' Rebecca could as little have stopped herself asking as a rabbit could have looked away from a stoat.

'He's taken off,' Una said over her shoulder, sliding a tray under the big grill. 'Didn't he say?'

Rebecca felt an icy stillness seize her. Taken off? She remembered his disgusted words, 'I'm out of here.' Had his anger been so deep? But to abandon everything here so near the end, to walk out on his job and his responsibilities. As he'd thrown up the Air Force when he'd felt ill used, she uncomfortably recalled.

'Well, fair enough, I suppose, he's more than due a couple of days off,' Liam was saying easily, beginning rapidly to assemble stores. 'Might have made his mind up a bit sooner, is all. That's what a bit of power does to a man, goes straight to his head, if it doesn't go somewhere else. Ah, Una, you're far too good to these lads, that sausage roll's food fit for kings, so it is . . .'

Had they noticed that she had been frozen to the floor for what seemed like seconds, Rebecca wondered, her hands shaky as she poured water into the coffee machine. So Dan would be back. The relief was enormous but the chill question remained – how would be face her?

'We're not quite so busy now, things are winding down. I half thought I might slip over for a couple of days. Would that be all right?' Rebecca felt desperately in need of comfort yet dreaded the associations of Edinburgh – and she was also aware of a deep resistance to the idea of not being here when Dan came back.

'Oh, darling, need you ask?' Esme exclaimed. 'I'd be absolutely delighted. Come whenever you like, of course. Only I'm afraid I'm a bit tied up for the next few days. Next week might be better. Would that suit you?'

'Um, well . . .' Rebecca hesitated. This wasn't what she'd needed; she always wanted to act immediately, pack, get going.

Esme, hearing with a small frown of concern that unchar-acteristic hesitation, added, 'However, I hadn't said, but I'm hoping to come over to Ardlonach soon anyway, if that's all right with Una and you. Would that work as well? Just after you closed, I thought, so that we could have time together.'

'That would be much better. I'd love it,' Rebecca said in instant relief. It made up her mind for her and meant she needn't go away from here. When Esme came perhaps she would be able to finish what she had so ineptly begun with Dan, safe from fear of rage or misapprehension. And if they could talk here, with time at last to walk, to wander, to share their thoughts, then there was no need to face the ordeal of returning to Edinburgh yet.

'The only thing is,' Esme was saying, sounding less certain than usual, 'I should like to bring a friend this time, if that's all right? Probably the last thing you'll want when you've just shut the doors is more guests in the house but we'll be perfectly happy to fend for ourselves, and we'll still be able to talk, I promise.'

'Of course that will be fine. No problem at all.' But who was the friend? One of the brisk golfing ladies with bobbles on their heels? Or some lank-haired teacher in sagging grey sweat shirt and dipping black skirt? Either way, it wouldn't matter, so long as whoever it was gave her the chance to be alone with her mother occasionally. The prospect of seeing Esme soon gave Rebecca something to cling to in the wretched days after she had so rashly blown her relationship with Dan out of the water.

Chapter Twenty-Five

The two days while Dan was away were strange and unhappy for Rebecca, though work didn't leave much time for thinking about what had happened between them, which was at once infuriating and a help. A lot of guests were leaving after the weekend but several hung around till after lunch in spite of successive squally showers and a most unpromising sky, and those staying didn't stir from the house. Luggage was carried out in rain and a whipping wind. Wet dogs barked on the wrong side of doors. Even the white-panelled office seemed dark and enclosed and depressing. And since they were now into October all the end-of-month accounts had to be run no matter what.

At the back of everyone's mind was the question of Tony. Would he reappear and if he did how would Una react and how would it affect their situation? All of them, whether they knew him or not, had a view but they were discreet enough to keep their comments from Una. She, poor girl, was so worn out that for once she let herself be persuaded to go up after lunch to try to get some sleep, and passed out so obliviously that Rebecca decided to leave her where she was and with Joanie's help saw Megan through a rather chaotic dinner.

Rebecca didn't achieve the escape of sleep so easily herself when she finally hauled herself up the steep stairs at the end of the gruelling day. Essentially a person accustomed to taking problems by the throat she felt unbearably thwarted by being not only at the mercy of Tony's whim but also left in mid-air on her own account, forced to wait to confront Dan, impatient for the chance to rebut his accusations, explain how she had felt, what she had meant. Apologise, even. For, as the day had ground endlessly along, she had come to see how she had deceived herself in pretending that she had merely wanted to share an important part of her past with him. She had seen more and more clearly that she had wanted to draw on his strength, exactly as he had accused her of doing, had even in some formless cowardly way hoped that he would tell her what she should do. Well, she had always wanted a tough man who wouldn't let her manipulate him or push him around, had been delighted to find one, and now she had discovered what that meant. Infringe the terms of their pact and he would walk away without a backward glance.

Would he be openly hostile when he came back? She feared he might. But after the break-up with Trudy he had maintained a friendly relationship. The circumstances were different there, though. He had known Trudy was lonely and had felt guilty because he couldn't give her what she needed and wanted. Also he had minded hurting her when he found himself more strongly drawn to Rebecca herself. Now compassion and guilt were not involved. Rebecca had attempted to break through the agreed boundaries, indulged in the unforgivable weakness of trying to enmesh him in her pain and need. That he could not tolerate.

Well, in practical terms it didn't change much, Rebecca tried to tell herself sensibly, thumping round yet again in the little bed which seemed now impossibly small ever to have held their two substantial bodies. In fact it left her exactly where she had been before, only without the happiness of Dan's company and the great delight of his loving, which it seemed she had barely had time to discover and enjoy.

She tried to distract herself by concentrating on Una's unexpected stand against Tony and the open-ended question of what would happen to Ardlonach itself. But Una, pale and silent, eating nothing, padding about doggedly with a bruised and beaten air, was in no state to discuss the future yet, and also Rebecca knew her own decision had to be made quite independently of what happened to Ardlonach.

Her sense of loss, her anger at her own stupidity, were not soothed by meeting Trudy in Luig the following day, a Trudy in obviously buoyant spirits whose face split into a huge grin at the sight of her.

'Rebecca, hi! Nice to see you! I just nipped out for some junk for lunch, I get so sick of healthy food. Come back and share it with me, shop's shut till two. Can you spare the time? And what's all this about Tony, I'm dying to hear.'

This piece of news, with all its ramifications, kept them busy as they walked back to the shop, jazzed up a couple of uninspired pizzas and put them in the oven, opened a bottle of wine and cleared from the low table a raft of letters, bills and papers so densely interleaved it could be lifted in one piece like a tray.

'So what do you think will happen?' Trudy asked, sliding the bubbling pizzas onto plates she'd left in the oven too long and swearing as she tried to pick them up without a cloth. Rebecca hastily moved the wine bottle and a jar of black olives out of the way as she rushed them to the table.

'I don't think she really knows yet. There hasn't been time to think properly, you know what it's like, we just hurtle from one job to the next. We're nothing like as quiet as we expected to be at this time of year. The good weather's helped, of course.'

'What good weather?' asked Trudy ironically. The rain was battering against the high windows and only a few yards of grey-green choppy water were visible beyond the wall, whose dazzling whitewash was today a thin blotchy grey.

Had Dan hoped to get some climbing? Where had he gone?

'Anyway, she seems definite that she won't get together with Tony again. That really surprised me; I hadn't had any idea she'd moved on that far. But she seems determined that either he lets her buy him out – she already has Daddy lined up to help – or they sell up. After that, I don't know. Run Ardlonach on her own? Big undertaking. Or do what? Or even do nothing, I'm sure she could afford to.'

'What about Tony buying her out?'

'No cash,' Rebecca said briefly, getting her mouth under a long rubbery thread of cheese then having to pick the tail of it off her chin anyway.

'What about the rest of the family then, could they help him?'

'To hear Caroline moaning and wailing you'd think she was in line for family relief or whatever it's called nowadays. Horse relief she probably means, there's no doubt who she'd allow to starve first. No, even between them I don't think the Urquhart clan could grub together that sort of money.' The cousins, she had meant. It struck her that Esme could, and suddenly she found herself longing passionately for her mother's calm sense and discretion and understanding.

'You'd hate Ardlonach to go.'

'I certainly would.' Now more than ever after the work and sharing and fun and the success they'd made of it. The house in its new character seemed almost more precious than the old because of all that had been put into it. Her world would be very empty with Ardlonach gone. But even so she supported Una whole-heartedly in the stand she was taking, and admired her for it.

'So where were you over the weekend?' she asked Trudy idly, as they decided they didn't have time for coffee but would have it anyway. 'Not holed up in this tip, surely?' Even for Trudy the crowded low-ceilinged room was unusually cluttered.

'What a way you have with words, Rebecca,' Trudy chided. 'But no, since you ask, I wasn't in this tip. In fact,' swinging round with an expression of uncontainable delight on her face, 'I haven't been in it much at all lately.'

'Trudy?'

Trudy, hugging the unfilled coffee pot to her big breasts, her expression an engaging mixture of rare shyness and irrepressible joy, nodded, 'I know. It's incredible isn't it, but it really seems to be happening.'

'You and Fitz? Honestly? Oh, Trudy, that's wonderful. When did it happen — and why didn't you let us know, you toad?' Rebecca hugged Trudy, coffee pot and all, in a great uprush of pleasure. This warm, generous girl, who had done her utmost to make the best of life alone, but who of all people was best fitted to be part of a loving and giving relationship, deserved happiness.

'Nothing's settled,' Trudy protested, scrubbing at her eyes with the end of her overshirt and smiling radiantly and damply. 'I mean, we haven't told anyone. We only decided last night. It still seems totally unbelievable to me. All morning I've been in a complete state of dither in the shop, wanting to say to everyone, "Here, take it, have it, it's yours, have two, have a dozen ..."'

'You lunatic. But Trudy, it's wonderful news, I'm so happy for you.'

'Let's have another bottle of wine. I can't be bothered to make coffee—'

'You should have told me straightaway. We should have been celebrating.'

'You don't think I'm mad? I mean, Fitz is such a — you know, so couth and elegant and all that, and well, look at me.' She made a large gesture round the flat which took a coffee mug with it.

'True, you do need a bit of civilising. No, you fool, I don't mean it, stop wailing. You and Fitz will be perfect together — what was that?'

'Oh, my God, the shop. Some totally inconsiderate person trying to get in to buy something. Yell out of the window at them to go away ...'

Driving home, for once not in a tearing hurry, Rebecca

felt first delighted at this prospect opening up for Trudy, then bleakly jealous, then furiously angry at her own meanness. How could she grudge Trudy the warmth and laughter and whirling pace of life she would find with Fitz? They were marvellously suited. But of course she didn't grudge it, it was the best piece of news there could possibly be. It just showed up in unbearable contrast the loneliness she faced herself. Even if Dan came back and they achieved some workable level of contact to see them through the next few weeks there had never been any future there. At best it had been an impaired, limited relationship and the constraints they had agreed on now seemed wholly artificial and unrealistic. Dan was a cold fish, knew it and accepted it; she just hadn't listened.

It was hard to meet him equably, to pretend that nothing had happened, but that clearly was what he wanted. His manner was almost that of the very early days, not quite so hostile, but watchful, withdrawn. He rapidly got through whatever work had to be done in the office, in silence apart from ordinary practical exchanges. To Una and Catriona he was friendlier, but only marginally. The courses, tailing off now anyway, found him daunting and unapproachable and even Liam got his head bitten off if he tried to be too rallying.

Una had told them, courteously going to each member of staff individually in turn, that all would continue as normal till this season's end but that she could tell them nothing yet about next year. They were all philosophical about it, being too tired to care much at present, and even Megan and Joanie, the most permanent element of the staff, shrugged off problems so far away. They were accustomed to working season by season; there would be the dole for now and something would turn up in the spring.

Rebecca had believed herself immune to the sense of isolation that ate into her these days. She had learned, she had thought, not to need interdependence and explicit affection. She had been able to enjoy physical relationships uncluttered by emotion. Only now, when that had been required of her, had she let the two become bound up together. And only now, at this distance, could she see that in fact previously she had not been alone as she had believed; her mother had been there, her love and loyalty never in question, never intrusive, never making demands.

To Rebecca, at odds with herself, dreading more every day the choices she would not be able to evade much longer, everyone in these restless days seemed safely cocooned in their own affairs. Fitz of course was quite out of hand with effervescent happiness and wanted everyone to share it. He had booked the dining-room for an engagement party and seemed likely to invite his entire panel of patients to it unless prevented. Trudy glowed, wrapping everyone up in big hugs on every possible excuse, casual about plans and more and more slapdash about the shop, lucky that her customers were so tolerant.

Catriona, in her newly-gained confidence, had agreed with Rebecca that for the time being help was more urgently needed there than in the hotel and was now dividing her time between them, a new challenge which was good for her and marvellous for Trudy, but which meant that Rebecca was almost as tied as she had been at the height of the season. Even when they shut there would be the books to prepare for audit, stock to take ... I'll have to set a definite date to go, she realised in panic, or I'll go on hiding behind all this for ever.

Una had said she couldn't face discussions or decisions till day-to-day hotel needs were finally behind them. There had been no word from Tony so the immediate dread of his walking in at any moment, making appeals, forcing her into harrying confrontations, had receded.

Thea and Paddy seemed to be moving up a gear in their relationship, Rebecca noticed with slight concern, then wondered if her own abraded emotions made her too ready to see this. But a comment of Joanie's revealed that it was openly acknowledged among the staff.

'Aye, we'll have tears afore long,' Joanie had said darkly one evening, nodding across the Coach-house at the two heads close together at the bar. 'It's no' going to suit that pair to be at the opposite ends of the earth.'

What would they do, Rebecca wondered, feeling a most unfamiliar melancholy grip her. It had always been known and accepted that Thea would go home at the end of the summer, and equally that Paddy had never had the slightest inclination to live anywhere but the west of Scotland, but suddenly it seemed hard to believe that they could part so arbitrarily. And perhaps because of their greater absorption in each other, or perhaps because his gentle single-minded devotion had at last worn her down, Sylvie was much kinder to Bern these days, going out with his group whenever she could, always beside him in any gathering.

Everyone has someone, Rebecca thought, then laughed at the self-pitying platitude. Catriona didn't, Una didn't, Lilias more and more restricted and in pain didn't, and Joanie battling fiercely through life on her own to bring up that huge family certainly didn't, to name but a few. Certainly Liam by this time had a girl from Luig in tow, and young Ellie the farmer's daughter found Ardlonach a useful place to meet a boyfriend her father didn't like, but surely she wasn't so pathetic as to be envious of *them*? She wished she could believe it.

One thing was certain, the engagement party wasn't going to be easy to get through in this frame of mind, and Rebecca winced to contemplate it. It wasn't going to be easy from a practical point of view either, since Fitz was now insisting that the entire staff should be guests.

'What does he think we're going to do, get in outside caterers?' Rebecca demanded irritably.

'Oh, no, that would be horrible,' Una and Trudy instantly protested. 'We can't do that.'

'But even keeping that night clear of other bookings he still wants us to feed about seventy people and most of them very reasonably want to stay the night so that they don't have to drive.'

'He just wants everyone to have a wonderful time,' Trudy explained fatuously and unhelpfully.

'We'll have a buffet,' Una said with decision. 'Everything can be done beforehand. Some of us can easily put through the washing up afterwards, there shouldn't be many pots to worry about. All the rooms will be ready, we needn't make down beds and next day we can just do the ones we need.'

'But Una, how on earth can we serve breakfast without setting up the dining-room? And all the other rooms will have to be tidied up. You know how much work is involved in a party this size.'

'We'll do a self-service breakfast down in the Coach-house,' Una declared, inspired. 'No one will be able to face much anyway if Fitz's party turns out the way he wants it to.'

'Our party,' said Trudy.

They laughed at her. 'It's Fitz who's got the bit between his teeth,' Rebecca assured her. 'You're nowhere. Better just sit back and enjoy it.'

'We've got all the set-up for making coffee and so on down there already,' Una was continuing, undeflected. 'Sockets for toaster and grill. We can set most of it up in the afternoon, take all the cereals and marmalade and so on down, then keep everyone out.'

'And make porridge in a haybox,' mocked Rebecca, nevertheless impressed by Una's positive approach.

'That's exactly what we'll do,' exclaimed Una. 'And we'll explain to everyone there's no real hotel service and charge them a cut rate. It'll work beautifully.'

Was this the Una who had been so terrified to find herself opening for Easter without her feckless husband?

'We'll do it,' Rebecca declared, abandoning her teasing. 'It'll work a treat. Good for you, Una.'

It was a memorable evening, the big house thronged and

buzzing and humming with music and laughter and voices. If only Esme had been able to come over, but Esme had been strangely hard to get hold of in the past few weeks, with her mobile either not working or switched off, and by the time Rebecca had managed to contact her she already had something on. She was still planning to come over when the hotel closed, however, and Rebecca consciously turned to that comforting thought as she stood alone watching the first, just within the bounds of good manners, descent on the buffet.

She felt hopelessly outside the scene, with something of the aloofness she had so determinedly cultivated during the Edinburgh years. Then it had made her feel safe, providing her with an armour no one could pierce. Now she felt isolated, excluded and for an uneasy moment once more unable to reconcile Ardlonach past and present. The big drawing-room had been cleared for dancing, just as it so often had been down through the years, and standing in the doorway watching the swinging circles she felt tears irrationally rise to recall the family sets for the reels and strathspeys, remembering the thrill of waiting for her turn, the delight of responding to the beat which began the figure that took her into the dance.

Don't be a fool, she told herself contemptuously, it was just boring old uncles and aunts, maddening cousins you quarrelled with half the time. But nothing could spoil the nostalgic picture, the later memories of evenings with John Irvine and Donald and Stephen there, Lilias with Gerald, and always Esme. For the first time in her life Rebecca had a glimpse, poignant and piercing, of how her mother must have felt to watch that family dancing with Francis gone. I must have been blind, completely insensitive, perpetually buried in my own affairs, she thought with a new shocked humility.

However, she was not left to watch many dances, and she took part with every appearance of pleasure. She filled in the gaps between with quick bouts of work and so, she gratefully saw, did every member of the staff, including the instructors.

Fitz himself, while apparently intent on dancing at least once with every female in the room, still found time to leap around every so often filling glasses, carrying laughter and an upsurge of happy sound with him like a Mexican wave.

Dan was there. Rebecca had not been sure he would come and then had been angry for tormenting herself over it. A decision about whether or not he came to Fitz and Trudy's engagement party could have nothing to do with her. And why shouldn't he come? His affair with Trudy was history. He and Fitz were good friends. Of course he was at the party.

He didn't dance with Rebecca. She bitterly resented being put through the hoops of hope, doubt and rejection as helplessly as a teenager but was unable to protect herself from the torturing sequence. She took a tray of glasses into the semi-darkened kitchen where the dishwasher roared and gushed, and stood there under the single striplight to wait for its cycle to finish. She slid out the clean rack, slid in the glasses, turned the switch to start up the thrumming again — and still stood there, head bowed, acknowledging her tiredness, her disappointment, her hapless sense of not belonging, which here of all places and on this evening crowded with friends, vibrant with happiness, was so bizarre and hard to take.

She made herself go back. This was Trudy's evening; she couldn't turn her back on it. Pushing open the swing door she heard the music of a strathspey she loved, the Glasgow Highlanders. As she reached the door of the drawing-room Dan was leading Catriona down the middle. He danced beautifully. It could still surprise her. Without warning her throat ached, her eyes stung. If only, this evening, he had allowed them to move back at least to friendship, to an acknowledgement that they had cared for each other. She had not done anything so dreadful, surely, that he should turn his back on her so completely. She had made no claims on him, asked for nothing beyond a few moments' listening. She had made no attempt to alter the status quo between them. How cold he was, to be able to slam the doors so implacably on everything they had enjoyed together, the companionship, the talk, the laughter and loving.

She could not sing tonight, though they clamoured for her and she saw Trudy's puzzled disappointment. She wished she could but knew that to stand up before them all, remembering what Dan had said about how her singing had moved him at the ceilidh, where their wonderful affair had begun, would hurt too much. She would not be able to get through it. Perhaps Fitz understood something of the sort — it would not have escaped him that Dan was treating her as badly or worse than he had treated Trudy — for he was on his feet, crossing to the band and the next moment his great voice was rolling out in 'Pickin' Time' sending himself up as usual, and in a moment everyone was tapping and nodding and beating time like happy clockwork dolls.

Rebecca slipped away, suddenly in urgent need of refuge. The library was usually a forgotten backwater on occasions like this but tonight a pair of bodies was entwined on the sofa. They didn't ever know she'd come in. She opened the door to the stone stairs but before she started down heard the click of a ping-pong ball and someone call 'eighteen fifteen' and someone else start arguing. The obvious retreat would be her own room and for a moment she was tempted to slip up through the quiet cool house and go to bed, hide away, not reappear at all. But she checked herself. It would be selfish to leave all the clearing up to Una and not very friendly to Trudy and Fitz to disappear. How could she solemnly undress, get into bed, alone when everyone else was gloriously in the swing of the party downstairs, sorry for herself, indulging herself, pathetic. She wouldn't give in now.

Going back to the drawing-room she saw Clare tucked up in a corner, forbidden to dance any more by both husband and host, and negotiating a way round the dancers went over to sit with her.

It wasn't until the party had wound to its close and the staff had gone weaving over to their quarters after a final drink that anger finally took over. Rebecca hadn't had much to drink herself. She had been far too busy for one thing. So this anger was cold, logical and very precise.

Dan had behaved tonight in a wholly unacceptable way. She had overstepped the bounds he'd laid down in the matter of personal confidences and he was treating her as though she had made some exorbitant demand on him. Tonight had been a warm, generous gathering of friends to celebrate Fitz and Trudy's happiness and he had superimposed on it his own emotional hang-ups. He had no right to behave in such a way.

Rebecca turned back down the stairs, unlocked the office and took her car keys off the hook. No picking her way along dim paths by starlight or torchlight tonight. She would have this out with him, now.

Chapter Twenty-Six

Dan was still downstairs. He had not drawn his curtains and was standing with his back to the fireplace where a small electric fire stood in the corner of the hearth. He stood feet apart, big shoulders hunched, head jutting forward, thumbs hooked in his belt, staring at nothing, his face sombre.

Rebecca didn't waste any time on assessing his mood or the scene. She took one look in at the window then reached to thump on the door. Dan's frown when he opened it didn't surprise her and didn't deter her. Actually Dan was so conscious of the gulf he had created between them that he assumed some emergency was on hand when he saw her there on his step.

'What is it? What's happened? Something wrong with the survivors?' They had been politely requested to make themselves scarce for the evening and entrusted with the minibus keys so that they might do so. Dan was already reaching for his jacket.

'Not the survivors and nothing's wrong. I've got something to say to you, that's all.'

Rebecca looked so grim herself, her tone was so belligerent, that Dan had stood aside to let her come in before he realised what he was doing. Rebecca hadn't taken argument about it into her reckoning, and her angry arrogant determination that if she intended to talk then talk she would was very compelling.

'You behaved like a total bastard to me tonight,' she opened up fiercely, swinging round on Dan as soon as she was well into the dismal little room.

'Rebecca—'

She didn't wait to hear. 'You didn't have to treat me like that. I don't care what personal problems you've got, you don't have to be so bloody hostile. All I ever did was try to share something I care about deeply because I felt we knew each other well enough for that. It's something I've never talked about to anyone, ever, not even to my mother, though I suppose to tell you that will make you run for your life again. It didn't mean I thought I had some claim on you, or that I was trying to worm my way into the locked recesses of your being, if indeed they exist, and if you didn't like it it really would have been quite enough to say so. To behave as though I've become some loathed enemy is completely out of order and to do it tonight, which was supposed to be a happy time—'

'Because people were there to see, you mean?' Dan wasn't used to being attacked and snapped at this implication instinctively to divert her fire.

'What?' Rebecca, halted in mid-tirade, gaped at him. What other people might have observed or concluded hadn't so much as entered her mind. 'No, you fool, that has nothing to do with it. This is about you and me. We were friends, we were lovers, and I don't accept that you can behave towards me as you did tonight. You can't go on hiding for ever behind that pathetic phrase of yours, calling yourself an emotional retard and imagining that lets you out of all responsibility. It's certainly no excuse for being cruel. There are still things like kindness and friendship and liking, in case you haven't discovered them, and I feel hurt and outraged about what you've done to me and I wanted you to know I do. That's it.'

Before Dan could draw breath to respond to this forceful torrent of words Rebecca had swung round to the door, eyes flashing and jaw set, an aura of vigorous and unmollified anger swirling round her like the folds of a cloak.

'Rebecca!' Dan leapt swiftly to stop her, grasping her arm.

She shook off his hand. 'Nothing more to say.' She had her hand on the door knob.

Dan slammed the door shut with his shoulder before she had opened it more than a couple of inches.

'There's plenty to say.'

They confronted each other, both breathing rather quickly, both rigidly still, two strong-willed people equally aware of being poised on some knife-edge, but neither able to gauge what the other would say or do next. It was Dan who deliberately let himself relax first, like a dog who has decided battle is an unwise choice.

'OK, I behaved like a bastard this evening,' he said, sounding more aggressive than he felt because that was the only way he knew how to respond when someone was having a go at him. And she'll never know how amazing those eyes are, he thought in spite of his defensive anger, wide, challenging, boring into his. He read in them, with a vivid consciousness of what he had lost blended with a reluctant appreciative amusement, her decision not to waste time pursuing that self-evident fact.

'I want to tell you something,' she said brusquely. 'Or rather, I want to finish what I started telling you before. It won't be of the slightest interest to you, I'm not even sure why I'm bothering, but it seems for some reason to matter to me that you should have the complete story, the true picture.'

Her tone was curt, clinical. Although she said this was important, she sounded as though it was some insignificant detail she wished to put straight. But Dan, not understanding her mood, exasperated at his own reflex reaction of anger, wanting only to keep her there till they got things sorted out between them, sensed something vital coming, something he might not like but could not evade.

'Well, at least sit down,' he suggested, sounding more impatient than he had meant to. Conciliation was not familiar territory for Dan. He moved away from her towards the fire, inwardly cursing his own ineptness. He gestured to a mean little wooden-armed sofa with thin concave foam cushions covered in ginger tweed. It faced the fireplace and seated two. If she sat there Dan would have to sit beside her, or stand over her, Rebecca realised. She stayed where she was, just inside the door. An icy draught twined round her ankles.

'My child wasn't adopted by her natural father,' she said abruptly. She knew it was futile and ridiculous, of relevance to no one but herself, to make this attempt to put the record straight, but some dogged inner compulsion drove her on. 'Ages ago I was engaged to a man called Ivor Dundas who later married someone else. They couldn't have a baby, tried everything . . .' Having rushed into her story she found, frighteningly, that she couldn't go on.

Dan, very still, said quietly after a tense pause when she could feel her blood pulsing, hear the purr of the fire like a roar, 'Go on, I want to hear.'

She didn't tell it well, was in fact remarkably incoherent for her and Dan knew that was a measure of her racked feelings. He didn't interrupt, made no movement, piecing together as best he could her halting account of that chance meeting with Ivor when she herself was pregnant by another man, on the precise day when Ivor had been told by the adoption society that because he and his wife had once had a temporary separation their application had been turned down. It had been ironic, though Rebecca didn't enlarge on this part of the story, since the separation had been a direct result of Rosalind's grief when she had found she would never be able to conceive. But no one had listened, the decision was final. Ivor had been pretty well at his wit's end that day, at the prospect of going home to tell Rosalind, and at the prospect of starting the whole process again with another agency, perhaps being turned down again, certainly looking at a lengthy waiting time.

They had talked for hours, Rebecca in her turn telling him about her own situation. Ivor had wondered, as Dan immediately wondered, why she of all people had not terminated the pregnancy. Ivor had asked. She had told him a great deal more about her disillusionment and grief than she revealed now.

'We'd expected to get married, or at least set up house together,' was all she told Dan. 'Then the father decided he couldn't face it, too late for me to do much about it.' Her succinct dismissal of this betrayal warned Dan not to offer comment or sympathy.

Rebecca's mind went back to that strange day, the hours of absorbed cathartic talk with Ivor in the little boulangerie with its spindly black-and-white furniture, the lozenge-shaped view of the castle high up through rain-streaked windows, the disregarded background coming and going, the smell of wet coats.

Dan watched her, aware of his own tension, of sick milling hope which even apprehension about where this was leading them could not quench.

'Everyone warned me you should never give your baby up for adoption to someone you know. They were quite right, of course,' Rebecca resumed tonelessly, her eyes on the small clutter of objects on the table in the middle of the room, a large screwdriver and a tiny red-handled one, a couple of apples, a sheath knife, a coaster with a picture of the Loch Ness monster's humps. 'I was pig-headed as usual and did it my way. There should never be any possibility of a way back ...'

She had gone far away from this room, from him, Dan knew, and seeing her resolutely gather her thoughts, control the distress that had sharpened her voice, make herself go on calmly, he felt more love and admiration for her than he ever had before. She went on tersely, determined to get this done, 'Ivor lives down in the Borders, he has a small estate there. He promised me, he absolutely promised me, that he would never bring her to Edinburgh, that I could live there safely, knowing I would never by any chance meet them. I trusted him. I really believed he would do that for me.' Her voice wavered up, the shock of that day returning. She bent her head, not even aware that she had stopped telling this out loud. He had not telephoned, he had not even come alone, but had been walking towards the flat with the child, his own need so overriding that he ignored not only their agreement but her complete defencelessness and the pain this would bring her.

'Of course he thought by then I would have got over it all. It had been more than seven years.'

No, Dan thought with perceptive compassion, you don't get over that.

'He came because Rosalind, his wife, had died. I hadn't even heard, had no idea. Pulmonary embolism, he said. I think it means a clot of blood in the lung. We didn't talk about it. He had come because—' Now she couldn't go on. Buried all these months through cowardice and fear, the huge question stared her in the face. She wasn't even aware of Dan moving towards her.

'Why had he come?' he asked gently. Perhaps because for once his own fear of inadequacy was in abeyance, subordinate to Rebecca's need, perhaps because he truly cared about her pain, there was something in his voice which reached and steadied her.

'He came to suggest that I went to live with him, married him. To be with Sophie; to be a mother to Sophie.' She looked up at him now, distress naked in her face. 'I *am* her mother!' she cried, and he felt his throat constrict.

'Oh, Rebecca, come here.' Very gently, alert to any hint of withdrawal on her part, he put his arms round her and to his immense relief she accepted them, bowing her forehead against his chest, making an effort to get her voice under control again.

'There are lots of things to be said for the idea, of course,' she went on after a moment, trying to sound briskly practical. 'Ivor and I were very fond of each other once. I'm sure he's a marvellous father. And it would be a wonderful place to live, a wonderful way of life. I'm supposed to be letting him know what I've decided when I go back. I told him I was committed here for the summer. Anyway,' straightening up but not meeting Dan's eyes, assuming with a huge effort a dismissive tone, 'that's it. I just wanted you to know. God knows why, idiotic really, you're the last person who wants to be bored with all this stuff, but anyway, thanks for listening.'

Dan kept his arms loosely round her. 'That's not all though, is it? Come on, I'm not letting you go like this. Have a drink or a coffee. At least sit down and get warm.'

'I don't want to keep you up any longer. Oh, God, all that clearing up tomorrow. Well, actually in a few hours,' she groaned. 'I'd better go.'

She seemed to have forgotten her original reason for coming. Or had this been the real reason? Whatever it was the implications filled Dan with a deep churning excitement which he did his best to put aside.

'You haven't talked about Sophie,' he said.

She stared at him for a moment as though not allowing herself to understand him, then though scarcely a muscle of her face moved he saw it slowly fill and crumple with grief. He wanted to enwrap her, physically protect her from this pain. He drew her with him across the room to the paltry welcome of the cheap sofa and folded her close.

'Come on, Rebecca,' he said again. 'Talk to me, tell me. How do you feel about Sophie?'

'I don't know,' she said fiercely, in a muffled agonised whisper. 'I just don't know. And I should, I'm certain I should. She's my child, my baby.'

'But not a baby now,' he said, following her lead, terrified of doing more harm than good.

'I don't *know* her!' Rebecca exclaimed passionately, jerking up out of his arms and running a hand back through her hair in a familiar gesture of frustration. 'She's been an image, an idea, all through these years. All my feelings for her were tied up with whether I'd done the right thing, with guilt and regret. I imagined her at Ivor's house, doing all the normal things, playing in the garden, riding, going to school, with her friends, all of that. But it was an imaginary child in those pictures, a child who didn't know me, a child who had a mother and father and grandparents and relations and a whole background of people and places I don't know. To go walking in on her life now would be just like any other stranger walking into it. Any stepmother. And if it was a stepmother, if Ivor met someone he loved and who loved him, they would have a real marriage not the pretence of one, not some shadow of a refurbished affair. It's appalling, but I don't know what to do any more than I did the day I met them, Ivor with the little girl who looked exactly as I used to look, or the day he proposed all this. I can't believe I can't decide. Am I an appalling moral coward? Am I unnatural? Wouldn't any normal mother simply take this chance at once?'

'I don't think you're abnormal except in the sense that you are capable of looking at it so honestly and subjectively,' Dan said calmly. 'You can see that for Sophie, who has no knowledge or memory of you, there can be no bond, and that's very brave of you. You can see the distinction between what you think you should feel and what you do feel. For you, just as for the child, there has been no actual person to love, only the image. I think the decision hinges on how you feel about – him – and by the sound of it you've seen that already.'

Rebecca leaned back against his arm and the first glimmer of a smile appeared on her taut face. 'For a man who's supposed to be bad at feelings you're pretty perceptive,' she remarked shakily.

The observation returned them abruptly to awareness of themselves, of the issues between them, and each found a small thrill of anticipation in that.

'You needed to talk about it to someone,' Dan said, keeping carefully to the matter-of-fact. 'You've a hard decision to make.' The excitement of a moment ago oozed away as he contemplated all that was on offer for her. Was there really any question of what she'd choose?

'You've been so good to listen, Dan. Particularly as I'd just been a bit uncomplimentary about your behaviour tonight.'

'You certainly came in loaded for bear,' Dan assented, and tension was released in laughter. 'Let's get the kettle on.'

'I really should go.' Rebecca didn't sound as though she meant it and in fact the last thing she wanted at that moment was to get into her car and drive back to her solitary little room.

'The night's in tatters anyway,' said Dan. 'What are you worrying about, you'll be able to sleep in November.'

'True.' She accepted the little stock joke and her coffee gratefully.

Dan didn't sit down beside her. Instead he prowled away to the window, then back to the fireplace to stand half turned away from her with his hand on the high mantelpiece, his face hidden.

She watched him, frowning. What was coming now?

'Listen, that night I flipped my lid when you started in about all this,' he began abruptly, and she let the way he'd put it pass. She unwrapped her burning fingers from her mug and put the other hand round it carefully, as though to think of this would protect her for a moment from what was coming.

'I've got a kid,' said Dan, his face still turned away and she found herself gaping at him, dumbfounded. 'A little girl. Five. She's with her mother.'

'But Dan – I didn't know – do you ever see her?' Rebecca asked, floundering.

'No.' A harsh rasp of sound above the faint buzz of the electric fire.

Without taking her eyes off him Rebecca put her mug on the floor and got up, moving to stand at his shoulder, slipping her arms round him, pressing her face against him. 'Oh, Dan, I'm sorry. I had no idea.'

He nodded mutely, not looking at her. She held him, leaning

lightly against him, tears unexpectedly in her eyes. This lesson could be repeated a hundred times and one never seemed to grasp it – everyone has hidden wounds.

After a few moments Dan turned, lifting his arm over her head so that he could put it round her, drawing her against him more comfortably but hiding his face still. She realised with shock and tenderness it was so that she would not see his tears.

'Let's go upstairs,' he said roughly.

For one panicky instant she resisted. That room had been where Dan had so violently flung away from her. She hated it, it was inimical, ugly. But at once the thought had gone, lost and unimportant. This was about Dan, his need, his vulnerability, not about four walls.

At last warm and close and safe they talked, or at first Dan talked, spilling out the hidden things that gnawed at him and had driven him to build a shell of aggression and contempt and self-sufficiency around him.

'I hadn't even realised you were married,' Rebecca said, having had time to prepare a light interested tone to muffle the jolt this fact had given her.

'Twice,' Dan said tersely. 'Taken for a mug twice, would you believe. Yeah, well.' He gave a little grunt of disparagement. 'First one was bog-standard service disaster. Meet in a club, never do anything together but drink and dance and screw, then bloke gets posted abroad and wifie's left to hoover the married quarter. She stuck it for a month, give her her due.'

Rebecca made no comment, sensing that this was not important to him, bitter though he still was about it.

'So then I did it all again, didn't I? Only this time I took my time, was engaged for a year just about, spelled out all the service stuff, particularly about being in the Regiment. You can't pick and choose where you go and most tours are unaccompanied, it goes with the job. I even got my mates to talk to her, and their wives, any that had stuck around. She was adamant that she knew the score, wouldn't mind, would be perfectly happy on her own — would be supportive. Good word, supportive. Well, she was still there when I came back from detachment in the Falkland Islands, and Lee had arrived by then. It's nice walking back into your quarter and finding your wife and kid there and the 'Welcome Home, Daddy' banner up and all that jazz. Glad I found out because it never happened again. Next time she was at her Mum's — she's there still for all I know.' The bitterness had turned to savagery and Rebecca put a hand on his chest, and was relieved when his hand at once came to cover it.

'She didn't bother about a divorce till I got into that court-martial mess, then she started running around like a chicken with its head off shrieking unfit parent, abusive husband and Christ knows what.' He put up a hand to his face, thumb and forefinger pressed against his eyelids. 'Oh, shit, you don't want to hear all this. That's why I went ape when you started to tell me about Sophie, that's all. Just so as you understand.'

'I want to hear it all.' Years of silence, so like her own. Who could understand this better than she?

'Nothing new about it.'

'Tell me.'

'Oh, she wanted out. Had another bloke only she was clever about that, I hadn't the faintest idea till a few months ago. She wanted a divorce only she couldn't leave it at that, she wanted to keep me away from Lee for good as well. And she succeeded, used that death in the live-firing exercise—'

'But she couldn't possibly! It had nothing to do with you as a father. And you were cleared.' In her consternation at this incredible injustice Rebecca pulled herself up on her elbow to look into his face.

She felt him shrug. 'Oh, there'd been plenty of shouting matches. I'd hit her a couple of times, nothing serious. She used to come at me with her nails, half out of her mind, I'd give her a slap to calm her down.' His indifferent tone told Rebecca better than any protestations how precisely accurate this was.

'Mum was there to tell all, of course. And the court-martial was still pending. She found someone to listen. Believe me there's always some half-baked, half-trained do-gooder to listen to the mother.'

'But she couldn't legally prevent you from seeing your daughter on grounds like those,' Rebecca protested, her mind refusing to accept such a proposition.

'I gave in,' Dan said briefly. 'Just wanted to get clear of the whole boiling. It'll probably be better for Lee in the long run anyway. Jesus, what kind of affection and stability could I give a child? And on the practical level, I don't even have a permanent job, I don't have a home to offer her, a future.'

Without difficulty Rebecca picked the kernel out of that. 'You know you're capable of giving affection. Your problem seems to have been that no one returned it.'

Dan was silent. Rebecca felt the strong beat of his heart under her hand. Somewhere behind the importance of what they were saying to each other a part of her rejoiced to be close to this magnificent body again, to feel his warm hand spread on her back, his powerful thigh under her drawn-up knee.

'Dan, all this business about being emotionally crippled is nonsense and you know it. It's just a blind. You just don't intend to get hurt again.' Even as she said it she realised how justified he must feel about guarding his emotions where she was concerned, in view of what she had just told him. Also, with a strange jar, the thought occurred to her that she was crippled in precisely this way herself, though she had not been honest enough to recognise it as he had done.

'Yes, well look at tonight,' Dan said bleakly. 'I knew I was behaving like a total shit, but I just couldn't handle it. I kept remembering that damned ceilidh and how I felt that night, and how good things had been between us, and the contrast just got to me. Then I was scared to death you'd get up and sing. I knew I'd have to get out if you did, I wouldn't have been able to stand it. Then watching you dancing with other people, and always so busy, chatting and laughing and involved, I didn't know how to break through. I knew I was being a fool, but I'd let us get so far apart. Every day lately I've meant to talk to you, ask you to talk, try and sort things out. Only I didn't see how I could without going into all this stuff and I couldn't face that—'

'Dan, it's all right, I understand and none of that matters now. It truly doesn't. We've both done the same thing, tried to pretend our scars didn't exist. We're both old enough to know that can't be done, and that's where we went wrong. You can't make arbitrary boundaries in relationships, saying so far and no further. We came up against them sooner than we expected, and then made a mess of dealing with that too. We were selfish and cowardly and childish.'

'Well, thanks for making all that clear,' Dan remarked, sounding happier than he had for a long time.

Rebecca laughed, swooping to kiss him lightly. His hand came up instantly behind her head and pressed her mouth back to his. In another second he was rolling her over and moving on top of her. Rebecca had just time to be amused – for the serious matter of the first love-making of the night Dan couldn't endure being in any other position – before sensation caught her up and coherent thought fled.

Chapter Twenty-Seven

The fortnight that remained of the season seemed to Rebecca in memory to stretch out for weeks, full of happiness and packed with events, while at the time it flashed by with a speed that made her long to clutch at the days, savour each hour. In retrospect it glowed with sun and autumn colour, though in fact for the first few days gales scoured the coast, driving white-capped waves up Loch Luig, sending huge breakers to smash against the cliffs of the island and whirl up in flying wind-torn patterns of white spume. Even at sheltered Ardlonach the garden received a battering which destroyed its rich end-of-summer beauty, chimneys went the wrong way and doors whipped out of people's fingers and slammed with a series of maddening thuds throughout the house.

Dan devised programmes which gave the final courses something more useful to do than squat in wet bivouacs with the wind howling over their heads or trog blindly across rain-soaked moors, and he was happy to do so since this kept them, and him, nearer to home.

He was high on an exuberance almost equal to Fitz's, though more reserved about it, and in his case too it was mixed with incredulous relief and an obscure sense of some dreaded test having been passed and left behind for ever. The days after he thought he'd wrecked his chances with Rebecca by allowing his anger and frustration to get the better of him, days filled with bitter regret, unable to see any way to resolve the situation he had created, seemed now a dark muddled dream. Talking, on each side, had opened sluice gates long closed; now they both wanted passionately to share, communicate, express the buried doubts and guilt to someone trusted to understand.

In each other's arms in Rebecca's bed, or down at Dan's cottage where although the comfort was meagre they could be sure of peace, or holed up by the library fire in the late evenings when after a day of coughing and belching it had settled to a warm red glow, or, when the gales relented, out on the hill or down at the jetty taking the Firefly out of the water after a last visit to the island, they talked unstoppably. Talked about the past, each privately marvelling at the simple way in which memories that had ravaged and harried them could step back, assume a new perspective, be looked at objectively and accepted as over and done with.

And they talked about the present, about the house Fitz was buying, about Catriona's wilder and often very funny aberrations in the shop, about Ellie begging to be allowed to stay on and work for nothing rather than go home to help her mother, who evidently drove her even harder than Rebecca did, or more pertinently be once more under her father's stern eye. Mona had gone back to her waster husband for another round of lager-inspired sex, conception, abuse, fights, police at the door, children into care and dippings into the public purse. Joanie shrugged about this, prophesying from long and bitter experience, 'She'll be back, just you see.'

They talked of the future only as it concerned Una and Ardlonach, each tentative still about it in relation to themselves. Tony, as Rebecca had told Dan he would, had run to Caroline, who had made one or two illogical, emotive and insensitive phone calls to Una on his behalf. During one of them Una had handed the receiver to Rebecca and simply walked away, trembling but definite. Rebecca, impressed, had let Caroline finish a long bossy speech about tolerance (I'm surprised she's heard of it, Rebecca marvelled) then said, 'Una's gone, Caroline. She got tired of listening to you. If you've anything constructive to say, say it to me.'

'Oh, Rebecca, you're impossible! I'm sure you put Una up to these things. She always used to be such a sweet gentle girl.'

'A malleable and long-suffering one anyway.'

'Well, since you're there there is something I'd like to say to you, as a matter of fact.' Rebecca pulled a face at Dan, who had looked up from his analysis of Tony's marketing results, grinning to see her sit down at the desk and square her shoulders for battle.

'Get on with it then,' she ordered Caroline.

'Well, if Una persists in this outrageous idea of buying Tony out, have you thought of the repercussions for the family?'

Rebecca's eyes gleamed. She said nothing.

'What I mean is,' Caroline's voice, since she was deprived of the encouragement she had hoped for, rose appreciably. 'Ardlonach won't be In The Family any more. That surely must have occurred to you. It is Tony's, after all, not Una's. She's only an Urquhart by marriage.'

'Just so. Tony married her and now she has a wife's rights to their joint property. They can sell up and divide the profits and then Ardlonach won't belong to an Urquhart at all.'

This simple fact seemed beyond Caroline's conception. 'But it's really Tony's. Una couldn't possibly do that. And I mean, think how it will affect the rest of us.'

'Worrying about her free holidays,' Rebecca said to Dan in disgust, covering the mouthpiece with a token gesture but not bothering to lower her voice.

'Rebecca, you know how George and I are placed, we're simply living from hand to mouth at present, I don't know when we shall ever get our heads above water, and the twins are no better off though I must say I always thought gynaecologists did terribly well but it seems not according to Leonie, and of course Malcolm likes to spend every penny he gets, what he and Fran go through on one trip abroad would pay my feed bills for a year, and then mother always pretends she's broke though I don't see how she can have got through everything father left her and she certainly hasn't passed much on to us yet, though George thinks she probably shouldn't leave it much longer. However, be that as it may, what we were thinking, I mean we all agree—'

'I do believe she's going to get to the point,' Rebecca remarked, holding the receiver a few inches away from her and raising her eyebrows at it.

'—well, you're family too and you care about Ardlonach as much as any of us. We were thinking if we all got together, round the table you know, and thrashed something out—'

Dan grinned more broadly, leaning back in his chair to watch the wicked pleasure fill Rebecca's face.

'Rebecca, are you still there? Well, you might say something, this isn't easy for me you know, I always seem to be left with all the disagreeable jobs . . .'

'Talking to me, you mean? No, Caroline, go on, I'm listening, just get on with it.'

'Well, we just thought it would be such a crime to let it all go, particularly when Tony's making such a success of it—'

'*What?*' Rebecca mouthed at Dan.

'—he tells me his plans for the activity centre have worked out brilliantly, says it can't fail to be successful and the whole place is really taking off at last.'

Rebecca's eyes had now narrowed and her jaw was truculently set. Dan watched her with enjoyment.

'Go on,' was all she said.

'If we all put in whatever we could, only I must say school fees have gone through the roof, what we originally set aside is laughable and I know Fran and Leonie find the same, but of course you don't have any such drain on your finances, and we thought Esme might be interested too. It would be an excellent investment, Tony's sure. We're just tossing ideas around at this stage, naturally, and what we all want most is for Una and Tony to make a go of it, a little give and take on both sides and all that, but if they *don't*, I mean if that's absolutely out of the question, this could be Plan B. We do all love the place so much ...'

Rebecca lowered the receiver and studied it as though it personally was responsible for this flood of banalities. Dan would not have been surprised if she had cracked it in two on the side of the desk. She pursed her lips, closed her eyes, made sure her temper was under control, then lifted it again to say briefly, 'Get Tony to do his own talking, right, Caroline?' before clicking it down with careful restraint.

Dan raised a forearm to protect his head. 'Don't take it out on me,' be begged.

'My bloody cousins, cooking up nice little schemes so that they can continue to enjoy "the family home" for a couple of visits a year apiece. What have they ever put into it, what do they contribute, what do they know about the work that goes into it? And what about some acknowledgement of what Una's done, or some hint of concern for her? Do you know, I'd rather see the place sold outright than let that lot get their greedy hands on it. And they're even thinking of tapping mother for cash just because she's had the gumption to get up and work all her life instead of depending on father's money ...'

Even as she let her hot indignation spill out a small part of Rebecca's brain noted that it seemed quite natural to talk of these family and financial matters to Dan, and equally he seemed to accept that she should. There was an unexpected comfort in this simple discovery.

'And to think Caroline actually started off by talking to Una about a reconciliation. What absolute bullshit, they want Una out, they want to make sure of Ardlonach for themselves.'

'As a hotel, as a going concern?'

'Oh, yes, even they will realise it can't just stand empty between visits. They'll send Tony back to run it. They've got to do something with him. I can't see him being much use in a training stables though I suppose he could drink gin with the owners and perhaps whitewash a loose-box occasionally, if loose-boxes get whitewashed these days.'

But fume and long for decision and action as Rebecca might, ultimately everything hinged on Una and Una had asked for time, which with loving sympathy and affection her immediate circle was willing to give her. Rebecca therefore with great self-discipline put the whole issue on hold and allowed herself to enjoy this interim of happiness, happiness with that edge to it of things ending which made it all the more intense.

Her own decision still lay in wait but she felt that many doors had opened in her thoughts and at last she could honestly examine motives and dispense with conditioned thinking. My baby, my child, my daughter; these words she could now acknowledge as emotional triggers which after all these years had no real meaning. It was time to think of Sophie as she was, a person in her own right, established and integrated in a setting Rebecca herself was now invited to enter as a stranger.

A relationship, marriage even, for that seemed to be what Ivor naïvely hoped for, embarked upon with a man who long ago had been her lover (God, I can't even remember what he was like, can't have been too riveting), in order that Sophie should have two parents, which seemed the sum of Ivor's thinking, could be no more than an intellectual compromise. A few months ago it would merely have meant exchanging one makeshift existence for another, but at least including the most fundamental bond of all, that of mother and child. Now there had been a glimpse of something else, a revelation of her own capacity for feelings Rebecca had not known existed.

Yet there was no way forward here either. In spite of the deeper understanding she and Dan had achieved, all that had really made clear was why there could be no shared future. Their affair belonged to the present, to these particular circumstances, to this season arbitrarily rushing to its close, and for the brief time left to them they gave themselves up to simple physical delight in each other.

Sometimes, inevitably, Rebecca's mind would swoop forward to tempting images of living with Dan, renting a cottage for the winter near the climbing lodge so that he could live out with her, or sharing the Inshmore cottage with him next summer if the survival school was still in existence. She even got as far as wondering, since Esme would be appearing very soon, what her mother would think of him, and realised that of course Esme would make no comment. Then, always honest, she considered what had lain behind the question. She and Dan came from different backgrounds, had been educated differently, had led different lives. If that concerned Esme at all it would be on the practical level of whether it would become a source of friction.

It was a useful exercise for Rebecca to look at the affair in this perspective, allowing her to distance herself from her absorbed obsession with Dan, his touch, his voice, his fit powerful body and just as importantly in the humour she could tease out of him, lighting his dourness and giving him a totally new air. She came to the conclusion, assessing their relationship with cool objectiveness, that in temperament, attitude and character she had never found anyone who suited her half so well. As an organised, punctual and energetic person she had suffered a good deal of frustration in her life from the casual, disorderly, last-minute scrambling of most of the people she knew or worked with. It was a surprisingly satisfying basis for a relationship to find that kind of frustration eliminated. With Dan, no matter how mundane the shared activity, there was an ease and simplicity which she increasingly valued.

Also, more difficult to admit to but more basic even than this similarity of approach, she knew that for the first time in her life she had found someone who would not allow her tongue or her temper to get out of hand. There was in that discovery the subconscious security of a child who knows there are set parameters to its behaviour, and Rebecca was not too arrogant to dismiss the value of it. Except with Esme (and, she saw with a little flash of surprise, in the friendships of this summer), she had wrecked most of the relationships of her life because she had always been allowed to get the upper hand. She had been sweeping, intolerant, accustomed from school onwards to others following her lead, but every time she had walked away, bored and impatient, there had been a small nagging core of dissatisfaction left behind.

Well, there was no question of having the upper hand if any relationship continued with Dan, she thought wryly, but would the opposite danger entrap them? Were they too alike and would they end up fighting to the death? Certainly there was no inclination to fight at present; they were on the crest of a wave of sexual pleasure and these fears seemed remote and irrelevant.

Even after the storm died down the days were not the mellow, golden, lazy days of autumn further south. They were keen and bright, with a whipping wind and a tingle in the air. Inland the great hills were outlined in white against clear pale skies and the cold nights sparkled with stars. Boats were taken out of the water at the Luig Marina; owners of holiday cottages gave rough lawns a final Flymo, secured windows, tidied dustbins and garden chairs into sheds and locked the doors; owners of letting cottages burned carpets and refurbished kitchens and got the paint-brushes out.

In the hotel everyone was luxuriating in the winding down feeling. Half a dozen dinners, enough room for everyone in the top bar in the evenings, no more hill lunches to make up, indeed on one occasion a day with no lunches of any kind. Una could come down at ten to eight to do breakfasts, one night they shut the bar before ten, they cancelled half the papers, reduced the linen stock, planned menus with freezer emptying as the chief criterion, returned surplus kegs of beer before they went out of date, and sat round for long chatty coffee breaks.

No date had been settled for Dan to leave (Rebecca didn't ask and didn't want to know) though it was agreed that Liam and Bern would go during the week after closing. Local staff would finish after the last day of guests, Thea and Sylvie would be around for a couple of extra days to clear up and pack. Although everyone counted off the days, groaned when unexpected guests turned up, muttered on a sunny Sunday which brought nearly as many bar lunches as August, there was somewhere in everyone's mind a contradictory tug of reluctance to have it all end.

Paddy, the only person whose job was secure since he worked through the winter on maintenance and the major job of cutting back the garden and preparing it for next spring, startled Una by giving notice. He was wooden-faced and embarrassed as he did so and Una, ever ready to respect people's privacy, took one look at his stony expression and asked no questions.

'I'm really, really sorry to lose you, Paddy,' she said sincerely, 'but thank you so much for all you've done. We couldn't have started up the Coach-house without you, and you've been marvellous about coming in whenever you were needed and turning your hand to so many things. I can't think what we'll do without you, to be honest, and I shall miss you terribly in the garden, but I do wish you well in whatever you do next.'

It was Rebecca who leapt to the answer. 'You're going out to Australia,' she said baldly.

To her immense surprise Paddy blushed, then visibly relaxed. 'I've wanted to tell you.' He turned to Una, still embarrassed but determined now to explain. 'I've got a couple of problems I have to sort out. It's, well, things aren't just that straightforward.'

Rebecca took one look at his troubled face. 'You're married,' she said calmly.

Paddy gaped, his jaw literally dropping, and Una turned to gaze at her in astonishment.

'How the hell did you know?' Paddy demanded.

'Can't be anything else.'

Una began to look alarmed as Paddy's face darkened with

an anger rare for him. It didn't seem the moment for Rebecca to be quite so blunt.

To her relief Paddy shrugged and grinned ruefully. 'Trust you, Rebecca. Yes, I'm married and I've got two kids into the bargain, well, hardly kids, one's nearly twenty. The wife and I were separated but we never got around to divorce, though I suppose we should have. She's been living with someone else for a couple of years.'

'Does Thea know?' Rebecca asked, sticking as ever to the point.

'She does,' said Paddy, and it struck Rebecca suddenly how accepted by them all her right to question him on this point had been. There was a certain protective care for the staff, irrespective of age or standing, which went with management and which seemed to be tacitly acknowledged as her area rather than Una's.

'And you want to go out there and see how things work?' she asked.

'Just,' Paddy agreed on a breath of relief that this secret was now in the open and no one was making a big deal of it.

Rebecca was delighted for Thea. There was nothing here that couldn't be straightened out. Paddy was so competent and reliable, eating up work at his quiet pace, that she had always felt he undervalued himself. The relationship with Thea had been good for him, though of late there had been the nagging worry about misery waiting for them both when the time came for her to leave. Well, it might work out, and good luck to them. At least Paddy had the sense to free himself of entanglements before he took off. What Thea's well-heeled family would make of him was the next question, but no doubt news of that would filter back in due course.

'What on earth will I do without Paddy?' Una wailed when he'd gone. 'He keeps the place functioning.'

'Well, it did just occur to me — and I don't mean to pre-empt any decisions — but Bern has nothing in prospect but the dole at present. Why don't you keep him on for the time being at least?' Careful to say 'you' not 'we'. Careful not to ask how far ahead Una was looking. 'He's conscientious and useful, you can rely on him totally and he really needs a job. He's saved nothing this season. You know how he sends every penny he can spare to his mother.'

'That's a brilliant idea,' Una said eagerly. 'Though I'm not sure I could let him loose on the garden,' she added in sudden alarm.

'He could do the heavy stuff, and he'll do exactly as he's told, that's one thing you can be sure of.'

And when she drove away from here, when this was over, at least she would know that Una wasn't quite alone.

'Did you know Paddy wanted to go out to Queensland?' Rebecca asked Dan rather breathlessly, as they rock-hopped out to the furthest point of the headland with a sweeping westerly in their faces, their faces dark red with its icy buffetting and their eyes shut to slits.

'Knew he couldn't let Thea go anyway,' Dan shouted back. 'Man's a goner. Those legs.'

'Do you think Bern will cope?'

'No question. He'll pant after Una now, instead of Sylvie.'

'Oh, God, I never thought of that!'

'Here, get down here out of the wind. I can hardly hear you.'

They sank down into one of the few clefts in the rocks that didn't have a pool of sea water in the bottom and huddled close, rubbing the drips off their noses and getting their breath back.

'Old Bern won't be any problem. You know that. I reckon it's the perfect solution.'

'I don't know how long it will last, though.'

'No, it's all a bit up in the air at the moment, isn't it?' Dan looked seaward, his face suddenly grim. He had vowed to himself he wouldn't ask Rebecca what she had decided but the question was never out of his mind, and he didn't really think there was much doubt about the outcome.

Rebecca said nothing, pressing her head back against his arm, shutting her eyes against the cold liquid touch of the wind. The decision was hers and hers alone and must be made on its own merits. Dan had never so much as hinted at any continuation of their relationship, let alone permanence. What she decided about Sophie, about Ivor, about that comfortable, secure, near-perfect existence open to her was an issue entirely separate and finite.

'Would you ever try to see Lee again?' she asked out of her thoughts, and feeling a tightening of the muscles in the arm that supported her reflected that even a few days ago putting such a question would have been unthinkable.

'Sorry, Dan, don't answer if that's too intrusive.'

'It's OK. But no, I don't think so,' he said levelly.

'Not even when she's older?'

'She'll be the product of – that upbringing.' He had never used his wife's name. 'Even if she hasn't been brought up to hate me, or to believe a lot of things that aren't true, she won't be any part of me. I've often thought that these reunions after years of separation – you know, people falling sobbing on each other's necks and all that guff – must be totally phoney. Nurture has to be what counts. Well, anyway, for a child. I mean, the adult has all the thoughts, longings, memories, the concept of parenthood fixed in his brain. But how can the child feel anything? Oh, Christ, love, I'm sorry, I was just thinking about Lee. That was a bit too near the bone, wasn't it?'

'It's so odd that we both have this to deal with,' Rebecca said, making a little gesture with her hand to accept the apology and show she didn't mind. 'You've made your decision. You're braver than I am.'

'Yeah, helped by the virtual impossibility of a father walking back into the scene after all this time and being granted much in the way of rights,' he pointed out cynically.

'I suppose you're right. One thing I have wondered though,' Rebecca pursued, 'thinking about all you've told me—'

'What?'

'Your leaving the Air Force, or rather leaving the Regiment, because that was obviously the part that mattered to you. Was it really because of this fight with your wife, more than feeling that the service had treated you badly? You seemed somehow to care about it too much to give it up for such a reason.'

'No flies on you, are there?' Dan rubbed his hooded head against hers in a gesture of rueful affection. 'Yes, I didn't tell it quite straight, about coming out. This business about losing Lee, it fucked me up completely for a while. I couldn't see straight. I just wanted to get clear. And then there was a new squadron commander, he didn't know me, he didn't give me the back-up I'd have got from the previous boss who'd known me really well.'

'Couldn't you have got in touch with him, the previous one? Surely he would have helped.'

'He was out in the Falklands by that time. I just couldn't get my head together to start the whole business of getting support from him.'

Dan's bleak tone moved Rebecca unbearably. He had lost so much. She reached a gloved hand to draw his head down and laid her icy cheek against his.

By popular vote the staff party was to take place at Ardlonach. Various suggestions had been made – a nightclub in Inverness, blue movies and carry-outs in the Coach-house, ten-pin bowling and kebabs, dinner in some local hotel.

'Why go and have lousy food somewhere else?' Thea objected, 'when we've got the best here?'

'Only then Una and Megan have to cook it,' Rebecca reminded her.

'I don't want any corny entertainment,' Sylvie said definitely,

'I like it when we sit around with Dan's guitar and Rebecca and Fitz sing.'

'Fitz isn't staff.'

'Oh, surely we're going to invite Fitz and Trudy?'

A flurry of comment but general agreement.

'But not my mother,' Rebecca took the chance to make clear. 'She knows we're having a party and she said she'd answer the phone or take herself off for the evening, whichever we preferred. She's got some friend coming with her anyway so she'll be fine.' Esme had merely said it was someone Rebecca didn't know, so that cut out most of the golfing cronies and her extensive dining circle.

So revelling in the luxury and freedom of having the house to themselves they turned to to arrange their own party, with a long table beautifully decorated and a menu of everyone's favourite dishes hotly and pleasurably fought over. Fitz and Trudy were invited, but no other outsiders, and Rebecca solved the problem of the incessant telephone calls by getting an answerphone. Nothing was going to spoil this party.

Chapter Twenty-Eight

❦

Esme arrived with her lover. He was a big burly man with a handsome open face, blue direct eyes and short thick tightly-curly silver-grey hair. He was wearing non-fashion jeans and a faded navy sweat shirt and could not have been a greater contrast in physical type to dark, whippy, dandified Francis Urquhart. He twitched his bag and Esme's out of the back of a hard-worked Vauxhall Frontera with an ease that made them look empty.

'This is Laughton Wallace, darling,' Esme said composedly.

He took Rebecca's hand in a huge grasp and his eyes met hers with an open enjoyment of the joke which made her laugh back at him. With one of the leaps she often made she said, 'Of D.J. Wallace?' a name whose scrolled brown letters had appeared at every major construction site in Edinburgh and the Lothians for two generations.

Esme laughed too, hugging her. 'Inn-keeping hasn't impaired your wits, I see. How lovely to be here. And here's Una.'

It was a moment that fixed itself for some reason in Rebecca's mind, vivid ever after. Soft, damp, lazy-leaf-twirling air; rain-dark gravel patterned with bruised yellow and tan and the soft tawny-red of wild cherry; the shaggy autumn look of the garden climbing above them; the faint pungent scents of decay and wet earth; Una coming smiling from the porch door. But what made the moment special was the heady new freedom of time being theirs, of knowing they could stand here prolonging the greetings at leisure, not obliged to rush off to the next job, answer some compelling summons. They could go in and have tea with Esme and this intriguing companion with his friendly keen eyes and his calm air of being his own man. They could sit and talk till bedtime, go out and walk if the impulse took them, have dinner whenever they liked, wear what they liked, eat what they liked. This forgotten freedom to do quite ordinary things gave a more luxurious feeling of holiday than Rebecca had ever imagined. And no ashtrays to empty, cushions to plump up, newspapers to straighten yet again.

'Now, where have you put us?' Esme enquired briskly, as they made a move to go in at last.

'There are a few beds made up here and there,' Rebecca told her blandly, amused to catch Una's appealing look. 'Perhaps you'd better tell us what your requirements are.'

'A large double bed,' said Esme promptly and Laughton loosed a big, happy, entirely unembarrassed laugh.

'I'm so glad they've come,' Una said as she and Rebecca came downstairs again.

'So am I — Una, you idiot, you're crying. What on earth's that about?' Rebecca demanded, stopping short and catching Una's arm to turn her to the light of the stair window.

'I just think it's so lovely,' Una explained, sniffing and unashamed. 'It's such a marvellous surprise and they look so — so sort of through and through contented.'

'God, you're sentimental,' Rebecca told her disgustedly, but beneath her own amusement at this astonishing development she too had been aware of a pang of — what? Nostalgia, it felt like, but that made no sense. Bitter-sweet. She felt herself backing off from the adjective like a snorting pony, but that was what had come to mind.

The staff thought Laughton and Esme marvellous and didn't attempt to hide the fact. Their open happiness, the way they held hands and sat close together or watched each other cross a room, gave everyone a great boost of pleasure and somehow seemed to sharpen all the emotions which were in any case running high.

'Make us seem like a staid old couple,' Fitz grumbled. 'We'd better get married soon and grab some of the attention back.'

'Any time you like,' Trudy said promptly, and put her hands up laughing to a flurry of, 'Oh, when?' and 'But we'll miss it'.

'But you didn't even hint to me,' Rebecca complained to her mother the first time they were alone.

'I wanted to tell you when I was here early in the summer, but there simply wasn't the opportunity, and in any case there wasn't much to tell. Then in August it was even worse. All the family about and such a brief visit. Anyway I realised afterwards it would have been impossible to describe Laughton or convey to you how I feel about him. Just a great sense of rightness, no doubts, no questions.' And none of the exasperation and jealousy and battles there had been with Francis, much as she had adored him, but that she would not say to his daughter. 'It just seemed simpler in the end to bring him.'

Laughton was a blunt no-nonsense man, encouraged by his father to work his way up in the business from the moment he left school, which he did too early for qualifications of any sort. He still ran the huge concern in an active hands-on manner, exactly as Esme did her business, and it was not hard to see how much they had in common.

Dan was the only person who seemed unable to handle the situation, taking refuge in a watchful reserve which disappointed and annoyed Rebecca. It did not occur to her, disciplining herself resolutely to accept the absence of any future with him in it, that he might have dreaded meeting Esme, and was disconcerted to find her happily absorbed in a love affair of her own.

One thing that did strike Rebecca, remembering her worries about how Esme would react to Dan, was how oddly alike, given their different generations, Laughton and Dan were. Both were powerful vigorous men, both with a look of health and fitness about them, both with an inherent air of authority and competence. Even in their choice of clothes they were alike, both apparently impervious to cold, eschewing collars and despising buttons. Rebecca, smiling as this occurred to her, was conscious of a subtle unwinding of tension, as though anxieties never properly examined had floated away and vanished.

It was Laughton's idea that he and Esme shouldn't disappear for the staff party. 'Far more point if we do the work,' he proposed at lunch. 'We're prepared for all the hard graft except cooking – waiting, pots, wash-up, whatever.' He laughed as every head swung to look at Esme. 'Don't worry, we did discuss it.'

'You all think I look too tidy,' she reproached them, laughing at the politely doubtful faces. 'Don't let that mislead you.'

I bet I'm not the only person here who feels like crying, Rebecca thought defiantly, tilting her head to look past the candles down the length of the table to Una facing her, looking pretty and glowing in her favourite dark red. In another of those strange blurrings of past and present which had beset her when she first came back, there came a memory of childhood parties in this dark-panelled room, where portraits of kilted Urquharts in the company of dead and living creatures still hung in their appointed places. She herself was the only Urquhart by birth in this room tonight, but she had never felt more at home here, more part of any group sitting round this table.

I love them all, she thought sentimentally. God, how much have I had to drink? But at once she crushed the flippant reaction; the word had been the right one to choose. She could hardly bear the thought of Thea and Paddy and Sylvie putting twelve thousand miles between them and Ardlonach, probably never to return. And the others would scatter, find different jobs. Whatever happend, this particular group, as it was now, would never be together again.

There was a stir, a general exclamation, loud applause, as Laughton came in bearing a huge flaming Bombe Alaska. He was dressed in one of Megan's white overalls over his jeans and though the chest capacity was big enough even for him the sleeves were halfway up his brawny forearms and both had split. Megan had shrieked with laughter at the sight; she didn't pay for them. Esme followed with a pile of plates, trim in a staff skirt and shirt and looking in the candlelight no older than Rebecca. She and Laughton had feared their presence might after all put some constraint on the party and this had been her solution, raising a laugh which had effectively done the trick. Now, having brought in the coffee, they resisted with great firmness all invitations to pull up chairs and join the party, retreating to the kitchen to wade into the washing up and enjoy a quiet supper of their own.

Had they guessed what would happen, Rebecca wondered a few minutes later, when everyone had coffee and port or a liqueur in front of them, startled to see shy Una, pink-cheeked and nervous, getting to her feet. With a sudden sick clutch of foreboding she knew, quite certainly, that this wasn't going to be the boss's conventional end-of-season speech.

Perhaps the tense look in Una's face, a slight trembling of her hands which she tried to conceal by pressing her splayed finger-tips on the polished wood before her, alerted the others to the same realisation, for the silence which fell was electric and every face was suddenly serious.

First Una did thank them for all they had done. 'At one point I really didn't believe Ardlonach could open for the season,' she told them. 'Rebecca persuaded me it could and she made it happen and I want to thank her for that and for everything she's done since—'

Rebecca's eyes prickled and the candlelight blurred as the smiling faces turned towards her and the glasses were raised.

'—but you all did your share—'

Is it really over, Rebecca wondered in swift illogical panic, as though the reality had never truly come home to her till now. She felt impressed and moved to realise that Una had seen this decision as her sole responsibility and had sought no help.

'I know it's been difficult for some of you, not knowing what would happen next year, and I'm sorry you've had that uncertainty, but there were a lot of things to be considered. Anyway,' visibly shouldering these thoughts aside and bracing herself, Una went on steadily, 'I have decided to open again, to keep both the hotel and the school going if I can. I don't know how many of you will be free to help me, or will want to come back, and sadly some of you will be too far away,' with a tremulous smile at Paddy on her right with Thea beside him, and at Sylvie across the table from them, 'but I would love to have you all here again if I could. I don't think I need to say that.'

Rebecca saw soft-hearted little Sylvie wipe at her eyes with her narrow wrist and Bern scoop her into an enveloping hug, looking not far off tears himself.

'Oh, don't, I can't bear it,' wailed Thea in anguish, turning to crush her face against Paddy's shoulder, releasing them all to comment and laughter.

In the excited babble, the applause, Catriona jumping up to hug Una, Fitz taking the port down to Liam since it kept getting lost among the females, Bern tenderly and unself-consciously drying Sylvie's tears with a grey handkerchief with blue and maroon stripes, Rebecca felt a huge bubble of admiration and love swell up and burst inside her. How brave of Una, how well she had done, and how truly impressive it was that she had not first canvassed or established the support she could hope for. She had seen this as her own challenge, and had made her own decision.

Rebecca turned to find Dan's eyes on her and felt her stomach turn over. There was so much implicit in what Una had just said, possibilities which till now no one had dared to bank on. Dan's job as head of the survival school was assured if he wanted it. Una was talking to Bern at this very moment, no doubt telling him he could have a job all the year round. Megan and Joanie now knew spring would bring them back after their hibernation on the dole, Liam would probably turn up again if it suited his nomadic existence when the time came. And I? Has Una counted me in?

But no, Una had made it clear that she had counted on no one; everyone was free to make his or her own choice.

I must say something, Rebecca thought, most uncharacteristically flurried and at a loss. I must join in the general delight and pleasure, meet Dan's waiting eyes. 'That's marvellous news,' she said to him, and heard with dismay how forced and artificial she sounded.

'You didn't know?' The watchful look didn't soften.

'No.'

'Una hadn't discussed it with you?' He found it hard to believe and showed it.

'No, not a word, truly. I think she's been terribly brave to make up her mind on her own.'

Dan turned to look at Una, being unwound from Trudy's embrace by Fitz who was pretending he didn't want a smothered patient on his hands. Rebecca had the feeling that Dan had deliberately looked for something to engage his attention and suddenly, unaccountably, found that her eyes were full of tears. She had one glimpse of Dan's startled face swinging back to hers, then he had her firmly by the arm and on her feet. 'We're going to push back some chairs in the drawing-room,' he announced. 'Time for a little activity here,' and he was walking her out of the room, his arm around her, his big frame blocking her from the eyes of the others, shutting the door behind them, drawing her along the corridor and into the dark recess of the doorway to the stone stairs.

Rebecca stood leaning against him, sobbing helplessly, and he held her gently, an ache in his own throat, but knowing he did not have the courage to ask her what had caused these rare tears. There had been no mention of her being here next year, no reference to her plans. His own brief euphoria to hear the school would go on and to know he could return to this job which had so satisfied and suited him, abruptly died. Could he bear to be here without Rebecca? He didn't think so.

He held her, his face twisted with pain, his head against hers.

Presently she drew in a ragged breath and said, 'I'm sorry, Dan. I'm not really sure what this is all about. Things ending, I suppose.'

'Yes, that's all it is,' he said, doing his best. 'Things ending.'

At last there was time to be with Esme, time to walk at their leisure along the shore and wait for the right moment for words. Laughton had gone up to Inverness on business for the day.

'Could that have been engineered?' Rebecca enquired dryly.

'Planned,' Esme corrected her, a smile in her eyes. 'I need to know what you think and feel about him, and about my being with him. And I want to know as much about your life as you feel ready to tell me.'

'Well, I like Laughton,' Rebecca stated, starting with the easy part.

Her mother laughed, taking her by the shoulders, pressing her cheek to hers. 'I cannot tell you how much that matters to me,' she said.

'Are you going to get married?' Rebecca asked, hugging her back.

'I think we'll just go on as we are for the time being,' Esme said serenely.

'Which is?' Rebecca enquired. 'I don't think I'm quite clear on that.'

'Living together,' said Esme, lifting her eyebrows in affected surprise, and they were both swept by laughter. 'We're in the flat at present, since Laughton inhabits a cupboard stuffed with technical magazines and machines that speak and whirr and burp, but we're looking for a house. You won't mind if I sell the flat?'

Extraordinarily, with shame, Rebecca realised that she did mind. In spite of her conviction of her own independence it had all the time provided the feeling of home base, and she hadn't even known. There suddenly seemed a large empty space in the middle of Scotland, and her own moment of choice came hurtling towards her, inescapable and terrifying.

And at last she could talk about it, talk about things even Dan hadn't heard, the desolation of the years when her heart had felt frozen, when her guilt at what she had done seemed to come between her and everyone she met, everything she thought or did. She told Esme what had driven her from Edinburgh last spring and what Ivor wanted. She also told her of the proposition Una had made this morning. Una had said her father would put up the cash to buy Ardlonach outright but that she would prefer Rebecca to come in as her partner.

On this day of revelations, which brought a great peace to them both, Rebecca and Esme also made time to go over and see Lilias, now spending most of her days in bed and with a full-time nurse living in, who of course spent most of her time fighting with Barbara Bailey. And they went out to Rhumore to visit a contented looking Clare, finding Donald, relaxed after a good stalking season, most unusually home in the afternoon and happy to blether over a lengthy tea.

But in all those hours together Rebecca didn't talk about Dan. If once she began she would inevitably reveal how she felt about him, and she knew it would concern Esme to be told in the next breath that Dan wasn't into commitment of any kind.

They went for dinner to Fitz's house high over Luig harbour, where a casual overlay of Trudy's belongings was beginning to blur the classic outlines of his elegant style. The Irvines were there and it was a lively gathering, with only Rebecca and Dan edgily conscious of issues still unresolved.

Dan's wariness of Esme persisted till the following morning, when she and Laughton came down to the boathouse to have a look at plans for putting in a sink and heavy duty washing machine. Esme, Laughton and Rebecca had all derived much private enjoyment from Dan's persistent referral to Laughton for his views when this was first discussed. Now Esme and Rebecca watched his face with anticipation as Laughton wandered off as soon as business began to have a look at the Firefly. Dan suspended his enthusiastic description of what he wanted in surprise.

'Carry on,' said Esme briskly. 'It sounds all right so far. You'd get a good run-off from here.'

'Will Laughton want to have a look——?'

'Take no notice of him. I'm the plumber,' she told him briskly, beginning to jot down measurements.

Dan turned to Rebecca, completely thrown.

'I told you she ran her own business,' she said in pretended surprise but her eyes were sparkling happily.

'You're going to hear about this later,' Dan promised her under his breath, knowing he'd been been set up but at the same time acknowledging a relief that had been growing in him that Rebecca's mother was nothing like the posh up-market female he had dreaded meeting.

Esme, busy with calculations, felt rather pleased with Rebecca, who could so easily have used this information to reassure Dan. Instead she had let them meet unedited, to make their own evaluation of each other. And Esme on the whole approved of Dan. He would almost certainly have his ugly moments but he could without question handle her difficult stroppy daughter, and not only was that a pleasure to behold but it was what no one else had so far been able to provide. Without that strength in a man Esme knew Rebecca would never be content.

She and Laughton left that afternoon, given a great send-off by everyone, Esme already busy on the mobile as the Frontera wound up the drive. They took Liam and his monster pack with them, to drop him off on the A82 to thumb his way up to Wester Ross.

Next to go were Thea and Sylvie, watering the platform at Fort William with their tears. Dan, seeing the mute misery in Bern's face, got him to help with taking the first load of his belongings across to the Spean Bridge lodge. This had severely shaken Rebecca. Somehow she had felt till then that her options were still open; or were at least her options. Now she was obliged to admit there was no further reason to delay, not even the excuse of work. All the boring jobs like stock-taking, stripping rooms for painting, booking sweep, carpet cleaner, maintenance visits for dishwasher and boiler, had been done. The moment had come.

She left early, heading east on a day when the first real snow covered the Nevis range and the Glencoe ridges, moving through a nearly deserted landscape under a sky uniformly grey and starkly cold. Pathetic fallacy to see in this some kind of omen, she mocked herself, but being prosaic didn't help at all. She felt hollow with anxiety and dread, with lack of sleep and a terrible sense of physical uprooting, of having no focal place where she belonged. Una, hesitant and dreading encroaching upon matters she felt to be private, had said only that she wanted Rebecca back more than anything in the world, but she had been careful to make clear that she would re-open Ardlonach whatever Rebecca decided.

Her sense of apprehension and of being totally alone was absurd, Rebecca knew, reminding herself that this journey could after all be taking her towards what she had dreamed of for so long and believed impossible of achievement – reunion with her daughter. Not today, of course, today she would talk to Ivor, today she would tell him what she had decided.

It was very dark. Rebecca felt her way with a hand on the rough harling of the wall. She couldn't see if there was a light on till she had nearly reached the window, then the blurred glow along the sill made her feel her heart had leapt into her throat. She raised a knuckle to knock then curled up her hand and drew it back against her chest, taking a deep breath to steady herself. This was a scene that had to be played lightly.

Dan's voice called casually, 'Come in,' and he was still sitting at the table when she opened the door, his hands stilling at the sight of her above the tangle of lashings he was sorting and whipping. He had expected Bern, she guessed. Indeed she had half expected to find him here herself, since he must be finding his cottage lonely.

She shut the door behind her and leaned against it, cushioned by a couple of Dan's jackets hanging there, absurdly comforted by having them behind her shoulders. Dan did not move, watching her with expressionless pale eyes, his face carefully blank. This suits us both, the thought flashed across Rebecca's mind with satisfaction; not to leap into each other's arms, to deal with this matter-of-factly.

'How did it go?' Dan asked, almost naturally.

'I'm back.'

'So I see.' It was not enough. This mattered too much for any misapprehensions.

'It was a dream. It wasn't reality.'

Still he watched her, but now there was a rigidity in his stillness which she well understood.

'You were right when you said nurture is what really counts—'

'Don't take any notice of what I said,' he interrupted sharply, almost angrily. 'This is your decision.'

'You were only saying what I'd already realised,' she said quietly. 'I'm a stranger to Sophie. It would mean no more to her if I married Ivor than if any other woman did; and it would be infinitely better for her to have parents who were truly happy together, and had a chance of staying together.'

'How about you having Sophie on your own?'

'Ivor would never give her up. He adores her.'

'But you'll miss out on all her growing up. It might make no difference to her now whether her mother is her real mother or adopted, but it might matter later. And it would matter to you.'

'Yes.' Rebecca felt suddenly exhausted, incapable of the effort it would take to try and express her empty sense of finality, but equally her conviction that to try to enter Sophie's life in the way that was available to her would be selfish and false. And would mean losing something just as precious; potentially, she suspected, more precious.

'So what are you going to do?' Dan asked, keeping his voice carefully flat.

She looked at him across the small room, oblivious of its drabness or the chill where the warmth of the fire did not reach, here by the door. 'I want to be with you,' she said, 'if you want that. Just be with you, for as long as it suits us. Anywhere. Here, if you like.'

Their eyes still intent upon each other's, without a glimmer of warmth or feeling as Rebecca was to realise afterwards, Dan came slowly to his feet, his hands setting gently back the length of rope on the pile. 'Do you mean that?'

'Yes. I know you don't want to be tied in any way, but I feel – I think – that we don't want to part yet. That's all. As long as we feel that, I'd like to be with you.'

He was coming towards her, his face like stone, and she found herself fighting down an impulse to cry out to him to say something, anything. Then he was gripping her by both elbows, bending his head down to her shoulder. But she had glimpsed his face and wrenching one arm free had pushed a fist under his chin, forcing his head up. 'Oh, Dan.' His eyes were wet, defenceless, and still he couldn't bear to let anyone see that, and shut them against her loving incredulous gaze. She reached up, wrapping both hands round his head, pulling it down to her, soothing and cradling it.

'Jesus,' he said, his voice muffled and rough. And, 'Jesus!' he repeated on an indrawn breath of disbelief. 'I thought you'd gone. I didn't see how anything in the world could matter to you once you were there, once – all that – was open to you, waiting for you to reach out and pick it up. Are you sure you don't need more time? This is a big thing. About Sophie, I mean, you must be sure . . .'

'I've known, I think, for a long time,' Rebecca said softly. 'I could never make myself think it all out with any kind of realism. My brain would just skate away. It was a fantasy I was clinging to, that's the only way I can describe it, Dan.'

*   *   *

'... and you'll be able to come out on the hill, do more on the sailing side, there's no point in getting stuck in the hotel seven days a week.'

'Catriona would like to do more days in the office, she told Una so.'

'Will Trudy be fighting for her time?'

'Oh, anybody can do the shop. She can afford help now anyway. Have you got anything else to eat?'

'There's a tub of cheese leftovers from the hotel. So can you face this dump next summer?'

'Won't bother me.'

Dan grinned, but he knew it was true. If it worked it would do for Rebecca. Well, it didn't have to be this hovel, but with a great lifting of his spirits he realised that all kinds of possibilities were open to them.

'Got a torch?' Rebecca was asking.

'Of course I've got a bloody torch,' he said. 'Where's yours?'

'Forgot to take it out of the car. Come and see something.'

Grumbling, but quite content to be led off into the dark night by Rebecca, he followed her along to the quay. She flashed the torch over a neat little Toyota 4WD.

'Whose is that?'

'Mine. Got it today.'

'What's happened to that flash orange object?'

'Oh, city girl's car, don't you think?' Rebecca said airily, turning into his arms.